# DEVILS

## — IN —

# SUNDAY HATS

Joseph D'Urso

Library of Congress Control Number: 2017918167
ISBN (paperback): 979-8-9875268-2-8
ISBN (hardcover): 978-0-9996852-6-6
ISBN (e-book): 978-0-9967899-5-0

Printed in the United States of America
First Printing January 2018

Published by Aether Press, LLC
Miami, FL 33133


www.joey-durso.com

# CONTENTS

*"It is a sad thing to be Christians at a supper,
heathens in our shops, and devils in our closets."*
—Stephen Charnock

# 1

"PRAISE THE LORD! Praise Jesus! 'Cause y'all know without 'im, y'all ain't got *nothin*'?"

With their chorus of hootin' and hollerin', the congregation couldn't have agreed more. The Reverend Jeffrey Shaw's amber eyes flickered with flame as they stared out into the hellfire; his costly cologne may as well have been the stench of brimstone. He stood brazenly behind the pulpit as a spiritual commander before an obedient army of believers. Upon his word they would eagerly march into battle for the unforgiving Christ he preached of, carrying their crosses of guilt on their backs and checks in their hands to be slipped into the collection box.

The Southern Mercy Bible Church had a reputation for producing the most persuasive of sermon givers, which, in the fiery brand of Protestantism of the American South, implied the most histrionic, the most terrifying, and naturally, the most lucrative. Levi Thompson had always hated Sunday service. It reminded him of when he was just a kid, his mother forcing him into uncomfortable slacks that never quite fit right and button-downs wrinkled from protest. It reminded him of hair slicked painfully to the side with an inexplicably sharp comb. The worst was that it reminded him of his mother at all.

He was eighteen, and for those eighteen long years every Sunday was the same. Mama dragged him to the local church with her hand clasped tightly around his wrist, scolding him in a cutting whisper. All the way there (she still drove, though Levi had held a license for a good two years), she criticized his poorly coiffed hair and the careless buttoning of his shirt, as a securely fastened top button was a sign of the utmost taste. She noted that he could have spent just a little more time in the bath scrubbing behind his ears. She drew attention to the spot he'd missed while shaving and that he'd nicked himself in another. Mama was a critic whose words were driven by the powerful judgment of God.

"…The Lord Almighty said to 'honor your father 'n mother!' But look at the country y'all live in! This here's a place that ain't got no *respect*!"

Mama slapped Levi on the wrist with a white-gloved hand when she caught him peering out one of the windows. They were plain— the congregation condemned the pagan décor that adorned the Catholic churches up north. He snapped his gaze back to the pulpit, Mama scowling at him from the corner of his eye. The Reverend stood shaking his fists in the air, drawing cries of agreement and righteous anger from the townsfolk of Clemency, Alabama.

Levi quickly lost focus again and watched Mama smooth a wrinkle in her yellow dress. She cleaned up very well for Sunday service. It was the one hour of the week when she could flaunt her God-fearing figure. Nobody could deny that Lenore Thompson was a beautiful woman. She had a kind of classic elegance that always managed to overpower the smell of whiskey on her breath, which lingered every day but Sunday. It was as if she'd stepped right out of the forties, when ivory-skinned women made it a habit to always look the part, and would never have been caught showing even the slightest bit of cleavage. Mama was a lady.

"Y'all try to raise these kids the way the Bible tells us, but with *Satan*, that great liar 'imself struttin' round the nation, what's it gotten y'all? Y'all done seen your boys 'n girls givin' it up to any ol' fool who walked by, shootin' up and cussin' like there ain't no one listenin'! I ain't seen no class in *ages*!"

"Amen!" cried out Victoria, the preacher's faithful wife. She stood up and spread her arms like a busty saint crucified for her overly public beliefs. With her head cocked back toward Heaven, eyes closed and smiling in divine rapture, she adamantly declared, "Thank the Lord for my baby girl, Sophia! Don't none o' y'all say we ain't got no hope for her generation!"

The churchgoers blessed her for her Christian parenting, and her daughter for her guarding her modesty. They lamented the degenerate state of society, no doubt secretly plotting just how to effectively chastise their children for their transgressions the second they got home. Most importantly, they affirmed the need of all Americans—no, the whole *world*—to accept Jesus into their hearts, or suffer dire consequences in the hereafter. It was a weekly ritual, one that had changed little over the course of Levi's lifetime.

"Pay attention, boy!" Mama hissed in a hushed whisper, more deafeningly than if she'd yelled outright—the church whispers. Levi dreaded them. They were a regular prelude to the barrage of criticisms that would strike him the whole way home in the old Cadillac. Levi didn't pay enough attention to the fire-and-brimstone sermon he'd heard so many times before. The volume of his singing was insufficient, if noticeable at all. Over eighteen years, he'd learned to ignore the attacks, and to thoughtlessly nod his head at the appropriate times.

"…Y'all ever thought about why the good Lord's punishin' this godless country? 'Cause America, ladies 'n gents, ain't nothin' but the new Sodom! The new Babylon! We done brought this plague upon *ourselves*, brothers 'n sisters! And we Christians are the only'ns who know we gotta do somethin' about it!"

••

If you took the highway south from Lillian, you'd see a sign about eighteen miles down the road. It'd be green and faded, posted on the right side just a few hundred feet past a flowery shrine to a teenager killed in a car crash decades ago. It'd read: CLEMENCY, AL. POPULATION: 128.

The highway was never that wide to begin with, but it narrowed even further when it transitioned into Main Street. A drive down that central road was like a quick pass through the 1950s. Small, outdated shops lined the aging pavement, some boasting fancier signs above their awnings, others left with only the dusty outlines of rounded black letters long since fallen off. The town's schools, branded with the names of dead governors, flanked the first intersection, implying an invisible, though formidable, town gate. The Gabriel Moore Grade School had hospital-green walls and stood across from the Israel Pickens High School, which was staffed with an immortal faculty of crotchety grandmothers who smelled of chalk and mothballs. But it was the two-story Parsons Bible School that eclipsed them both, towering over the centers of secular, degenerate education with a sky-scraping flagpole and halls full of wholesome teenagers and silently broken hymens.

Straight ahead was the Swayne Public Library, stale and musty with the scent of unread books. Like a string of colorful banners, the ratty T-shirts hung up at the windows of the All Ye Faithful Thrift Store flapped in the breeze and caught the gaze of poor folk and regular passers-by alike. Their reflection danced on the foggy glass windows of the one vacant storefront, which used to be a bank well before any of the horny kids fornicating in its empty vault were even born. And just before a succession of mom-and-pop stores like J&G Hardware and the Hometown Market was the geographical and spiritual center of town: the Southern Mercy Bible Church.

Cars seldom passed down Main Street. Even the church, as packed as its pews might have been, lacked a parking lot. People walked, as there was little laziness on the day of rest. Meager crowds filled the road twice a week, both times on Sunday. In the morning all of Clemency gathered at the shallow steps of the simple church and bottlenecked through a single white door for service, only to pour out an hour or so later back into the world of the flesh. And in the evening—seven o'clock, on the dot—the crowd returned to the church, transforming it from a house of charismatic worship to an improvised town hall. The Reverend Shaw stepped down from the pulpit after sunset to make room for all those who chose to dabble in local politics, however ineffective or mundane. When the townsfolk walked home, the church became, once again, a shrine to God and the timeless American South, which didn't need to rise again, as it'd never fallen in the eyes of the Almighty in the first place.

A quick turn left from the doors of the Southern Mercy Bible Church and past the heart of Clemency, over the rusted tracks of the defunct railroad crossing, came a tiny dirt road on the left: Shiloh Path. And at the end of Shiloh Path, a ways into the untamed woods, was the Thompson house. It was nestled in a dim clearing, the edges of which were draped with hanging vines and tall, unkempt grasses. The Thompsons kept the mosquitoes out with screens lining the porch. Some still managed to slip through. Over the years, the screens had begun to boast many small holes.

Two deep trenches cut into the uneven dirt driveway, compliments of Mama's old Cadillac, which always managed to get stuck in the gooey mud on a rainy day. The squeal of its tires was just as awful as the grating squeaks of the house's front door. A permanent trail of footprints led down the road back toward the far end of Main Street. The first marks appeared a year and a half ago, when Levi could finally pass for twenty-one. It was then that he was able to walk down to Backwater Spirits without Mama's presence, his pockets stuffed with her wrinkled dollar bills.

••

"You're a *squatter*! That's what you are!" Mama barked from the parlor, her throat strained and voice hoarse from an evening packed with cigarettes and liquor. It wasn't froglike, though Levi expected such croaking decades down the line, but the smokiness rivaled that of the sultry blues singers who lived on in Mama's old records. But unlike them, her tone was far from soothing, and neither was it like the soulfulness of her church hymns. She sang sweetly on Sundays. The rest of the week she was a howling foghorn, or a smokestack spewing black clouds of drunken anger and regret. And Levi's bedroom door wasn't the best gas mask.

"If you're gon' live at my house, the least you can do's go down to that there store 'n pick up another bottle, boy! Make yourself *useful* for once in your sorry life!"

He nudged the door open with an aging creak; he poked his head out to ensure that he could make a clean escape. His feet slipped easily into his worn, dirty sneakers, and he pattered across the wooden floor of the hall, snatching up the few dollars Mama had so generously tossed on the ground. It didn't feel like enough as he shoved the cash into his back pocket. He dashed back to his room to grab his father's old leather wallet off his bed and made a break for the back door. Again, he'd have to dip into his own savings just to buy some cheap whiskey. The screen door snapped shut behind him, and the echo of Mama's voice faded out. It was like a baby's cries for milk, and Levi had grown tired of the sound.

The liquor store was closing within the hour, but it was only about a half mile up the road. The dirt path he called both his street and his driveway was uneven beneath his feet, strewn with pebbles and lined with tire treads, winding through the gauntlet of swampy trees that led straight to Main Street and his family's dusty white mailbox. A street sign marked the border between Mama's bleak, hazy domain and the fledgling Jerusalem of northern Alabama, called Clemency. The trail turned to smooth pavement, and after a quick right came the rusty railroad tracks that hadn't seen a train pass over them in years.

The tiny standalone shop stood on the left, set right along the road at the curb with no room for a sidewalk. Painted by hand on the green and white–striped awning was the name that Levi had come to resent over recent months: *Backwater Spirits*. He paused, took a breath, and pushed open the dirty glass door that was streaked with cheap window cleaner. It was his third time there that week. He didn't want any questions. Mama had managed to keep her vices a secret from the nosy churchgoers and gossipy customers at the Americana Diner, and Levi knew that tearing down her façade, no matter how unwittingly, would invoke an ungodly wrath like no other.

The old black man behind the counter looked up and nodded his head, which was crowned with short, grayed hair. He kept to himself. While Levi shopped for Mama's liquor he mostly stood at the register, drumming his rounded fingers on the wood and fixing his forest green bowtie.

He easily kept an eye on everything in the store. It was small, nearly suffocating. Rows of fully stocked shelves lined the walls and their dark wood paneling, each labeled with handwritten paper signs carefully posted with masking tape. The yellow legal pad flags swayed with the rush of air from the opening door, fluttering over stockpiles of boxed wine and hard liquor. Vodka and gin found a home on the left wall; whiskey and scotch stared back from the right. Levi walked in their direction, guided by a hanging light bulb that shone a deceptively angelic beam down over the devilish poisons.

The plastic bottle Levi pulled off the shelf buckled inward as he squeezed it. It was the cheapest he could find, and Mama's usual brand. She was a creature of habit. The owner had slapped a small orange label over the original price tag, marking a four-dollar discount. The stuff was absolutely foul. Mama always got what she paid for.

Levi brought his purchase up to the counter and set it down. The old man eyed him up and down, though he recognized him as a regular, for sure. He didn't card him; in that small town, the drinking age was still eighteen and Eisenhower was still president. They said little as Levi counted his money. Mama was two dollars short.

The man suddenly broke the silence. "How you holdin' up tonight, young man?" he asked. Even such a simple, polite question was startling when Levi was used to a consistently wordless exchange.

"Good enough," Levi answered. He hesitated, unsure of what to say. "Still alive, sir."

"Glad to hear it," the man said, cracking a smile. His teeth were brilliantly white, in stark contrast to the freckled brown of his skin. He reached out his hand with its equally clean fingernails and took the money, and opened the cash drawer with the ring of a classic bell.

"So, all this whiskey you buy every few days," he said, "it's for you, or for that good-lookin' mama of yours?" The drawer slid closed and he handed back the change. "She don't seem the type, so I'm guessin' you're just a young man enjoyin' himself on the town."

"With all due respect, sir, that really ain't your concern," Levi replied.

He shrugged. "I suppose it ain't."

••

Levi left the store with a dampened mood and a brown bag in hand. There was little light to guide him on his way back to Shiloh Path, so he kept one foot scraped against the edge of the highway pavement with each step he took. He crossed the road and stumbled over its lip onto the bumpy, unpaved trail. Along the road, stretching to just before the Thompson house, was a waist-high wooden fence, its oak beams rotted and crumbling, slick with cold, moist moss. Levi put his hand on it, careful not to press too hard to avoid the splinters. He followed the fence until he caught his foot on the trenches left by squealing tires. They were permanent scars in the dirt.

Through the open windows he heard Mama's old records playing. Ella Fitzgerald beckoned him closer, reeling him in with an enticing hook of a bridge when her voice gave way to piano and sax. For the first time in a while, he entered through the front door. There was little reason for subtlety or stealth. Without a doubt, Mama was waiting for him—rather, waiting for her bottle.

He set the brown bag down on the coffee table, covering a small black mark left from a fallen, smoldering cigarette. Her ashtray, with its engraved heart at the center, was filled to the brim. He stepped away. Mama reached over and stopped the music, cuing a question with the abrupt scratch of a record.

"Where's my cigarettes?" she asked, uncharacteristically calm. She looked up and shot him a look of cautious suspicion.

Levi grew quiet and visibly apprehensive. "You never asked for 'em, ma'am."

"Never asked for 'em?"

"No, ma'am."

Mama stood up. Levi took a slight step back.

"In Jesus's name I pray, boy, that you done remembered you been gettin' me them cigarettes every time you go down to that there store."

"I'm sorry, ma'am," Levi conceded. "But I didn't have no money for 'em."

"Y'ain't got no money for 'em?" Mama asked, her voice turning deeper, more grating. She began her approach. He stood his ground, however foolishly.

"Then maybe y'ain't workin' hard enough," she snapped. "How hard is it to pump that gas? Y'ain't got the smarts to do that right, neither?"

Levi risked a response. "I been workin' hard, ma'am, but it don't pay too well," he explained to little benefit, "and I had to put down some money for that bottle o' yours, too. You didn't give me enough for it, pardon my sayin' so." He instantly regretted running his mouth. Back talk wasn't something Mama took lightly. The Lord didn't like children who had a mouth on them, and she, in God's image, disliked them just as much.

"Now I know y'ain't talkin' to me that way, boy."

Saying sorry would have been a waste of good summer air, so he didn't.

"What was that? Y'ain't even gon' repent for it? You wanna talk about sorry, boy? Y'know what *I'm* sorry for? For lettin' your lazy, useless self stay in my house. *My* house, boy. Y'hear that? *My house.* And don't you forget it."

Mama lunged forward and smacked Levi in the side of the head. He tried his best not to flinch. He wasn't a child anymore; she wasn't about to pull out the belt, he knew. She hit him in the shoulder, pushed him. He didn't budge.

"Lord as my witness, boy, y'ain't good for *nothin*! Y'eat *my* food. Y'use *my* water. You got a roof over your head, and y'ain't payin' no rent—no *nothin'* for it! I got me a right mind to throw y'out into that there street. Maybe the Skinners'd take y'in, if you lucky. If y'even good enough to live with that trash!

"Y'ain't gone to no college. I ain't never seen them high school grades o' yours, neither, but I reckon they was as sad as that good-for-nothin' job you workin' down the road. You gon' do that for the rest o' your sorry life, boy? Pump gas?"

Without her dismissal, Levi turned and headed toward his room, but she followed him, still smacking him in the arm. He didn't say another word to her, nor did he look up. He slipped into the bedroom and locked himself in, his back against the door. She'd soon grow tired of yelling, Levi told himself from experience. Without seeing his face, she'd get little satisfaction.

"That's right, boy, lock yourself in there!" she yelled through the thin wooden door, rattling it with a flat palm. The peeling white paint always clung to her hand when she pulled away. "While you hide in there, I'll be out here workin' in the real world, makin' sure you got a place to stay! I swear, boy, if only your Pap could see what a sad, sorry man you become, I bet he'd leave all over again!"

••

Over the years, Levi had become particularly skilled at slipping out his bedroom window. He'd learned exactly how to arch his back to avoid hitting his head on the glass with the lights off, and where to put his feet to push himself out without having to look. He hopped out and heard the sparse gravel crunch as his feet hit the dry earth. He left the window cracked so he could sneak back inside, and to air out the smell of whiskey that always seemed to linger in the doorway. With a little luck, it'd be gone by the time he got back, though he didn't know where he intended to go, or for how long.

The flashlight's switch clicked with the chirp of the crickets hiding in the woods and under the old porch. He held it out in front of him. It provided only a small circle of light on the path before him; he'd gotten it cheap from AlaCo's convenience store, and it was, in all likelihood, meant more as a keychain light for finding fallen lighters in the dark depths beneath a car seat. The moon picked up the slack, shining bright and full over a sleepy Southern town.

With no clear destination in mind, Levi reached the end of Shiloh Path and stepped out onto the open road. He looked both ways, though he knew there'd be no traffic at that hour, or at any hour of the day, really, but it was a habit drilled into him from elementary school. He set his sights on the cluster of shops in the distance. He spat on the ground as he passed the liquor store.

"It ain't polite to spit, y'know," a voice from around the store reminded him.

"Jonah?"

"Yours truly."

He was sitting on the grass with his back against the wood shingles, eyes closed and arms folded across his chest. Standing up to meet Levi, he first tossed a crushed and chewed toothpick into the grass. He was just slightly taller than Levi, only by a few inches; his working boots pounded the pavement as he stepped into the road. Jonah held out his hand to greet his childhood friend after wiping a smudge of dirt off his worn khaki shorts. Levi offered his to oblige.

Jonah Young lived on the next block over, Lebanon Lane, just a short walk away. Levi had known him since he was just a kid, running a string with two plastic cups through the small patch of woods between their houses, playing spies with the neighbors' son. His family attended church as regularly as Mama did, and a mutual fear of God and the Reverend's scrutinizing stare did well to create an unbreakable bond between two young sinners. If there was any person in the world who could understand just what Levi had dealt

with that night, it would be Jonah. Levi felt a bit of guilt in piling his worries on his best friend. Stories of Mama's slurred reprimands had likely begun to bore him over the course of their friendship, though when they were little, such grim tales hadn't yet been written. It was a happier time.

"There a reason you been sittin' out here in the dark?" Levi asked, smirking.

"I reckon the same reason as you," Jonah said. He stretched his arms back behind him, stood on his toes. "Y'always just walk into town this time o' night without an escort?"

"Mama's been drinkin' again."

"Ain't that a surprise."

Levi looked down, scraping his foot forward to push around some gravel. "Care to join me? I ain't goin' nowhere special. Truthfully, I ain't goin' nowhere at all."

"You been walkin'. I'd say that's goin' somewhere. Sadly, our lives don't seem to be goin' nowhere, and that's the truth."

Levi smiled, but even a short laugh couldn't mask his uneasiness. "I ain't in a mood for that smart mouth o' yours. Not right now."

"Might as well make me a stranger, then, since I ain't shuttin' it anytime soon."

"Now you're soundin' like my mother," Levi noted. He pushed the small pebbles into a crumbling mound, then kicked them off the road into the grass.

"Except I just like the sound o' my own voice," Jonah retorted. He smiled proudly. "Your mama don't shut her damn mouth 'cause she chases her bullshit with whiskey. Betcha the most quiet you get is when she's busy takin' a sip."

"Or hangin' over the couch."

"She probably don't even know what a hangover is, seein' she ain't ever sober enough to get one. That mama o' yours is a piece o' work, ain't she?"

Levi winced.

Jonah gave him a slap on the back. He put his arm over his shoulder and guided him forward with a firm nudge. "Alright, let's get outta the dark."

"Ain't no gettin' outta the dark in this town."

"Well, ain't you the optimist," Jonah said. "I'd say there's a beer at Gene's with your name on it. Maybe a nice big tab, too. But don't you go sayin' the bottle's half empty."

••

Gene's was the only bar in town, and though no one knew whom it was named for, it was generally accepted that Gene must have been a low-class drunk who cared little about appearances. It was a seedy, one-room establishment, with wood paneling on the walls put up in the 1970s and never replaced or maintained. The permanent cloud of cigarette smoke did well to cover up the unsightly details, masking the tiny centipedes that too often managed to find their way inside, and the decade-old stain in the back corner left by a lush with a full bladder. Thankfully, that smell had faded over time, but Gene's always provided some other stench to sting one's nostrils.

"Ain't it a little weird for me to drink to forget Mama's drinkin'?"

Jonah took another gulp from his beer and set it down on the bar, exhaling sharply. "I ain't gettin' you piss drunk. One or two won't kill you. Speakin' of, I think I need myself another."

He looked over to find the bartender. The regular had left for the night, and Ms. Valerie Skinner had taken his place. Jonah scowled.

"Second thought, I think I might be good on that." He turned and put his hand on the bar, preparing to stand up. Neither he nor Levi were in the mood to deal with one of the Skinners. The whole family was bad news, except for the five youngest children, who were born into a crack house more for the welfare checks than for their parents' happiness. And of all the degenerates who lived on the north side of town, Valerie made Jonah the most uncomfortable.

"Well, well, well, if it ain't Mr. Young at my little ol' local."

Ms. Skinner had both hands on the dull wooden countertop, leaning forward with the insides of her scarred, scabby arms exposed. Her clumsily cut neckline, hanging down, presented the sharp ridges of her ribs at the center of her chest. Overall, she showed far too much skin for someone with such a leathery complexion and who was about forty pounds too thin. With a slender, skeletal hand she pulled another bottle from under the bar, popped it open and slid it in Jonah's direction. He caught it with one hand.

"I'm done drinkin' for the night, ma'am, but thank you kindly." Jonah held out the beer, as if to return an already open bottle, though at Gene's, the next patron probably wouldn't have cared even if it'd been half finished. Ms. Skinner didn't accept it, and waved her hand in casual rejection. She cracked a crooked, discolored smile.

"On the house, boy," she said, pushing it back in his direction. She rapped a yellowed finger against the foggy brown glass.

"I'm sorry, ma'am, but I don't think I can accept it."

Ms. Skinner frowned and took back the beer, then offered it to Levi. He, too, waved it away.

"Tough crowd tonight," she laughed. Sighing, she stepped back from the bar. "Ain't no skin off my nose, Mr. Young. Just tryin' to thank you for lettin' my sweet Gabriel court that pretty little sister o' yours. Y'ain't the senseless brother type, I reckon."

"Hannah'll do what Hannah'll do. Ain't much sense in tryin' to change it."

"Smart boy," she replied. "And just like your sister, Gabriel'll do what Gabriel'll do. Ain't much you can do 'bout that, neither. But don't you worry your handsome self—he'll take good care o' her. Me and my Reggie done raised that boy right. He ain't never hurt a fly, that'n. Or no fly that ain't had it comin'."

Jonah held back his response and looked to Levi for an exit strategy.

"It's gettin' late," Levi announced, standing up. "I got work in a few hours." He pulled out some cash from his back pocket and slipped it onto the bar. "Thank you for the beers, ma'am. And for offerin' my friend here one on you, even if he got too much pride to take it. Very kind o' you. Ain't that right, Jonah?"

Jonah nodded. "Very kind, ma'am."

Ms. Skinner pushed a gel-crusted strand of wiry blond hair behind her ear and smiled just a bit. "Don't y'all worry about it. And Mr. Young—take care o' your sister. Gabriel's took quite a likin' to her, and don't none of us wanna see him get hurt. You, least of all."

••

Levi slipped a pack of cigarettes into his back pocket as he and Jonah left Gene's. He'd gotten it from an old vending machine in the back of the bar, set behind the men shooting whiskey and the few women present who filled the air with smoke. It had been stubborn in accepting his wrinkled dollar bills, and it took a few slams of his fist into the plastic window before the red-branded label of Byron Clays finally dropped down into his waiting hands.

He sprinted a few steps to catch up with Jonah, who was marching with hateful determination, his clenched fists shoved into his pockets and shoulders hunched. The small rubber flap on the back of Levi's sneakers, half torn from constant wear, clicked and snapped against the pavement as he picked up his pace. It was like the ticking of a bomb, and Valerie Skinner had lit the fuse.

"What's the matter?" Levi asked. "Y'ain't still thinkin' about Hannah now, are you?"

"Course I am," Jonah grunted. "I thought she done ditched that son-of-a-bitch."

"I reckon that piece o' trailer trash ain't goin' nowhere soon, given he sounds like he ain't got his sights on no one else. Your sister's a pretty girl."

"And young enough to take advantage of without much tryin'."

"And also young enough to ignore anything her brother says to her. Hate to say it, but I ain't sure what you're expectin'. She ain't gonna listen."

"I ain't about to save my breath and sit back."

"Then you're gonna get yourself into a whole assload o' trouble," Levi warned. "Gabe don't seem the type to get outta the game just because big brother said so."

"So, I'm fucked no matter what, you're sayin'."

"Hannah'll come to her senses. Just wait it out, or you're gonna ruin it."

Jonah looked away toward the trees and sighed. "Too much time with that sack o' shit and she'll lose her senses entirely. Then there ain't no goin' back."

The two of them fell silent for a second, and Levi had no words to rekindle the conversation. Jonah was restless, tapping his foot lightly as if, at that moment, he was incapable of standing still with the threat of a junkie's unwelcome presence in his driveway just a little bit up the road. His thoughts of his sister's bad judgment were practically loud enough to hear, and his scowl left a lingering sense of desolation that thickened the air until it became even more oppressive than the summer humidity. Levi did his best to break the silence.

"I guess we'll be callin' it a night, then."

"Sounds like a good enough time as ever."

Levi shook his head as Jonah headed down past Shiloh Path, his back turned to a night that'd proven to be more disquieting than relieving. As his friend faded into the dark up the road, Levi reached into his pocket, pulled out his flashlight, and clicked it on. The old white mailbox greeted him with a dirty grin of peeled paint and mud splatter.

He crept up to his bedroom window and slid his fingertips through the thin opening he left for himself. When he climbed inside, he swiftly checked the door: it was still locked. Mama hadn't drunk enough to try to tamper with it. He opened it carefully and walked slowly down the hall, into the parlor. Mama was asleep, slumped back on the couch. The wood floor beneath her feet was wet with melting ice.

Cautiously, Levi approached her. He slipped the pack of cigarettes out of his pocket and set them gently on the coffee table. She'd find them in the morning when reaching for her glass.

# 2

THE WHITE PICKUP sat idling outside the Young family's home. It wasn't quiet. The old, overworked engine rumbled. Black smoke billowed from the rusted exhaust pipe; someone had written a vulgar word on the rear window, tracing a finger through the thin layer of kicked-up dust, but even that had begun to become foggy with moisture. The inside of the truck was just as humid as the summer air that rippled with the engine's heat. Gabe Skinner was sitting in the driver's seat, up to no good, as usual.

Jonah stopped and scowled. He never enjoyed seeing Gabe. Even in high school, a year prior, Gabe was the kind who was best to be avoided. Rumors circulated back then that he'd set a preppy girl's hair on fire in chemistry class, all because she'd mocked the dinginess of his hand-me-down clothes. The chemical stench of his father's smoked meth and summer sweat was nothing compared to the oppressive odor of Amber Calhoun's perfectly coiffed hair bursting into flame, they all said. Jonah wasn't sure if he believed the story or not, but there were too many alleged witnesses to outright deny it, which only added to Gabe's social infamy. The eldest Skinner boy developed the kind of presence that made you feel smaller, more insecure. More uncomfortable.

Jonah slowly approached the house, trying his best to stay in the shadows. Subtlety was simple, because the engine's shaky clatter muffled his careful footsteps. He made an effort to peer through the rear window, but the dim lighting worked against him, and whatever Gabe was doing remained concealed by darkness and dirt-splattered glass. Giving up, Jonah picked up his pace, and walked briskly past the pickup with his eyes set on the house's front door. He told himself not to look back, but couldn't fight the urge.

Gabe's face was slick with sweat, his sickly skin shining pale in the harsh glow of the headlights. His chest, with its concave deformity, heaved with heavy breaths, as if he were recovering from strenuous movement, or a sign of an impending overdose. Hannah sat beside him, eyes wet with tears, filling the role of one of many girls who were far too young for him, but whom he managed to effortlessly manipulate.

The two were talking—or at least Hannah was, since Gabe had more of a penchant for shouting—but they stopped abruptly when Hannah caught eyes with her brother. Gabe shot his gaze up at Jonah and sneered, his unsightly teeth like fangs. Unsure of what to do, Hannah raised her hand to quickly wave and acknowledge Jonah's arrival, but Gabe snatched her wrist and forced her hand down against the seat. She winced, and leaned back slightly against the window, fogging up the last sliver of clean glass with her breath.

Jonah began to fumble with his keys. They jingled as he shakily pushed one into the keyhole, but, even in his nervousness, he still turned his head to keep an eye on Hannah. The two were talking again, with Hannah reaching for the door. Gabe gripped her shoulder before she could open it and pulled her to face him. Forcefully dragging a hand over her chest, he leaned in, and, probably to his disappointment, Hannah pecked a hurried kiss on his cheek before swinging open the door. She hopped out and dashed from the truck; Gabe held the natural scowl his eyebrows made, shaking his head. He violently threw the pickup in reverse and hit the gas, the wheels scraping against the dusty ground before he shot backward toward the highway.

Jonah took his hand off the doorknob and left the keys hanging from the lock. He crossed his arms, waiting for Hannah to scale the two steps up to the creaky porch.

"And what was that, exactly?"

Hannah looked down, reluctant to answer.

"I hope things ain't gettin' serious with you two," he said sternly.

"You smell like beer."

"Quit it," he snapped. "This ain't about me."

His sister pouted like the little girl of fourteen that she was. "I know."

"How long were you two campin' out here? Do Ma 'n Pa know about it?"

"Not too long," she murmured, biting her lip. Jonah squinted, suspicious. She wasn't a talented liar; she gave up the act quickly, rolled her eyes and dropped her shoulders. "Fine," she sighed. "An hour. Two, maybe. I don't know."

"Just talkin'?"

Hannah nodded. "Yep."

"So what? That kid just came on over here to talk?"

Clearly uneasy about the prospect of telling another lie, she replied, "No, he picked me up after school let out."

"Seein' that it's midnight, you were out for nine whole hours?"

"We went drivin' south of town."

"I know you ain't told Ma 'n Pa you were out doin' God-knows-what down in Hebron all day. So what'd you tell 'em? They sure as hell know you weren't studyin'. There ain't much he can teach but how to find a good vein."

"I told 'em I was with you."

"Jesus, Hannah," he groaned. "You pulled me into this stupid lil' lie of yours? Now I gotta cover for you, too? And for what, so you 'n Gabe Skinner could get some time to yourselves? Christ, he's got six years on you." He whispered sharply, trying to keep his voice down.

"He ain't that bad," Hannah whimpered, shaky-voiced.

"What, once you get to know him?"

"Yeah."

Without warning a light went on in the house, the glow softened by sheer, white cotton curtains. Even with hushed voices their confrontation had woken their parents. Jonah prayed for his sister's sake that it hadn't been Gabe's squealing tires that summoned them out into the living room. At the same time, he wondered if she might benefit from being caught. If the jig were up, then maybe she wouldn't start at it again. But in her youth, she was too prideful for that.

"Get yourself inside before Ma 'n Pa see you sneakin' in so late," he advised, lightly grabbing Hannah by the shoulder and pushing her toward the door. "They think you're the 'smart one' in the family, so start actin' the part. You'd best be thinkin' about what that Skinner kid really wants from you. I bet you it ain't nothin' good."

••

Levi hadn't caught much sleep by the time his alarm went off. At five in the morning, the light passing through his bedroom window was bluish and dim. The harsh blare of music too loud for such small speakers echoed off the naked walls. Picture frames might have helped dampen the sound, but Levi had none. Shutting off the radio with an ungraceful swat at the snooze button, he opened his sleep-sealed eyes.

He pulled his legs over the side of the bed and pushed himself up to stand. The room lit up with the tug of the chain hanging from the naked light bulb above. The brightness stung his eyes, and he made his way blindly across the room, covering his face with one hand and reaching out with the other. The closet was open wide, the sliding door pulled aside, but Levi's shirt was draped over the top of the dresser. He never bothered to hang up the stained tank top he wore to work. Any other employer would have been horrified by his manner of dress, but working in the hot Southern sun at a gas station didn't warrant formalwear, of which Levi had little, anyway. Only three wire hangers of a dozen or so held a dress shirt—each a button-down reserved for Sundays. Grabbing the work shirt and pulling it over his head, he caught sight of the broken picture frame he'd carelessly covered, the only one he owned. A crack in the glass ran across Pap's face, ending at a young Levi's chest, with Mama smiling, untouched.

Levi pushed his legs into his jeans, put on his still-tied shoes and headed through the house and out the door. His wallet and keys were still in his pockets, and his pants smelled of stale smoke, compliments of Gene's and his mother. He left the door unlocked.

It was unseasonably cool outside, and the chill of the early morning air dropped a slick film of moisture on his skin. He ran a hand over his bare shoulder and flicked the dampness away. As he headed northward into town, sweat, in spite of the cold, beaded at his forehead. AlaCo was just under two miles from home, but Levi found himself wishing each day that he had a car. After four years of working (or was it five?), he'd never gotten a ride from Mama, and Heaven forbid she allow him to drive himself. She was fiercely opposed to the idea of him behind the wheel, unwaveringly convinced that he'd find himself guilty of vehicular homicide. She never expressed much concern that he himself might die in the crash, but there was a fear in her eyes that undermined her act of not caring. Besides, the old Cadillac could barely handle the short drive to the diner.

That diner—the Americana—was the only open store on Main Street at that hour. Mama was probably working. She always left the radio on when she was home, even when sleeping, and Levi hadn't heard classic blues seeping through the paper-thin walls that morning. Mama was queen of the graveyard shift, taking whatever hours she could. Levi could only imagine how she spent her time. There were only so many milkshake glasses to line up across the shelves.

Past the diner came the gas station. Its bland, square sign, bearing ALACO in red, white and blue, towered over the road, illuminating it with only a soft flicker of dying neon light. The dark speckles on the glowing banner were a mix of dust and dead insects. Levi still couldn't quite figure out how they made it inside the sign, attracted by the light, only to starve and drop lifelessly to the bottom. Maybe if the pile of desiccated husks grew high enough, one hopeless bug might manage to crawl over its fallen comrades and escape the filthy plastic prison.

In the center of the tiny parking lot stood a lone gas pump covered by a rusted metal awning, where Levi was to stand for twelve grueling hours in the sun, talking to foul-mouthed truckers on their way to Birmingham and churchgoing families who wished he'd pump faster. He'd get his shoes soaked in carelessly spilled gasoline bubbling from the swollen tank of a pickup, and would have to plunge them in a bucket of water outside Mama's back door when he got home. And he'd need to scrub his skin three times in the shower to get rid of the dirt and lingering smell of fuel.

All in a day's work, he supposed. The sun was rising over the trees off the highway, and it was met with the sliding-then-crashing sound of the garage door opening. Levi's boss stood to the side, his huge hand on the switch. Russell—or Rusty, as he'd usually assert—was the lead mechanic. He'd taken over as the manager as well, and the extra work hadn't taken much of a toll on him, given that he had a mere five employees working under him. The real owner of the gas station never frequented his franchise; Levi had never even met him. He suspected the mythical owner might have been invented by Rusty himself, just to blame the poor working conditions on a fictional scapegoat whose existence no one could ever disprove. Levi always wondered why Rusty couldn't have come up with something better than Mr. Smith, choosing a name that was ironically synonymous with anonymity. It made Mr. Smith that much more dubious.

"Mr. Smith's the one who's dockin' your pay," he'd insist when Levi's paycheck came up short.

"Mr. Smith thinks minimum wage is bad for business," he'd say when Levi questioned his rate of pay compared to that of the country at large.

"Mr. Smith says we can't afford to hire more help," he lamented when Levi had worked two and a half weeks straight, and had been hoping for one day off, even a half day.

Levi had learned not to complain over time, but there always came a chance day that the pump didn't work, a driver was obnoxious, or his tip was pitifully small, and then he'd appeal to Rusty, who blamed his problems on the managerial bogeyman. Levi had tried to find other work, but Clemency was an economic graveyard, and sadly, he couldn't climb out of the early grave he'd dug for himself. College would have been a viable means of escape if he'd had the money for it. Maybe he didn't pay rent, but he paid Mama's bills on the regular, though she would readily deny it. He couldn't afford to leave. Education wasn't an option, and the only learning he'd continued was in watching Rusty work on cars, and even that never paid off. He was stuck in his role as pump attendant, and his window of opportunity was closing as fast as the drivers' windows after they'd begrudgingly slipped him a tip.

Rusty looked out the garage and caught sight of his most overworked employee, and proceeded to walk outside to greet him with orders. He nearly had to duck down because of his height. He opened his mouth to speak, but a truck in the distance honked its horn at a daring squirrel, interrupting him. He tightened his arms, puffed out his chest, then pointed out to the highway. A Mack truck, its exhaust pipe spewing gritty, black smoke, slowed down before turning in to the parking lot, hissing as it came to a stop at the pump.

"First catch o' the day," Rusty noted, chuckling at Levi's tired frown. He turned around and slipped back into the garage, disappearing into the comfort of the shade, of which Levi would grow jealous by noon.

Levi approached the driver's window, looking up to meet the man's gaze. The glass slid downward and a strongly muscled arm against the door preceded the driver's face, iconic in its ruggedness and topped off with a baseball cap bearing an obscure beer label. He'd seen the driver's type before, more times than he could count over the past years. But this one wasn't smoking a trademark cigarette. That didn't bother Levi, who tried his best to avoid being choked by clouds of smoke, or worse, being killed in a massive explosion when the gas caught fire. The trucker paid and went on his way before any disasters could strike.

Hours passed until the sun was at its peak and sweat beaded on Levi's brow. Saturday traffic to and from Lillian and Hebron gave him plenty of work, and Rusty got his fair share as well, the garage flashing with sparks and rumbling with the thunder of drills and ratchets. But when a short line grew and an impatient von Braun family began honking their horn, the morning of toil reached its privileged and condescending climax.

They pulled up in their shiny black Bentley, completely out of place. Living like royalty high on a hill on the west side of town, the von Brauns were exiled travelers from the foreign country of New York who'd settled in what was easily, in Levi's view, the most irrelevant town in the American South, and by no means an appealing destination. They'd moved to Clemency when their son Jimmy was in high school, the same age as Levi, but after his graduation they fled the boondocks for unknown reasons. Many suspected that George von Braun, the wealthy patriarch and sly entrepreneur, had run himself into legal troubles up in the Northeast after their abrupt disappearance. Consequently, they'd recently returned to Clemency to reclaim the textile factory a few miles out of town, which George had once owned and refused to give up so easily.

His decision to relocate back to the middle of nowhere was one that Jimmy von Braun outspokenly resented. He sat in the back seat with his sunglasses on and his baseball cap tipped down, club music blasting from his headphones so loudly that even Levi could hear it. For once, he was quiet, silently biting his fingernails instead of accusing everyone around him of trying to steal his parents' hard-earned income to pay for their classless lifestyles. In front of him sat his mother, Charlene, who was busy talking on her phone, her polished nails clicking against its stylish case. She'd chosen to treat Levi like a waiter, and a woman of her wealth and status never looked a waiter in the eye.

"Fill it up, premium," George ordered, sitting behind the wheel. "I'm sure you've got plenty."

Levi sighed and pulled off one of his work gloves, saying, "Given we ain't never had premium here in the first place, I'd say you're mistaken."

George turned to Charlene and told her the bad news. She covered the phone with her hand and slipped off her feline sunglasses, leaning over her husband to get a look at Levi. "Listen up, young man: What's your name?" she asked impatiently.

"Levi, ma'am."

"You do have last names down here, don't you?"

Levi rolled his eyes. "Thompson."

Jimmy tore his headphones from his ears and tossed his sunglasses on the seat. "Is that Levi Thompson over there?" he laughed, grinning with sick satisfaction. "Of *course* it is! I see life hasn't changed much, has it?"

"You're ridin' in the back o' your mama's car."

"Father's car," George interjected.

Charlene shook her head. "Mother's car."

"Point is," George continued, "regular isn't going to cut it."

"We'll be taking our business elsewhere," Charlene announced as if to upset Levi, who couldn't have cared less. She put the phone back to her ear and apologized for her rudeness, then continued her conversation.

"Well put. Guess we'll have to fill up when we get to Lillian, then," George said. "So long, Mr., um... Tompkins, is it?"

"Thompson, sir."

"Right."

"You know how to get there?" Levi asked, shifting his weight onto one leg.

George pointed behind him and opened his mouth to speak, but Jimmy cut him off with his know-it-all mouth. "It's, like, twenty miles north of here. Isn't that hard. It's probably just one road, too, right? I bet you people even call it a highway."

"Eighteen miles, really. But ain't no one's countin'."

Jimmy squinted. "Eighteen, then. That's two less miles that we have to worry about running out of gas on the side of the road. Who knows what kind of degenerates live out in the woods up there?"

"Gun-totin' cannibals, mostly," Levi replied, "with a taste for the over-privileged, I hear. I reckon you'll make it through, though. A quarter gallon'd probably get you to Lillian no problem in that new car o' yours."

"German-made, young man," George added, pointing and winking.

"It's British-made," Jimmy corrected, smacking the back of George's seat.

George shrugged. "Whatever make it is, it cost me a pretty penny."

"More than that washed-up mother of yours has probably made her whole life," Jimmy sneered. George shook his head but said nothing, whipped by his own child.

"I'd say you're probably right, but that ain't really none o' your business. I sure as hell wouldn't ask Mr. von Braun over here 'bout his pay. Ain't polite where I'm from."

Charlene sighed, "It *was* a lot higher—"

"Drop it," George snapped. "The factory's keeping us comfortable now *and* it's holding this entire town together. You remember that, Charlene. And you too, Jimmy."

"So now my husband's an altruist," she scoffed, breaking away from her private conversation on the phone once again. "Where did I go wrong?"

"You tell your mother she's always welcome to apply at the factory. I don't believe she works for us, does she?" George asked.

"No, sir."

"She's over at the Americana pouring burnt coffee at two in the morning," Jimmy laughed.

The thought of caffeine seemed to intrigue George. "That diner down the road? I'd say we've been idling here long enough, running on fumes. It's about time for something to eat, even if it's just a simple, one-star American burger. Mr. Tompkins—"

"Thompson."

"Of course. Mr. Thompson, I think we'll be paying your mother a visit—if she's working, that is. Otherwise I'll have my omelet served by someone else." George put the car in gear and looked up at Levi. "Work on getting that premium, alright? Go tell your boss that he's losing business without it."

"Most importantly, *our* business," Charlene added.

"Just think about it," George said. Then he pulled out into the road and headed toward town, the wheels of his shiny car scraping on gravel at the lip of the pavement. Mama had a rough time in store for her. The von Brauns would probably ask for roasted pheasant and fine, imported wine—except for George, who seemed content with eggs, even powdered ones from the Americana, and maybe Jimmy, who'd order a diet soda to stay at the edge of his forced starvation. Mama would share in Levi's suffering, and they'd be the most unpleasant customers that day. It was the first thing the two of them had shared in a long time.

••

Levi's mother always sat the two of them down toward the front of the Southern Mercy Bible Church. They sat alone, always ahead of the Youngs. That Sunday, the Young family sat directly behind them, with Jonah within whispering distance. Communicating during Sunday service was always risky business; while the Youngs only glared at Jonah when he'd been caught red-tongued, Lenore Thompson was a wrist grabber. Jonah always joked that Jesus's suffering was nothing compared to the abuse Levi suffered every Sunday morning. Lenore nearly fainted the first time she overheard.

Jonah glanced up at her to make sure she wasn't looking, but she was too involved in singing spirituals to notice any sacrilege on his part. He leaned forward and tugged on the back of Levi's shirt, drawing a subtle glance.

"You ain't gonna believe what happened after Gene's," he whispered.

Levi turned his head slightly. "She's sittin' right next to you." He pointed back at Hannah, who sat with legs crossed, hands in her lap, tapping one foot.

"She ain't listenin'."

"*I'm right here, Jonah*. I can hear you," Hannah declared, frowning.

"Well she ain't gonna say *nothin'* about this, now, even if she *is* listening," Jonah growled, jabbing his elbow into her arm. "Ain't that right, Hannah?"

"You hit a bruise, moron," she groaned.

"Is that part of the story?" Levi asked with genuine concern.

"*Y'all need to shut up.*"

"The Lord's listenin'!" Lenore snapped, slapping Levi on the wrist. He recoiled out of surprise and focused his attention on the Reverend Shaw, startled and obedient. John and Debra Young glanced over at their children with suspicion.

Jonah waited a little before making a second attempt at contact. He leaned in and whispered, "Caught the two of 'em gettin' all cozy and whatnot out in the driveway."

"Cozy and whatnot?"

"We ain't doin' *nothin'*," Hannah asserted, kicking her legs in frustration.

"Well *before* y'all was doin' nothin' out front, Gabe brought you all the way out to Hebron," Jonah elaborated.

"Is that true, Hannah?" Jonah's mother asked, turning her head to examine the look of horror on her daughter's face. Hannah froze. She turned pale with fear.

"Well—"

Levi unexpectedly came to her defense and spared her the futile effort. "It ain't," he whispered to Mrs. Young. "Gabe Skinner drove up to Lillian, but he was drivin' alone. I seen him myself, and filled his tank, sorry to say."

Jonah stared at Levi in complete shock. His mother seemed satisfied and went back to her singing. Hannah gave a deep sigh of relief and smiled at her rescuer. At least for another day, she remained safe at the top of the pedestal her parents had put her on, for better or worse.

Punching Levi in the shoulder, Jonah hissed, "What the hell are you doin'?"

Lenore turned her head and glared with righteous wrath. He shrugged at her, smiling innocently. She turned the page in her songbook and fixed the back of her hairnet before rejoining the congregation in song.

"You really wanna cause a scene here?" Levi whispered.

"Do *you?*" Lenore snapped, pointing an accusatory finger at him. Levi waved his hand in the air and dismissed Jonah and the whole graceless dialog.

The singing died down and the congregation took their seats again. The Reverend Shaw approached the pulpit, fixed his tie. He put both hands on the wooden frame and leaned in toward the mounted microphone; his words were fiery and powerful, enough to burn away the sins he found in everyone he met, but he still found himself dependent on the technology of the modern age he cursed so viciously.

"Y'all remember what Paul meant when he said, 'Never avenge yourselves, but leave it to the wrath of God?'" he asked, holding a hand out to procure a response. Someone in the back let out a howl of excitement.

"Seems simple, don't it? But I read my Bible day 'n night, thinkin' thoughts o' God and His Holy Word, and I gotta tell y'all, I done come to a new revelation, brothers 'n sisters!

"We been waitin' and waitin' but we ain't seen our sinful enemies cast out by the judgment o' God! We turned the other cheek to the atheists—"

"*Godless!*"

"—the homosexuals—"

"*Sinners!*"

"—and anyone else tryin' to say that America *ain't* a Christian nation and that God ain't got no place in runnin' this country," the Reverend testified. "We didn't do nothin' to 'em, even when they beat us down, callin' us 'racists' and 'bigots' and 'homophobes' and all sorts o' nasty names that we most certainly ain't, all 'cause Jesus taught us to!"

*"Praise Him!"*

"But y'know what, ladies 'n gents? I done realized that we been doin' it *all wrong!*"

*"Forgive us, Lord!"*

"We been waitin' for the hand o' God to strike them down, but *we're* the hand o' God!"

*"Glory to God!"*

"And it's us who's gon' sow his wrath upon this heathen nation! And when they's weepin' and wailin' for all their transgressions, us Christians'll be weepin' tears o' joy!"

*"Amen!"*

"So *raise* y'all voices up!" he shouted with conviction, and he summoned up a tempestuous roar. "And sing that song o' joy before y'all walk back out into that sad, sorry world!" The organ sounded and the faithful took their parts in one last hymn, the men singing low as rumbling thunder, the women singing high like white doves that fed on godless carrion. Jonah sat out on both the singing and the shouts and the prayers that followed, which felt as long as Leviticus.

The chatter of mingling church ladies rose over the shuffling of songbooks and paper bulletins being tucked away into purses and coats, only to be thrown out in kitchen trash cans. The throng of modest women stepped out into the sun with their white hats tipped forward, funneling through the open door that discerned entrants with more scrutiny than St. Peter. The Youngs stood up and walked single file down the aisle into the daylight. Lenore and Levi lagged behind.

Jonah waited on the steps for the two to finally come outside. Lenore appeared first, her white heels clicking on the concrete. Levi followed and passed Jonah without taking notice of him. Jonah stood and made himself known.

"Where y'off to?" he asked.

Levi looked to Lenore, who was walking toward their old Cadillac, weaving through the crowd that'd clustered in the road. She was too busy scolding an energetic little boy who'd accidentally knocked her purse to the ground to notice her son's brief absence. Levi turned to Jonah and replied, "Back home, I reckon. Mama don't stay out for long."

"To hell with your mother."

"Jonah, we're leavin'," Mrs. Young called out from the sidewalk. "You comin'?"

"I'll catch up," he answered, and his mother, unconcerned, continued walking with her husband and daughter down Main Street. They, like most people in Clemency, made it a habit to walk to Sunday service. Lenore, however, always had to be the first to get to church, and flew there on rusted eagle's wings built by a less-than-godly General Motors.

"What'd you have in mind?" Levi asked, curious but reserved.

"Haven't a clue, but with that mama o' yours, I'd say you need a break, and ain't no matter where." He glanced at Lenore, who'd stopped walking and was doubling back to claim her son. He nodded his head as a warning to an unsuspecting Levi. "Church is over, and for her, it's already five o'clock. I'll swing by in an hour or so, once she's out of it. She won't even know you're gone."

"The Lord done took your legs, boy?" Lenore barked. She snatched her son's wrist and pulled him away, unafraid of a dislocated shoulder. "This ain't the place for you," she scolded, then looked Jonah in the eye. "*Neither* o' y'all."

Jonah opened his mouth to respond, but Lenore never gave him the chance. "My boy ain't goin' nowhere with you today, Mr. Young. Sunday's a day for family, and I bet yours would agree." She waved her hand to shoo him away. "We're goin'. Y'all can offend the Lord another day."

••

The Cadillac's passenger door creaked when Levi pulled the handle, its hinges thick and brittle with rust, or maybe caked with mud kicked up by the whirling tires on Shiloh Path after a heavy rain. Whatever the cause, Levi failed to open the door completely. Its fussiness forced him to squeeze through the narrow opening and slip onto the seat. It took two tries to successfully close the door, and it slammed shut with an unpleasant bang.

Mama's door, however, swung open without a hitch. She sat down and put the key in the ignition, fiddling with it until the motor sputtered and roared. Pulling out of the high school parking lot, she turned right onto Main Street and drove slowly without her foot on the gas, as churchgoers crossed the road without looking in either direction. Since the Thompsons were one of the handful of families that actually drove to Sunday service, most weren't used to dodging cars. Levi saw Mama hold herself back from slamming her fist on the horn, tempted to force the crowd to scatter like pedestrian devils before an angel's trumpet.

They proceeded slowly through town. Mama hadn't said a thing yet—it was a silence that left Levi more than concerned. From experience he'd learned she could erupt at any second, putting Mt. Vesuvius to shame, and unfortunately, Levi was trapped in a mobile Pompeii. Only on Sundays was he thankful that Clemency was so small, and that the drive, even with foot traffic, would last five minutes at most. But only Mama could manage to turn five minutes into an agonizing hour, as time seemed to stop the second she opened her mouth.

The Americana was coming up on the right and Levi braced himself for an imminent attack. That diner was one of many triggers that lit Mama's fuse. When the window banner advertising a limited-time, two-dollar pancake breakfast came into view, Levi gripped the door handle like someone bracing for a violent collision. Mama turned her head. There it was.

"That Jonah Young's a bad influence," she began. "Ain't got the fear o' God in him." She didn't draw a response. Instead, her son only stared out the window at the passing storefronts.

His silence didn't deter her. "I done raised you right, boy," she said proudly, "because y'ain't gonna turn and spit in God's face. Y'ain't done nothin' to anger the Lord, 'cept maybe your bein' lazy. Work ethic, boy. Y'ain't got one. Idle hands—"

"—are the Devil's playground. I know."

"I reckon y'don't," she judged. "If y'did, I wouldn't be payin' for you every day." She seemed unaware of how wrong she was. For her, it wasn't even a lie. She really believed it.

Rolling his eyes, Levi kept his gaze away from her. They passed the intersection of Main Street and Gilead and the foot traffic dispersed; the town was dead beyond that point. Mama hit the gas slightly, shortening the rest of the drive by just a little, but still long enough to draw her routine Sunday lecture to a close. The Reverend Shaw's sermon always had an encore, and she had the honor of delivering it after a bump over the railroad tracks.

"Y'ain't honorin' your mother, makin' me work all night long just so you can take advantage. Y'don't ever thank me, neither."

"Ain't it 'honor your *father* and mother?'" he asked.

Mama's face sunk. "Maybe. But he ain't around to be honored by no one."

# 3

FOR THE MOST PART Jonah didn't mind his job at the library, though the silence was starting to get to him. He used to find it calming, and enjoyed the minimal human contact he engaged in, as he'd first gotten the job while he was in high school, back when he was the center of several social circles. It was a reprieve from impressing others with his seemingly effortless sense of humor and his natural athletic prowess, and was the one time throughout the day when he didn't draw attention to himself. And though few were aware, he enjoyed reading the books that didn't have many handlers. Math might not have been his strong suit, but he was more literate than most gave him credit for, though his intentional sabotage of his English grades didn't help. At that time, he expected that the number of field goals he kicked was more important to girls than the number of books he read. Sadly, football was a thing of the past, and no one really cared about how talented of a quarterback he was two years ago.

Swayne was quieter than the average public library, hearing less polite whispers because of Clemency's rapidly shrinking population of readers. Jonah couldn't say he was surprised by the recent trend, having considered the town backward at best for most of his life. His boss, Mrs. Lewis, cited a nationwide decline in literacy as the cause. Locally or nationally, there was no denying that any time the bell jingled as the front door opened, the customer was sure to be elderly. No one Jonah's age read anymore, and while he had a disorganized pile of books beside his bed, he pretended to be just like his peers. When young people of his generation did read, they read what Mrs. Lewis called "societal excrement," making them, in her mind, just supporters of cultural saboteurs who destroyed American literary heritage one smut story at a time. It was the bookstore across the street that sold such degenerate propaganda, she claimed, accusing Chickasaw Books of being a hotbed of low-class writers who penned their manuscripts in crayon. The store was expected to go out of business soon enough, and Mrs. Lewis was proud to have contributed to its entrepreneurial demise. Chickasaw was her failed rival, and she reveled in the clatter of its front door, rusted from neglect and disuse, because she likened its noise to the sound of nails driven into a coffin.

Mrs. Lewis, or Susan, as she informally preferred, was a woman of seventy or so, and one of only a handful of retirees from Israel Pickens, as the majority of high school teachers preferred to stand at the blackboard until the day they died. She'd quit the business of education before Jonah's time, preferring to work in an environment where people voluntarily kindled their literacy; she'd also recently quit smoking, a fact that she liked to remind people of over and over when she judged them as weak-willed. However, her long, faux fur coat, which nearly touched the ground when she walked, still stank of stale cigarette smoke. It looked like a carpet, under which she strung her pearls around a wrinkled, shaking turkey neck. The only time he'd ever seen her clean the coat was when she'd gotten a smudge of her blotchy red lipstick on the white trim. Even then, she didn't manage to get the smell out.

That day, she was sitting at the front desk with a stack of books to her right. She kept records by hand, as the library's computer had broken several months ago, and a lack of county funding kept her from buying another, though she probably wouldn't have known what to shop for, anyway. Susan refused to use the public computer desk that the library uselessly boasted, holding some hope that more people might come and make use of it. She didn't want to be in their seat when that day finally came, but because that day hadn't yet arrived, Jonah worked silently, uninterrupted, organizing books on their shelves and fixing those with broken bindings. There hadn't been a shipment of fresh books in months. Consequently, many had loose pages, some of which had faded and dried until they nearly crumbled when handled by an occasional reader. Most of the time, that reader was Jonah himself.

Sometimes his mother stopped by when she was on her break at the Hometown Market. A florist, she always smelled like flowers, and the scent that followed her was a pleasant break from the mustiness of aging paper in the humidity. Although her husband worked within walking distance at the local grade school, she could never visit him, as he was too busy mopping old tile floors and emptying trash cans stuffed with pencil shavings and notes passed by fifth graders just learning how to gossip. Sometimes when Jonah stayed late at the library, he'd see his father walking home in his blue uniform, a tired look on his face put there by the degradation he suffered daily. The teachers there seemed to think he was their personal butler, and consequently had no shame in giving orders.

There were those days when Jonah felt like a personal servant to Susan, but she paid him well—certainly much better than Levi's boss paid him, because even though Susan cursed the county, the state and the country for failing to properly fund her scholarly mausoleum, she still believed in minimum wage laws. While Levi was out pumping gas for wages anyone else would have reported to the Department of Labor, Susan was compensating Jonah at the legal requirement, but always under the table for reasons she never bothered to explain. A shrewd manager with a mind for business, she thought herself pretty clever for an old woman. Jonah learned it when he first started working at the library, when Susan consistently laughed at her own intentional puns about paying him "off the books." She milked that joke for months, to the point where Jonah would finish it for her, driving her to put him right back to work, bitter that he'd ruined her side-splitting punch line.

Yes, his job of stacking books was easy, and no, he didn't have to question his weekly earnings, but Jonah still ended up daydreaming as a natural means of escape, far too often for Susan's comfort. The sun shone through the front windows, enticing him to stare desperately through the glass toward the lifeless street. That day, the once modern buildings seemed to gleam for the first time in half a century. It was almost too much to bear for someone stuck piling books in the back of a musty library that'd had only one customer that day, and who'd left without a single book in her hands.

Jonah slipped their only copy of a popular erotic novel onto the shelf, which he imagined had been discarded by an unsatisfied buyer in some nearby town, given that it was in immaculate condition. It was one of a few dozen in his unsorted bin that afternoon, which filled up every day, though he never personally saw enough customers enter or exit to actually produce such a large pile of returns. He was suspicious that Susan took books at random and acted like someone from Clemency had actually rented it, just to make life less boring for her sole employee. She probably didn't really need his help, but Jonah figured she liked the company from ten to five.

But at two o'clock on the dot, when Jonah, like clockwork, looked out the window once again, Levi made his appearance. He came walking from north of town, presumably from work. He avoided going inside and unwittingly jingling the bells mounted to the bottom of the door. Instead, he just waved and pointed out toward the street, and, by a stroke of luck, Jonah happened to notice. Jonah shrugged, arms out—a wordless *"What do you expect me to do?"* Levi pointed again, this time toward the back of the library, to the freight door that hadn't been opened since before the sandy-haired boy had even been a thought in his then-sober mother's mind. But before Jonah could make a break for it, he took a peek at Susan. She was quietly stamping and cataloging books, adding even more ink to the purplish stains on her fingertips. She never quite seemed able to wash it off.

Jonah made his way through the small maze of bookcases and slipped into the narrow corridor at the back of the library. The freight door loomed at the end of the hallway, more like a massive slab of ruddy, crusted metal than a door, past the one-toilet bathroom with its half-ply toilet paper (if such a thing existed), and a closet stuffed full with a mess of cardboard boxes and banned books pulled reluctantly from the shelves. Its metal paneling was so untouched that the padlock had become rusted and brittle and fell to the floor in two pieces. He carefully gripped the handle and slowly raised the door. It lurched and shuddered with a graceless bang when it reached its meager limit.

"What in the hell was that, kid?" Susan yelled from the front end. "There ain't a single book heavy enough to make that kind of fracas!"

"Thought I heard somethin' out back!" Jonah answered. It wasn't really a lie: Levi stood outside the open door, covering his mouth to hide his laughter, which still slipped out as muffled breaths through his fingers.

"That Reggie Skinner better not be rummagin' through our dumpster again!" Susan shouted, though it'd been a few weeks since they last saw the Skinner patriarch searching for food or needles in the garbage, as if a public library had any to dispose of in the first place. Susan cackled in her smoky voice, "Ain't he got enough trash at home?" Levi burst out into hysterics, and Jonah cracked a smile. After that, they didn't hear another word from the bleached-blond librarian.

"Ain't you supposed to be workin'?" Jonah asked, arms crossed. "I'm sure there's a line o' truckers in need of servicin', not to make you sound like a prostitute."

"There ain't no cars to fix today, so Rusty generously took it upon himself to take over."

"Probably ain't in your best interest to go home just yet, though. That mama o' yours is gonna accuse you of bein' a lazy sack o' shit."

"She's outta whiskey, I think. I seen her milkin' a few drops outta last night's glass."

"You tellin' me you're gonna buy her liquor before she ain't even asked you yet?"

"A preemptive tactic. If it pushes back a war till tomorrow, then yeah, I'm willin'."

"I'm out in a few. I'll meet up with you after."

"What you got in mind?"

Jonah shrugged. "We ain't never got plans to do nothin' but always end up findin' somethin' to keep our sorry asses busy," he noted. In a town like Clemency, creativity was a necessity for the younger crowd, who had to live the childhoods of those who grew up decades before them, when first-person shooters and other expensive electronic distractions weren't an option.

"Sounds alright to me," Levi said. "Meet me at Jericho and the railroad tracks when you're out." Jonah nodded and gave a thumbs-up as he pulled the freight door shut. It made an even louder clatter than before. He walked back through the library and got started on another stack of books, beginning with a novel in French that he couldn't believe anyone in Clemency was capable of reading.

"What took so long?" Susan asked, taking off her horn-rimmed reading glasses and setting them on the desk. She squinted suspiciously. "Either that Reggie was too doped up to leave without a fight, or you done clogged up the goddamned toilet."

"Took me a good while to rid us of that junkie, ma'am."

Susan chuckled and rolled her eyes. Slipping her glasses back on, she said, "Hope he found somethin' good in the dumpster, then. Lord knows he's gotta feed that family o' his somehow."

••

Levi reached into his pocket to find his money before opening the door to Backwater Spirits. He had it tucked away into his father's old wallet, which otherwise held Levi's license and a loyalty punch card for the Hometown Market, of which all ten purchases had been clipped by a hole puncher. It entitled the holder to one free bouquet of flowers, of any variety but roses, since they were a little too expensive. Levi never bothered to claim his father's untouched reward, figuring that such an offer expired back in the early nineties, when that first bouquet had been bought, only to later be tossed in the trash, withered and unsightly.

He stepped inside and looked over at the store owner, who was slipping a piece of yellow paper into a book to mark his place. He looked up at Levi and said kindly, "Good afternoon, young man. Whiskey, I take it?"

Levi cracked a halfhearted smile. He was disgusted to think that his mother had forced a reputation upon him. "Ain't it always?"

"I'll ring it up right now."

"I take it by now you know the brand and all."

"You're like me, boy: a creature of habit. You, or the lady you're shoppin' for."

"Like I said last time, sir," Levi answered as politely as he could, "ain't really your concern."

The store owner raised an eyebrow and grinned. "And like I said last time, young man, I reckon it ain't. But it don't hurt to try and converse."

"Y'ain't got much customers, do you?"

"I'd say you're one of a handful o' regulars. Guess these God-fearin' Christians ain't got much of a taste for drinkin'. After all, Jesus must've turned water into grape juice."

"I ain't much of a fan, neither," Levi confessed, "but it ain't out of a fear o' God."

"A fear of somethin' else, maybe?"

"Sir—"

"Ain't my concern, I know. Pardon me for askin'. Just ain't never met a kid your age who ain't a binge drinker o' sorts. You're a bit too young to be livin' like me, sober and happy about it."

"Y'can't tell me you're a liquor store owner who don't drink." Levi was growing curious.

"Ain't touched a drink in a long time. Comin' on twelve years, if I ain't mistaken." With clanging bells the register burst open even before Levi had put the bottle on the counter, and just as quickly, the owner slammed it shut. "Don't pay no mind today, young man," he said. "On the house."

Levi shook his head, refusing the offer. He pulled the money from his pocket and hoped he'd be able to shove a few crumpled bills into the man's hand and slip out the door. "I'm sorry, sir, but I can't accept."

"Oh, yes you can," he replied. "And you will. I gather y'ain't much of a talker, but I ain't had much conversation with no one for what seems like months. Besides, I'd say you're a regular by now, and giveaways are good for business. Keeps 'em comin'."

Levi smiled and slipped the bottle under his arm, concealed in a brown paper bag that only made its contents more obvious and even more clichéd. "Y'ain't got to worry 'bout keepin' my business, sir." He reached out his free hand. "Levi Thompson, by the way. I ain't caught your name yet."

The store owner clasped Levi's hand. His light-skinned palms were thick and rough. "Elijah—Elijah Green, Mr. Thompson. Been a pleasure."

The realization ran through Levi's mind that it'd taken him over a year to learn Elijah's name. He felt a tinge of guilt for not having said much before. "Well, I'm off, Mr. Green."

"Elijah."

"Yeah, Elijah. I'll see you around. Thanks a million."

"No thanks needed," Elijah replied. Levi was just about out the door when the man called out again. "Oh, and Mr. Thompson—"

"Yes?"

"—let me know if your mama's interested in tryin' somethin' else. I'm thinkin' of orderin' a new brand in the future, but I wouldn't want it to go to waste. Change is good every once in a blue moon."

"Sir—"

He laughed. "Ain't my concern. I know."

••

The sun was starting to make Jonah sweat. Sunset was a few hours away, but the suffocating heat hadn't subsided by even half a degree. He loosened one more button on his shirt, leaving it open at the base of his ribs—an act of immodesty the Reverend and his wife would have harshly judged, because any more than one loose button was promiscuous at best. The shirt had been white when he first wore it. Now it was dull and tinged with gray; it wasn't stained by perspiration, but by the dust that wafted up from open books, which seemed to bind to its fibers like glue. The fabric didn't breathe well, either. Lucky for him, Susan lined the library walls with buzzing floor fans. They were old and shaky, and Jonah feared that one day a stray blade might fly across the room and decapitate him, making him a martyr for literacy.

He waited where the railroad tracks met Jericho Road and looked down the street in boredom. Just after five o'clock, all the schools along the road had already let out. He suspected, though, that there was at least one after-school club meeting in the Parsons School library, the shelves of which were stocked more with End Times fiction than textbooks. Usually the students who frequented the library after hours were studying each other, not intelligent design, and certainly not evolution. Despite their illiteracy in sex education, the Parsons kids had no trouble figuring it out themselves by trial and error, with some help from the pornographic—and commonly forgotten—parts of the Bible. King Solomon was their guide and his Song of Songs was their manual. The forbidden fruit they tasted was as delicious as they'd imagined, and many boys searched the classroom orchards for the pomegranate trees most easily climbed and ripest for the picking. Few returned from the harvest empty handed.

But after graduation, the trees were uprooted and brought far away to be planted and pollinated in the fertile soil beneath the windows of college dorms, and Jonah was left with an empty field and only rotten fruits to pick from. The girls were gone, and so were their chasers, except for Jonah, who, like Levi, remained bound to Clemency with nothing to eat but the spoiled food of his own memories. All they gave him was a sour stomach and a hunger that he couldn't seem to satisfy. As far as he was concerned, he'd gone hungry for too long. If someone were to manage to sway him into going to college, however unfeasible, then the prospect of a hookup a week would certainly be a strong motivator.

His stomach growled—never mind the metaphorical starvation he'd suffered: he hadn't eaten lunch that day. He put his hand to his belly and grimaced. If he weren't waiting for Levi to show up, he'd run over to the Americana and grab a sandwich to go. There was no way he'd be willing to sit down at a booth and risk being served by Levi's mother. Not only would leaving a tip be awkward (especially knowing that Levi wouldn't see a dime of it), but Lenore's glares of blatant judgment would be enough to spoil his appetite. A ham and cheese sandwich with Christian guilt on the side wasn't his idea of a satisfying meal.

That's when—*Finally,* he thought—Levi came walking around the corner to meet him just where he'd told him to wait with growing impatience. His face held the lingering pout that always dulled his eyes after he'd done something that made him feel guilty: most often, it was a fight with his mother, but Jonah knew there hadn't been time for such a disaster to strike. Jonah saw it on him after he'd bought a bottle of whiskey, harboring the sickening regret of tacitly condoning his mother's mistakes and hastening her downward spiral. He'd seen it more times than he could count. The day when Lenore would stop leaving lines on her son's face, or when Levi's skin would thicken enough to render her words powerless, couldn't come soon enough.

"Y'look like shit."

Levi rolled his eyes, light browns disappearing beneath tired eyelids. He kept on walking and Jonah followed at his side. In his hand he carried a brown paper bag, with the neck of a whiskey bottle peeking out into the thirsty world around it. The two both stepped over the rails and followed the rusted lane southward back into town. Levi picked up the pace.

"Is that for us, or your mama?" Jonah asked, clearly knowing the answer, and he sprinted a quick burst to keep up.

Hands thrust into his pockets and his head held low, Levi met Jonah's gaze without stopping and shrugged. "My shoes still smell like gasoline. I ain't goin' home yet to wash 'em off."

"Don't you wanna drop off that bottle before your mama starts gettin' thirsty? I'll tell you what: slip somethin' in her drink next time 'round. I got plenty of eye drops at home that'd give her some wicked runs. She ain't gonna notice you out back when she's hauled up in the bathroom." He drew a slight smirk out of his friend. "Just somethin' to think about."

"She ain't pulled out the belt in years, but I guarantee I'd have a raw back real quick."

"Y'look like you got somethin' in mind for us to do," Jonah noted, "seein' as you're walkin' so damn fast."

"Gotta wash my feet off," Levi replied. "And get off the street, carryin' this paper bag. I don't want no reputation as a travelin' drunk. I swear, it don't run in the family."

"We got a tub at home, y'know."

"I ain't gonna be a burden on someone else, too," Levi groaned. Jonah suspected Levi was reluctant to break their unintentional (and strange) tradition of having never set foot in each other's houses. Their superstitions had grown over the years as a way of rationalizing the irony of childhood friends and next-door neighbors knowing next to nothing about the color of their respective bathroom walls or kitchen floors. To find out firsthand would be to violate a near-sacred divide.

Levi pointed toward the woods to the side of the tracks. "That there creek ain't gonna be cold this time o' year. Ain't no one's gonna bother me there, 'specially that woman." He parted a thorny bush and pushed his way into the trees. "Not without gettin' cut up real bad when she stumbles in screamin' for what's rightfully hers."

••

Levi pulled off his shoes and socks and dipped his bare feet into the cool water of the creek. The soft caress of the trickling stream washed away his concerns like those last dregs of gasoline taken by the current. He sat down at the pebbly edge of the water, his jeans pushed up to his calves, and leaned back with his weight on his hands. He heard the crunch of the earth beneath him. It felt good to be away from Main Street, out in the wilderness where animals were meant to be animals, and not among the human beasts that wandered in their spiritual wasteland.

Jonah, about twenty feet away, took a seat on top of a large rock jutting out from the mossy soil, a smooth plank over a shallow sea. His legs hung from the edge and he laid back onto the stony surface, chewing on a toothpick, one of many he kept in a bundle in his pocket. He cracked it in half accidentally with his teeth. Drawing another from his supply, he flicked the pieces of the first into the creek. The shards floated on the surface, and brushed against Levi's foot as they traveled away downstream.

"How's the water?" Jonah asked.

"Ain't bad," Levi said. "Not that you got any real interest in jumpin' in, anyway."

"Sorry if I ain't got a death wish," Jonah shot back. "I'd break my neck jumpin' in from up here. I got news for you, buddy: we ain't kids no more. I betcha it don't even reach past your waist by now."

Levi laughed, closed his eyes and felt the sun's warmth on his face through the swaying trees. He missed the days when he and Jonah would take a walk over to the woods instead of coming straight home after grade school let out. In the summer they'd strip down and swim naked in the creek, the water swallowing them up to their shoulders; the winter saw the exchange of double-dog dares to sprint across the ice without falling through. Levi got caught waist deep in the frozen stream only once. Mama was horrified when she saw him dripping wet at the door with frost clinging to his legs, convinced he'd been frostbitten to the point of losing a limb. Pap just laughed and fetched a dry towel for his shivering son. He had to spend an hour convincing his wife that an amputation wasn't necessary, and that they didn't need to invest in a wheelchair. She finally calmed down when Levi's lips lost their bluish tint.

He remembered the sound of Mama striking matches to light their old, grease-splattered gas stove when she fixed him some tea. Six years old, he didn't much care for it, but Mama insisted that while the ice on his skin had melted, his insides could still be frozen without him even knowing it. The feeling of the hot drink flowing down into his stomach was paradoxically comforting and unpleasant, like the opposite of a hot glass splashed with ice water exploding in the washer's hands. Mama even made him stand on a chair with his hands held over the blue flames fluttering on the stovetop. And right then, sitting at the side of the creek, Levi heard that crackling sound of a sparked match again.

It came from Jonah, who was cupping his hands over his mouth with a lit match in the other. He shook the flame out and tossed the charred stick aside. Wisps of smoke tumbled from the glowing tip of the joint he revealed, the sweet, skunky odor drifting down from his perch.

"Really?"

Jonah squinted as he took a deep drag and inhaled sharply. Exhaling, he shook his head. The smoke rose and curled into a hazy halo above him. "Just 'cause you never got a taste for it don't mean I can't partake a little," he argued, throat clenched.

"Hope your little sister ain't thinkin' the same way," Levi said freely.

Sitting upright, Jonah glared. He took a quick hit and blew the smoke to the side. "If she knows what's good for her, she ain't."

"A Skinner's a Skinner, and all o' them older ones is always fixin' for somethin'. I betcha that Gabe just gets his outta his mama's purse."

"Her panties, I'd wager."

"Y'know damn well that walkin' infection don't wear no panties."

Jonah choked on the smoke, sputtering with clouds blasting from his nostrils like a dragon's breath. Levi continued, "What I'm sayin' is there ain't no way Gabe ain't smokin' or snortin' or shootin' up somethin' he shouldn't. And you best make sure that sister o' yours ain't dabblin', too."

"This coulda been over with if you hadn't went and covered for her."

"Just talk to her about it before things get ugly."

Jonah climbed down and stood at the water's edge. He snuffed out the smoldering joint on the rocky soil and, after making sure it was extinguished, put it behind his ear. "Only Levi Thompson could kill a high like that."

"Hate to piss in your corn flakes, but it's for your own good," Levi concluded.

"And a big hit or two would do *you* a whole lotta good. This ain't your problem."

"I—"

"And I know what I'm doin', so don't you work yourself up over it." He held out his hand to help Levi stand, who was shoving his wet feet back into his shoes. Jonah took the lead back toward town with Levi tailing him, his footsteps soft and squishy. During their walk, Levi said nothing more on the matter.

SUNDAY CAME TOO QUICKLY, and before Jonah knew it, he was dragged to the Southern Mercy Bible Church by his mother, who held a nervous look on her face as they were the last ones to enter the sanctuary. Hannah had demanded hot water for her shower, and it ran out right before she stepped in; she blamed Jonah, and Jonah blamed the boiler, and his mother blamed the both of them for her headache. To add to her stress, she scuffed up her heels on the way over, determined to arrive at the church at least a minute before the rest of her family. It was debatable if such hurriedness would absolve her of the cardinal sin of tardiness. It was just as detestable that she allowed her own children to arrive even later than she did, as it was a clear sign of ineffective parenting. She'd failed just as miserably in getting her son to keep quiet during service. Levi, though, was the real instigator.

"You say somethin' to her yet?" Levi whispered from the next pew over. "Seriously—don't no one wanna see this lil' affair get any uglier."

Jonah shook his head. Levi glared, visibly frustrated that his friend hadn't heeded his advice, as if it were that easy. He snapped his attention back to the pulpit when Lenore, sitting beside him, dabbed her eyes with a white handkerchief now blotted with black. The Reverend Shaw, too, had tears in his eyes, raising arms to God with clenched fists, begging forgiveness for the sins of His people and vengeance upon those who persecuted them. The spiritual leader of the Southern Mercy Bible Church rarely turned the other cheek.

Hannah didn't catch on to what Levi tried to whisper but couldn't keep adequately hushed. Jonah sighed with relief, apprehensive about bringing up the subject, because no time or place really seemed right for that line of questioning. He'd considered tailing her to see exactly what she was doing with Gabriel Skinner when they disappeared for hours. The family car was available, and all he needed was the keys, not permission. But jumpy Hannah, easily startled, would probably notice if Gabe's pickup was being followed by the Youngs' familiar Ford.

Lenore drew a compact mirror from her wristlet. With a click she opened it and took a quick look at the rivulets of mascara running from her eyes. She calmly put the mirror away and looked over at her son, who, from what Jonah could tell, was trying his best to focus solely on the sermon and shut out his mother. In a rare breach of ecclesiastical propriety Lenore stood up from her seat and tiptoed her way out the side door. She clutched her handkerchief over her heart as she disappeared to find the bathroom.

Jonah leaned forward and put his elbows on the back of the wooden pew. "Waitin' for the opportune moment," he whispered close to Levi's ear. He wasn't lying, either.

"You best be tellin' the truth, now. Your bullshit stinks worse than most."

"I'm insulted," Jonah said, feigning offense. "I ain't the lyin' type."

Victoria Shaw's sudden outburst interrupted their exchange. She stood up on top of her seat and trembled with sublime gratitude, ready to beat her chest to the rhythm of her racing heartbeat. She went into her usual rapture, one she'd scripted over the years, though perhaps the Holy Spirit just had a set routine from which He rarely deviated. "Can't y'all see that the Devil 'imself's tossin' all kinds o' temptations at y'all's sons 'n daughters? Who they gonna turn to when sin's all around 'em, if y'all believers done raised 'em right?"

*"Christ Almighty!"*

She snatched her daughter's wrist and pulled her up from the seat beside her, holding her arm high in the air as a sign of victory. "I done put the fear o' God in my baby girl since the day she was born, and she ain't never gon' be a Jezebel! Ain't no boy's gonna get her to turn her back on the Lord! So go 'n tell *that* on the mountain!"

The congregation whistled and shouted in celebration of their spiritual leaders' success story of good, Christian parenthood. Victoria let go of Sophia and waved for the choir to stand and sing songs of hope and joy that their children might resist the snares of the Devil, which came in the guise of low-cut shirts and miniskirts. Sophia humbly sat back down, with the flowing white robes of the singers billowing and red sashes swaying behind her. Jonah couldn't take his eyes off her. He saw her like a portrait with an ever-shifting background, though the face before it stayed the same.

She played with a lock of her long, black hair and smiled insecurely, looking up at the pulpit. Her eyes were the rich amber he remembered them to be. He had shyly caught eyes with her across the table all the time during Sunday school. He even sketched them crudely in crayon in the margins of the lesson pamphlets. When his teacher caught him, he always claimed them to be God's eyes watching over the world. His excuses to hide his crushes worked back then, but that was a long time ago.

"You better make that 'opportune moment' come pretty damn quick, 'cause it ain't easy to doze off when they're singin'," Levi murmured. Jonah didn't answer; Hannah snored and, for a second, woke herself up. Her head fell back down again.

"Your sister's sleepin'," he said again. No answer. "Hello?"

He finally caught Jonah's attention. "Sorry. What's that you were sayin'?"

Levi rolled his eyes and looked ahead. At that same moment, Jonah caught eyes with the Reverend's daughter a second time. She smiled at him—right at him—and waved, fluttering her fingers delicately out of her mother's sight. Victoria rolled with the Holy Ghost and couldn't have noticed. Her eyes were set on Heaven, with nothing but a bright, white light at the end of her tunnel vision.

Jonah smiled back. Levi took notice. He raised an eyebrow, drawing a simple shrug. "What?" Jonah asked.

"You're playin' with hellfire, there."

Lenore returned with her makeup looking perfect as ever. She apologetically pushed her way back to her seat and sat as gingerly as she could manage. Levi's attention to the songs of worship and Jonah's silence were enough to satisfy her. She took up her songbook and joined in effortlessly, as if she hadn't missed a single beat. It was then that Jonah decided that, for the first time in eight years, he was going to attend the coffee hour after Sunday service. He wasn't even going to bring his family. All he wanted was to find out what Sophia's smile was for, and risk a public whipping for the sake of a crush he thought he'd gotten over long ago.

••

Jonah poured a little too much bitter, black coffee into the Styrofoam cup, filling it precariously to the brim. He considered taking a mini powdered donut from the open package, but felt the balancing act would be too dangerous. The thought of spilling scalding coffee all over Victoria Shaw's designer shoes was paralyzing, and he had no intention of risking such a catastrophe, at least in public. Unfortunately, he couldn't walk away with just his coffee; Jeremiah Hodges was whining up a storm, and kept Jonah at the table as he listed his myriad complaints against the people of Clemency.

The local pharmacist was a lanky man with thinning hair and an excessively square jawline, and he had plenty of grievances to dump upon an unsuspecting young churchgoer who was only there for the mingling. He lamented his ongoing cold war with Dr. Noah Lee, who barely prescribed medication to his few patients, leaving Jeremiah with a stockpile of painkillers he couldn't distribute. In fact, the whole situation gave him such a migraine that he humored the idea of using the pills himself, since they were nearing their expiration date, anyway. He cursed his lack of high-income clientele, saying a booming population of pill-poppers and well-groomed junkies was good for business, and that he'd grown sick and tired of selling condoms to horny teenagers. Jeremiah eyed Jonah and speculated that he himself was probably one of those teenagers once, and meant no offense.

When Jeremiah reached for a donut Jonah leapt through his window of opportunity and made his way past the herd of gossipy women who made sure to laugh twice as hard at each other's insipid jokes. Sophia Shaw was sitting on a metal folding chair against the far wall, sipping cautiously on a cup of breakfast tea with milk. A paper plate sprinkled with muffin crumbs sat tucked behind her feet, and she crossed her legs at the ankles to hide it in shame. Her purse sat on the chair next to her, one of a whole row with only a few takers, much to Jonah's relief. Eavesdropping was one of the holiest sacraments at the Southern Mercy Bible Church, and all were expected to take part in the rite.

Jonah crossed the room and caught on to Sophia's act of pretending not to notice. He stood right in front of her, about to ask if the adjacent seat was taken, though he knew the answer. Sophia beat him to the punch.

"No, Mr. Young, it's not taken. If you're going to show your pretty face at coffee hour, then at least have the social skills to make the first move." She smiled, grabbed her bag and placed it in her lap, offering up the empty seat to a subtly emasculated Jonah.

He blushed a bit and obliged her. "Seen you lookin' back there. Y'know, I betcha them parents o' yours taught you it ain't polite to stare. Leads to covetin'."

"Like old times, you're thinking," Sophia said. "From what I remember, you weren't exactly the model Christian boy, drawing all over your books like Mephisto painting a masterpiece. In fact, you've got such a devilish reputation that my parents would probably throw a fit knowing I'm making idle chit-chat with the likes of Jonah Young."

"People can change, y'know," he suggested.

Sophia laughed. "So, this is when you tell me that little boy finally grew up into a fine, respectable man." She wasn't about to buy into his cliché. "A boy chases girls at church because he hasn't got a subtle bone in his body, just like writing a girl's name over and over again in his schoolbook for the whole class to see. A man, on the other hand, is supposed to be cool about it. I think you've just gone and proved which one you are, Mr. Young."

Jonah smirked and looked down at his coffee, raising it to his lips. It burned his mouth. "Shit!" he yelled. Sophia jumped back in surprise. The surrounding chatter died down; the throngs of church ladies glared at him, appalled. When they acknowledged that he at least had the personal restraint to keep from taking the Lord's name in vain, they returned to their rounds of polite slander.

"You sure know how to get a girl's attention," Sophia said.

"My apologies," Jonah mumbled as he wiped hot coffee from his mouth with a rough, one-ply napkin. He put the cup and the trash on the ground. "Didn't mean to embarrass you, there."

"You ain't seen nothin' yet," Sophia whispered in mock dialect, but nervously. She stood up and greeted her mother, who floated in without warning with one hand on her hip, carried on the wings of graceful cherubim. She had perfectly straight, black hair that she always kept pushed behind her shoulders, blending with a black dress that flaunted her figure but exposed little. The way it pinched in at her ankles gave her the appearance of a Bible-toting Morticia Addams. She commanded Jonah's attention and smiled politely with the regal poise of a theocratic queen.

"I know I didn't raise a daughter who would neglect the flock like this," she declared, shaking her head, and apparently, shaking off her accent with it. "These people need their shepherds' baby girl. Think of the kids."

The Reverend's wife reached out her hand, jingling the fan-like necklace crusted with silver and crystal that hung at the base of her slender neck. "I don't believe we've met," she said, shaking Jonah's hand cordially. Her hands were cold. She hadn't done much laying on of hands that day.

"Jonah Young, ma'am."

"Ah, yes. Mr. Young. I've heard a lot about you, and I'm sure my Sophia has, too." She took her daughter by the hand. "Now excuse us. Sophia has some catching up to do with Gracey. She hasn't seen her in quite some time, and I'm still hoping my girl might learn to cook. And what better teacher could there be than an Italian?"

"Pleasure to have met you, ma'am."

"Likewise," she said curtly. Off she went with her daughter right behind her, but Sophia turned her head to look back at Jonah, who half expected her to turn into a pillar of salt. She shrugged and whispered forcefully: "See you next Sunday, then, sitting right in the front like a good Christian boy."

But Jonah didn't feel like a good Christian boy. Really, he never had. And he certainly didn't plan to start now.

••

It was the Tuesday after Jonah had signed his death warrant by laying eyes on the Reverend's daughter, and Levi was on his way back from AlaCo, his shoes reeking of gasoline. He had the displeasure of filling the Reverend Shaw's tank that day, and spilled a little fuel while finishing up with his brand-new convertible, which he'd promptly purchased after a month-long fundraiser to replace the church windows.

Levi had to explain to Victoria, who spoke over her husband from the passenger seat, what Jonah's intentions were and what his upbringing was like. He couldn't answer either question, and certainly didn't want to speak for Jonah, whose intentions with a woman were fairly consistent. He hoped that this time would be different, out of genuine concern for Jonah's safety. The townsfolk of Clemency had contemplated implementing biblical law before, though Leviticus already set the boundaries on their social lives. The Reverend and his wife dictated morality, and Jonah too often jumped the fence into the fields of immorality, which they would no doubt learn soon enough through the grapevine.

The heat was relentless, radiating from both the summer sun and the smoldering eyes of Victoria Shaw, and Levi found no mercy from either. His shirt hugged his body and clung to his skin, damp with sweat. The droning buzz of cicadas hidden in the trees rang in his ears while he worked his menial job through the worst part of the day. The light of midday left him with fresh color on his shoulders and natural highlights in his sandy blond hair. It also left him with a lingering sense of pointlessness, as he toiled beneath a bright sky that he rarely had the opportunity to admire on the shores of the Gulf. In fact, he'd never been there, but the silvery mirages on the pavement served as a fleeting reminder of a vacation he couldn't afford. His daydreams proved more than useless.

It was pointless to tuck his pay away in a coffee tin knowing that he'd never find use for it. The only time it saw the light of day was when he'd dip into his savings to cover what Mama didn't give him for cigarettes and alcohol, and those times when unpaid bills piled up in the mailbox with Mama denying their very existence. He slipped cash into pre-stamped envelopes when the water was shut off while she was at work and he was left standing in the shower with soap suds running down his legs. If the dealerships weren't miles away, he'd have bought a car by now, and if the state revived the local rail, he'd be in Birmingham with two thousand in his pocket and his life in one small bag. But with no car and no ticket, he walked his way to nowhere.

If it were any later in the day he would have followed the back roads home, but traffic was light in the early afternoon. By six o'clock the army of factory workers would come rolling into town in wave after wave of tired cars. Levi tried his best to stay out of sight when he could, because he'd prefer to be wearing something nicer than a dirty undershirt if someone were to notice him. It was bad enough to have to pray on his walk to work that he wouldn't have to do business with someone he knew, and after a long day of worrying, he didn't want to carry the same worries home with him. Each car that passed by the gas station was one more that could be carrying a prominent churchgoer, the parents of a high school acquaintance, or even those acquaintances themselves. He thanked God that Rusty didn't force him to pin a name tag on his chest. With his luck, it would have been the bold, unforgettable red of Mama's Sunday lipstick, matching her signature smudges on the mouth of every glass scattered across the parlor.

All he wanted was to be an oil-smeared mechanic working in the dingy garage—not out of any interest in cars, but to hide underneath them with his face obscured by broken axle rods. No one could recognize him when the only thing visible was his shoes. He wouldn't have to worry about awkwardly accepting a tip from an ex-girlfriend's parents, or forcing conversation with one of those judgmental exes, or worse, the condescending boyfriend of an ex who'd somehow identified him. He wouldn't need any more lies about waiting for a fictional semester to start, or imaginary, salaried jobs lined up out of town that maybe—just maybe—he'd one day be able to actually find.

Levi coughed as a passing car kicked up dust in a gritty cloud. He wiped the dirt from his eyes and regained his balance. The car stopped up ahead. Its brake lights flared red and it sped into reverse, barreling backward toward Levi with the grinding crunch of tires slipping on decades-old tarmac. It came to a short, violent stop right beside him.

"Well, look who it is!" Jimmy von Braun exclaimed from the driver's seat. He reached for the volume dial and turned his mobile disco back to a regular quarter-million-dollar sports car. "Mr. Levi

Thompson himself, walking back from another proud day of making a solid three figures."

Levi kept on walking. "After taxes, might as well be two."

"I see *somebody's* comfortable in their poverty."

Jimmy kept his foot light on the gas and crawled at Levi's pace. "You know, I had to drive all the way up to bumblefuck to fill up, all because your boss thinks that urine's a legitimate fuel source."

"Ain't y'already in bumblefuck?"

"Honey, this country dump is so far off the map that I feel like goddamned Amelia Earhart plunging into the south Pacific where even the Democrats couldn't find her." He laughed at the idea of evading tax-hungry tyrants and corrupt regimes. "What, are you offended on behalf of your beloved party?"

"I ain't the political type."

"And *I* ain't never met a poor family that didn't vote Left. I dare you to tell me with a straight face that your welfare-queen mother *isn't* siphoning money from my parents' bank accounts as shamelessly as you do with your petrol. Tell me: Is it legal to buy McDonald's with food stamps these days? Or maybe booze?"

"Ain't it enough to sit back and watch us from up on your hill? Or is it just too damn boring up there with all your neighbors throwin' their cocktail parties and soirées?"

"Trust me," Jimmy choked, fighting a fit of laughter, "the crowd up there couldn't spell 'endive' even if their lives depended on it, and they sure as hell wouldn't know how to pronounce it. Maybe they've got money by *your* standards, but in this town, that's like placing first in the Special Olympics. At the end of the day, you're still a retard bumbling down a track."

Jimmy rolled past the stop sign at the intersection of Main Street and Jericho to keep up with Levi, who crossed without a hint of hesitation. Levi looked over. "You missed your turn," he pointed out.

"Well, I'll be damned," Jimmy said. "Looks like I'll be following Mr. Moneybags home, then." He snickered at his own joke and looked away to change the song on his iPhone, turning up the volume a bit. The pounding bass that shook ecstasy-fueled German raves overseas rattled his windows. He rolled the rest down with a flick of a switch, continuing, "You know, if you weren't covered in shit and oil, maybe I'd be willing to offer you a ride. But I don't imagine it'd be very good for the Italian leather, wouldn't you agree?"

"Wouldn't know."

"But if you did, I'm sure you'd understand." He raised the volume even more, so loud that he had to shout over the electronica. "Try not to work too hard, Thompson. I'm sure the Nanny State will pick up the slack."

Jimmy's tires squealed as he careened down Main Street and made a sharp U-turn at the corner of Gilead. He honked his horn when he flashed past Levi and blew the stop at his turn toward the hill. The car he recklessly cut off stopped short, avoiding a devastating collision by only a few inches. The damage Jimmy's lawsuit would do to the driver's life savings would eclipse any injuries suffered.

Levi walked down the driveway and through the back door with a bad taste in his mouth, worse than the vodka Jimmy kept in his car in a plastic water bottle. He stepped into his room with heavy feet and rummaged through the closet. The coffee tin was under a pile of towels. He popped off the lid and carefully arranged the day's tips in ascending order before depositing them in the can, which he promptly tucked away again, to wait for the day that he might finally withdraw it for a purpose that was purely his own. Unfortunately, that day seemed far away. And spoiled brats like Jimmy von Braun only served as a rude reminder of it.

••

The bench next to the yellow flower bed seemed like the best spot to wait for Hannah. Jonah sat on a bronze plaque that had lost its shine, bearing the names of Eileen Hitchens and Jacob McCain and the dates of their tenure at Israel Pickens. He couldn't figure out how Mrs. Hitchens was deemed worthy of immortality, the miserable, old bitch that she was. Taking a seat on her name was his last means of revenge. It'd been over a year since he saw his last scarlet letter branded at the top of an exam. He readily admitted that he wasn't meant to be a mathematician and made no excuses for it, but she was cruel in her witch hunt against ineptitude.

*Y'can kiss my ass once 'n for all,* he thought.

He guessed that the engraved date of her retirement was also the fateful day he had long prayed and hoped for during calculus class. The passing of a Pickens teacher was like the appearance of a comet's bright, dusty arc in the sky, seen only once a century by those longing to witness it. Jonah imagined that Mrs. Hitchens's own celestial beacon would have been fiery and foreboding, a bloody gash across the night sky, spilling red like her pen on every ill-prepared student's homework. Mostly his.

While Jonah couldn't reap the benefits of her demise, he felt happy for the students who once had the pleasure of greeting Mrs. Hitchens every morning, and enduring her academic interrogations, her flabby arms undulating as she pointed fingers at the incompetent, and her punitive grading policy. The new students wouldn't have to worry about her trend of teaching a different grade each year, ascending all the way to high school, and the unending torture of sitting in her class for half a decade. Every day, the ten o'clock bell became more and more comforting. But that day, as he sat there waiting, the bell wouldn't be a source of comfort anymore. If anything, it'd be a call to arms, the casus belli in a war of two siblings.

The distant sound of its ringing in the halls was Jonah's signal. He looked up and kept the front doors firmly in his sight. Her yellow backpack would give her away: the mess of flower stickers and pop culture logos lining its sides rendered the bag unmistakable. And when she'd come walking out, hands on the straps, giggling with one or two other teenage girls with their insecurities masked by makeup, Jonah would be there to intercept her and finally lay down the law.

He waited, and the yellow flash of Hannah's backpack came from behind a small congregation of jocks with hairline acne and girls with tissue-stuffed bras. She was walking alone, a marble notebook clutched against her chest. From what he understood she wasn't an unpopular girl, though she didn't walk among the ranks of golden-haired cheerleaders and their comatose athlete boyfriends. Jonah stood up and stayed in front of the bench. Hannah didn't notice, her gaze fixed on the gray pavement. He held out his arm. She jumped when she walked into it.

"Figured you'd want some company walkin' home. You *are* goin' home, ain't you?"

Hannah glared. "What do you think you're doin' here?"

"Embarrassed to be seen with your big brother? And here I thought I was bein' nice."

"Y'ain't here to be nice. I ain't five."

"No, you're fourteen, so it ain't appropriate for you to go skippin' around with the likes of you-know-who. You should be gettin' home or I promise you'll regret it."

"His name's *Gabriel,* and I ain't seein' him now, anyway. Not that it's any o' your business."

"And I ain't five neither, you little brat. You expect me to believe you're seein' friends or somethin'?"

Hannah crossed her arms and pouted. "As a matter o' fact, yes."

"Maybe you got Ma 'n Pa fooled, but don't take me for some ass who'd ignore the fact that his sister's fuckin' up her life."

"Why're you pickin' on me so much?" She looked down and rubbed her eyes.

"There ain't much I can do with that thick skull o' yours," Jonah replied. "But believe me when I tell you that if you'd been born a boy, I'd be beatin' the livin' shit outta you right now." He grabbed her chin and pushed her up to look him in the eye. Her eyes were heavy, sagging above the folds of dark circles beneath them. "Y'look like y'ain't big on sleepin' these days."

Hannah slapped his hand away and pushed a stray strand of hair behind her ear. "I've had a lot o' schoolwork to catch up on—I don't need Ma 'n Pa thinkin' I'm takin' after my dumb older brother. I *do* have priorities, even when you're runnin' around sayin' I ain't got any. Y'don't know shit about me."

"Watch your mouth," Jonah snapped. "And look, I've gone and spewed my fair share o' bullshit back in school, and there ain't no way you can bullshit a bullshitter and hope to get away with it. You're as good of a liar as you are a judge o' character."

"I don't need to take this from you," Hannah groaned. She clasped the straps of her backpack and headed toward the street. Jonah scowled and followed.

"You should know by now that home's that way." He pointed down Main Street at the far side of town, where the family house was tucked away on Lebanon Lane. The better-off residents up on the hill passed by it on their way south without ever considering that a small dirt path could possibly lead to a family with a protective son and a tragically misguided daughter. But Gabe Skinner, living in the shadow of the western hill, never had any trouble finding it, even with vision that Jonah assumed was blurred by needles meant for diabetics or five-dollar glass pipes from head shops out of town.

Hannah turned left at Main Street despite his protest, clenching her fists in frustration at his determined pursuit. She glared back and headed straight toward the Skinners' decaying house. Jonah, furious with Hannah's complete disregard for his repeated ultimatums, sprinted after her. With strides much longer than hers, he caught up easily. She recoiled when he reached for her arm.

"What the hell's the matter with you?" he barked. "Why're you so damn jumpy?"

Hannah tore her arm from Jonah's grip and tried to walk away. He snatched her wrist and pulled up her sleeve to the elbow. Her forearm was patched with dark bruises. Some were fading; others looked fresh.

*"Did Gabe do this to you?"* Jonah shouted, letting go of his sister. She pulled down her sleeve and rubbed her arm. "It's him, ain't it? If that piece o' shit's gone and laid a hand on you, I swear to God, Hannah—"

*"I'm fine.* I can take care o' myself," she asserted. "I don't need your help, and I ain't a kid anymore. So leave me the hell alone."

"As far as I'm concerned, you're still a clueless little—"

*"I don't need you anymore, Jonah."*

Jonah stared as she turned her back to him and walked away. He held himself back from running after her and dragging her home kicking and screaming. And as he watched Hannah shrink into the distance, he sighed knowing exactly where she was headed. Not too far up the road she'd find Midian Lane—leading to a dilapidated mobile home defended by rusted chain-link fences, and surrounded with balding grass and plastic lawn ornaments. It was the dirt path littered with cigar guts and cigarettes that ended right at the Skinner's front door, and up that procession way, Hannah was marching toward her cliff.

# 5

IT WAS TOO HOT to sleep that night. Levi's room felt like a swamp, with warm, humid air seeping through its open windows, missing only alligators prowling his floor. The comforter and sheets sat in an unfolded pile beside his bed, but throwing them aside hadn't done much good. The summer weather still left Levi tossing and turning in bed. He struggled to draw the thick, heavy air into his lungs. It felt like being waterboarded, and he never fully caught his breath. When he did manage to fall asleep, it was more like passing out from lack of oxygen, and he had no dreams.

He slept for an hour or so when the sun was just starting to peek through the trees, but the sound of Mama slamming the front door behind her woke him. Jumping up in bed with a sharp gasp, he heard the Cadillac's door crunch shut and its engine roar. Mama was out for the day, working the morning shift. Her black apron, speckled with the crusty white of old ranch dressing, had been taken from its spot on the kitchen chair. He tried to wash it for her once, but the stains were stubborn, and no matter how much skin he lost through scrubbing, the apron still looked wretched. He'd considered buying her a new one, but knew she looked at it like some well-loved security blanket, while at the same time cursing it for being a blindfold on her dreams, if she had any.

For once, Levi actually hoped that Mama hadn't left a drop of hot water for him. It was even difficult to peel off his damp undershirt with its sheer cotton dragging along his flushed skin. He pulled the curtain back and stepped into the shower, his eyes closed as he listened to the groaning of old pipes preceding the first trickle of cold water from the shower head. The water surged and splashed onto his body with an icy sharpness. Levi did his best to enjoy it. He expected it'd be his only relief from the heat that day, which was already starting to paint mirages on the road by the time he reached the railroad tracks.

The rusty air conditioner at the front of the Americana Diner rattled and hissed. Through the windows Levi saw Mama pacing between tables, replacing empty ketchup bottles with full ones and topping off overused salt shakers. He wondered if she ever expected to be waitressing into her forties. He imagined she'd once had greater hopes for herself. When he was a child, she seemed happy. And though he didn't remember much about his father, he knew enough from the few photographs in the house that he, too, seemed content with his life, and that his wife felt the same.

Seeing Mama at work was strange, to say the least. She rushed back and forth behind the counter in her pale pink dress. She unpacked blue crates filled with warm coffee cups and replaced sticky soda fountain spouts. But even though the Americana had low expectations for its employees' appearance, Mama still did herself up as if she were headed straight for church. The red of her favorite lipstick always drew attention away from the plainness of her dress. It brought out the blue of her eyes and an extra dollar for her tip when she waited on a man.

Levi had a similar day in store for him at the gas station up the road, but the tips he accepted seemed to be given out of pity rather than gratitude or, often, perceived obligation. And sometimes the drivers just dropped the money out the high windows of their trucks and let it hit the pavement. He couldn't just slip it into an apron after snatching it up from beneath an empty glass; instead, he'd have to pound his foot on it just to keep the exhaust from blowing it down the highway. They didn't have much concern for a dollar or two. Levi suspected they used most of it to pay tired, old hookers, anyway, though AlaCo was no such truck stop. Granted, Valerie Skinner did live only a short walk south of there, but her driveway wasn't wide enough to accommodate an 18-wheeler.

It was noon when the first talker of the day pulled in. The sun seemed to stop at its zenith and scorched the weeds that slithered up between cracks in the concrete, and the midday heat lingered. The drivers who came before her were quiet and reserved with little desire for conversation, which Levi didn't mind at all. But he was resting with his back against a metal beam when Mrs. Thatcher arrived, sitting with the driver's seat pulled up so close to the steering wheel that she could barely fit. Levi hadn't seen her since he sat in her eighth-grade English class. Her tiny teeth looked exactly how he remembered them (*Chiclets*, the kids called them), but her bushy, fake eyelashes had grown longer, making her eyes into the gaping mouths of two tasteless Venus flytraps. He prayed they wouldn't catch him in their sights. He wasn't that lucky.

"Hey, ain't you the Thompson boy?"

*Shit*, Levi thought. Two options flashed through his mind: he could throw in the towel, caught red-handed, and admit that he was, in fact, Levi Thompson himself, or he could lie. Denying his identity was, as far as he was concerned, the best way to avoid the judging stare of past teachers who were wondering where they, or Levi's mother, had gone wrong. The conversation would quickly run dry.

"A Thompson? No, ma'am." He focused on unscrewing the gas cap.

Mrs. Thatcher pointed her finger at him and squinted, smiling. "Yeah, Levi Thompson. Eighth grade—a long, long time ago. He probably wouldn't remember me, anyway."

"Sorry, ma'am, but we ain't never met before. And I ain't never met a Levi Thompson, neither. Hope I should take it as a compliment." He cracked a smile, but Mrs. Thatcher didn't return one. She sat with her hands on the wheel and her eyes scanning Levi up and down. He expected that she didn't believe him, but after a few uncomfortable seconds, her face relaxed and she looked satisfied.

"Good-lookin' kid. Smart, too," she said. "Take it as a compliment." She winked at Levi, or tried to—her eyelid trembled under the weight of her fake lashes, turning the wink into a shaky grimace. She handed forty dollars to Levi and started the car. "Keep the change."

Levi coughed from the rush of black fumes. Mrs. Thatcher mouthed an apology and pulled the car out into the road, catching her bumper on the lip of the pavement with a thud.

The hours of operation sign clattered against the glass as Levi pulled open the door to the station convenience mart. He inserted a key into the register, slid it open and deposited the cash he'd accumulated in his back pocket over the course of the day. The drawer closed with a metallic crash.

"Careful in there," Rusty called from the garage, the door wide open. Levi heard the clinking of a drill bit on cement, then Rusty's heavy footsteps. The smell of cigars, sweat and cedar was his introduction. With no cologne in the garage, he made due with air freshener. He walked into the room and tossed a blotchy towel over his shoulder, black with motor oil.

"Should I still be callin' you Levi, or are you someone else for the day?"

"Y'heard?"

Rusty crossed his tree-trunk arms, grinning. "I didn't take you for one to lie."

"If lyin' means keepin' gossip outta church, then I'll do whatever's necessary."

Rusty rubbed his chin, and the scraping of his fingers on heavy, black stubble was loud enough for even Levi to hear. "Well, while you're workin' for me, I'll be callin' you by your real name. There's a car waitin' outside, *Levi Thompson*. Get to it." He pulled the towel off his shoulder and slapped it against his thigh. As he disappeared back into the garage, he dabbed his forehead and matted down his wiry hair. The whirring pulse of his drill echoed behind Levi, who had returned to work for just under minimum wage. And when he unscrewed the gas cap and clipped it onto its holder, he reflected on the fact that he, too, was getting screwed.

••

Jonah was Swayne's human alternative to the Dewey Decimal System. He found the system antiquated and unnecessary, since he spent so much time organizing that he'd committed it all to memory. It also helped that the shelves were more like the Vatican archives than a useful library, because they served as a place of archaeological preservation from which books were rarely removed. So when Gracey and Joe DeRosa came through the door and asked for a manual on hardware and a mystery novel fit for an old woman, Jonah knew just where to look. Any potential reader that walked into Swayne was rarely under the age of sixty.

The DeRosas spent most of their time talking with Susan. She made a joke or two about them being the only Italian-Americans in town, who, ironically, didn't take out books on cooking or organized crime every time they paid Swayne a visit. Gracey laughed; Joe didn't seem amused, but remained polite nonetheless. Susan avoided using any of the ethnic slurs that she frequently dropped in private. Gracey and Joe were, after all, two very friendly guineas, however unfortunate their lack of a New York accent was. To swear in front of them would be just plain rude, and Susan, of course, was a lady of manners.

Jonah picked up a book they'd decided not to take. *Dwell Within* was its title, and a quick scan of the back cover identified it as a Christian-themed horror novel and a blatant plagiarism of *The Exorcist*. "Someone at church told us about it," Gracey had said to Susan, "but I don't think I can read it. This old heart can't handle no night terrors." Jonah expected it was just a tacky attempt at stirring up a stronger faith in the reader, and he figured it'd only be a matter of time before it spread like wildfire through Clemency. To Jonah, if the townspeople were so easily frightened into obedience by a messy compilation of Bronze Age myths, then a contemporary work of fiction might leave them just as shaken.

"I don't imagine a crappy book like that would be enough to get you back to church," Susan shouted from the front desk.

"I'm there every week," Jonah replied, approaching the front end.

"Maybe to keep your family happy," she speculated, "but you ain't goin' there for yourself."

"Since when'd you decide you know so much about me 'n God?"

"Since I seen you roll your eyes at that there book," she answered. She stamped the inside cover of an encyclopedia and dropped it with a thud into the return bin.

"Well, damn me to Hell, then."

"Calm down, kid," she sighed. "No need to be so defensive. I myself just go to hear the dirt those Bible broads talk about each other. Y'ain't never seen such a wretched beehive of bitchy, ol' WASPs."

Jonah took the encyclopedia out of the bin and turned his back, but Susan hadn't had her fill. "Y'know, back when I was an educator, us teachers had a whole boatload o' gossip about our students. I doubt those ladies have changed their ways since my time."

"I reckon I gave my teachers a lot to talk about," Jonah said. "Sexual exploits 'n all."

"Now I know you don't mean you bedded your teachers," Susan laughed. "Those crotchety grannies are drier than the Sahara, I'd wager." Jonah smirked, but neglected to mention the one thirty-year-old biology teacher with whom he'd earned some extra credit. That teacher didn't last long at Israel Pickens High School. Her colleagues didn't appreciate that she still got her period while their own ovaries had long since shriveled and died. Jonah, though, was thankful and relieved.

"Y'know, it's mighty strange that you got yourself such a playboy reputation," Susan remarked. "You're a smart kid—book smart, at least, more so than you get your due credit for. Ain't got much common sense, though." Jonah, distracted, put the encyclopedia on the wrong shelf. "That goes over there," Susan corrected him. He moved it to its designated place. "That's better," she said. "You ever thought about goin' to school?"

"I went to school. Graduated, too."

"I meant college, and watch that smart mouth o' yours. Gracey 'n Joe's son—Lord bless those delightful dagos—went off to college and got himself a nice, cushy job up in Tennessee, and from what I hear, *his* kids are doin' pretty damn well for themselves, too, and I'm sure they ain't workin' at a library for a crazy, ol' bat like me. Y'know, it ain't outta your reach, kid."

"Maybe one day, when I ain't got so much shit on my plate."

"Then quit shittin' on your own damn plate," Susan advised. "One o' these days I'm gonna fire up that there computer and sit you down to fill out some applications. This library ain't big enough for the two of us."

"But until that day," Jonah answered, "I'll be here minimizin' my potential."

Susan laughed. "Just say the word, and I'll plug it in for once."

Jonah couldn't help but think that it was too late for him. Like a good Christian past his prime with no chaste girl to marry, he felt all he'd face was rejection. He didn't expect that his academic record would do him much good, other than prove that he was far more dedicated to popularity than his future. Any recommendation from a past teacher would only depict him as an apathetic student with no desire to apply or push himself, other than pushing himself into a Parsons girl, if the writer were to tell the truth. He doubted that he could sway one into lying on his behalf. So, sure of the hopelessness of his cause, he only prayed that Hannah wouldn't follow in his footsteps. The Hannah he knew was sensible enough to forge her own path, even if her big brother was too busy watching over her to get his own life together. But sadly, he wasn't sure if that side of her would be around for much longer.

••

Levi always seemed to walk through the liquor store's front door right before closing time. The warmth of the setting sun on his back was familiar, as was the glare on the window that made the business hours sign difficult to read. He was quite familiar with the store's schedule, however. Over a year of visiting Backwater Spirits at sunset gave him a sense of structure, though he wished he could have organized his life on his own terms, and not around store hours or the weekly Sunday service. Looking to make his purchase quick as to not inconvenience Elijah Green, he went straight for the whiskey, snatched it off the shelf and approached the register. As was his way, he greeted the older man with little more than a nod, but for once he felt compelled to utter a few words, however idle.

"You ever judge a person by what they're buyin'?" he asked.

Elijah raised an eyebrow. He shrugged and rang up the whiskey, and, without stating the price, took Levi's crumpled money and produced the change. "I try to live by the idea that if you gonna judge, then you gonna be judged. But that ain't to say you can't deduce a bit about a person based on what they're drinkin'.'"

"Then what've you deduced about me?"

"Well, for one, I know it ain't you drinkin'. But it don't take a psychic to figure that out, since you done told me that already. I'd say, however, that whoever's sendin' you to buy that stuff is just tryin' to feel a buzz as quick as can be. It ain't about savorin' the liquor. Only someone who's drinkin' to enjoy it nurses a glass all night. Everyone else is drinkin' to forget."

"Maybe that's somethin' I should take up, then. Forgettin' don't sound too bad."

"Forgettin' is an easy out. Y'ain't fixin' the problem, though. Even if you don't recall it, it's still there. And you can't get those around you to forget it, neither. They're the memory you ain't never had."

"You got a family?"

"Married forty-three years, young man, and even in a drunken stupor, I ain't never forgot it. Proud to say that even at my drunkest I ain't never laid a hand on my Mary Ann, sure as Hades. I loved her ever since the day I first seen them gray eyes o' hers in that polka dot dress. You'll get it one day."

"Ain't nowhere close to that day, thankfully. Takin' a girl home to meet Mama ain't easy on a romance."

"Any mama, or just yours?"

"Most ain't on their third glass by noon," Levi replied. "A drunk, Bible-thumpin' mother and a sorry job at a gas station. I'm a real catch."

"Ain't no such thing as a 'sorry job,' young man," Elijah insisted. "Work is work, and you'd best keep from lookin' down on an honest livin', your own, included, and don't you let no one look down on you, neither." Levi stayed quiet. "Y'ain't stealin' money from no one, and y'ain't out dealin' drugs around town like I'm sure some o' the boys your age is doin'. So don't let nobody tell you that what you doin' ain't good enough. As small a role as it may be, it's important. A necessary service, even. People gotta drive."

"Just didn't expect myself to be doin' this for so long."

"Play with the hand you're dealt, and quit thinkin' about the rest. You're gonna make yourself sick one day with all your 'would haves' and 'should haves.' All that matters is what you gotta do right now in this moment, and that's for you to decide. Ain't no one got the right to tell you your obligations, 'cause the only obligation you got is to live your life and thank God every day for it."

Levi picked up the bottle in its wrinkled paper bag and put it under his arm. "I'll keep that in mind."

"You do that," Elijah said, standing up from his seat. He walked over to the door and held it open for Levi, his last customer for the day. "Good night, Mr. Thompson."

Levi wished he could take a step back and look at his life the way Elijah did. He couldn't imagine ever loving his job, and maybe he didn't have to love it, but he struggled to find any shred of pride in pumping gas for next to nothing. Was he as necessary as Elijah insisted? Without him, the motorists would be inconvenienced at best, since they'd have to begrudgingly fill their own tanks, but it wasn't like they'd stop dead in their tracks on their way to Birmingham or Nashville or wherever they might have had their sights set. There were other gas stations along the way, and there were other pump attendants, all of whom probably hated their jobs as much as Levi did. In his mind, at least, misery loved company.

After sunset the temperature plunged, and the walk home was unexpectedly chilly. Levi rubbed his arms with the bottle against his chest, nearly sprinting down Main Street to find his unkempt driveway. The ground alongside the road was rocky and uneven. A car flashed past him with its lights exploding through the dark, and he lost his balance. The bottle of whiskey slipped out of his hands and tumbled down the pavement. The car stopped short and swerved to the shoulder, the bottle bouncing off its back tire and landing in the dirt. Luckily, it was made of plastic.

"You're gonna get yourself killed one of these days," Jimmy von Braun yelled. He tore off his seat belt and got out of the car, his music still blaring in the background. Reaching through the open window, Jimmy hit the volume knob and cut the sound. Without acknowledging the young aristocrat, Levi headed toward the bottle that lay just out of reach.

Jimmy noticed and asked, "And what's that, there?" He stepped in the way and picked it up from the roadside. "Drinking by yourself after a long day at work? My God, Thompson, I've never met anyone in my life that could beat me in being a complete train wreck. It's a humbling experience, I have to say."

"Hand it over," Levi demanded, in no mood for Jimmy's antics. Jimmy laughed right back.

"I guess this is how the other half lives. Me, my nose would be numb right now from all the coke, but what can you expect from someone who's wanted to be Kate Moss since he was five?"

"I'm sure you got much better liquor than that in your wine cellar."

"You keep *wine* in a wine cellar. That's why it's a *wine* cellar." Jimmy looked down at the bottle he held in his hands. "You sure you haven't cracked into this yet?"

"Ain't mine," Levi said, stepping closer. He reached out his arm, but Jimmy pulled the bottle away. He held it upside down from the neck.

"Don't tell me your mother's drinking this garbage. On appearance alone, she seemed classier than that when I met her." Jimmy tossed the bottle through the car window and it bounced onto the passenger seat. He opened the door and got in. "Really, I'm doing her a favor here. And if you're lying to me and you really *are* drinking alone, then it's *you* I'm helping out. Call it an act of kindness, if you want. This shit's been known to kill." He put on his seat belt. "Try something over ten bucks next time. Liquor store's behind you."

Jimmy threw it into gear and shot off into the dark. Two points of light, cut in half by the car's silhouette, raced down Main Street toward Hebron and disappeared, concealed by the thick tree line. Levi kicked himself for not having laid a hand on Jimmy, but he worried about what Charlene and George von Braun would do if they knew their son had even been lightly shaken up, fearing legal action as either a paid-off arrest or a fierce offensive in court. He'd much prefer to get home on foot than in the back of a squad car.

He slipped through the back door, announced by the tireless chirp of summer crickets in place of wailing sirens and flashing lights. Mama, as always, sat in the parlor, but she'd opted for television over music that night, and sipped on a dwindling glass with the blue and white light of the screen flickering over her face. Levi sneaked into his room and closed the door, careful not to let it slam shut as it was known to do. A pile of wrinkled laundry sat on the bed, so he pulled off his work clothes and threw the mess onto the floor beside him. He slipped under the covers, the cool, dry sheets a welcome relief, though they'd be damp with sweat by morning. Closing his eyes, he tried his hand at sleeping, but was forced to pretend. Sleep wasn't going to be an option for very long. He considered it only a matter of time before Mama noticed that he'd come home empty handed.

IT WAS RAINING the night Levi's father disappeared. Though what he recalled was filtered through the eyes of a six-year old, he remembered the rain, because of the way his stuffed bunny felt soggy after having been left beneath an open window. It was a hot night like many others before and after it, and there'd been thunder and lightning, but what made that night memorable were the muffled shouts of a husband and wife. They surged in tides as they lost control, then thought of their sleeping son, then lost control again. Over time, he'd lost what little he caught of their words, shouted and whispered. More than anything, his surprise dominated his memory. Mama and Pap rarely fought. At that age, when he, like all six-year olds, thought himself the center of the world, he couldn't imagine that they were arguing about anything other than him, their only and dearest child.

There was the startling slam of a door, and desperate sobs filled the parlor. Curious, he peeked out from his bedroom and saw Mama, with dried riverbeds of black makeup running from her eyes. He remembered the stains her mascara left on the edges of the pillow she clutched to her cheek, and the smell of her perfume, more sour than usual, or perhaps it'd been her breath. There was a bottle on the coffee table, empty, if his memory served him. And he remembered her taking him in her arms, but not what she said to him, if she'd said anything at all. Maybe she just stayed quiet. It would have been the last moment of silence shared between them from that night onward.

*"I know you're in there, boy!"*

Her shouts snatched him back into the present and he woke as violently as a sleep-deprived soldier. They exploded like mortars on the battlefield, and Levi instinctively stood at attention, his eyes fixed on his locked bedroom door. Mama shook the doorknob with a mind to break it off. Her words, though, were a fit enough battering ram.

"You done proved yourself useless once again!" she barked, banging her fist against the thin wooden door. "This ain't the first time you was too stupid to remember the one thing I ask you for— or just too lazy to do it!"

The thud of her hand on the door covered the creaks of the floorboards while Levi crept over to the window and carefully slid it open. He crawled over the frame and hopped down onto the ground outside his bedroom. He had to admit that he felt emasculated, hiding from his mother in such an adolescent fashion, but sighed with relief as her shouts grew fainter. Leaving just a small crack for his fingers to slip through later, he pulled the glass just short of shut. He hoped that it'd be a couple of hours before he'd have to make his shameful return, head hung low, for hopefully no one to see.

He fled, just like his father, or so Mama would have said. She refused to talk about it at length, and even at eighteen, Levi knew as little as he did when he was six. She kept him from the truth, whatever that truth was, and, when asked about her husband, or ex-husband, or late husband, she replied only with accusations of abandonment. "He left us," she'd say without further detail. That was her truth, but Levi couldn't accept it. For Mama, reality and fiction found themselves mixed together in a glass on ice, both so foul that neither was easily swallowed. Over the years, Levi began to resent what he viewed as personal propaganda. Mama was lying. She'd kicked Sam out and regretted it. She made him into the aggressor, and herself, the victim. It was easier on everyone if the blame was pinned on someone who couldn't defend himself. She did the same to her own son, who found himself stumbling through the woods just to spare himself the chastisement.

The tall, rough stalks of forever-nameless plants and their rugged leaves brushed against his legs; he regretted having worn shorts. In the daylight, crossing through the wall of trees made his walk to Jonah's house just a bit shorter, but that night, it was a bad decision. He reached the Youngs' property with no less than five cuts across his ankles. In the suffocating humidity, they'd probably stay fresh for an hour, leaving his socks the rusty color of dried blood. Lucky for him, his shoes were so plain that no one was likely to look down to admire them.

The cheap flashlight fought at first, but Levi clicked it on and shined it straight at Jonah's bedroom window. It wasn't bright enough, so he took a few steps closer to the house, walking out from the cover of overgrown weeds and slender, swampy trees. The glass reflected the hazy beam and scattered it in multiple directions. Levi hoped it'd be enough to catch Jonah's attention, if he were even awake to notice it flashing on his wall. The last thing he wanted was to be forced to toss pebbles at Jonah's window to lure him out like a star-crossed youth in Verona, only to disappoint him with both his identity and his reason for being there.

The window scraped against its frame as Jonah raised it to answer the call for attention. He leaned out, saw his friend— "Gimme a minute," he whispered. The window slammed, and after that minute had passed, Jonah slipped out the front door, careful not to let the screen door snap back. The iridescent white of his gym shorts, meant for sleep, not socializing, shimmered in the light; he zipped up his sweatshirt, having just pulled it over a bare torso while he walked out unprepared onto the porch. He tiptoed down the three front steps and met Levi in the driveway, who held the flashlight up, casting shadows on both of their faces.

"Hope you're in the mood for a drink," Levi said. "We're goin' to Gene's."

Jonah rubbed his eyes and stretched. He looked down and ran his hands over his clothes. "I look like shit."

"Well, lucky for you, Gene's ain't got much of a class-act clientele. You'll fit right in."

"There's more to this night on the town than just drinkin', I'd bet. You got a story to go along with it?"

Levi motioned toward Main Street with the flashlight in hand, its battery teetering on the edge of burning out. "I'm buyin' you a beer or two, so save the questions for later. I got some business to take care of. Just don't go gettin' all pissed at me when I'm the one doin' all the talkin' for once."

••

Crossing the threshold into Gene's was like passing through Dante's infernal gate. Jonah had read the *Divine Comedy* many times at work behind the back bookshelves, and Gene's never failed to stir up quotes and scenery in his mind: *Abandon all hope, ye who enter here*, he thought. The front door was narrow and plain, and certainly nothing like the ravenous mouth of Hell, but when it swung open on its shaky hinges, it revealed an underworld of tasteless horrors. The wisps of cigarette smoke were the fumes of burning brimstone; the cackling of drunks was the weeping and gnashing of teeth. The dive bar was a bottomless pit in a town that strove to ascend to the highest realms of Paradise through booze and bad conversation, but it was resented and outright condemned by the heavenly choirs singing hymns right down the road.

"You gonna tell me what exactly's goin' on?" Jonah asked as he and Levi entered the degenerate establishment. He smacked his friend on the arm. "Hello?"

"We gotta get a bottle o' whiskey for home."

"For your mother."

Levi grunted affirmatively and stepped up to the bar, taking a seat. Jonah sat down beside him on a creaky stool. He rocked back and forth each time he leaned forward because of the seat's uneven legs, probably glued back on after the stool was smashed during one of many bar fights. "You fixin' to get one here?" he said. "Y'know, there's a liquor store right down the street."

"Closed," Levi replied. "And after I left there before, that piece o' shit von Braun kid showed up and ran off with the bottle."

Jonah laughed and wrinkled his face in disbelief. "You tellin' me he grabbed that thing right outta your hands, and you didn't do nothin' to stop him? Jesus Christ, Levi, I'm embarrassed. He's gotta weigh a buck ten at the most. Anorexia ain't much help in a fight."

"I dropped it and he picked it up off the road. And I ain't about to go chasin' after a Benz down Main Street," Levi snapped.

"And what the hell's he gonna do with a cheap-ass bottle o' whiskey like your mama's?" Jonah scoffed. He leaned back and the seat clicked against the wooden floorboards when he shifted his weight from one wobbly leg to another. "I reckon he's got some top-shelf poison in his house. Imported wines and everything."

"You'd think he was in college stealin' shit like that," Levi said.

"You'd think we should be," Jonah added grimly.

Valerie Skinner swooped in out of nowhere like a crackhead harpy from the clouds. "Well, good evenin', boys!" she exclaimed, hustling over to their side of the bar. She tossed aside the towel she'd been using to wipe up the sticky remnants of spilled shots. "And here I thought y'all went 'n fell off the face o' the earth or somethin'. Y'ain't came round much these days. Ain't never met two handsome-lookin' boys your age who wasn't out drinkin' every weekend to pick up a girl or two, not that you got much to pick from round these parts."

"We both got full-time jobs, ma'am," Levi answered.

"Consider y'all selves lucky," she advised. "The best I can get is this part-time gig right here. Startin' to think that's all there is, anyway—ain't much of a choice. But with all the hours y'all are puttin' in, don't a nice, hard drink sound pretty damn good about now?" When neither replied with much enthusiasm, she gave them a second option. "Or beers, if you ain't out to get shitfaced, as disappointing for me as that may be."

Jonah nodded without Levi's consent. "Thank you, ma'am. That'd be perfect," he said, and Ms. Skinner walked off to fetch their drinks. He leaned over to whisper, "Let me do the talkin'. Y'ain't got much of a talent for sweet talkin' women, no offense."

Levi sneered at the thought. "You gonna try and flirt with the likes o' that ol' Skinner bitch? It ain't gonna get you nothin' but a trip to the free clinic. I'm just gonna throw her some cash for the bottle and get the hell outta here."

"Don't doubt me," Jonah advised. "Watch and learn."

Their hostess returned with two slender bottles in hand, carrying them with the necks slipped between her bony fingers. She threw down two cheap napkins and set the beers on top of them, which were already starting to sweat. The napkin stuck to the bottom of the bottle as Jonah pulled it toward him. He tried his best to fake gratitude and cordially tipped his beer at Valerie before raising it to his lips. A good Southern boy, he addressed her as "ma'am." He should have known better than to remind a woman like Valerie of her age.

"Please, I can't take this 'ma'am' and 'Ms. Skinner' shit no more. *Valerie*, please—Val, if you want—I don't care. Y'don't need to be so formal with me, Jonah Young. After all, we're almost family now, wouldn't you say?"

Out of the corner of his eye, Jonah saw Levi place his hand over his brow and look away in discomfort. Jonah picked up his beer and took another imperative gulp. He wished he could avoid the inevitable conversation, but he didn't have the same luxury that Levi had: not having any contact with the worst family in Clemency, which was a title agreed upon by every townsperson gossiping at coffee hour about Valerie's track marks or Reggie's legendary sloth.

"With new relatives as lovely as you, I dunno if I'm gonna be able to handle that kind o' kinship," he joked with a weak smile that betrayed his disgust. He nudged Levi in the side to grab his attention in a time of conversational need.

Valerie snorted and stroked Jonah's wrist, just for a second, but long enough to leave him with the same revulsion as finding a spider crawling in his sheets. "Flattery might work on teenage girls round these parts, but it ain't gon' get you nowhere with me. But I do appreciate your compliments," she cooed with a wink. "Go on as long as you'd like."

"It ain't flattery," Jonah insisted. "It's just the gospel truth."

"My Gabriel finds that little sister o' yours to be a *very* lovely girl, and I gotta say, I can't deny that fact, neither. Y'know, it's damn adult o' you to be so understandin' o' what them two got goin' on together. Leavin' Gabriel alone when he's chasin' a girl's always the best way to go. He ain't the type to give up so easy. He's a fighter, that'n, and he always knows just what he wants."

"Just like his mother, I take it," Jonah speculated. He drank to it.

"I got a will o' my own, but all I got to show for it is my darlin' Reggie, sittin' on the couch doin' jack shit and drinkin' his life away, just like he is right now, I'd wager. Gabriel's done took after his father, 'cause just like him, he don't give a damn what you think, one way or the other."

"He must o' gotten *somethin'* of yours," Levi interjected.

Jonah glared at him for his late contribution and rushed to find something to say. He wasn't about to let Levi eclipse him when he'd spent so much time arguing that a woman couldn't ever refuse his sweet talk. "Good looks, maybe?" he proposed, and immediately regretted the tepid response he'd offered.

Levi forced a laugh without much effort at hiding it. "And I think my friend here just mighta gotten his pathological ass-kissin' from one o' *his* parents," he jested. Valerie slapped her hand on the bar and cackled, but her laughter unexpectedly turned to a coughing fit, which Jonah figured to be the result of decades of smoking cheap cigarettes from the Indian reservation forty minutes out of town. Her throat sounded about as slimy as her son's personality.

"I'll just get right to it, ma'am—Valerie," Levi continued. "We were really just lookin' to get some whiskey off that there shelf."

"Direct, and right to the point—I like that," Valerie noted, nodding her head with a crooked grin. Her teeth had a permanent yellow crust at the gum line, and they looked a little too short, as though she'd worn them down to stumps from grinding them too much while flying high on God-knows-what. "Y'might get somewhere with the ladies if you'd go and act more like your friend here, Jonah."

"I'll keep it in mind," Jonah replied, seething and uncharacteristically quiet, his voice strained in a fight to keep himself from snapping back.

"So what'll it be? Just two shots?" She winked at Levi. "Or maybe three?"

Levi shook his head. "No, we're lookin' to buy the whole bottle."

Valerie frowned. "Y'know, there's a liquor store right up the road."

"And that liquor store's closed," Levi retorted.

"It ain't really house policy to go 'n sell bottles off the shelf, with all these damn laws concernin' drunk drivin' and all."

Jonah jumped back into the conversation with enthusiasm. "Well, seein' as Levi ain't got no car, I'd say that ain't much of a concern." He smiled widely at his friend, but felt a touch of guilt for cutting him down, though there wasn't any need to impress such an unimpressive woman.

"We walked," Levi clarified.

"*And* we sell liquor by the glass, not the bottle," Valerie added.

"Lemme get a look at it," Levi proposed. Valerie obliged and pulled a bottle off the lowest shelf. Levi held out his hand to take it, but she set it down on the bar instead. Wrapping his fingers around its neck, he examined the label. "Seven hundred 'n fifty milliliters. Now, we're Americans, and we ain't got much use for the metric system, but I'd say that's about… what, round twenty-five ounces and change?"

Valerie scratched behind her ear in ignorance; Jonah just stared silently. Levi continued, "How much you sellin' shots for these days?"

"For that shit? Four bucks a pop, but I'll settle for three—family discount, y'know. I reckon the boss won't mind a bit." Val winked at the two boys from across the bar. She took the bottle out of Levi's hands and tucked it behind a barrier of dusty napkin holders and uncovered dishes of bone-dry lemon wedges, which were a busy breeding ground for fruit flies.

"That's very kind o' you, Valerie. A single's about one and a half ounces, ain't it?" Levi asked. Jonah shrugged, unsure, as he was accustomed to drinking liquor, not quantifying it. Valerie peeked at the bottom of a shot glass, pointlessly searching for a volume count. She slipped it back under the bar with no such luck.

"So, if I ain't mistaken, you could get us about sixteen or seventeen shots outta that there bottle. And with your gracious family discount, it'd run me 'n Jonah over here 'bout fifty bucks for the whole damn thing." He looked over at Jonah, whose mouth was at the edge of dropping open in disbelief. "What?" Levi asked, insulted at Jonah's shock. "I do math every day, givin' change 'n all. It ain't like we got a register out there."

"I must say, Mr. Thompson," Valerie interjected, "them fancy calculations o' yours done lost me there. Never quite finished all my schoolin', gettin' knocked up at fifteen 'n all." She looked to Jonah for confirmation. "He right, Jonah?"

He wasn't sure one way or the other, but knowing that Levi's previously unheard-of math skills were the only chance they had at keeping Lenore happy, he stood behind the hypothetical price. "I reckon he is."

Levi wasn't finished outsmarting Valerie. "So, if we fork over fifty bucks and a hefty tip for Gene's nicest bartender, ain't it the same as buyin' by the glass? Or the shot, I guess." He smiled at the Skinner matriarch; Jonah figured that if her skin weren't so chalky and dull, she'd be blushing, like the old slut she was. "Y'know what? We'll even pay the full four bucks just so you don't get yourself in trouble. Sixty-eight it is." He reached into his pocket and pulled out the worn leather wallet that had once belonged to his father. Rummaging through crumpled receipts and an old punch card for free flowers at the Hometown Market, he found what he was looking for and slapped the roll of cash onto the bar. It didn't look like enough. Extending an open palm, he expected Jonah to cover the difference, for the time being.

Jonah glared and produced the rest, for both their sakes. "Guess we're payin' at a premium."

"And *I* guess an extra seventeen bucks is well worth keepin' my mother from screamin' loud enough for you to hear from the next street over," Levi whispered harshly, his voice soft but sharp as a knife. "Quit your bitchin'. I'll pay you back."

Valerie took the money and flipped through it like a thin book still too thick for her to read. "This is eighty, boys."

"Keep it all," Jonah replied, taking command. "For all the trouble we done caused you. And not to ask for another favor, but could you get us a bag?"

"I got an empty box, if that's good enough for the two o' you," Valerie said, bending down to pull out a flimsy cardboard container that once held a slim bottle. "And you best remember, Mr. Young, 'bout that time good ol' Val helped y'out when you damn well needed it."

"And I bet Gabe's his mama's son," Levi added, "since generosity runs in the Skinner family, don't it?"

Jonah withstood the urge to slap himself in the side of the head, having thought that to follow a cliché with a cliché was an act of pure, tasteless excess. Levi's shit-eating grin made it even worse.

Valerie looked back with her face gleaming in satisfaction, then turned to Jonah, awaiting a response. He felt obligated to continue the flattery. He just hoped he had the stomach to finish the job without spilling vomit all over the bar.

"And if he's anything like his mama, I'd say I ain't got much to worry about with my little sister," Jonah said, the words like sour bile bubbling up from the pit of his stomach. They left just as bad of a taste in his mouth. Even the entire bottle of bottom-shelf whiskey couldn't rinse that flavor away.

"You bet your tight lil' tush you ain't," Valerie giggled. "Gabriel always treats his gals like a goddamned princess. Sure as hell ain't got *that* from his father." She slid the box across the bar. "Well, enjoy yourselves, boys. Whatchy'all drinkin' to, anyways?"

Levi took up the box and held it under his arm, the thin cardboard buckling as he pressed it firmly against his side. He looked to Jonah for an appropriate response, which Jonah couldn't rightly find. His mouth open and emerging voice unsure, Jonah held up a single finger as he began to offer his unplanned answer. Valerie beat him to it.

"Come to think of it, I reckon it ain't much o' my business. Even more so, I s'pose two kids y'own age ain't in need o' no reason for drinkin' whenever y'all please," she said, completing her own line of questioning.

"In this here town," Jonah interjected, "there ain't no set occasions for drinkin', anyway. Just ain't biblical, y'know?"

"So we ain't got no choice but to make our own," Levi concluded.

Valerie nodded and straightened a stack of one-ply napkins as rough as sandpaper. "Sounds like a good enough motto as ever," she commented. "I'd join the two o' you, if work ain't gone and got me stuck here all night. Y'all ain't never seen a real party till one o' the Skinners done showed up. And I mean me, specific."

"We'll go 'n take your word for it," Jonah replied.

"And if my Gabriel ain't gone and dated himself into your family, and if I ain't gone and married my wretched ol' Reggie, and if my folks ain't gone and raised me a real, class-act lady, I dare say I'd come after at least one o' y'all."

"That's a whole lotta 'ifs,'" Levi remarked.

"Thank God," Jonah muttered under his breath. Levi noticed but Valerie didn't. She was busy flicking her eyes up and down from their shoes to their faces, scanning them and their bodies for something to suggestively exploit in conversation. Jonah pulled the zipper on his sweatshirt just a bit higher and prayed that his nylon shorts weren't too sheer, shifting in his seat to hide any hint of a reward for Valerie's self-declared generosity. For once, he wished he'd taken the Reverend's constant calls for modesty to heart.

"Seein' as you can't rightly join us, I guess it's about time for us to leave," Levi said. He stood up from his seat and met eyes with Jonah to hint at him to do the same, who quickly rose on cue. "Thank you for sortin' out this whole mess for us, Val."

"Anything for lil' Hannah's big brother—and his cute friend, too." She winked. Jonah came close to gagging. He could only imagine how painfully Levi's guts were churning. Based on the grimace Levi poorly tried to hide, he concluded that it was only a matter of time before he and Valerie became witnesses to a public shitting accident.

"Just remember that there shiny ring on your finger," Levi advised with a grin, jokingly wagging a finger at Valerie, whose ring looked like it came right out of a cereal box. "I ain't about to be a part o' no scandal. Clemency ain't the place for chasin' married women."

Valerie laughed, pressed her hands together in prayer and looked desperately up to Heaven. "I know, I know—God's a-watchin'," she said with mock piety. "Though He might just be tempted to join in."

"That's right," Jonah affirmed, his face smug. "God's a-watchin', and my friend right here always seems to get stage fright. Have a good night, Valerie. We're gonna go off and be two good Christian boys. There ain't much room for fun with the Reverend breathin' down your neck."

••

With the sticky feeling of sexual harassment lingering on their skin, Jonah and Levi called it a night. Levi went on with his overpriced spoils in hand, ready to give it to a thirsty and belligerent Lenore, who was never satisfied with her son's willingness to enable her while most other boys his age would have simply told her to go fuck herself. Despite the quality of Jonah's advice, he'd never learn. It'd take a miracle to get Levi to give up on his mother and accept just how hopeless her situation was—that, or a tragedy that'd leave her dead on the parlor floor, or in a hospital. It was a terrible thought, but it was the truth. No matter how true, though, Jonah couldn't bring himself to say it out loud.

Jonah could judge all he wanted, but in the back of his mind he knew that he had his own share of issues to deal with: Hannah was in love with a junkie. She was too young to know what love was—granted, Jonah had never experienced the feeling, either—but teenage infatuation was impossible to break, especially that of a hormonally volatile girl. Jonah wasn't about to feed into her interpersonal addiction, but no matter how forcefully he protested, she only clung to her precious Gabe even more tightly. Even their parents couldn't have done anything about it, though they were completely out of the loop. She was their good little schoolgirl, acing every test and passing every class with flying colors, who spent her nights studying diligently and certainly not sneaking out with the town's dregs. And as furious and concerned as Jonah was, he wasn't the type to run to his parents for the sake of getting his little sister in trouble. He was too old for that. He'd bluff, for sure, but he wasn't a rat, even when his sister was dating one.

Fatefully that track-marked vermin came scrambling out of the dark. The pickup's headlights glared out of the shadowy driveway and the tires ground against the dirt, kicking up dust mixed with stinking exhaust fumes. The engine rattled and whistled, and Gabe Skinner, red-eyed as ever, pulled out into the road. Jonah, a little drunk and a little too bold, stood right in his path. The bright lights tempted him to look away, but he let them sting his eyes and stared the driver down. He heard the roar of the engine as Gabe hit the gas. Jonah didn't prepare himself to jump out of the way into the grass; instead, he stood his ground and waited for Gabe to be the loser in this dangerous game of chicken. The tires squealed and the pickup came to a painful stop. Jonah emerged the victor.

"Is you a fuckin' retard or somethin'?" Gabe snarled, leaning his head out the window. He tossed his glowing cigarette onto the pavement and got out of the truck, slamming the door behind him. "I swear, pullin' a stunt like that, y'deserve to get ran down."

"Maybe if y'ain't smoked before gettin' behind the wheel, you woulda seen me sooner," Jonah said with a shrug. It was a lamer response than he'd intended. "Ain't nothin' wrong with smokin' a joint or two, but little girls ain't the best company for it, if y'ask me. And why'd you wanna be around 'em in the first place, I wonder?" He grinned with squinting eyes in the glare of the headlights, though it lent to his sardonic expression. "Family problems? Makin' up for a shitty childhood?"

"She ain't a girl no more," Gabe sneered. "I took care o' that a while ago. And don't you go gettin' all pissed just 'cause you'd rather be a faggot who runs around with another guy instead o' findin' himself his own woman to fuck."

It wasn't the degenerate's accusations that left Jonah seething in anger: it was his insinuations about Hannah's womanhood, and his cutting her girlhood—her childhood—short. He struggled to find the right words, but Gabe's mother had clouded his head too much by serving him cheap beer. "A real woman—y'know, a *grown* one— wouldn't be caught dead with a track-marked junkie if she knew what's good for her. Hannah ain't dumb, but she's impressionable, and y'ain't foolin' no one 'bout your intentions. Y'just get off on takin' advantage of a kid who don't know no better."

"She knows what she's doin', and you best believe she loves it," Gabe insisted. "I dunno what them parents o' yours did to 'er, but I ain't never met no one who's so willin' to do whatever I say, and I ain't a borin' man, with dime bags or in bed." He slipped a tiny plastic bag out of his back pocket and pinched it between his fingers, flaunting it and its half-finished contents: a gram or two of white powder, the chemical identity of which Jonah could only speculate, however irritably. "Finished half of it 'erself this afternoon. With an overbearin' queer for a brother, ain't no wonder she's fixin' to escape any way she can. Don't matter, though—I like 'er better that way."

"Guess you ain't datin' her for her mind, then."

"She's better off tweakin'. Cries less when I'm fuckin' her—a lil' blow does a virgin some good, but you wouldn't know nothin' about that."

In his mind, Jonah swung his arm hard and landed a solid fist in Gabe's pockmarked jaw; he stomped a heavy foot on his throat and kicked him in the ribs until he broke more bones than a free clinic could fix. Then he hopped into the pickup and threw it in drive, hit the gas with furious intent and heard the satisfying thump of Gabe's twisted body under the squealing tires. He put it in reverse and hit him again, rocking back and forth in the road until Gabe was just a flattened puddle of skin, guts and shattered bone. But it was all in his head, and he wasn't in any state to pick a fistfight. The best he could do was clench his teeth and keep himself from making the situation any worse with a snarky line or two that he'd later regret when he sobered up, not because they'd pissed Gabe off, but because they'd be jumbled and embarrassing. The buzz of the beer erased all wit and dulled what could have been a razor-sharp lampoon, and if there was one thing he wouldn't do, it was let Gabe get the last cutting laugh. Unfortunately, Gabe's sly grin proved that he knew he'd won this time.

"Stay outta my way and we won't have no problems," Gabe ordered, offering an ultimatum that couldn't possibly be heeded with a clear conscience. "Ain't no other guy's gon' look at any girl o' mine, even if he's 'er brother." He climbed into the pickup and lit a cigarette, flicking away a glowing cherry that landed at Jonah's feet. "Enjoy your night, big brother—I know I already did."

Jonah stomped out the embers and looked upon the black smear of ash on the road, and swore to himself as the pickup's red taillights disappeared into the distance that when all was said and done, he'd do the same to Gabe, and make him just an ugly stain on the bottom of his shoe.

# 7

Sophia Shaw always had a halo around her. It was as delicate as sunlight sparkling over the creek when she smiled. When she pouted, as she did that day just after Sunday service, it was more of an iron curtain that even Jonah's proud talent for conversation couldn't part. And as she sat there in the corner—once again, alone in her palpable boredom that every coffee hour evoked—the heavenly barrier that separated her from the world of the flesh was impenetrable. Jonah was physical, material and base; an angel would never lower herself to the level of worms in mud.

He planned to approach with caution. He'd gulped down his coffee right at the table, caring little about the upset he'd soon feel in his empty stomach. The cup went right into the trash. He wasn't about to spill scalding coffee all over himself again, or worse, onto Sophia's conservative skirt, but he'd worn black that day just to be safe. He wouldn't let a stain ruin his chances at making an improved second impression. With an unfamiliar nervousness, he eyed her from across the room. He'd never had trouble wooing a girl before, and he couldn't decide if he should attribute his social gracelessness to romantic rustiness, or legitimate affection. The fact that he couldn't tell the difference unnerved him even more.

Jonah prepared himself for his psychological run through a treacherous gauntlet of big-mouthed old ladies and their husbands, who'd loosened their belts to accommodate two or more helpings of coffee cake. A talkative obstruction could cross his path at any moment, and it was unfortunate that his parents had gone home after service, as they could have been useful as human shields against the gossip queens, or worse, the Reverend Shaw and his darling Holy Roller. Ma and Pa could have been the chaff to Victoria's sin-seeking missiles. So instead, Jonah had to avoid her with the best counter-maneuvers he could perform.

A puff of powdered sugar struck his side when Mr. Spaulding clumsily dropped a donut onto the table; it bounced and hit the floor like plates his waitresses dropped at the Americana, whom he always forgave and gave a second, third or fourth chance to. Howard Spaulding was the owner of the Americana Diner who was too often criticized for his lack of Greek heritage. He had a chubby face, though his body was disproportionately lanky. The dark circles around his eyes and high-arched eyebrows led many to say he looked like a clown, though they never dared say it to his face. The donut had grazed Mr. Spaulding's tie and left a streak of white powder; much to his relief, he'd chosen not to wear the American flag tie he usually wore to work. Jonah, too, was scathed by the donut, and he rubbed out the stain in hopes that the dusty blast hadn't left even a hint of white on his black shirt. As such, he kept his left arm pressed against his hip while he crossed the room, all while worrying that the awkward stiffness of his stride would only draw more attention to his sugary assault. He opted to sit to Sophia's right to hide it—if he could ever make it to the seat. Victoria Shaw, however, had other plans.

"Mr. Young," she said, rigidly addressing Jonah as she ambushed him from the side, previously undetected behind a cloak of chatty septuagenarians.

"Mrs. Shaw." He outstretched a hand to greet her. She didn't reciprocate. He uncomfortably withdrew his open palm.

"Once again, it's a pleasure to see you mingling with the flock. You are *mingling*, aren't you?"

"I was plannin' on it," Jonah replied. He peeked behind Victoria to catch a glimpse of Sophia. When the Reverend's wife continued, he half expected her to snap her fingers to condescendingly grab his attention.

"Talking to the one pretty girl in the room isn't the kind of mingling I'm suggesting."

Jonah fell silent for a second. "I hope you don't think—"

"Oh, I don't *think*—I *know*, Mr. Young. I know what unfaithful little boys like you do when their parents aren't looking. I only hope you keep in mind that—"

"God's a-watchin'?"

A sly, satisfied grin spread across Victoria's face. "Maybe all those years of Sunday school weren't completely wasted on you after all," she replied. "But I'm sure you don't know your Bible as well as you should. Matthew 5:27 to 28. Can you remember *that*?"

Jonah shook his head, bit his lip. Victoria sighed. "I suppose that would be expecting too much of you," she lamented. "Evidently, reading isn't your strong suit, but God willing, you'll learn something today. The verses go: 'You have heard that it was said to those of old, "You shall not commit adultery." But I say to you that whoever looks at a woman to lust for her has already committed adultery with her in his heart.'"

"Matthew 5:27 to 28," the Reverend Shaw interjected. He crept into the conversation from behind Victoria and put a hand on her shoulder. Like a God-fearing Goliath, he towered over her and Jonah. "But you know, Jesus didn't stop there. He went on to say—"

"If your right eye causes you to sin, pluck it out," Victoria quoted.

Her husband nodded. "And your right hand, too. Any part of you, in fact."

"So, Mr. Young, if you were to *finally* follow the Lord's command like the rest of the flock, you'd be left with only one eye, one hand, one foot—"

"And nothing to fill your drawers," the Reverend concluded. He subtly gestured toward below Jonah's belt. "You've only got *one* of those, I hope."

"Lucky for me, the Devil went and gave me a spare," Jonah jested, seizing his chance to speak amid the Shaws' scriptural onslaught. He laughed nervously but neither Shaw appeared amused. "But I ain't fixin' to go under the knife anytime soon. Ain't no need, seein' I ain't exactly on the prowl here—'specially not for your lil' Sophia over there."

The Reverend looked reluctantly satisfied; Victoria, on the other hand, tried to hide her burning scowl with a narrow smile. Her husband took his hand off her and thrust it into his pocket, taking a single step away. Jonah expected he'd fended him off.

"Now if you'll excuse me, Reverend—and Mrs. Shaw," Jonah said respectfully, "I'm gonna go 'n lighten up your daughter. I gotta say, she ain't lookin' too happy at these brunches lately. Can't imagine why, given such good company." He left Victoria standing there with eyes filled with hellfire. An ensuing chat with Gracey would dampen the flames searing his back, if only for another thirty minutes. Victoria would spin herself a fanciful little web of white lies and forget all about their little encounter. Mingling, naturally, always took priority. For her, idle talk wasn't ungodly, but the very foundation of a small town's happy façade, which was her burden to build.

Her daughter, however, was doing her best to avoid idle talk altogether: she'd fled the scene and was nowhere to be found, having disappeared before Jonah could even call out her name. She couldn't have gone far, because she'd left her purse sitting on the chair next to an unread church bulletin. Jonah sat down, two seats away, as to not be too suspicious, both in his intentions toward the absent Reverend's daughter and in his proximity to an unattended bag with no one to protect its contents. He hoped that there wouldn't come a curious churchgoer who was interested in striking up a conversation with a lonely-looking young man sitting by himself. Then Levi emerged from the congregation and stood before him. Of all obstacles, he was the last that Jonah expected.

"Can't let you do that," Levi said with a concerned grimace.

"Do what?"

"I know that bag ain't yours, unless you've been hidin' a transvestite lifestyle from me all these years. She's a nice girl, I'm sure, but you're askin' for trouble."

"All I'm askin' for is a minute alone with her. Ain't nothin' questionable about that," Jonah countered. "I'll catch up with you later. I only get one shot at this a week, and I ain't about to blow it like last time."

"I'm sparin' you another failure by gettin' you outta here."

"Second time's a charm."

"The Reverend and his wife don't believe in second chances. I saw 'em grillin' you back there, and it's only gonna get worse. They ain't gonna turn the other cheek to some boy who's goin' after their perfect virgin daughter."

"Who said I got any interest in violatin' her?"

"You got a reputation for it, that's why."

"Maybe it's time to change that."

Levi shook his head and looked back toward Victoria, who was letting out a perfunctory laugh at one of Mr. Hodges's bad jokes, all while eyeing Jonah with suspicion. "Now, I ain't never been a cock block, but this time I gotta get in the way before you do somethin' you regret. We both know y'don't always think with your head." He pointed behind him at the Reverend and his wife. "Mama's been sayin' I should listen to the preacher for a while. Maybe I should call him over and see what he's got to say?"

Jonah scowled but surrendered in the face of Levi's threats. He reached for the bulletin on Sophia's chair and opened it to the last page, which was filled with simple block-print ads for local businesses, as it always was. He folded the paper and tore out a coupon for use at the Americana Diner. On a Wednesday two weeks away, Howie Spaulding planned to offer any coupon-bearing customer a free milkshake between four and five o'clock in the afternoon. It was a strangely short window of opportunity for such a special, but not particularly uncharacteristic of Mr. Spaulding, who didn't have much of a mind for business. Jonah took the frayed clipping and placed it on top of Sophia's black purse as Levi turned to leave. With any luck, Sophia would find the ad and know that he was the one who'd left it. And with even more luck, Jonah would see her walk through the diner door, and know that he hadn't been sitting alone for an hour for nothing.

••

Sunday service may have had a history of crawling at a snail's pace, but the week always passed by disappointingly quickly. Before he knew it, Levi had woken up on a Friday morning, and not only cursed the thought of dragging himself out of bed to drudge over to the gas station, but dreaded the coming sermon just forty-eight hours away, which would be more imbued with cries of damnation than his own daybreak mentality.

Clouds veiled the sun that day, and the summer heat gave way to a welcome chill in the air. Levi relished the comforting sensation of a dry shirt wrapped around his body; too often it constricted him, tight with his own sweat like wet cotton in a dryer for the first time. Sadly, it wasn't the first time, but one time out of hundreds, thousands, even, and there wasn't a final one to come anytime soon. He'd come to accept that he'd likely die with the odor of gasoline, not formaldehyde, lingering on his remains, and that he'd be dressed in the same old clothes he'd worn for years with little concern for a new wardrobe to ruin with oil stains and dust.

"Ain't a glamorous job, I know," Rusty admitted when he'd seen Levi scrutinizing the stubborn stains. "But ladies love a man who works with his hands, I can tell you that." It was easy for a mechanic to say. For Levi, however, working with his hands meant pumping gas, and it was lonely work, which wouldn't translate well into prowess in the bedroom, unless he was in bed alone, as he too often was.

The light rain fell when he stepped out into the road, his shift over but encroaching on unpaid overtime. With the gentle trickles of water over his brow and shoulders the stench was sluiced away, and he imagined the little puddles he left beneath his feet had a yellowish tinge, jaundiced with petroleum, or the rainbow sheen of motor oil on pavement. For once, the air smelled fresh; the humidity broke and breathing became enjoyable, not laborious. Every so often he caught a flash of light, at first fearing that it might be sunlight, which would usher in a new wave of heat and complaining, but each time the bursts proved to be the glare of headlights passing through the mist. He thought of the haunting glow of a mountain lion's eyes in the night each time he saw the piercing pairs emerge from the hazy distance, watching him, as did the drivers on their hunt, who no doubt recognized him as the hopeless young man who pumped their gas with a forced smile, the victim of a devastated economy and a town that hadn't grown since its inception.

A den of lions loomed off the road at the end of decrepit Midian Lane: the Skinner family, perhaps not regal enough to be called lions, but rather hyenas, jackals or any other mangy, detestable creatures. They were a pride that was proud of their name, though it inspired only disgust and contempt. The churchgoers condemned them as degenerates and drunks, while even the poorest and lowest class in town judged them as a destitute blight on the once honorable name of Clemency, because while they themselves had very little money, they at least worked for their low wages, as productivity was their means of distraction, not drugs. The Skinners, however, were only as regal as lions in their reputation of being the most majestic of welfare queens. Reggie, the patriarch whose power was derived not from inherited wealth, prominent ancestry or even a noble family name, built his crooked-roofed castle on parasitic foundations, preferring to live in a flimsy house of EBT cards. On the other hand, his son Gabe, when not dealing drugs, did work a part-time job as a line cook at the Americana. His wages, however, went straight into the pockets of shady characters who lurked on the street corners north of town, who peddled brief escapes from the defeatism all of Clemency knew so well.

*"That's right, bitch, run off!"* roared the cub from his den. *"Y'ain't gon' be gone for long!"*

The shaky door clattered when it swung back and hit the cheap vinyl siding. The frightened cries of the Skinners' newborn sounded out from the dimly lit mobile home. But while his sobs were simply those of a startled infant, Hannah Young wept with an overwhelming mix of contradictory emotions. She ran toward the street in tears, her face in her hands and a hateful bruise on her neck. Levi was no stranger to love bites: after all, he'd noticed them on Jonah's neck countless times in high school, and each time evoked a feeling of disgust toward someone who didn't even have enough shame to wear a scarf. But the marks that Hannah carried on her as a brand of victimhood weren't left in the inconsiderate heat of passion. If anything, it had been the heat of anger, the kind that made one want to choke the life from someone, and apparently, even a teenage girl too young to be in such a predicament in the first place.

He wasn't sure if she was ignoring him or if her tears clouded her vision so thoroughly that she couldn't see him standing in the road. Her desperate sprint dwindled down to a tired shuffle when she crossed the threshold of the Skinners' blighted yard, and she dragged her feet with a fatigue that suggested not just physical exhaustion, but emotional defeat. Levi didn't have to jog to catch up with her. He walked alongside her, tempted to touch her arm to grab her attention, but found himself too worried about pressing the wrong bruise and drawing out another yelp.

"I'll walk you home," he said without introduction. Hoping to find a way to wipe away her tears, he thought of the old rag he kept dangling from his back pocket, but it was far too sullied for use as a much-needed handkerchief. Her cheeks were already blotchy with running mascara. She never wore makeup—her parents, like most in Clemency, had no desire to see their daughter gallivanting around like an unrepentant Magdalene—but it seemed she'd tossed aside her spiritual obligation to modesty for the sake of making Gabe Skinner happy. It was an ironic thought, that Gabe expected his girls to look like models while he saw no reason to present himself as the handsome young gentleman that he never was, and likely could never be. After all, with a father who probably taught a thirteen-year-old Gabriel to shave with a piece of glass for lack of razors, such self-respect from the eldest Skinner boy was both unrealistic and unfair.

"You'll tell my brother everything," Hannah predicted, her tone leading Levi to conclude that she was desperate to pour her unspoken problems upon a willing listener, while at the same time far too terrified of the consequences to do so. From what he understood, she had her friends, but it wasn't a stretch to assume that to admit Gabe's myriad faults to them would diminish the allure of a dysfunctional relationship with an inappropriately older man. She was probably their idol at that point, a symbol of true desirability: to immature schoolgirls, even Gabe would seem unattainable and, therefore, extremely attractive. It didn't matter that he was a cockroach cloaked in dull human skin; it was irrelevant that his intentions were as pure as a fisherman dangling a delectable worm before hungry catfish. He was a catch, for sure, and Hannah had reeled him in, at least in their inexperienced, impressionable heads. Neither she nor they seemed to realize that it was Gabe who towed the line, and who was perfectly willing to throw each girl back into the sea after he'd cut them open and left them to cloud the water with blood.

"I know y'ain't gonna believe me, but I swear I won't say nothin'," he promised with imaginary fingers crossed. He knew it was a vow he couldn't keep, and that, in all honesty, he wouldn't want to. He'd at least let Jonah know a piece or two of the story. Unless Hannah was about to wear winter clothes for the next few weeks, it was inevitable that her brother would notice the bruises that could only have been spread by Gabe Skinner's yellow-fingered fist. The most Levi would have to report was that he saw Hannah at the end of Midian Lane, and her fate would be sealed. He worried, however, that Jonah's reaction might be as emotionally destructive as Gabe's was physically. He was even more concerned that Jonah might do something stupid—not to his little sister, but to a drugged-up sack of shit who had nothing to lose. Even if Gabe got his ass kicked, he'd still find a reward in emergency room morphine.

"He wanted me to hang out with his friends," Hannah muttered. "But I met 'em before and I don't like 'em. There's somethin' off about 'em. And now he's mad at me, 'cause he says I'm doubtin' his judge o' character, or whatever."

"Well, at least you're growin' up enough to recognize when somethin' ain't right about someone," Levi noted. "I know you don't wanna hear it, but maybe you should be turnin' that intuition in Gabe's direction."

"Y'don't understand," Hannah snapped. She hung her head low, regretful. "None o' you do."

"Listen: all teenagers, 'specially girls, think they're misunderstood," Levi explained, "and maybe some o' you are. But *you* ain't. I know you don't wanna believe it, but y'ain't. Jonah's tryin' his best to look out for you, believe it or not, and maybe he can come off like an ass when he's doin' it, but y'should try to listen more."

"Gabe's got a temper but so does—"

"Your brother ain't never beat nobody. But he sure as hell might if he knows what your boyfriend's been doin' to you."

"He says he don't like to see his girls act up. Says he's teachin' me manners."

"Don't tell me you really buy into that shit."

"He also says it's in the Bible, so it's okay."

"There's a lot o' fucked up stuff in that book," Levi groaned.

"So you sayin' we shouldn't read it, then?"

"No," Levi sighed. "It's got its points. I guess you gotta take the good with the bad."

Hannah stopped in her tracks and, as though she'd finally reached the point she'd always hoped for, answered: "That's what I'm tryin' to do with Gabe." And like their walk down Main Street under the cloud of a darkened mood, their discussion came to an end, and it was the last that Levi heard from her on that matter for some time. Jonah, however, went on with his life, unaware of the events that day. Levi told him nothing. Ignorance, though, wasn't always bliss—especially for Hannah, whose naïve delusions weren't enough to keep her safe.

••

Susan Lewis taught Jonah to stack the language reference books on the top shelves of the travel section. It was near the ceiling at the apex of a bookcase that was far larger than normal; some books he had no choice but to turn on their sides to fit, as they were too tall for the miniscule gap between the chalky, crumbling tile boards and the matte metal shelves. They were a donation from Hebron's flourishing school system, just a small part of a larger shipment that Susan not only seemed disdainful of, but also perfectly willing to hide among the older books that had been organized and untouched for years. She was resentful of literary hand-me-downs, citing them as evidence of a sort of separate-but-equal relationship between Clemency and the prosperous districts to the north and south, though her town's faithful considered themselves to be more equal than others in the eyes of God. And even if the books had been written, published and printed in Clemency, Susan would still have put them in the most inaccessible spot, as the library's clients—all half-dozen of them—wouldn't find much use for them.

"If they're gonna gather dust, they might as well do it out of sight," she said. "These people don't even know half a language."

Jonah wasn't short but the step ladder he'd pulled from the back closet wasn't going to cut it. Three shaky steps weren't enough for the job, and when he took up a book in his hand—*Learn Beginner's French*—he had to hop up with his arm outstretched as far as he could without dislocating his shoulder. After a few tries he managed to slip it between two old German books that had been there since it was studied as the language of the enemy. On some level, he regretted hiding the French book away, flanked by two volumes that it would most certainly surrender its attention to, as they had much bolder spines. He'd taken French in high school, thinking it was an instant ticket to bed, and, in fact, it had worked. But there were no more classes for him to take, it being a year after graduation, and no one to whisper poorly pronounced but seductive phrases to. He forgot most of the words he knew and overused. Even if he wanted to brush up, he'd never be able to get that book without risking a broken back.

"Y'know, your little sister wanted to take out a book on Spanish once," Susan remarked, emerging from behind the bookcase that might soon prove to be the cause of Jonah's early demise, or at least full-body paralysis. "Said it was for school. Guess our district's gettin' cheap with providin' its students with shit textbooks."

"Is that so?" Jonah replied, grunting his words as he twisted his body to put away another book. He lost interest and tossed it up with no concern for organization. Susan couldn't even see it to criticize him.

"You weren't there that day, and this ol' lady wasn't gettin' up on that ladder for a lousy *lee-bro day es-pan-yole*. Told her unless she was plannin' on cuttin' lawns for a livin', there ain't a single reason to learn Hispanic."

"I took French." He stopped to catch his breath.

"Plain, ol' English is good enough for me," Susan concluded. She pulled a book from the pile that was yet to be sorted and decided that a Mandarin-to-English dictionary was as useless as a pecker on a pole ("There ain't a single Chink from here to Tennessee," she claimed); Jonah reached out to take it from her, but she threw it back, leaving him stretching down empty handed with a scowl.

"That brainy lil' Hannah ain't been round here in a terribly long time," she noted, having changed her mind on walking away in disgust at America's reluctance to declare an official language, which, at that point in history, had a seventy-percent chance of being Spanish.

Jonah flexed his calves and arched his feet but nearly lost his balance. "There ain't much use in readin' when you're hangin' round the most illiterate family in town," he said shakily, clinging to the edge of the shelf for dear life.

"That's a damn shame," Susan muttered as she shook her head in disappointment. "I'm guessin' she's callin' herself the oldest one's girlfriend. That boy ain't—"

"Nothin' but trouble. Believe me, I've heard it, and it ain't like I disagree or nothin'."

"So what are you plannin' on doin' about it?" Susan asked, arms crossed.

Jonah, in a fit of frustration toward the pointlessly fat textbook on some obscure language that even his young muscles could barely lift above his head, dropped it with a grunt onto the ground and kicked the cart of books. With a shaky clatter, it drifted away and crashed into another bookcase, which, luckily, was so heavy with Bibles and scriptural commentaries that a giant on crack couldn't even knock it down. He stepped down from the ladder and set his feet firmly on the floor. He stood his ground before an assailant with blotchy lipstick and a penchant for criticizing the most insipid details of his life. Now her biggest grievance was his unwillingness to be his little sister's gallant white knight, clad in a poorly fit button-down in place of shining armor.

"I don't wanna talk about it," he stated half-firmly, scratching the back of his head. He felt as though his hair was salt-and-pepper with book dust: he felt an itchiness on his ears and neck that he could only attribute to the powdery patina that built up over the years, never to be wiped away.

"You don't have a plan, do you, kid?"

"Don't need one. She'll get rid o' him sooner or later, once she realizes that he don't care about nothin' but his next high, or his next sorry, pathetic girl."

Susan chuckled and the cloudy pearls around her neck clicked like an aging hooker's heels on pavement. "I might be old, but I ain't lost my sensibilities. He ain't goin' nowhere and she ain't gonna let him go nowhere, neither."

Picking up a cardboard box of light paperbacks and balancing it on his shoulder, Jonah pushed the step ladder aside with his foot and resumed his task on a less ambitious lower shelf. He cleared his throat but had no intention of speaking. Susan paused, waiting for a response that never came. She filled the silence herself.

"You know, she's just like a younger me, except I was a hell of a lot bustier," she noted with a wistful tone. "If only you'd known me in my prime, kid. I was quite the bombshell in my day."

Jonah grimaced. "Not needed, ma'am."

Susan looked up with nostalgia in her eyes and continued, lacking any concern for Jonah's growing nausea. "I'll never forget Peter. Oh, Petey—wasn't much of a catch, I'll admit. Met him back when those goddamned trash collectors up in Lillian decided they were skilled laborers who deserved a schoolteacher's pay. His whole family was poor—the poorest in town, with a reputation as bad as the Skinners', but at least they weren't drug addicts. I suppose what made it worse was that the economy was boomin', unlike these shit times, so people had to sit around and wonder why in God's name the Johnstone family couldn't even scrape up enough money to buy their kids new clothes more than once every half a decade.

"But anyways, his father came up with a lil' opportunistic business plan, and went round with his run-down truck collectin' people's trash for two bucks a pop. Didn't give two shits about that useless trash collector union callin' him a scab and smashin' his windows in—he needed the money. Naturally, these nasty ol' Clemency WASPs circulated all sorts o' rumors, sayin' the Johnstones must've been pickin' outta the trash, searchin' for things that changed each time the story got told: food scraps, expired medicine for any kind o' condition, broken toys for their newborn. Even back then these people were hypocrites, 'cause no matter how much judgment they passed on Petey and his family, and no matter how many rumors they spread, they still had no problem handin' over their bags o' garbage every Saturday mornin' for a measly two dollars.

"Turns out Mr. Johnstone couldn't figure out where to dump the garbage, so he ended up throwin' it all off the side o' the road halfway to Lillian. Was only a matter o' time before he got caught, and the cops caught stinky wind o' his operation and locked him up for a few weeks for litterin' on a scale they ain't never seen before. But Petey wasn't about to let that stop him, so he kept on drivin' his dad's truck round town and made a regular Mount Everest o' black trash bags in his own backyard. Pretty soon those sour juices seeped outta the bags and into the ground, and their well water got real putrid; they couldn't use it no more, so there ain't no way they coulda washed that smell outta their clothes then. Didn't matter to me, though. Sure, it was foul as a rottin' duck in a puddle, but you get used to it. Smelled like capitalism to me, and money makin's the best cologne, even when the stink it's coverin' up makes you wanna retch.

"First time I noticed him—he didn't go to school, you see, for reasons I ain't never figured out, even to this day—it was a Saturday and he was in front o' my house, liftin' a big, aluminum trash can over the back o' his dad's truck. All that heavy liftin' gave him some muscles to die for, and I was ragin' with the hormones of a crazed teenager who'd rather listen to her body than her parents' alleged sensibilities. I swear, if I'd had the chance I woulda hid myself in one o' those trash cans like a stripper in a goddamned cake. Ma 'n Pa did their best to be conservative with their garbage, thinkin' it was responsible or some nonsense, but I started throwin' all sorts o' stuff out—spring cleanin' in the fall, tossin' out anything I could find, just to force Petey to stay a few more minutes out front flexin' his muscles and gettin' a few more drops o' sweat on his brow.

"Pretty soon I was chit-chattin' in the street and makin' a fool o' myself with my double-entendres and insinuations about him probably havin' his way with girls and throwin' them out, too, but it didn't take a psychic to know that most o' these Clemency girls would rather drown themselves in a river than get a single stain on their Sunday dresses from his rough, manly hands. Sure, he was a poor kid who spent his days around real trash and his nights around white trash, but the more Ma 'n Pa noticed me socializin', the more they objected—and the more interested I got. Wasn't long before I made that boy a man—until those goddamned trash collectors cut their strike short and Petey 'n his dad went back to bein' unemployed and even more undesirable.

"Guess he wasn't the best match, and maybe he was more o' my means o' rebellin' than a real shot at young love, but at least he wasn't no degenerate like that Gabe Skinner. Sure, Ma 'n Pa hated him, but in the end everyone knew he was harmless, and they were just tryin' to protect my modesty, whatever that means. But your parents must really hate that Gabriel, 'cause he ain't even got the ambition to take advantage of a bad situation, even if it means pickin' up people's trash. He ain't no capitalist: he's a pathetic, lil' parasite. God knows your parents would do anything to keep your sister from a useless bloodsucker like him."

"They ain't got a clue about him. God knows my best friend's been coverin' for Hannah anytime the truth's about to come out. But I guess I ain't said much, neither."

"Well, then your sister's only gettin' grief from you," Susan deduced.

"Most likely."

"I got grief from *both* my parents—Ma 'n Pa, both of 'em together. A united force to be reckoned with. But you know what? They couldn't stop me from doin' nothin'. They really found out about it when they caught me in the back of Petey's truck doin' the horizontal shuffle, but in all honesty, those dried-up Puritans mighta learned a thing or two."

"Jesus, Susan. You really doin' this to me right now?" He cringed, and looked down at the books in his hands, having lost his train of thought. "You ruined my whole damn process of organizin' this bullshit."

"I know, I know—Mrs. Lewis was an easy teenager. Hard to grasp, ain't it?"

"I got more boxes to stack, and you're too much of a distraction for it," Jonah said hurriedly.

"But then can't you tell with my good tastes? I used to rope 'em in left and right," Susan laughed, and, pulling on the sleeves of her long fur coat, modeled it with a quick spin around. The coat swung back and forth, so oversized that it almost swept along the floor. The downy, white trim on the bottom seemed to turn black with dust; in his head, Jonah saw a musty cloud billowing around her, like the smoke of hellfire beneath a harlot who was too enthralled in her own pleasures to see that the flames at her feet were not the fires of passion, but punishment.

"Not a single one o' these Clemency boys could stop themselves," she jested, though she was more serious than Jonah was willing to accept, "so I had to shoot a good number of 'em down. Ain't appropriate for a young lady to give *that* many kisses."

"Please, ma'am, I've had enough," Jonah pleaded.

"That's what they all said, kid," she cackled. "Wore those boys out good. But take solace in knowin' your lil' sister's only rompin' with one boy, no matter how deep in the gutter him and his wretched family might be."

Susan walked away with a devious smirk, leaving Jonah in an unshakable state of shock. But she couldn't help herself, and called from behind another bookcase: "Don't you fret, kid. I ain't pullin' any tricks on no one, especially you, so don't go bitchin' around town about sexual harassment in the workplace. Aunt Flo's gone and she ain't never comin' back, and Lord knows without her I ain't got a single spark left in this old body. Without me, this town's drier than the goddamned Sahara—except for that bitchy lil' oasis o' skankery, Charlene von Braun, if the church rumors are true. Hard to validate, though, since she ain't the religious type, and she don't barely ever come down from that bougie hill of hers.

"Nothin' good can come of those Skinners, o'course, but be thankful Hannah ain't hangin' with Charlene's type. Your lil' sister's just goin' for Gabriel out of insecurity—what teenage girl ain't insecure, except for me?—and eventually she's gonna learn somethin' and move on, and maybe even be stronger for it. But women like Charlene von Braun just fuck around for the hell of it, 'cause they're too bored with their fancy lives to fuck their husbands. A skinny bitch like that might just suck a dick for a diet Coke. Any smart man would stay clear o' the likes of her. There's worse things than syphilis out there: a schemin' slut like that will cut a man down like it's nothin', since people are just her pawns. Sooner or later Hannah's gonna learn how *not* to treat others, once she gets it in her naïve lil' head that a boy like Gabe don't know a thing about how to treat a lady. But if she starts actin' like Charlene, then you got a real problem. A girl like that don't give a shit about what others want or need, and she sure as hell won't stop harassin' a man till she gets what she wants: and it ain't nothin' to be proud of."

••

When a young Levi had grown big enough to wear the dress shirt he had now owned for years, he remembered the material feeling thick and suffocating, as though it were made of woven plastic and rubber strings. Fabric softener didn't do much, and neither did washing it again and again, each time more furiously, until he'd gone from gently scrubbing it in a tub of soapy water to nearly tearing it into pieces with his raw hands. Over time, however, the shirt began to wear down, and though it was impeccably clean—Mama would have never allowed him to step foot in church with a single stain on his shirt, as it was evidence of a stain on the soul—its color had faded considerably. The fabric was softer these days than it had ever been, but Levi couldn't be sure if it had truly gotten sheerer, or if the skin of his torso had become so calloused from its roughness that he could no longer feel it.

Whatever the cause of his unexpected comfort in his Sunday clothes, he stood at the counter in Backwater Spirits without much thought as to his state of overdress. Anyone else would have thought it strange that his first stop after Sunday service wasn't the diner or a quiet brunch at home, but, like his shirt, he was used to it.

"I ain't never seen you in church," Levi noted as Elijah Green slipped the all-too-familiar bottle into an equally familiar paper bag. "There ain't many people in this wretched town who've got the balls to skip Sunday service. Worse than riskin' an eternity in Hell, you're beggin' for the social wrath o' the Shaws—and they make the Old Testament God look real kind."

"My church days are over," Elijah replied. "Born and raised in it, and I'm as much of a believer as any. But there comes a point where you can't keep justifyin' the foolishness that comes outta that Reverend Shaw's mouth. I don't know what Bible he's been readin' all his life, but the Lord Almighty should sue the publisher."

"They drop Jesus's name in every other sentence, but I ain't never heard them read much outta the Gospels," Levi observed. "They're more o' the Leviticus types, I reckon."

"Sadly, there's a whole lotta people like that these days," Elijah sighed, looking out the window toward the Southern Mercy Bible Church, "and maybe you could blame it on illiteracy like the Northerners would, but I'd wager they're just tryin' to justify their own anger, and their own hate, by twistin' God's words and pullin' out any which quote they need. And I don't need none o' that in my life. I know a thing or two 'bout anger and hate, but if there's anything I learned outta readin' that book, it's that you gotta let go, or it'll consume you."

"My whole life's been one big mess o' hate, but that's my Mama's doin'."

"Maybe so, but holdin' on to it ain't gonna do nothin' to her—you're just hurtin' yourself."

"That ain't what the Reverend Shaw would say," Levi said with a shrug.

"I ain't gonna tell you what to think or believe, but I'm gonna give you some advice: don't listen to a thing that man says, or his wife, or any o' those churchgoers, who'd all call Jesus a pacifist hippie if he walked among 'em. The two o' them and their flock have got a right mind to steal the hog and sell the feet for alms. They're all devils in Sunday hats, and there ain't nothin' more to it."

"I've been listenin' to his sermons all my life, and all he's done is make me think it's all a crock o' shit."

"Watch your tongue," Elijah said with a benevolent wag of his finger. "Don't confuse what they're sayin' with the truth. Their false piety don't make real piety any less real. Trust in God, but don't for a second trust those who claim to speak for Him. You think the Reverend don't have himself a drink every night, or think about good-lookin' women like your Mama when his faithful wife ain't payin' him no mind? I know a hypocrite when I see one. He can run his mouth all he wants about my store bein' open on Sunday evenin's, but those words don't mean nothin' when they're slurred."

"Well, it ain't like I can skip church like you," Levi lamented. "Y'ain't got a zealot of a mother like I do."

"No, I don't. And I reckon freedom ain't your mama's cup o' tea. But y'ain't gonna be here forever, are you? Ain't nothin's permanent, but I s'pose the words 'this too shall pass' ain't never come outta your mama's mouth, and 'specially not the Reverend's."

"If there's one thing I wish I could believe, it's that."

Like a nervous tick without the nervousness, Elijah began to twist his wedding band around his finger, making two full rotations before he set his hand down on the counter to stop himself. "The only thing you can't change is change itself," he explained as a kind of indisputable fact, though one that, coming from him, Levi was inclined to accept. "Y'can't avoid it, no matter how hard you try. A boy like you's gotta know that just as the people in your life can disappear in the blink of an eye, and that happiness—real happiness—can turn to sorrow before you know it, it don't change the fact that the reverse is true. But the only way you're ever gonna turn that sadness into joy is by forgivin'—forgivin' others, and 'specially forgivin' yourself, if there's any guilt you're holdin' on to, whether y'know it or not. The only purpose anger serves is as a chain y'can't break, and all that resentment's gonna do is lock away the future. Y'can't keep wishin' for it while bindin' yourself to this town with your hate. That's all this town knows, anyway. And they're perfectly content to make it into a prison for people like us."

with your hate. That's all this town knows, anyway. And they're perfectly content to make it into a prison for people like us."

THE POORLY PLANNED promotional event at the Americana Diner wasn't set to begin for another fifteen minutes, but Jonah decided to arrive early, as he wasn't sure what time Sophia Shaw would make her appearance, if ever. He found himself a booth to claim for the two of them and sank into the old, red vinyl seat, which didn't sport too many holes, despite its age; the one tear he noticed had been patched over with a piece of maroon-colored tape that didn't quite match the fading tone of the cushions. The place was chilly from the shaky air conditioner shoved through one of the windows, from which a cluster of frayed ribbons fluttered to prove that Mr. Spaulding was, in fact, making enough profit to run the air conditioner consistently without bankrupting himself with electric bills. Despite the cold, Jonah was sweating—not profusely, but enough for the backs of his legs to stick to the vinyl, and his hair, in need of a good trim, to leave him feeling itchy behind the ears.

He'd had a difficult time choosing what to wear, since the diner was devoid of a dress code, though on Sundays it saw throngs of churchgoers boasting colorful dresses and well-pressed suits, looking to fill their stomachs after filling their souls with Christ's conditional love. And it was, after all, a Wednesday afternoon; the handful of customers who sat scattered around the dining area were clad in work clothes and housewives' plain frocks. Even in shorts and a checkered green button-down, which he made even more casual by rolling up the sleeves as far as his biceps would allow, he was more finely dressed than that day's clientele. He knew, however, that no matter what he wore, Sophia would outshine him. He had no desire to one-up her when it came to appearances, because not only did he appreciate a woman better looking than himself (though he had come to understand that he himself was pushing on a solid eight), he also knew that modesty was something she aspired to but found impossible to achieve.

It was too early for alcohol and the Americana didn't have much of a selection, anyway, but Jonah would have benefited from a few ounces just to numb his nerves a bit. He had to admit that he wasn't much of a dater, and courting a woman wasn't exactly his specialty: he had much more experience with encounters that required no romance and no potential for love, in which he got what he needed and a girl got what she wanted, with no questions asked and no expectations imposed. But to sit down with someone, actually talk to her, and, more awkwardly, actually listen to her, was a concept he had never really had a desire to put into action. In the past, it'd seemed like a waste of time. He wasn't afraid to admit it to Levi or any boy his age, in high school or at present, but it was an immaturely male attitude that he was reluctant to reveal now that Sophia had entered his life and caught his attention more than anyone ever had, as absolute a thought it might have been. He generally avoided absolutes. Nowadays, though, he was absolutely sure that he had the potential to throw his history away and perhaps finally shed a reputation that he once embraced, but now only wanted to leave behind, so he might finally be taken seriously.

Lenore Thompson, peering out with a scrutinizing glare from behind the register, had found it impossible over the years to take him seriously and forgive him his youthful sins. Jonah was resentful of her presence, somewhat guiltily, as he understood that she needed the money. He sympathized with her financial burdens, though from what he'd been told by Levi, she paid for very little of their expenses, and left her beaten and broken son to pick up the tab. She'd come to work early, taking on a double shift that would stretch far into the silent, lonely hours of the unprofitable graveyard shift; her consistent disappearances into the back of the diner led Jonah to believe that she was seizing opportunities for smoke breaks, not picking up hot plates for serving from beneath the heat lamps of the kitchen. Despite all his judgments, he had a hard time believing that she would be so reckless as to sneak a swig or two from a flask, all in a hopeless escape from the customers who shook their heads in pity at a middle-aged woman who still worked in a diner for meager tips and paltry wages. But if there was anything he'd learned from his years of friendship with her son, it was that she cared little for the opinions of others, except for their reaction to her classic dresses and flawless makeup each Sunday morning, which were consistently positive on the part of men, and envious on the part of women.

"A-a-a-anything t-to drink?" asked the only other waitress in the diner at that hour, standing at the end of Jonah's table with a kind smile. She was apologetic that she'd caught him by surprise, having broken his focused stare at the drunken monster who'd tortured his best friend for most of their lives. Much to his relief, Lenore was not his server; instead, Abigail Foster had come to give him a glass of ice water, meekly, with a shy trembling of her hands. Her age was somewhat of a mystery to Jonah, as her jowls led him to believe she was at least in her late fifties, but she had an unbreakable glitter in her eyes that reflected both youthful hopefulness and a tinge of something sad, like insecurity or embarrassment. She spoke with a stammer, so she tried her best to speak as little as possible, though a job as a waitress wasn't the best choice of professions for a woman as soft-spoken as herself. Some of the ruder church ladies were quick to mock her speech—unfortunately, the majority of church ladies were rude, parading rudeness as righteousness—but she never failed to spread a proud smile across Jonah's face when she sang from their hymnals. It was the one chance a week that she had to raise her voice without fear. When she sang her praises to God, her stutter disappeared, and her words were as fluid as holy water over a baby's unblemished brow.

Jonah could only assume she was slow in taking orders, because she was careful with her speech in an effort to minimize her stutter.

Whether her efforts proved beneficial, Jonah couldn't be sure, but he tried to have enough faith in humanity to believe that most wouldn't have judged her for what she couldn't help. Sadly, many women in that town deemed her a village idiot of sorts, or at least the victim of a terrible accident that left her with irreparable brain damage, though neither was even close to the truth.

As she passed to her next table, at which sat a group of four factory workers whose hands were covered in old, peeling Band-Aids, she received a reaction that was patient and sympathetic. Jonah smiled, and cursed those women who condemned all men as selfish, inconsiderate pigs, but who, in reality, tended to be far kinder than their female counterparts. The women at her last table were not so understanding of Abigail's manner of speaking, and snapped their orders at her before she could even finish repeating them back to be sure that she'd understood them correctly. Apparently, they were in a rush to get their cranberry juices, which they claimed to be drinking as part of a body-flush fad diet to lose a few pounds, though the so-called juice served at the Americana had little semblance of juice, and was more sugar water tinted with dye than nectar squeezed from a ripened cranberry.

Then entered the reigning monarch of starvation diets, Jimmy von Braun, the enemy of all things physically healthy and mentally sound, who tortured those who were too poor to buy liquor off the highest shelves, and who struggled day after day to make the ends meet that his wealthy parents had welded shut years ago.

"Jesus Christ," Jimmy groaned upon noticing Lenore Thompson behind the counter, her face flushed not from rouge, or embarrassment (she didn't hear his blasphemies), but from something else that Jonah couldn't guess: perhaps thoughts of an impending mid-life crisis, or regrets of her innumerable poor choices before that mid-life. Jimmy turned to the three friends he'd brought along with him and snickered, "Let's see if I made this place more productive by saving her from that poor-man's booze the other night. The owner should start giving me a cut of the profits for pulling this dump of a business out of its downward spiral."

His three cohorts scoffed at their surroundings, though Jonah detected a hint of obligation, as though they tried their best to placate Jimmy even if his humor was less than polished. By the looks of them, they'd come from out of town—not just out of town, but out of state, even, maybe on the other side of the country that had grown so large and divided that a Northeasterner was as foreign as a Chinaman to someone who'd grown up in the allegedly honest simplicity of Clemency. They easily could have been a trio of bastard clones designed and grown in fluid-filled tanks in some abominable lab, as they all sported the same orangey tan that was so unnatural that the sun shook itself in disappointment. Their legs, skinny as a sapling growing out of the urine-soaked dirt in the cracks of a New York sidewalk, were made even skinnier by the dark jeans that constricted them like a tourniquet; if they hadn't been wearing a mix of Chucks, suede and moccasins (their only distinguishing features), then they would have exposed the blue tint of their feet, the kind that foreshadowed festering gangrene. Jonah imagined, too, that they were impotent, without a single viable sperm left in their pinched ducts. The thought was alright with him. He preferred that their kind not breed and spread entitled progeny across the earth.

The elitist ringleader of the aristocratic circus freaks flaunted himself as their wellspring of good genetics and style; perhaps the clones had been formed from cheek cells taken at Jimmy von Braun's exclusive medical spa. He was taller than Jonah, though not by much, with sandy blond hair that he spiked up with quasi-cement whenever he was fixing for a fight, and left down and swept to the side on those days when he was too drunk or high to care. But unlike his figurative sons, his skin was fair, denying him the rotten sweet potato appearance of his associates. He was the kind of pale that was once valued in the regal days of Louis XIV, when porcelain skin was the mark of the upper class, who spent not even a minute in the fields laboring beneath the oppressive sun. Even indoors he wore sunshades to protect himself from the most harmless bit of light. But on those rare occasions when he slipped off his glasses (usually a few minutes before midnight), his eyes flashed an icy blue that he inherited from his equally cold mother, reflecting the frigid personality she so proudly made known.

"I don't know how you do it," remarked Peon #1. "There isn't a single Starbucks within a seventy-five-mile radius of this shithole."

"How do you live without your double-shot soy skinny salted caramel mocha with no whipped?" asked Peon #2 in disbelief. "I don't think I could go on living."

"I doubt they have vegan here," speculated Peon #3. "Looks like no lunch for me today."

"Bitch, I don't even eat," Jimmy bragged. The three lauded his bravery for the sake of achieving the perfect Holocaust figure. "But if you're so desperate to get fatter, then go home. This town can barely handle *me*. They sure as hell can't handle all *four* of us. These food stamp fucks can smell a dollar from a mile away."

"Like old times," swooned Peon #2. "You're a lot skinnier now, though."

"Shut up. I told you to burn all those pictures, traitor."

They helped themselves to a seat at the booth directly behind Jonah's, too impatient to wait for Lenore's begrudging invitation. If she were to make her appearance, Sophia would have their obnoxious chatter in her ears—the perfect way to ruin a less-than-perfect place for a first date. It was difficult enough for Jonah to accept that he'd be wining and dining the preacher's daughter at a run-down diner in lieu of an upscale Italian ristorante that didn't exist, but now any and all hope of making the Americana just a little bit endearing was completely sabotaged. Even without their unwanted presence, however, Jonah wouldn't have blamed Sophia if she showed up at the door and quickly turned away. She was too pretty for this atmosphere, and she had too much class—not like Jimmy, who claimed to know class, though it was the one vital thing that his parents' money couldn't buy.

"I'd ask if this seat was taken," announced an angelic voice, "but we both know the answer, Mr. Young."

Sophia stood at the booth with a smile on her face that flooded the room with light. She was petite and dressed flawlessly, as usual, letting her long, straight hair fall over her slight shoulders and checkered blouse. At that angle, it was impossible not to notice the breasts he'd admired for quite some time, though he had every intention of averting his eyes as far as he could; she didn't present herself immodestly, but no matter how hard she tried to cover up that which God so cruelly endowed her with, the more enticing she became. Jonah looked up at her in disbelief, and merely extended his hand to invite her to sit. She did so without his approval, knowing she didn't need it. With him, she could do what she wanted, and he, a desperate young man who was only just beginning to realize his helplessness, would obey her every command with gratitude.

"What if I'd said yes?" he asked.

"I'd call your bluff in a second," Sophia replied, slipping her purse onto the vinyl seat. "No self-respecting girl would ever accept a date if it's been proposed by you."

"An ironic sentiment, wouldn't you say?"

Sophia smirked and scanned the dining area, drawing attention to its barrenness in terms of patrons. "If anyone asks, I'm only guiding the unfaithful back to the flock, just like my mother would do. But I don't think I've got much to worry about. Gossip isn't a blue-collar pastime."

"You really think I'm that bad?" Jonah asked, trying to pass it off as casual and uncaring, though on the inside, he wondered if his reputation really did matter to her. The thought that she'd lie to cover her purpose for sitting at the Americana with an unlettered playboy of the past weighed heavy on his confidence. He didn't take her for one to lie, though. Maybe she truly did view their date as a mission, a means of turning a sinner back to God.

"You said you've grown up a little, so I'm just here to see if that was the truth, or a shabby pickup line. Either way, it'll be fun to see my parents squirm a little." She grinned and pointed across the street to the Southern Mercy Bible Church. "Just get yourself ready for an awkward sermon this Sunday. We'll both be sitting there knowing they're talking about us in generalities."

"I know I got a reputation, but y'know, yours is that y'ain't never disobeyed your parents. Can't imagine you ever been the subject o' their weekly damnations before."

"Yes, 'honor thy father and mother' and all that. I do what they say, and I'm not afraid to call myself a good Christian girl, but don't you go taking that as meaning that I'm impressionable or too innocent to see a wolf prowling in the woods. I'm not about to let a man take advantage of me—you, especially, no offense."

"None taken," Jonah replied. "Those days are over for me."

"By choice, or because there's no more sheep left to hunt?"

"A little o' both."

Silence ensued, and Jonah couldn't tell if it was an awkward pause, or a pensive one. Sophia seemed to be examining him, assessing his honesty, and after a moment of scrutiny under the gaze of her rare, amber eyes, he chose to make the next move, no matter how ungraceful. "Y'look real nice today."

"Small talk isn't my thing, but thank you," she replied, and though she tried to shrug off his compliments as insipid and commonplace, she still blushed, and held back the smile of a girl who didn't often hear that she was pretty. "Took me an hour just to get my hair straight."

"Awful lot o' preparation for a date y'say y'ain't too excited to go on."

"Never said I wasn't excited," she corrected. "Just being careful, that's all."

"Y'know, y'don't have to be."

It took a little time, but soon enough, Jonah had convinced Sophia that he meant her no emotional harm, and that he was not about to get in the way of her relationship with God by tempting her into abandoning her purity, whatever that meant. It bothered him that it took her so long to lower her defenses: he didn't blame her, but blamed himself. There was always the possibility that Sophia was simply one to play hard to get, and that she wasn't as concerned about his intentions as she claimed. His intentions, he insisted, were perfectly innocent, and he only relished the opportunity to socialize with a girl his own age who was considerably more interesting than the rest of Clemency's mediocre stock. For once, he spoke honestly, and wasn't just trying to convince himself out loud that he had no desire to see a girl throw away her principles for the sake of having a good time. He hoped that he could offer his best company and conversation to Sophia that day, sitting in a booth at the Americana with two milkshake coupons at the ready, and not find himself drawing blanks when asked to actually converse, as he was used to less verbose encounters.

Jonah was relieved to encounter fewer dams in the flow of conversation than he'd fretted over. They talked about their childhoods, and all the irreverent jokes Jonah played while their Sunday school teacher tried her hardest to instill a healthy fear of God in her preteen students. They revealed backstories to events like the day Jonah showed up to class with his sleeve torn off, even though class started only a few minutes after service; he'd ripped it clean off to force his parents to bring him and Hannah home, but just to teach him a lesson, his parents sent him to class anyway, in spite of whatever rumors might have circulated about the quality of their children's clothes. Jonah found endless amusement in recalling the smallest details of their teacher's appearance: Mrs. Sanders, an aging soccer mom whose kids never proved to be pro soccer material and who highlighted her hair poorly with her own kitchen tin foil, was "a little in over her head" (said Sophia, referencing Jonah) and "a dumb blonde who thought that Jesus discovered America" (said Jonah, drawing a guilty smile from his date). Sophia laughed at the memory of a young Jonah pretending to tear a page out of his Bible, then looking down in horror at Mrs. Sanders sprawled out on the floor, having instantly gone into shock—something he'd almost forgotten.

"If she thought *that* was bad," Sophia laughed as Abigail brought over a glass of water that she didn't spill, despite her shakiness, "then she should see how you turned out."

"She'd be floored knowin' I turned out to be anything at all, and that God ain't struck me down with lightnin' or somethin'." He grinned, but thought to himself that if he'd been struck by anything, it wasn't a divine thunderbolt, but something else, though he wasn't about to be as quick as to call it budding love. After all, he wasn't even sure he'd recognize the feeling, or if he was meant to, if predestination was as legitimate as Mrs. Sanders contended. But he did feel something growing, and for once, it wasn't in his pants.

"Don't worry, you're not going anywhere," Sophia promised, putting her hands together in prayer. "I'll put in the good word for you. There's nothing like being vetted by a preacher's daughter."

"Ain't worried about gettin' through them pearly gates, are you?"

"Didn't you know?" Sophia said, extending her hand to present the exquisite sights of Clemency just outside the diner window, as though they were a gift to behold. "This here's Heaven on Earth."

"*Fucking hell!*" barked Jimmy von Braun, his screeching voice accompanied by the percussion of shattered glass. "*You're gonna pay for these shoes, you stupid bitch!*"

Lenore Thompson stumbled back and caught herself on a standalone table. Her dirty apron sported a fresh stain: she had soaked herself and Jimmy's designer kicks with diet soda and lemon juice. Broken glass was scattered across the old carpeted floor and on the table, where it was so indistinguishable from the spilt ice cubes that Jimmy's pawns all threw their hands up to avoid slicing their impeccably manicured fingers. Flustered and red in the face, Lenore bent down and held out her apron like a coffee-spotted hammock, and began to scoop up the larger shards of glass with her bare hands. From a pocket, slipped behind a thin notepad with only a few carbon copies remaining, fell a tiny bottle of dark amber that hit the floor and slid over the cold puddle to directly beneath Jonah's seat. He cursed under his breath and froze up; Sophia saw his look of panic and reached under the table, scooping up Lenore's now public vice in one swift motion.

"Oh, my God," Jimmy von Braun laughed, astonished.

"Are you drunk?" Peon #1 asked in the harsh whisper of someone in church, though he would be caught in no such place.

"She's drunk!" Peon #2 exclaimed, pointing an accusatory finger straight at her, and covering his mouth with the other to pointlessly muffle his hyena-like cackling.

"She's not red 'cause she's embarrassed!" Peon #3 noted in a fit of hysterics. "It's a drunk flush! She's wasted!"

"Wasted at work!" Jimmy scoffed, struggling to breathe. "And I thought I was bad! No wonder she's so poor! Bet she's been fired from every job she's ever had for getting hammered!"

Then came the moment Jonah was dreading: Lenore looked up and met eyes with him, eyes filled with such a devastating maelstrom of emotion that he couldn't stand to behold them for more than an instant. Through the chemical veil that left her blue eyes as dull as the ocean on a cloudy day he saw a sadness he had never expected nor hoped to see her express. On her most irascible days, when she tore his best friend to pieces while still expecting him to facilitate her crash landing to rock bottom, Jonah found it easier to imagine her as a being who knew hatred and nothing else. To demonize her, to dehumanize her, and to describe her as such to her son was the simplest way to shrug off the blame she placed on Levi for nearly everything that had fallen apart in her life. But now, Lenore herself was broken on the ground, surrounded by glittering blades that crunched beneath her heels as she ran off to the cover of the kitchen.

"I ain't never liked her much," Jonah muttered to Sophia, "but she don't deserve this shit, 'specially from the likes o' those ritzy douchebags."

"Don't make a scene," she insisted, presenting the bottle in her palm for a second before hiding it in her purse. "And don't you dare think about telling your friend about this."

"Why not? He don't know she been drinkin' at work—and I didn't, neither, till this here mess happened and ruined the whole damn day."

"What good will it do to tell him?"

"Maybe he'll lock her up till she detoxes or somethin'."

"He's probably been dealing with this for most of his life, right? So what makes you think that he's gonna be able to do anything about it now? I know it sounds cruel and un-Christian of me, but maybe he should just let her run her course. And if you say anything about her making a fool of herself in public, and even worse, in front of one of the von Brauns, all you'll do is get him all worked up. She'll never learn her lesson if she has her son screaming at her about how horrible of a mother she is. She needs to figure that out herself."

"Now I just gotta figure out how to keep our second date scandal-proof."

"There's no way to keep a date with Jonah Young scandal-proof," Sophia quipped. "And who says I'd even agree to a second date?"

"Like I tell my empty-headed sister: don't go tryin' to bullshit a bullshitter."

"She's young—there's time for her to bulk up that brain. I don't know if there's much hope for you, though. The pretty ones tend to be dumb as rocks."

"Well ain't you a glutton for irony."

"I'm a glutton for people who actually know how to use that word, Mr. Young. At least I can say the conversation was good." Sophia glanced at her phone and drew attention to the time, and that she'd spent a great deal longer than she'd intended reminiscing on the days when she was pious and Jonah was irreverent, though in that regard, little had changed. "People in this town have their roles, and most of them play them till the day they die, for better or worse. I'm always gonna be the preacher's daughter, the Reverend's always gonna be my father, and my mother's always gonna be looking down on you, I'm sorry to say. Is that something you can handle?"

"I'm used to it. That's what you get for bein' the town's infamous, nonbelievin' son, who's pavin' his path to Hell with women scorned."

"I'm sure there's more heretics out there than you think." She scribbled a number on a napkin and pushed it across the table, drawing a victorious smile from her date, who was ready to throw in the towel and begrudgingly accept that first dates weren't his forte. "And don't tell the Reverend that his daughter finds the sheep who've gone astray to be a lot more interesting." She picked up her bag and looked down at Jonah, who was staring at her phone number, a sign of both mercy and triumph inscribed in blue ink, with wide eyes that erased any hope of portraying himself as coolly unsurprised. It was a rude but welcome awakening that he wasn't as confident as he'd thought, after all. Since when had he ever been pessimistic about the prospect of a second date?

Maybe because he'd never had one, or even a first—but times were changing, and the impromptu note he folded and slipped into his pocket was his ticket to a new life where he was more than looks, and more than his past.

••

Levi was walking the fine line between curiosity and intrusiveness as he made his way down Main Street with his eyes set on the Americana Diner ahead. He had no intention of being a stalker, peering through the windows framed with red, white and blue banners to catch a glimpse of Jonah on the job. He supposed part of him was merely concerned that Sophia Shaw might not take his friend up on his offer, leaving him sitting alone at a booth with an untouched drink before him and a scowl of unprecedented disappointment on his face. If that were the case, and he'd been stood up for the first time in his life by a girl who wasn't so easily enticed by whatever it was they all saw in him, Levi could always swoop in and spare him the shame of dining without company. He then realized, however, that that wasn't a viable option: Mama was at work, scribbling unhealthy orders in her notebook, polishing unpolishable glasses, or performing any number of menial, interminable duties that kept her life stagnant and paid little, both in wages and a sense of fulfillment.

Had it always been that way? Clemency was, ultimately, a place where time stood still. The buildings that lined Main Street had changed little over the decades, if at all, and when a change did occur once in a blue moon, it was the removal of a sign above a bankrupted business, or the falling of a once neon-lit letter from a store name that hadn't been spoken in years. The American dream was dead in that forgotten town, all while its townsfolk praised that fleeting dream. It was one of the few wellsprings of hope that continued to flow, no matter how meager its trickle, and Clemency was the parched stone from which poor families drew their water, only to be left endlessly thirsty while telling themselves it was all in their heads.

*"Take therefore no thought for the morrow: for the morrow shall take thought for the things of itself,"* they read from their holy books, but failed to consider that perhaps God preferred His creations to take care of themselves before He chose to take care of the rest.

Those who escaped the stagnant pool did so by marching confidently through the doors of the army recruiting station on the south end of Main Street. They were young men fresh out of high school, convinced of their own immortality, who sought the glory that accompanied a return from a valorous tour overseas. SSG Eddie Sharpe, the bald-headed recruiter that sat behind a desk with a baby face that hadn't matured over his twenty years of military service, tried his best to encourage the naïve prospects' aspirations, and considered each signature on his roster to be more evidence in his case for Clemency's unshakable patriotism. He refused to acknowledge, however, that many had been swayed by their parents into surrendering their freedom for the sake of preserving that of others. Most parents around the country would be horrified by the idea of their sons caught in the crossfire of clashing civilizations. Those in Clemency, though, considered any war a holy war for the country that was God's appointed policeman, and longed for the day that Bible verses might be etched on their bullets. Few were willing to accept that the deepest roots of their fierce loyalty wasn't a love of country or of God: it was the inescapable need for the poverty draft, one that was the most insidious of widow-makers, which took sons from their families to alleviate financial burdens but left only heavy hearts that were much more difficult to bear.

Some of Levi's friends had traveled down that road, scribbling their names in a teenage boy's chicken scratch on military contracts without taking a second to read what they were signing or to consider the consequences that came from spilling imperishable ink on paper that could be neither torn apart nor burned. He had no desire to follow them; only once, in a moment of desperation for an escape of any kind, had he strode through the doors and snatched SSG Sharpe's pen off the desk, ready to rashly add his name to a steadily growing stack of applications. SSG Sharpe eyed him with suspicion but made no effort to stop him. He simply sat with his hands folded, his chest puffed out, swelling up the bulky kind of body that could have either been padded by muscle or fat, though it was difficult to tell. Levi judged it as pudginess, as he only ever saw SSG Sharpe in motion while he was at church or wandering within a hundred-foot radius of the recruiting station, venturing no farther, to staple propaganda to telephone poles. His rain-soaked literature warned the good people of Clemency of the signs of the End Times, which they eagerly devoured in their devotion to the Book of Revelation, which was undeniably the most important book in the Bible. He never made mention of an Antichrist, a Beast, a False Prophet, or even divine judgment, but they found ways to connect nuclear war with two-thousand-year-old verses that clearly had nothing to do with mushroom clouds. The flyers he publicly pinned were no doubt his own creation: the consistent spelling errors identified them as unofficial military material, unless the Army was growing cheap with its marketing.

SSG Sharpe stared at Levi with the bloodshot eyes that seemed to bulge out of their sockets, which were not red and lifeless from post-traumatic stress disorder, but because of his chronic keratitis that he refused to properly address. Levi was just about to put pen to paper when the staff sergeant began to ramble on about an impending World War III in which all developed nations would be annihilated, leaving only the Third World to pick up the pieces and rebuild human civilization. He rubbed his eyes with each paranoid exclamation, not shedding tears for the looming doomsday to be wrought at the hands of politicians and shadow governments, but from his repulsive eye disorder. When he declared that he would rather suffer painful, itchy eyes for the rest of his life than take medication, which was all part of a federal mind-control project, Levi realized the man was delusional, and that he himself was just as delusional to think that surrendering his life to the U.S. Armed Forces was a sensible way to leave his problems behind.

While his mother was insistent that he would be a cut-rate soldier who would only be good at catching bullets in his chest, he was not driven to prove her wrong. Deep down, he felt he had to stay. He knew it was foolish, and the sense of pointless self-sacrifice was not only easily criticized but also rightful to condemn, but Mama needed him. She had lost her husband; he couldn't bear to let her lose her only son. It wasn't even his own life that he was concerned for. It was hers, and he stuck around to watch over her, though he readily admitted that he was doing a poor job at it. In spite of her drinking, her willingness to destroy her own life and her son's, she was still alive, and life in any form, no matter how painful or heartbreaking, was better than death. And without him, death was all that would be left for her. All men were dying men, Levi knew, but it was selfish to hasten the process simply because one didn't want to deal with life's ugliness, which accumulated like whiskey bottles in the garbage can outside his rickety back door.

It was only after Pap vanished from their lives that she began to frequent the liquor store, up until the day Levi could pass for legal age, at least by small-town standards. She tried her best to move on from her past marriage, which, as she claimed, ended when Samuel Thompson decided one day to abandon his son and, more importantly, leave his wife to fill the house with the sharp smell of whiskey and bellowing shouts that never brought about any change. It was only her own guilt that could push her to such extremes, Levi had come to conclude over the years; he was gone because she'd slammed the door in his face for reasons that still eluded their son. Not knowing the motive was worse than whatever it was that Mama felt Levi had no right to know, whether she was doing it to protect him or otherwise. When he tried to put pieces of faded memories together and finally draw all the necessary connections, he found that it was too long ago to ever really know the truth. Those brief flashes of recollection revealed a story that seemed far too simple.

*"There ain't nothin' here for us,"* Pap once insisted at the dinner table while a kindergarten-aged Levi orchestrated a waltz between a fork

and spoon. *"God as my witness, I ain't never gonna let him grow up into a nobody."*

Even earlier, at four years old, if he remembered correctly, he sat on Mama's lap as an old game show flashed with colorful, brain-rotting lights on the far side of the room, with Pap on the armchair in the warm glow of a table lamp. *"Faith,"* she'd said, touching her son's brow as if to baptize him with her own aspirations, *"That's what he'll get from this town."*

It seemed that not only did Levi inherit Sam Thompson's sun-catching, light brown eyes, but he also grew up to form the same opinion of Clemency, a prison that held captive sons born to captive fathers. "Future" was a word absent from the town's social dictionary, except for a future in which the Third Temple stood tall in Jerusalem and a thousand years of peace graced the whole of the earth—Pap knew it, Levi now knew it, and Mama blurred any sense of time with each swig from a lipstick-stained glass. But it wasn't possible that Pap would have stormed out the door one night because of his resentment, at least without carrying Levi under his arm on the way out. Still in his postman's blue uniform, his fingers blotchy with ink from the hand-addressed envelopes he delivered to every judgmental, paradise-bound townsperson, Sam would have rescued his son even with his stubborn wife clinging to his ankles. Levi was always the center of his world, his attachment outshining any love Mama ever held for her only son; Mama, however, praised the Lord that her husband never had the chance to see his beloved son grow up into an abject failure, but Levi knew it was a lie, though it still stung each time she hurled her insults his way.

Anyone who'd been witness to his childhood would have predicted a far different outcome. There was always the possibility that his career might not be one to boast of, but at least he'd have the luxury of saying he'd left Clemency behind the second he stepped out of Israel Pickens High School in plum-colored robes, cheaply printed diploma in hand. Pap spoiled him to the furthest extent his meager income would allow, not in such a way as to make him an entitled, sniveling brat like Jimmy von Braun (his salary didn't allow it), but enough that he always had a new toy truck under the Christmas tree, new sneakers when his toddler shoes became pockmarked with wear, and a different vest for the first Sunday of every liturgical season. He'd never been punished, even when his mother, having caught him demolishing toy block cities like an infant god or using her lipstick to paint a masterpiece on the walls, threatened: *"Just wait till your Pap gets home."* When he did get home after a long day of delivering overdue electric bills and stock art calendars meant to entice timekeepers into surrendering donations, he never brought the punishment that Mama had promised. Levi was Samuel Thompson's only son, the heir to and preserver of the family name, and Clemency's patriarchal roots still ran deep to that day, for better or worse.

Maybe Pap would have been disappointed with him; maybe Mama had been right all along. At least he couldn't blame himself for his father's absence, though in the same breath, he found nothing else to blame, other than what he suspected but couldn't prove. In spite of all the happy memories he held of a past that had slipped away in an instant like spilt liquor from a broken glass, it was that last night that took the forefront in his mind: when he heard a husband and wife's shouts and sobs of despair, the clatter of a bottle on a countertop and the jingle of car keys, then the slam of a door that never closed properly since. Mama and Pap were not so different once, but with that one, single fight, one black mark on six years of witness to a marriage impervious to criticism, Levi firmly ingrained an image in his mind of a father who was not only the complete opposite of his wife, but the savior from her glassy-eyed tyranny who'd been martyred before he could bring redemption. Pap's identity was either founded on truth, or on hindsight through the eyes of a young man who was ashamed to admit that if he could trade places with him, he would.

Samuel Thompson was free of the monster that Mama had become. It didn't matter where life had taken him, to what city he'd escaped to, or what had driven him—or forced him—away. All that mattered was that his son, who looked so much like him and dressed in his clothes on Sundays, was still made to serve his own head on a platter at Mama's request, because he was obedient and mindful of the Fifth Commandment, though he was irreverent of the rest. If anything, Pap would be proud that Levi honored his mother in the present and his father in memory. He'd left his son to continue his vow to support Mama for the rest of her days, though the blame rested not on him, but on that woman who denied him the chance to do it himself.

THERE WAS A NARROW PATH that led away from the Thompsons' house into the woods, one that had become hard to notice over the years, though it was once good for walking. Weeds claimed hold over the trail that was never cleared by human feet, but by the scurrying animals that slipped through the brush and stomped out new growth; a young Levi continued their efforts, with the clumsy footsteps of a child who probably shouldn't have been wandering alone but had too trusting of a father. As an adult, he never ventured along the game trail he once followed, and rough, spiny plants rose up from his past footprints, sporting crowns of colorful flowers that, no matter how beautiful, would never inspire a person to call them anything but a weed, invasive and undesirable. But with no cultivated garden to compete with, and no aesthetic elements in an unkempt yard other than neglected cans of garbage (which did not stink, as empty bottles could never spoil), neither Levi nor his mother paid them much notice. If anything, they were the most beautiful feature to be seen through the frayed screen of the squeaky back door.

Winding through ferns and shaggy vines that dangled from swampy trees like drapery, the path made its way to an open field, not sprawling like a nobleman's dynastic tracts, but fit for farming, though the only crops that reached for the sky those days were cornstalks that could no longer be considered domesticated. Few knew of the stretch of land, even those who waded waist-deep in the stream that ran just to the northwest, save Levi and Jonah, who'd known about the farm for years, though it was beginning to fade from memory.

Levi had nearly forgotten about it, spending too much time looking down the desolate road he followed to reach the flickering sign that marked AlaCo's fractured parking lot; nature was something he'd put out of his mind, except for those times when he suffered Jonah's clouds of pot smoke by the creek. And as for Jonah, he had more concern for human nature than that which grew wild outside his bedroom window, and more specifically, the basest and most primal expressions of that instinctual human nature—or at least he used to, before he started asserting that such things no longer interested him.

Just as abandoned as Jonah's past priorities was the decaying farmhouse at the far end of the untended field, which shed cracked, wooden shingles like an old man's falling hair. The paint that Levi remembered as a pale blue had faded to a sickly gray in the light of the sun, peeling away to expose the melancholy nakedness of a home that once embowered a family Levi imagined as happy and whole, but who left one day without a word, never looking back. Levi never knew them, and never saw them when he ventured through the woods to run wild through the rows of corn that looked like they would scrape the sky, to a boy as small as him. He'd chosen not to investigate, out of respect for the nameless whose crumbling house remained as a solemn testament to how ephemeral life could be. He'd once peered through foggy windows out of curiosity and saw floral-patterned couches still sitting in the parlor, speckled with mildew and dust. It was as if the owners had surrendered all their belongings to the past, seeking a future with no ties to what was behind them, even in the simplest of objects. Photos still hung on the walls, but from a distance, they looked only like frames filled with smoke, faded memories of times someone wanted desperately to put out of his mind.

The house wasn't a symbol of poverty, or some microcosm of the greater nation in which so many had lost their livelihood, if they'd had any to begin with. It wasn't some image to be photographed by an artist or a journalist, to be published as evidence of a failed ideology, of an American dream that had taken centuries to wake up from. The family that left it to rot in an open field wasn't driven out by a lack of money: if they had been, then they never would have left their precious belongings to be veiled by gossamers, lit only by moonlight through cracks in the ceiling. Even the banks would have cannibalized their property and rendered the rooms barren, devoid of any sign that someone had once slept in them, ate in them with family around the dinner table, or loved in them. There were no foreclosure signs posted bitterly on the porch, or yellow tape crisscrossing the window frames, or even a lock on the front door. Perhaps it was the complete accessibility that kept out even the most promiscuous of Parsons students—it wasn't condemned, and they weren't trespassing on private or state property, and everyone knew that rulebreaking was the best foreplay. The past owners denied them such a turn-on, intentionally or not, but it helped Levi relax a bit, knowing he could wander the field alone without cries of wild abandon sounding out in the distance like mating cicadas in midsummer.

He didn't know what had drawn him through the woods, to risk a tick bite on his bare legs as weeds and bush branches brushed against his body. When he pushed past the last line of natural barbed wire, cursing quietly as the plants made their final attempt at holding him back with a sharp thorn to the ankle, he stepped out into the sunlight and stood still, relishing the warmth of summer. It was the first time in ages that he'd taken a moment to enjoy the sun he too often claimed to despise, but knowing that there were no rusted gas pumps to be found among the unruly lines of corn plants gave him a peace of mind that he'd never trade in for anything.

Main Street and its passing cars were far out of sight, and the suffocating tension of Mama's presence in the parlor was swept away by the fresh air and the gentle breeze of midday. AlaCo's lifeless pavement, running with fissures that Rusty had never seen fit to seal with bubbling tar, and upon which Levi stood for hours on end with sore feet and nowhere to sit, was an unsightly but irrelevant feature of the past, at least at that moment. Abandoning himself to the earth he foolishly claimed he was too busy for was a means of release, like the feathery dandelion seeds that wafted through the air. He let his thoughts escape with them, though he doubted they could ever take root and grow into the reality he'd wished for over the course of his adult life. The soil in Clemency was far too barren for such cultivation, and futures only withered and died in its blight.

He saw a sign in the sky, like some divine metaphor: a kite, bright yellow and emerald green, floating high over the field and eclipsing the sun with its slender silhouette. The black line that kept it bound it to earth, no matter how high it soared, stretched out from behind the rows of crops, so thin that it seemed a strong gust of wind might break it and set the kite free of the anchor that held it back, even if it seemed to be flying by its own will to those stuck on the ground. The kite's arrowhead shadow slid over Levi's body and swept along with no concern for his presence, indiscriminate in its painting black the world below, unstoppable and without blame; he followed the pointed guide through the cornstalks, toward the fifty-foot chain that kept the kite from scraping the midday sun, held by a dark-skinned hand raised to the sky.

"Y'found me," Elijah sighed with a smile. "Ain't usual for us to be meetin' in broad daylight like this, but it's real pleasant, I'd say."

"Y'know, when you first asked me who all that liquor's for, I was fixin' to tell you to go fly yourself a kite," Levi jested, "but looks like I didn't have to."

"Every Sunday, when these blue laws gimme the time," he explained.

"Service let out two hours ago," Levi reminded him. "Your store's set to open soon."

"So it is. But it can wait. My most loyal customer's already here."

It only took a second or two for Elijah to apologize, having seen Levi's lighthearted smile contort into a subtle grimace that was just enough to convey how unappreciative he was. Asking Levi to excuse him for having stepped out of line, he unraveled an extra foot or so of the towline from around his hand and let the kite drift a bit higher. He looked up at the colorful visitor among the clouds and said: "My son always loved this. Thought if he jumped off the ground holdin' the line, he might fly away with it. Called it 'Big Bird,' 'cause of the yellow."

"Didn't know you had a kid," Levi said.

"*Have* a kid," Elijah corrected politely, insisting that the tense of a verb was a matter of considerable importance. "Jacob. Looks just like his mother, with them gray eyes."

"I take it he got the hell outta Clemency."

"Oh, he's round here somewhere," Elijah said, gazing off into the distance. "Just ain't seen him in a long time. Memory ain't the same as close company, but it's better than bein' alone in your heart, too. Ain't got no doubt that I'll be seein' him soon enough. Just took some time."

He didn't have to elaborate for Levi to understand that Jacob Green wasn't out wandering the field, hiding behind rising walls the color of his family name. Anyone else who'd stumbled upon an old man staring up at the sky with a cord in his hand and a wistful glitter in his eye would have hastily described him as either a pitiable senior stricken with dementia, or simply a crazy, old fool with no excuse for his behavior that could ever inspire sympathy among the sane. Jacob wasn't a figment of Elijah's imagination, the ghost of a child he regretted never begetting, or a delusional invention he spoke to late at night when he was overcome with grief. Maybe Jacob had escaped the wretched town and his father was too heartbroken to accept it. But even more heartbreaking, Jacob's name might have only been spoken by a nostalgic father, or by the lips of a passer-by reading the words upon a tombstone.

Levi didn't have the heart to pry into the man's business and ask if his son was wandering the overgrown fields of Clemency or fields of a more Elysian sort; if Elijah had the same penchant for backtalk as Levi, he'd simply quote his favorite customer and remind him that the subject of his invisible son "ain't his concern." But the ever-sober liquor store owner looked upon Levi with a smile and a crinkle of his eyebrow that implied he could read Levi's thoughts as clearly as he could see a bright kite among white clouds. He began to reel in the soaring memorial to his son's memory with a twist of his wrist, wrapping the cord around his flattened palm; as it descended and brushed the feathery tips of corn flowers the wind carried it toward the old farmhouse. Elijah brought it to a dead stop with a jerk of his arm, and the kite rested still, held up on the shoulders of crops with no one to tend to them or cut them back, pointing straight at the front door, which neither Levi nor Elijah showed any interest in opening.

"Done for the day?" Levi asked, reaching up to retrieve the kite. He handled it gingerly out of fear that he might break it, as a date, written in the shaky handwriting of a child clutching a permanent marker, read *"1976"* on its underbelly. "How long've you been out here?"

"Haven't a clue. Always lose track o' time out here," Elijah chuckled, taking Jacob's toy from Levi's hands. "So bright out here, the sun might as well be standin' still—I don't pay it much notice. Time's a worry for people who are too busy countin' down till its end, thinkin' they're maximizin' what time they got left, when they're too busy wastin' it keepin' tallies on the wall."

When they headed back into the trees and passed through the brush, the sunlight flickered through the leaves from all directions, and with no source creeping toward the horizon, he understood, for a moment, how time didn't always pass so quickly, if at all.

••

Around the same time every year—right after the first full moon of August, though it was doubtful they consciously observed it that way—John and Debra Young would take a weekend trip to a little town south of Hebron, where they leisured for one time out of the year without giving a single detail of their excursion to their children.

When Jonah was too young to watch Hannah, who still crawled around in diapers whining like a brat who could never be called a brat because she was just an infant, of course, the exhausted parents left them in the care of visiting family. Jonah's cigarette-smoking, tumbler-sipping great aunt never passed up an opportunity to show her grandnephew her own twist on parenting when his actual parents were too far away to interfere. Aunt Jolene, herself his mother's aunt and the only source of good humor on that side of the family, taught Jonah what she considered to be some of life's most important lessons: "Always drive the car before you buy it, and the same goes with girls," she said to him when he was ten; "You can't possibly expect a boy to be a man when you live like one o' these sexless Puritans," learned a fourteen-year-old high school freshman, taking that truth with him ever since.

Finally he was old enough to take care of himself and no longer required such unorthodox supervision, and this was fortunate for more than just Jonah's own sense of relief: Aunt Jolene had died not too long after his coming of age, having perished in a house fire started by a cigarette dropped in her sleep. Apparently, if she hadn't spilled cognac on her flower-patterned dress before dozing off in the armchair beneath the window curtains, she might have lived, albeit with burnt legs that probably would have turned black from diabetes, anyway. Such was the tragic tale of smoky-voiced Aunt Jolene, who left such stubborn imprints on Jonah's mind, and whom Debra Young mourned for less than three days.

Now Jonah's mother was off enjoying a far-from-luxurious holiday that was well needed regardless of its simplicity, and naturally, her more destructively flighty daughter passed in and out of the house as though she were just taking out the trash, throwing dirty clothes in her room and slinking away with fresh ones. She couldn't have been so stupid as to think Jonah didn't notice her obvious comings and goings. Half the time she made such a racket catching her foot on the leg of a misplaced chair or bumping her shoulder into the edge of a doorway that she woke Jonah up, startling him out of a recurring and satisfying dream where he'd been poking at Gabe's greasy skin as he slowly turned on a spit with an apple stuffed in his dead-toothed mouth. He scowled in bed in the light of the moon, knowing it wasn't the dark that made his immature little sister stumble sloppily down the hall. He never caught the unmistakable scent of weed following in her wake as she turned to leave; he could only assume she was dabbling in things he'd never keep in a hollowed-out Bible beneath his bed, and the thought made him furious. It inspired diverse and increasingly more absurd plans in his head to keep her in the house, short of tying her up and gagging her with a sock.

She was out again, God knows where. She'd left while Jonah was showering, scurrying past the bathroom window like a spider in fear of the newspaper looming ominously upon the table. He'd punched the tile wall in anger and slipped in the soapy puddle at his feet, bruising his ass and catching his sister's attention: she hissed, "Hurry up!" at her driver and slammed shut the passenger door, mistaking the crash of his body on the floor for the slam of the front door, preceding obscene shouts from her older brother in hot pursuit. By the time he'd struggled his way into a shirt and shoved his wet legs into a pair of water-spotted jeans, Gabe's pickup had shot off into the night, leaving the haze of airborne dirt to obscure the road and a slimy feeling in Jonah's head that made him want to shower again.

Fifty-five halfhearted pushups and numerous uncounted crunches later, he still had the house to himself, and the only sounds that broke the silence were the ever-present *clink-clink-clink* of the leaky bathroom faucet, and his own heavy breathing. All that joint smoking was taking a heavy toll on his lungs, he figured, but the thought didn't hold him back from lighting up in his dimly lit bedroom. With open windows and a shut door, he saw nothing better to do than to lie back with a smoldering clip in one hand and a Stephen King book in the other, though he much preferred the weed over a book that could have, and should have, been at least a third of the length that it was. He forced himself through another chapter without making so much as a dent, and burned a tiny hole in his checkered comforter with a fallen ember. Tossing the book onto his nightstand and snuffing the joint in a cup of dirty water, he fell back and sighed, desperate for and devoid of a way to kill the time. He supposed it was pointless and borderline obsessive to wait around in the dark for Hannah's shameful return, simply for the sake of catching her in the act and giving her a good verbal beatdown.

*'With an overbearin' queer for a brother, ain't no wonder she's fixin' to escape any way she can,"* had been Gabe's snide remark. With each unseized second that passed by, Jonah was only bolstering Gabe's argument. At least there wasn't anyone to see it, and if there had been, they would have found him stoned, irritated and stark naked in bed, staring idly at the ceiling. But abruptly he heard an irate knocking at the front door.

The car parked in the driveway was a dated station wagon with a replaced bumper of a noticeably different color, and Jonah didn't recognize it, or the shadowy figure in the driver's seat whose pale face was only briefly visible in the light of a struck match. A younger Jonah would have hid under a table and kept his mouth shut to discourage the unexpected visitors, as he and his mother had when pamphlet-toting Jehovah's Witnesses came to their door, before they were driven out of town by a mob of true apostolic Christians.

With modesty as a concern left for daylight and a pair of swishy, nylon gym shorts too loose to stay put without vigilant readjustment, he made his way down the hall. He pushed his hair back over his ears as a last-ditch attempt at composure and slowly opened the door, and a rush of humid summer air brought him right back to an oily state of dishevelment, though upon seeing the faces of the two pockmarked visitors, he knew he had little reason to be self-conscious.

Methamphetamine found its human incarnation in the greasy degenerates who stood in the open doorway, their ages indiscernible, though probably much younger than their dull, blemished skin led one to believe, maybe even around Jonah's own eighteen years. The foul creature to the left wore a black T-shirt with a death metal band logo that hung from his skeletal body like a rag on a wire clothes hanger. His associate at first appeared to be wearing a dark turtleneck, though the collar turned out to be a tattoo in illegible Blackletter that wrapped around his long, veiny throat. While the bleak rock enthusiast had little hair at all, Mr. Cheap Ink sported bangs that had begun to curl after growing out too long and being shampooed too infrequently, and they swept outward from a widow's peak toward his temples. Red blotches covered both their faces—whether acne or scabs, Jonah couldn't tell, but maybe an unsightly mix of both—and though they were not the type to smile, their lips caved inward in such a way as to suggest that their teeth's days were numbered.

"Where's Hannah at?" the leftmost disaster demanded. Manners, Jonah judged, were not something contractible through the sharing of a dirty needle.

"I figure you'd know better than me," Jonah replied with a disdainful scowl. He scratched an itch on his bare shoulder; meth heads had the same psychological effect as the thought of crawling insects on one's skin. "She drove off with Gabe a few hours ago, and ain't come back since."

The greasy-haired creature to the right jabbed his wiry cohort in the ribs and hissed, "That fucker ain't told us shit 'bout that, givin' us the runaround."

Rubbing what could easily turn into a bruise with a bitter grimace, the would-be roadie muttered, "I swear, I'mma beat his ass for ruinin' our get-together. Guess the guests are gonna have to settle for some extra ice to make up for it." He reached into his pocket and examined the dime bag he'd kept hidden, along with an empty matchbook and some small change. Looking to his sidekick, he asked, "I hope you got some, 'cause this ain't gonna cut it."

The tattooed corpse snickered at the word "cut," then replied regretfully, "Fresh out."

They both turned to Jonah with hopeful looks in their glazed eyes. "Hey man, you got any you willin' to part with? We'll drop off some bills after the party. You got our word."

"Figure you owe us, lettin' your sister go off with that asshole, when we already got plans with her," added the other one, picking at his fingers unconsciously. "Some judgment you got."

Jonah gripped the edge of the door until his knuckles were ghostly white and all the blood was displaced to his cheeks, which felt flushed and hot. "Y'all at the wrong crack house," he snapped, grabbing Tats by the throat and swinging his clenched fist straight into his stomach. The wide-eyed addict fell back coughing something awful, struggling to breathe, and his wide-eyed crony stared at Jonah in shock. Crashing down from a high, he was in no place to fight back; the two of them had lost their chemically induced aggression. The car's headlights flashed on behind them, reducing the startled dregs of society to spindly silhouettes. The driver revved the engine after Jonah flipped him the finger and pulled the screen door shut with a shaky clatter.

"Tell your sister we missed her real bad," the one said between hoarse breaths, still clutching his belly. "And we expect her to make it up to us. Y'ain't got to worry 'bout Skinner no more, big brother," he sneered. "He ain't the only one who's got a claim to 'er. We got his blessing, and soon enough, we're all gon' get yours, too, even if we gotta beat it outta you."

••

It was Charlie Parker with a full orchestra playing soulfully in the parlor when the fight broke out. Yes, it was summertime, and the heat drove all people over the edge, but life for the Thompsons was anything but easy; Levi had no father, let alone a rich one, to save him from Lenore, who was indeed good-looking but with eyes clouded with liquor and abject disgust. She was disgusted with her son for what he'd so shamefully become; she was disgusted with the man who'd left her to rear such a difficult, useless child; she was disgusted with herself for not having foreseen Levi's future as a squatter and a leech ungratefully latched onto her purse. Perfectly executed scales rose and fell behind her, strings and piano surged and subsided, and the alto sax squealed with its final, altissimo note, closing the song but opening the next litany of complaints shrieked across the kitchen table, and the percussion of a glass precariously slammed onto the faded wood.

"You think I *wanted* this?" she barked, pointing a shaky finger at the sink that held two lightly dirtied plates and a fork she hadn't given Levi the chance to wash yet, though he had every intention of doing so; she swung open the refrigerator door and cited their dwindling groceries, as if Levi had eaten them all, when in fact neither of them had had the time to replenish the shelves. "Ain't no mother wanna see her baby boy grow up into a sorry, useless man—if I can even call you a man!—who holds on to his mama for dear life and food and water and a roof over his head, and can't even be called a 'mama's boy' since he sure as hell ain't got no respect for her!"

Her forceful lamentations had little to do with Levi's own life, present or future; he was sure she was right in saying that there wasn't a single mother on the planet, or at least in traditional, family-oriented towns like Clemency, who would want to see her child stagnate on the border of adolescence and adulthood, with a foot sunk in quicksand on either side of the line. But Mama's slurred keening was for herself, as it always was: she couldn't have cared less about what became of her son, because he had his good-for-nothing father's eyes, and every time she looked at him she saw a reflection of the man who was said to have abandoned her. Lenore Thompson was dissatisfied with her own life, not her son's. And so long as he remained in her home and bled her dry like some kind of gas-pumping vampire (though he did nothing of the sort), she would be forever doomed to convince herself that she truly supported him against her better judgment.

Levi mustered up the audacity to respond honestly, for the first time in months, maybe years. The look on Mama's face was priceless. "I respect you more than you deserve!" he growled, exhilarated by the unleashing of what he'd built up over so long. "So much that if you told me to get out right now, I'd do it! And with a smile on my face, too! Ain't nothin' in the world would make me happier, so just say the word and y'won't have my burden no more!"

At a loss for words, Mama washed away the taste of her son's spiteful retort with a splash of whiskey, pausing just long enough to turn the tension from palpable to outright suffocating. She exhaled sharply, the hiss of a cat too full on milk to successfully pounce on a back-talking rat; if she waited any longer, he could easily slip out of her red-lacquered claws. "Y'ain't got the money to run off," she muttered clumsily. "Y'can't even survive in the grown-up world without your mama changin' your diapers, and now y'think y'can survive the streets?"

"What if I got some money saved up somewhere?" Levi hinted with a smirk; it wasn't a complete bluff, as the coffee tin in his room did hold a nice cushion for such a scenario. But his deviant satisfaction rapidly turned to regret, realizing that Mama might plunder his room in search of the alleged treasures buried in his closet, tightening his chains and rendering him just as powerless as he'd been as an unemployed student. When he saw her peeking in the direction of his bedroom door, he caught her attention again: "Just watch. I'mma pack up my things right now and get outta here, all 'cause I see what I do to you"—the guilt card, absolute genius— "and I love you too much to see you sufferin' on my account."

"*No!*" Mama cried, scrambling to the open doorway to block his exit, though he hadn't yet turned to leave. "Y'ain't goin' *nowhere* till I let you out. God as my witness, boy, it's gon' be on *my* terms, not yours."

"Why not now?" Levi asked innocently. "Ain't it as good a time as ever? Let's just get it over with. We both want it and I'm just tryin' to make it quick 'n easy."

"It's the middle o' the night! Y'know better than to run off in the dark!"

"I ain't gonna get hit walkin' on the side o' the road, if that's what you're thinkin'."

"I mighta let you get lazy and take me for granted, but I ain't about to let you make your Pap's mistakes!"

"The only mistake he made was thinkin' you wouldn't kick him out."

"I ain't kicked 'im out!" Mama roared, throwing her glass to the floor; it shattered, its shards as sharp as her tone. "He *left* us! He left *me*! You was just too young to remember!"

"Well then I guess I'm just followin' in my father's footsteps," Levi concluded with an apathetic shrug. "So it means one o' two things: either you done picked a sorry-ass husband and raised a sorry-ass son, or you done drove both of 'em out with all your problems. But it don't matter much in the end. Soon enough y'ain't never gonna have to deal with me again, just like Pap, wherever he is. Maybe not tonight, and maybe not tomorrow, but one day you're gonna come home and I'mma be long gone, and you'll have to walk up to that there liquor store all by your lonesome. Good night, ma'am. And pardon any rudeness on my part. Wasn't my intention at all."

••

For years Jonah and Levi had wanted to believe that the creek out in the woods was their little secret and theirs alone, where they might regroup after long days of unfulfilling, menial work, which left no impact on the people who passed in and out of their lives, let alone human history. There were times, however, when they intruded upon couples who were themselves intruders.

That day was one such example, because as the two young men stepped out of the overgrowth to take a brief repose in their hideaway, they stumbled upon an uncouth tryst that neither had any desire to witness. The anonymous girl was surprisingly quiet, her face pressed against the smooth bark of a maple tree, hidden from recognition; the boy was much louder, moaning comically as if it were a necessity in the act of teenage lovemaking (after all, it was an essential element in pornography). But he, too, kept his face covered in his partner's long, dark hair, baring only his clenched behind to the two peeping Toms who tried their best not to peek, and who knew no one by the name of Tom.

"Go on, get outta here!" Jonah ordered, Levi snickering behind him. The girl finally made a sound—"*Shit, Cody! Grab my bag!*"—and pulled up the capris that lay bunched up at her ankles. They scampered off into the woods, the boy still naked, covering his blue balls with a dirt-streaked shirt. Jonah couldn't help but holler one last piece of advice: "And stay in school!"

He laughed at the absurdity but did not mean to mock it; after all, he couldn't with a clean conscience, filled with memories of similar deviant acts in the same remote, open-air bedroom. But it was his place, shared only by a select few, and if he had to piss on every tree at the streambed's edge just to mark his territory, he would have, and maybe the teenage animals might have steered clear of the pungently claimed spot in the woods. It was the one place he and Levi could call their own, and he had no intention of opening it to public use. He'd lost claim over his own home when Hannah decided she was too grown up to heed his warnings and decrees, and it seemed that though Gabe Skinner hadn't ever stepped through the front door, he was the new master of the domicile, who reigned with a backhand and poison dripped slowly into his young victims' ears.

Levi, too, had nowhere to hide from his mother, who filled their parlor with the stale stench of cigarette smoke, and who didn't permit him to ever assume the role of man of the house, which they both thought his long-gone father would have wanted. To the creek they were destined to go, to wash away all those undesirables from their minds. And Jonah certainly wasn't about to let a couple of Parsons kids ruin it for the both of them, littering the streambed with dirty clothes and used rubbers that would take a thousand years to decompose.

Jonah kicked off his shoes and plunged his aching feet in the running water, the shadow of the trees crisscrossing his toes like sore lines left by sandal straps. There were no fish in that creek to nibble at his soles, though some in the town deceitfully claimed it was a natural hatchery for crawfish. Paddy Tucker, the foul-smelling, hairy-armed attendant at the Hometown Market's seafood counter, consistently claimed that he caught the bottom-dwellers in the creek with his own nets, though Jonah had never felt a single one tickling his toes. The sputtering station wagon with Louisiana plates that periodically pulled into the back of the market was a dead giveaway that his catches came from out of state, and that he'd one day get caught in a lie like his crawfish in a net outside of New Orleans. Local or imported, it didn't matter; Jonah wasn't a fan of seafood, anyway. He'd drawn too many comparisons between the stink of old fish and the unfeminine musk that surrounded Gabe Skinner's unkempt mother behind the bar, and consequently found such a diet repulsive at best.

There was, however, a scent he was particularly fond of: the sourness of the smoke that swirled up from the joint he promptly lit and held up to admire. Just as Jonah began to feel a warmth around his eyes and brow and a pleasant tingling in his feet, Levi held out his hand and ordered: "Hand it over. I ain't about to let you hog it all."

He willingly surrendered the smoldering joint with a sly grin, remarking, "Rather uncharacteristic o' you, Levi Thompson. What changed your mind?"

Squinting his eyes in a sickened grimace, Levi took a deep drag and fought a wicked cough. "This shit's s'posed to screw with your memory, right?" he asked, trying his best to keep from sputtering up a cloud of smoke.

"So they say."

"Good," Levi replied, passing it back to his eager friend, who was more than ready to smoke himself stupid—it seemed that Levi was, too. "Beer's gettin' old. And it don't work no more."

"Looks like you're finally wisin' up, bud. I've been sayin' that for years."

"More than wisin' up—steppin' up, maybe. You shoulda been there when I spat Mama's words back in her face."

"Finally!" Jonah exclaimed, nearly dropping the joint in the creek. "Levi's grown himself a pair o' balls. God knows it took long enough for 'em to drop." Levi's eyes began to fill with red: not from anger, but from what was, in Jonah's opinion, nature's greatest gift to mankind. Far from insulted, Levi burst into a fit of laughter, the kind that couldn't be contained as easily as tree in cheap rolling papers.

"What'd you say, in your newfound manhood?" Jonah asked, almost shouting over Levi's cannabinoid hysterics. "Hope you told her to go to that Hell she's always goin' on about."

"Told her if she thinks I'm such a burden, then I'll just move out."

"Nice bluff," Jonah sneered. "But where'd you go if she called you on it?"

"Don't know. But she sure as hell didn't like that prospect. That woman tries her best every damn day to push me out, then when she's finally got me on the brink o' doin' so, she backtracks real quick.

Maybe the walk to the liquor store's too far for a stumblin' drunk or somethin', I don't know. She's got me for the time being, though, for better or worse."

"Worse, I'd wager," Jonah judged, flicking the clip into the water, which had burned down so low that it burned his fingertips. The thought of abandonment crossed his mind: Levi leaving his mother in the dust, and himself, as an older brother, carrying the guilt of almost abandoning Hannah, though she'd given him little choice in the matter. He didn't want to beat a dead horse, however—that carcass was so beaten that it was more like a pile of ground meat than a horse—and avoided the subject. It was better to let Levi spill his anxieties like Lenore's cheap whiskey out of a broken bottle, because each passing day, Levi's spirit seemed to be sporting more tiny fissures, until he shattered, out of pain, anger, or both. Even as a friend, there was little he could do to mend those cracks. And as Sophia had advised, perhaps it was better to let Levi's conflict run its course, until Lenore could no longer deny that she was the root of the problem. Jonah didn't mention any of it that day.

"Eh, I'm over it," Levi declared, more likely to convince himself than anyone else. "How'd your date go? I hope Mama didn't ruin it for you."

*If only you knew*, Jonah thought with an awkward smile, doing his best to keep a secret that he never would have been able to keep in the past. "Didn't lead to nothin' inappropriate, if that's your suspicion," he reassured Levi, who was reaching out to take a clip that'd been long since tossed away, much to his disappointment.

"Didn't know that word was in your dictionary."

"Just added it. Word o' the day, I guess. Maybe word o' the year."

"Try your best to keep it in mind," Levi advised. "With all the weed you're smokin', it might be the type o' vocabulary you always got on the tip o' your tongue, but can't recall quick enough to say when the time comes."

"Well, eloquent or not, looks like things might be lookin' up for me in this God-forsaken town. For once in my sorry life, I ain't fixin' to get out any which way I can. It ain't just a lack of opportunity keepin' me here this time. Right now, it's my choice. And I ain't never had much freedom o' choice before." Thinking about it, he just hoped he could handle it. He wasn't used to having options, other than a choice of short-lived fish in the sea. Making real decisions was something he'd surrendered, not to God, but to hormones and boredom. And for the first time in his life, he was ruled by neither, and no one insisted otherwise.

# 10

THOUGH THE GULF OF MEXICO saw plenty of vicious storms throughout hurricane season, Clemency, situated in the lower Appalachians at least two hundred miles north, suffered only the relentless heat of summer and light snows in winter, but little else. That week, a tropical storm threatened the southern coast, tearing across the Gulf bearing a harmless-sounding feminine name, as such storms always did. Meteorologists confidently insisted that Tropical Storm Sookie was far too weak to cause any damage more than a few miles past the coastline, and that the worst the area around Clemency could expect was a dreary, cloudy day. However, this did little to quell mass hysteria, as the people of that northern Alabaman town had a tendency to interpret all natural disasters as signs of the End Times, no matter how minor or predictable.

While most, if not all, of Clemency's churchgoers were secure in their belief that they would be saved from the horrors of the apocalypse, taken up to God in the miraculous Rapture, they still prepared for the exceedingly slim chance that they might be left behind. Canned vegetables and candles flew off the shelves, and families filled their bathtubs to the brim with lukewarm tap water. Most extreme of all was the line of cars at the gas pump, which began as two or three before sunrise, but by noon had grown so absurdly long that Rusty had no choice but to impose strict limits on fuel distribution, and not a single car left with a full tank. No one was able to explain how they intended to drive away in their aging sedans under ten feet of water, as many believed might flood the land. If anything, bedsheets should have been the most valuable commodity, as they could be used as sails for makeshift rafts, carrying faithful refugees to the safety of the mountains.

*"But as the days of Noah were, so shall also the coming of the Son of man be,"* they recited, as the modern Deluge was coming, and nothing could stop it—other than topped-off fuel tanks, apparently, which could part dangerous seas and deliver the Lord's chosen people to the undefined Promised Land somewhere up north. Levi was only a hindrance to their exodus. His tips amounted to less than ten dollars that day.

"What do you mean 'no more than four gallons per customer?'" snapped an old woman with a purplish wig and wrinkled hands with so many multicolored veins that they could have been a road map of her evacuation route.

"I ain't been waitin' in line for three and a half hours just to fill up my tank to where it'd started before I been *idlin'* all damn day," bitched the beater-sporting, bathroom cologne–wearing man with armpits that hadn't been groomed since puberty.

"So you want my kids to *drown* when we ain't got enough gas to get outta town?" gasped a bloated, big-haired blonde with three sweaty bastard children in the back seat, who instinctively took a noisy gulp from her XXL diet soda.

"Ain't no way I'mma die in this storm all 'cause a high school dropout was too lazy to pump more than four gallons in this heat," growled an overweight, tan-skinned professional in a tweed business suit who hadn't noticed that the pen in his chest pocket had sprung a leak, staining his left tit blue.

"Fine—keep your gas, you little prick. You'll need it when the Rapture comes and you're left behind to rot," promised the gap-toothed trucker who had a cross dangling from his rear-view mirror and mud flaps with naked ladies on them guarding his back tires.

"Now, I don't expect you to know kindergarten math, but a fifteen percent tip when you only lettin' me pay five bucks for two useless gallons don't add up to much, so y'ain't gettin' shit from me, boy," declared the leathery old man who had flecks of dried spittle at the corners of his gaping mouth, his eyes so cloudy with cataracts that he nearly struck a street sign as he drove off with his adult diaper in a twist.

"Get your manager out here, kid. Either you been lyin' about rations 'cause you're a troublemaker, or you're too stupid to follow the rules—either way, you deserve to get your ass fired," demanded the shapeless black woman with chalky white lipstick and zebra striped press-on nails, who was so overweight that her breasts, like the pendulous, pancaked teats of an orangutan, had to be tucked into her pants so she could buckle her seatbelt.

Rusty, who was walking out of the convenience store with a sweating water bottle in one hand and a set of car keys in the other, overheard the call for parley. He stuffed the keys into his back pocket and took one last swig of cold water, and promptly approached the faded red car, which was idling despite the hose still dangling from its tank, asking bluntly, "What's the problem, here?" As was his favorite stance, he crossed his bulging forearms, obscured by a cover of dark, Mediterranean hair, and stood his ground. He was not the type to let the customer tell him how to run his business (he being the de facto owner in the absence of the mythical Mr. Smith). The customer was rarely right. If she was, he'd still deny it.

Fighting her way out of the confines of the driver's seat with a roll of doughy flesh stuck behind the steering wheel, the scowling woman snapped between labored breaths, "You'll fire 'im, or y'ain't gettin' my business again," as though such a weightless threat could sway the ruddy-skinned giant that towered over her. Meaning the most casual disrespect, he pulled a cigar out of his pocket, one third already smoked, and lit a match with a quick flick of the wrist. He made sure to blow the offensive smoke right into her face. Probably asthmatic, it would have done her well to get back in the car and roll up the window to avoid respiratory arrest.

"Ain't gonna happen," he promised, "so take what you can get, then drive the hell off." He pulled the hose from the car and slammed it back onto the shaky pump, and slapped the car's trunk as though he were a baseball player slapping his teammate on the ass for good luck. "'There's a storm brewin'!' y'all are sayin', so count your damn blessings and wait it out. Now give this young man what you owe 'im," he instructed, pointing a black-stained finger at the knock-off designer purse minding its own business on the passenger seat, "then y'can take your unwanted business elsewhere."

He turned to the next customer, who sat impatiently behind the wheel of a pearl-white SUV with temporary tags, and shouted amicably, "You, ma'am! Wouldn't you like to finally take your turn?"

The driver, a rail-thin black woman with buzzed hair, white gold hoops and a face so sunken that it gave her horse teeth, called back, "I got a right mind to *beat* her fat ass! Get that slob outta here!" Then, grumbling unspeakables under her breath, the stubborn, morbidly obese customer put her car in drive and slithered away toward Main Street, seen off by an angry mob who'd left their torches and pitchforks in their trunks. Rusty gave Levi a thumbs up, and left him to his duties. He cut short his march to the garage, however, when he heard slurred curses of another sort sounding out from the crumbling parking lot. He stopped dead in his tracks. Levi froze, and the blood drained from his face with a wave of prickly cold.

*"You'd best be listenin', you sorry, son-of-a-bitch!"* Mama screamed from the driver's seat of the old Cadillac, steadily cruising in her son's direction. The tires, caked with dried, flaking mud, ground against the pavement that was already sprinkled with gravel and dust, and along with the metallic scraping of unknown moving parts in the decrepit engine, the sounds rose up over an eerie, awkward silence. Most of the customers in line wouldn't have known her name or face. From that day on, however, they'd never forget her, or the look on her son's face as she made the Cadillac into a barricade, parked callously in a gap between cars just fifteen feet from the pump, which clattered as fuel trickled from the hose like mascara from her bloodshot eyes.

Beside Levi, the skeletal, dark-skinned woman muttered to herself, expecting her gas to be pumped in a timely fashion, "Ain't no white bitch is gonna hold me up, I swear to God." She leaned her head out the window and barked in the voice of a woman three times her size, *"Get in line! Y'can wait four goddamned hours like the rest of us!"* A thunderous chorus cheered her on, praising her bravery, because they were all too curious to act on their own. Gossip, it seemed, was a more valuable commodity than fuel during a shortage.

*"Mind your business!"* Mama barked back, hitting the horn as an extension of her tempestuous voice. "It's a crime before God to get between a mother and her *son!*" With one sentence, Mama had revealed Levi's identity for all the world to know, to pity, or to ridicule. The black woman's face, once contorted with spite, now reflected a sense of the utmost sympathy. When Levi met eyes with her, he felt as though he were in a spotlight on a stage of circus freaks, looked upon with equal pity and revulsion. He wanted neither from her, or anyone.

"There ain't no runnin' away this time!" Mama sneered, clasping her hand around the door handle. She tried to swing her legs out of the car and push herself off the seat, but she stumbled and caught her arm on the seatbelt; in frustration she drove her fist into the steering wheel, snatched up an empty glass bottle from the passenger seat, and smashed it on the pavement. Glass scattered in all directions, but the entranced stares of the onlookers were focused solely on her, far from distracted.

She held her face in her hands and rocked herself as would a homeless woman seeking to inspire sympathy, but it wasn't an act of manipulation. It was real—it was honest, as were her tears. And though her audience looked to Levi to act on their behalf and be the one to console her, behaving like a true son, he couldn't oblige them. In his head he'd been sent back into the past, to his childhood when he heard her sobs through a cracked bedroom door. Back then he could crawl into her lap. But now, a young adult who couldn't bear to spend more than a moment beside her, he couldn't be that source of innocent solace. He wasn't sure how to be anything for her, other than a doormat or a punching bag that offered little resistance when each blow came his way.

"I won't let you leave me," she murmured, her voice suddenly soft and fragile. "Sam, you *can't...*" Her dark hair fell out of its professional bun as she pulled it in anguish, letting it tumble over her shoulders in a way that she'd never let the public see before. She was no longer the prim and poised churchgoer famed for her unwavering propriety. She slurred her words as she cried out, "Samuel Thompson, *listen* to me! You can't put me through this again!"

Levi did look so much like his father.

"Go home, Mama," he whispered, with the kind of softness that could either mark it with compassion, or the utmost embarrassment, and even he wasn't sure which. She deserved no compassion, he reminded himself, because she herself had never offered it. Was she worth feeling embarrassed over, if it meant that he did, on some level, care about her, even if that caring was in the form of disdain? And when she surrendered and left him to tend to an ever-growing line of customers who shook their heads in judgment, both critical and seemingly sympathetic, did she really mistake him for his father, whose brown eyes he'd inherited, and which were filled with the same wistfulness that he'd always imagined as Samuel Thompson shut the front door, never to return again?

••

There was a hill on the far side of town, over which the sun never seemed to set, as darkness did not fall upon the wealthy. The hill had no official name, as it was hardly an impressive geological formation, rising thirty feet above sea level at best. It only towered over the poor folks because of the cluster of three-story houses at its peak, like shrines at the apex of a gently sloped ziggurat, dedicated to some modern Moloch who demanded outsourced jobs as tribute.

Among those whitewashed chapels was the Reverend Shaw's far-from-humble abode. It was a shiny new castle nestled in a town of crumbling antebellum homesteads, in whose double-door garage rested two silver luxury cars, one German, and one British—neither one American, though their owners were such zealous patriots. The front door was stained glass in the glow of the porch light, shining with the reds and blues of a beautiful, inlaid pattern. The house's vinyl siding appeared iridescent, like mother-of-pearl decorating the scrollwork of a monarch's chest of gold bullion. Evidently, there was one blatant inaccuracy in the Bible: the Third Temple wouldn't be rebuilt in a New Jerusalem, but on the hill on Clemency's western border, where Yahweh's high priest and priestess served him with such opulent devotion.

At the end of the gray brick driveway, between two stout, stone pedestals that supported the graven images of a snarling lion and a scowling eagle, stood Jonah with his lit phone in hand. He was both the man and the ox missing from the fourfold guardians: the man whose newfound nobility had led him to Sophia's door, and the ox who, in his unwavering stubbornness, refused to leave her alone. He'd called her earlier that evening, while still dripping wet on the bathroom floor after a hot shower that was hasty but got the job done. She'd picked up after just one ring—their date had piqued her interest—but broke some unpalatable news.

"No, I'm staying home tonight," she announced with recognizable regret, and when he abruptly inquired as to her reason in his dwindling confidence (was it him?), she explained, "Not by choice, so don't go beating yourself up. I wouldn't want to see your pretty face sporting a self-inflicted shiner, now."

"Guess a trophy with a dent don't do you much good."

"Don't flatter yourself. A trophy doesn't mean much when every other girl's already won it."

"Ouch."

"And besides, I never said you're my boyfriend."

"Not *yet*, at least."

She laughed it off but didn't address the implication; neither did she fully explain why she'd been imprisoned for the night, locked away in a den of lions. He could only assume that her terrible crime had been sitting at a diner booth with the likes of him, and given that he was an accomplice to her transgressions—both angering a jealous God and even more jealous parents who were to be honored, not disobeyed—it was his moral obligation to break her out.

Unfortunately, he would have to capture her, maybe even against her will, and for the same reason: for her own good. She wasn't about to sneak out, she'd asserted, not just because it was an activity reserved for childish high school students, but because the Reverend and his wife were light sleepers, as good Christians must be ever-vigilant, lest they be caught drooling on a pillow when Christ descended from the clouds to bring swift judgment upon mankind, and mouth-breathers, especially.

Maybe the light of the returned Messiah could expose him, but Jonah stayed away from the lamps that made the driveway a softly glowing path to Heaven, or Hell (the line between them seemed to be growing thinner by the minute). One window on the left side of the house cast warm, yellow light upon the young lilac bushes beneath it, which sported delicate flowers just high enough to brush the underbelly of the windowsill, but had no sweet fragrance until Jonah had drawn closer.

The grass was damp with cool dew, and his sneakers slipped over the shadowy carpet and squeaked like walking on linoleum. He felt water on his bare ankles but resisted the urge to flick it away, as his eyes were firmly set on the light at the end of his tunnel: an enticing glow, radiating from beneath a stoic, black lampshade, which stood at the edge of the window.

A couple taps of his fingers later, he announced his arrival by text—not his favorite means of communication, but presently necessary. Even in a succinct message he was determined to write properly. One of his biggest pet peeves was the mobile slang used by so many of his functionally illiterate peers, the kind that somehow managed to work its way into essays and book reports. Clearly sarcasm was inexpressible without an amicable, triliteral interjection, as if anyone truly laughed out loud to it.

*"Come outside,"* he'd written her, *"I'm by the window, like a creep,"* including the apostrophe that millennials were all too willing to omit, knowingly or not. Maybe one day he'd write her a real letter, in the eloquent language he always meant to use in English class but didn't out of concern for social status—which, as it so happened, could only be achieved through the use of abbreviations and consistent misspellings, and maybe even facial expressions shaped with bastard punctuation marks. He'd write it by hand, in spite of the masculine crudeness of his penmanship, and send it off with a stamp and a tight seal, even if her mailbox was a quick walk from home.

The Reverend, however, would intercept it before it could ever reach its intended recipient. It'd end up in their marble-framed fireplace like a heretical text in a good, old-fashioned book burning, tossed into the flames by the hand of a modern Inquisitor who meant to protect his daughter from all forms of alternative—or free—thought.

Her literal window of opportunity opened wide, not with the dramatic crash of a prison cell torn open for the first and possibly last time, but quietly, with the gentle touch of a girl who was careful not to blow her only shot at a brief escape, even if it was only in the form of a whispered conversation she wasn't meant to have. Her black hair billowed outward in the breeze, wavy and natural, flowing free from the bondage of public scrutiny. Jonah smelled her coconut shampoo, a mellow undertone to the bright floral of lilac flower perfume from the bushes over which she peered. Her smile dazzled in the moonlight, and her skin was just as luminous as the silvery veil of clouds that passed over the face of the full moon.

There was something about the simple way she dressed for sleep that made her more enticing than even the most provocative lingerie ever could. She wore a plain, sky-blue T-shirt so suited for nocturnal repose that it barely hugged her body, and soft sweatpants that showed the curve of her hips but nothing more. She looked the part of the girl next door, innocent and honest, with the most genuine beauty that needed no makeup to be brought to the attention of wide-eyed boys. With no concern for sex, she was effortlessly sexy; no girl had ever set his body on fire without the use of a lighter in the guise of lipstick or tight clothing, but she'd done it without even flicking her thumb over the aesthetic trigger. All the water in the Mississippi couldn't have extinguished what she'd kindled.

"You know, of all people, I would have thought you'd understand 'no means no' more than most," she whispered, turning the brightness of the lamp beside her just two clicks dimmer.

"Only when it counts," he replied.

"You mean my wishes don't always count?"

"What I mean's that you been wishin' for an escape all these years, and I'm gonna give it to you, even if you're too proud—or scared—to take it."

"Slipping out my bedroom window in the middle of the night isn't the dignified freedom I've been praying for."

"Beggars can't be choosers. A thank you might be in order."

"I never beg, Mr. Young. I'm not what you're used to—I can promise you that."

"And what exactly do y'think I'm used to, after all these years o' deviance?"

"Excited, little middle schoolers who think sneaking out of their parents' house is the highest kind of thrill, I imagine."

"Middle schoolers? I ain't no pederast."

"You *were* in middle school once, weren't you? Jonah Young wasn't always the grown man he now claims to be."

"Funny, comin' from a girl whose parents still treat her like a child."

"Filial piety isn't childish: it's proper."

"Then maybe it's about time you get down in the mud like the rest of us trash."

He hadn't meant to imply that Sophia considered him low-class, as he was far from offended. Even if she had, it was something he'd become accustomed to, anyway, and he'd grown particularly thick skin. At first grimacing with regret, then relaxing upon realizing that she hadn't deeply insulted the young man who waited at her window, she replied: "Well, as of our last rendezvous, my parents have judged me as just another addition to the dregs at the bottom of society's barrel. A travel-sized bottle of whiskey hidden in the depths of a purse would make anyone think that, though, so I can't blame them that much."

*Great,* he thought. *Now Lenore's ruinin' more lives than just her son's.* The old Jonah would have cursed her for keeping him (and Levi, of course) from ever getting laid again. This time, however, he lamented only the punishment the Shaws had so mistakenly imposed on their only daughter. Love always had its obstacles, he knew, but a stranger's backroom vice shouldn't be one of them.

"I reckon I shoulda expected them to snoop around through your stuff," he admitted.

"All part of a routine inspection, military-style," Sophia sighed, with a defeatism that revealed a forced acceptance of the inevitable. "Condoms and birth control are the worst kind of contraband in the Shaws' squeaky-clean barracks. You know, the only safe sex is no sex. Maybe you should enlist—you might learn a thing or two."

"Buzzed hair ain't my style," he jested, tussling the wavy, brown hair that hung over his ears.

"Maybe not, but it's a small price to pay for gaining some respect for authority."

"Authority?" he scoffed. "Now I know y'ain't referrin' to God Almighty. There ain't nothin' in this world He loves more than a rebel against the establishment. His own Son was the biggest rulebreaker in history, remember?" He held out his hand and smiled, baring white teeth in the moonlight that suggested both honest encouragement and youthful deviance. "So why don't you walk in the footsteps of Christ and climb out that window?"

Sophia reached for the lamp to switch off the light, then stopped herself, leaving her finger lingering over the plain, black lampshade.

"I hope I don't need to remind you that just because we're in the cover of night, doesn't mean we're about to do what couples do behind closed doors, with all the lights off—not that we're a couple, of course."

"Don't have much plans on what we'll be doin' once you're down here, but trust me, that definitely ain't an option. All I'm askin' is for you to take that leap o' faith," Jonah replied earnestly, extending his hand once again. "Don't worry: I'll catch you."

"You're sounding an awful lot like Satan," she remarked as she shut off the light, enveloping all but her feline eyes in darkness. "Are the angels going to hold me up, lest I dash my foot against a stone?" She sat down upon the windowsill and sighed. "The Devil's a liar, but he's a damn good one. So maybe I'll dance with him—just for one night."

The Reverend's daughter reached down as if to pull Jonah up to her window, but he, like he had so many times before, chose to help her set her feet on the ground, at his level, among mortals and mice. The curtains inside swayed in the wind and lapped at her body. It wasn't much of a drop to the grass, six feet at most, but when a petite girl who'd become so accustomed to being placed on a pedestal fell to earth by choice, it might as well have been like BASE jumping from the top of a crude and deviant cliff. And was it really reassuring to have a young man with a newfound insecurity ready to catch her, when he was far more skilled at letting girls lie on their backs beneath him?

Without a word, hesitation or an expression of fear, Sophia jumped. And although Jonah stood with his arms wide open, ready to be the one to guard her carefully and lift her up in his hands, she was a girl with no need for a man to protect her from harm. Whether a sprained ankle or a broken heart, she could heal both on her own. She landed on her feet, but stumbled; her white sneakers, streaked with green from the grass beneath her, slipped on the dewdrops in the dark.

She fell right into Jonah's arms and found her balance in his embrace, her cheek pressed against the firm muscles of his chest for only a moment. A smile spread across her face, meek, with humble reservation. Her amber eyes caught the light, filled with an excitement that Sunday service never seemed to give her. Like a natural reflex commanded by unconscious modesty, she pulled away and pushed her hair back, regaining her calm, sensible composure. Jonah still felt the warmth of her body lingering on his skin. He couldn't suppress his grin, no matter how many times she rolled her eyes at his penchant for being so easily pleased.

By no means was he a stranger to an old-fashioned, youthful leap out the bedroom window in the cover of night, but he'd never been the one to hold out his hand. In the end, was he the one carrying her to earth, or was she raising him up, in the hope of self-redemption?

Even with years of high school trysts and covert escapes through a house of sleeping obstacles, he felt a rush of eagerness, excitement, or maybe even true courage. The radiant sense of honest victory was not from conquering a girl who yearned to be conquered (the Reverend's daughter was unconquerable, and in need of no one); it was in knowing that for the first time in ages, perhaps ever, a girl had answered his call, and let him act the Romeo without Shakespearian prose. She allowed him to walk beside her in a search for something deeper than an hour or so of shadowy deviance that never brought true satisfaction, at least on his part.

With his eyes on the unlit road ahead, and even with all that sense of innocent freedom, the sickly sensation of guilt remained, a reminder of all those times past. He was doing nothing wrong, and he was not coercing her into doing something immoral, but why did he fear punishment, expecting it with dread, but almost eagerly? The path to Hell was paved with good intentions, he'd been told all his life, and at that moment, he had the best of intentions. At least he'd get there without calloused feet or a hardened heart, having been strolling down a smoothly paved road that began at Sophia's open window, and led into the dark where anything was possible.

••

Billie Holiday was a guardian angel of sorts, a phonographic spirit guide who never really left Levi's side. She sat on his right shoulder, serenading him in the ear he kept on the opposite side of his pillow. When he humored spiteful thoughts of Mama, she was there to remind him that even a cruel creature like Lenore Thompson could appreciate beauty.

It was a timeless beauty, one to be beheld on vinyl, CDs or intangible MP3s, though Mama chose to preserve her soulful siren on the records that had first made her immortal and lent a quality to the sound that could never be imitated by any other technological medium. She channeled that dead woman's words beneath a wobbling needle, and with their supernatural powers she brought a heavenly peace. There were those times, though, when Billie and Ella were angels of death. They called out in the night from behind Levi's back, lest he forget that no matter how many times he snuck away from Mama's wrath, there was no escaping the inevitable. Death and whiskey: both were horrors he was fated to face.

The voice faded away as he headed down the driveway, the emotive miasma still surging and receding like the tide, but now more like a light trickle of notes like rain off a tin roof. There was little reason to run, because there was nowhere to run to. The Ten Commandments, a code he once thought universal, were enforced no matter where he went. Mama's house was a temple of honoring a dishonorable mother, and the town of Clemency, sleeping in the distance, was a city-state bound to the rest of God's rules. To be honest, of all biblical commandments, the Fifth was the only one he'd been adamant on obeying. As a violator of the rest—he placed his resentment before his love for God, and he coveted his more fortunate neighbors' property each day on his walk to work—he was in danger of social excommunication from the Southern Mercy Bible Church, which was a worse punishment than an eternity in the fiery pit.

Those who'd been rejected by God's true followers were an odious lot, and though Levi had long believed that church was to be a place of sanctuary, not judgment, he couldn't fully blame the pious churchgoers for wanting to separate themselves from the ranks of the Skinners and von Brauns as far as spiritually possible. He had no place among the Skinners, whose Eucharist was a tab of ecstasy on the tongue. And the von Brauns—they thought themselves so high above the inconsequential, suit- and dress-clad nematodes at their feet that even God Himself must have looked like a meddlesome, pointless insect, worthy of nothing but a designer shoe dropped upon Him.

However, Mama saw little difference between her son and the excommunicated. It was only a matter of time before the Reverend caught on to Levi's disinterest in the fiery Sunday service that everyone else looked forward to all week. Levi would be barred from

Paradise forever, as the Reverend Shaw had St. Peter on speed dial. Mama would never again be able to show her face in public, with irreversible shame imposed upon her family name by an ungrateful and ungodly son, and she would be forced to spend each Sabbath day alone in the parlor in a yellow dress for no one to see. For them, the Sabbath was a day of restlessness, when God sat so idle as to allow Levi's once happy life to fall into disrepair.

No one was ever truly happy, he told himself as he kicked an empty beer bottle into the ditch beside the road. Anyone who said otherwise was either a drunk, an addict, or a salesman. Anything they used or peddled could bring a smile to one's face, but in the end, it was just an unacknowledged wince of pain. The beer bottle clattered against a growing mess of cans and broken glass, the debris left when a teenage meteor came crashing to Earth after a brief, bright glow in the night.

The smell of piss-warm beer and cheap vodka never lingered, washed away when the rains came, but the place stank of debauchery. The parents who thought their sons and daughters were out studying, shopping, or praying in the pews must have known that the landfill by the railroad tracks was their children's monument to their own rebellion.

A lonely brown bottle lay sideways in the center of a circle drawn with a finger in the dirt, like the hand of a crude clock; it pointed toward the destitute station platform, past an imprint on the ground where one lucky pervert had the good fortune to be sitting, and received an obligatory kiss, grope, or worse. Levi followed the glass arrow with little else to do. He grumbled when he stepped on the gold foil of a condom wrapper. For one lucky teenager, it'd been the golden ticket, though there were far too many in the world for it to be considered valuable.

Only once in his sophomore year of high school had he attended a rail party, as they'd called them—granted, he'd only been invited once, and not because he was anyone's first choice, but as an understudy for Jonah, who'd declined at the last minute in favor of a private, two-person gathering by the football field. At that point in his life, Levi wasn't much of a drinker, having only had a sip or two of the single beer that Jonah had snuck out of his parents' house to be drank and spat out in the woods. The partygoers didn't know the extent of his inexperience, however, and he was determined to prove his manhood the only way American teenagers knew how: by achieving a blood alcohol content of roughly 0.299 and making a series of regretful sexual decisions that boys called embarrassing and girls called borderline rape. Those decisions were not always made by choice, but by chance, determined by fate in the form of drawn straws, toothpicks or playing cards.

He'd pulled one such card and as misfortune would have it, the other gambler holding a spade was a dyed-blond boy by the name of Gregory Andrews—a closet case with a closet door made of the cleanest, most transparent glass. Levi nearly had to shout his protest over the howling laughter cued by the Queen of Spades. Convinced Gregory had somehow managed to rig the game, Levi swayed the group into giving him a second draw. With the Ten of Clubs in his left hand and his right clasped tightly by an eager and glassy-eyed Lizzie MacDowell, he disappeared off into the bushes, Gregory pouting like a bitch in the glare of an upturned flashlight.

With too little light to see much and double vision too severe to have allowed it anyway, Levi's other senses seemed heightened. He heard the snap of an unclasped bra against bare skin, felt slender fingers grazing his arm, and smelled a pop star's juvenile brand of perfume, mixed with the sour stench of bile bubbling up from his gut to his nose. Before Lizzie could even draw her lips close to his, he spun around and unleashed a torrent of soupy vomit all over a blossoming forsythia bush. In fact, that bush was still there as he walked down that beaten path years later, but in his mind, that overwhelming odor still stung his nostrils.

He remembered debating with himself while Lizzie cried out in horror, emitting a series of sympathetic dry heaves: should he claim he was too drunk and expose his true identity as a lightweight, or should he confess that he was too nervous, and build a reputation as the awkward boy who was simply too much of a pussy to act on a girl's sloppy advances? Certainly the latter was not an option, as it wasn't true at all. In fact, he'd lost his virginity a year earlier, though he had to admit the experience had left him with a child's comical excitement and a curious sense of dread, as though God, the original voyeur, had been scrutinizing him with every clumsy thrust.

For whatever reason, Lizzie felt it was appropriate to lie on his behalf, and when the pair emerged from the shadows of the overgrowth she brusquely announced that she felt far too nauseous to risk swapping not saliva, but putrid chyme. Maybe she worried her peers would conclude that she was a failed seductress that couldn't even rope in a teenage boy who, like all boys their age, should have been horny enough to touch anything that sported two, one or even three breasts (they weren't picky). Luckily, there was an alternative to sending Levi off with his original, male partner, though Gregory's face once again sunk into a grimace of the utmost disappointment. The most popular among them pointed ominously toward the railroad tracks, in a spot below an overhead lamp that was too dead to even flicker eerily. "Five minutes. We're countin'," they whispered gravely, some snickering in the background. "Y'ain't comin' back till Bloody Bethany pays y'all a visit."

Bloody Bethany was one of those local myths circulated by stupid, superstitious teens, who earned an adjective that so many other ghosts around the country carried before their names: Bloody Mary was certainly the most popular, showing her face in mirrors and on polished headstones upon the uttering of her name. Bethany, as the story went, lived twenty-five years ago (always twenty-five, even as the years passed), the daughter of abusive adopted parents who locked her in her closet and gave her paper cuts between her fingers with pages from their family Bible. Apparently, Bethany's only escape from their cruelty was the boy next door, to whom she confessed her undying love, hoping he might whisk her away and save her from such terrible suffering. He rejected her, with no hesitation or apologies.

Heartbroken and hopeless, Bethany made her way to the railroad tracks in the middle of the night and threw herself in front of a passing train. Allegedly, she died right in the spot where Levi and Lizzie were forced to sit in silence. Town records couldn't corroborate the story, but facts didn't matter to kids who were so bored that they were willing to wait in the dark for the pitiful spirit of a young girl who'd lived a tragic life and died an equally tragic death. Needless to say, Levi saw no such apparition. Even in death, Clemency's townsfolk fled as far as they possibly could, and no amount of conjuring could convince them to return to that rough notch in the Bible Belt.

Several years later, however, as he walked the decrepit path of the railroad tracks, he heard the tortured moans of some discarnate spirit echoing out from behind the station platform—right under the dead lamp that marked the site of Bloody Bethany's demise. But unlike the local folklore, this voice was a man's: a whining, bratty man, who seemed to feel he was privileged enough to be chauffeured personally by Charon across the Acheron to a lavish afterlife without paying a single drachma.

"Take me now, you useless God!" Jimmy von Braun shouted into the darkness. "Either take me up to you, or send my bitch mother back to the fiery pit she came from! Or the Bronx! I don't give a damn, as long as that scorpion woman gets what's hers!"

Even on his intended death bed his phone sat beside him, its screen the only source of light. Though the von Braun family heir always wore the very best designer clothes that money could buy, this time he looked especially ostentatious, lying in the dirt in a meticulously fitted button-down, perfectly pressed slacks, with a dark, skinny tie like a silky noose around his neck. Of course, even in the cover of night he wore mirrored aviator sunglasses, because a young man of his wealth and status was too lofty to allow St. Peter to look him directly in the eye. A silver wristwatch gleamed in the glow of his phone, as did the slender bottle of clear liquor standing upright and dignified on the ground. It was half empty. No doubt Jimmy would never have considered it half full, ever the pessimist parading as a realist.

Seeing Jimmy in a position of the utmost weakness was, in a sick way, the most uplifting sight Levi could have beheld that night. Holding back snide laughter, he interrupted Jimmy's drunken supplications, informing him: "A train ain't ran through here in years. You'll die o' starvation before y'ever see headlights comin' your way."

Jimmy scowled, his icy blue eyes smoldering with disdain. "I've been starving myself for years, and I'm not dead yet," he groaned, picking up the bottle of vodka to take one quick swig. "But I intend to be soon enough. Get out of here, Thompson. I'm not about to be stopped by some redneck who can't even keep his mother from drinking herself to death."

"Suit yourself," Levi answered with a shrug, unfazed by Jimmy's insults. An aspiring suicide with a lack of good planning was in no real place to hurl criticisms his way. "Y'know, if your mama's such a bitch, then she ain't gonna be cryin' over you when you're just a splat on the railroad tracks—not that that's gonna happen anytime soon."

"Maybe I'll go jump off a bridge, then. Plummet, even."

"Ain't no bridges round here, neither."

"Jesus Christ, Thompson!" Jimmy snapped, pushing himself up off the rails to get back on his feet. "This town's just a big, fucking joke. It drives you into suicidal ideation, then doesn't even give you the means of acting on it! What am I supposed to do, hang myself with a Versace tie? Slit my wrists with a piece of broken Swarovski crystal?"

"Y'could always chase a bottle o' Valium with the rest o' that there vodka."

"I've been taking that for so long that it might as well be children's Tylenol." He reached into his pocket and withdrew a leather-bound cigarette case, then looked up with wide eyes that reflected some kind of morbid epiphany. "I have an idea! *You* can put me out of my misery!"

"And how do y'expect me to do that?"

"I don't know, be creative! I'm sure you've had to improvise things for years, seeing as you're far too poor to afford anything new."

"So after the deed's done, I'm gonna have to improvise a shiv in jail, then."

"Oh, come on, Thompson!" Jimmy pleaded, holding a long, skinny cigarette to his mouth. "Prison would be like a *hotel* for you, given what you're used to. Prison slop's going to seem like a goddamned gift from Julia Child, and honestly, a little bit of sodomy every so often is a small price to pay for a solid roof over your head, if you ask me, especially since you've already been getting raped every day as the only child of a worn-out booze bag. Guess we *both* should be going to a sexual assault support group, shouldn't we?"

"Ain't never put nothin' up there, and I sure as hell don't plan to. Life ain't great but it sure ain't bad enough for me to make that kind o' trade."

"Wish I could say the same. Could have spared myself a whole lifetime of visits to my proctologist," Jimmy muttered, flicking his lighter to produce an eerie flame. It gave him the semblance of a white ghost who kept his pale complexion by smothering himself in the strongest sunblock available. "Wait a second—are you really going to stand there and tell me you didn't have an abusive childhood? Cheap whiskey doesn't make for a life of kindness."

"No offense, but I ain't about to confess no weaknesses to you, of all people."

"Lighten up, Thompson. This is the one chance you're ever gonna get to have the closest thing to a heart-to-heart with me. Savor it while you can, before I sober up and run you down with my quarter-million-dollar car for wearing five-year-old sneakers."

"Fine. Y'ain't the only one with a bitch for a mother. Happy now?"

"Far from it. You'd think my classy attempt at suicide would have made that pretty clear by now. But it's nice to know I'm not the only one who plots his mother's murder every day."

"Ain't *never* said that."

"You're right—you have no reason to. I'm sure Mama Thompson doesn't have a massive life insurance policy for you to collect after her untimely demise." Grimacing with disgust as he took another drag, Jimmy pulled the cigarette from his mouth and examined it. The cherry smoldered unevenly, sizzling away the paper along the underbelly of the carcinogenic cylinder, while barely progressing above it, lending to puffs of caustic, unpleasant smoke. He tossed it disdainfully upon the ground and stomped it out, though he'd only burned a small bit of it. In light of his wastefulness, he turned to Levi as if to teach him a life lesson, explaining, "There's nothing more tragic than a poorly lit cigarette. And remember, Thompson: it's shameful and classless to try and fix it." He pulled out another and smiled, satisfied as a wise sage of tobacco wisdom. "You want one?"

"No thanks," Levi replied, waving away the cigarette Jimmy held his way.

"Oh, come on," Jimmy whined. "I get them imported from Liechtenstein."

"I ain't the type to cave in to peer pressure."

"The von Brauns don't have peers. Only peons."

"Must be a lonely existence."

"The truth hurts, I guess," Jimmy conceded with a shrug and a sigh. "I've got Charlene to thank for that. Bitch isn't afraid to tell it like she thinks it is. When you're wearing diamonds and Jean Patou perfume to bed, reality is whatever you want it to be."

"Better than stinkin' o' whiskey at four in the morning. Now that's when reality gets real twisted."

"You know what? You're right, Thompson," Jimmy confessed, flicking ash from his cigarette; he shuffled back in a panic when he saw the embers falling toward his impeccably shined shoes. "At eight hundred dollars an ounce, a 3.4-oz. bottle of *Joy* is basically carte blanche to be the most rancid bitch this side of the Mississippi. But ten cents an ounce for bong-water booze doesn't give you much of a right to do anything, let alone call yourself a judge of character. But she still calls her only son a failure, doesn't she?"

"Every damn day."

"Same here. Well, maybe she's right—maybe you are a failure. You failed at getting yourself a real education and a good-paying job. Hell, you failed at getting the fuck out of this little landfill you call home. You know, all this time I've been thinking you were perfectly content with your miserable life as a beater-wearing pauper. But looks like I've been proven wrong."

"Your sudden epiphany ain't helpin' me much, no offense."

"But we're *both* failures, you and I, Thompson! I let that bitch take her chocolate diamond shits on me all my life, all while complaining about the wrong things: not buying me that three-thousand-dollar designer jacket, not paying for my six-thousand-dollar lipo on these goddamned leftover love handles, not buying me a new Mercedes after I totaled the first after one of the best nights of partying I've ever had. I guess I *should* have been complaining about having her for a mother, at least to her face! Instead, I'm bitching about it to someone who's never had to worry about getting his parents to pay him what's rightfully his."

Levi propped himself up on the edge of the crumbling train platform and shook his head. "I can't believe I'm givin' you the satisfaction of hearin' this, but I'd kill to have your life."

"More money, more problems—don't you forget it," Jimmy reminded him. He took a seat next to Levi and lit himself another cigarette, this time igniting it perfectly on the first try. "Believe me, you don't want to live your life knowing you spent nine miserable months inside that harpy's ice-cold uterus. I'd rather have risked fetal alcohol syndrome and come out with eyes on the side of my head than have Charlene pass me off to one of her wetback maids. Don't you dare repeat this, to anyone—or I'll have you and your mama thrown out into the streets—but your simple, unpolished life sounds more appealing every day."

"Simple?" Levi said, dumbfounded. "Yeah, my life's simple: get up at the ass crack o' dawn, walk down to the gas station, get beaten down till the sun sets all while contemplatin' all the things you did or didn't do to deserve the embarrassment, then come home with less than minimum wage in your pocket because you're too much of a pussy to tell your boss he's breakin' the law, and have your mama waitin' for you with an empty bottle in her hand screamin' up somethin' awful 'bout how it's your duty as a Christian son to head down to that there liquor store to fetch her what she values over what's left of her family. Simple's knowin' that you ain't got a car and ain't never gonna get one, 'cause you're payin' for your mama's bills without her knowin' it 'cause she's too drunk to care 'bout the letters pilin' up in the mailbox, and since y'ain't got no car y'ain't bought new clothes in ages, and you've ruined what shirts you got with gasoline and oil and that black shit that comes off o' people's worn-down tires."

He slid his thumb under the shoulder band of his shirt and drew attention to just how dingy its white fabric had become; he stuck out his foot, and pointed to the sneakers whose soles had worn down to a paper-thin layer of rubber. "I lie to customers every day 'bout who I am once they recognize me—'Levi Thompson!' they're yellin', like they're excited to see me or somethin', but really they're just happy they got somethin' new to gossip about after Sunday service, since Mama's been doin' a pretty good job o' hidin' her vices behind her songbook. So please, tell me again how my 'simple' life's so goddamned desirable."

"I've never said this before in my life, but don't worry about the clothes so much," Jimmy advised as he took one oversized swig of vodka, so excessive that he nearly spat it out instinctively. "There's nobody in this backwater Sears's sales rack to impress, anyway—other than me, of course, and though you're reasonably cute, you're not my type. And *that's* why your simple life's something to be envied, believe it or not: no pretenses, no two-faced bitchiness, and best of all, no dinner parties with Wall Street bankers and Manhattan real estate agents and bored, Orange County housewives with bad face jobs to impress with all your achievements, which, in the von Braun family's language, means how little empty space you have in your third bedroom walk-in closet."

"My closet's only half full."

"Better than half empty, like this goddamned vodka!" Jimmy screeched in frustration, guzzling the poison he'd imported from some sterile part of the former Soviet Union. "Don't you know what I'd give not to have to dress to the nines every day, and spend an hour every morning picking out what to wear? How can that bitch Charlene expect me to be decisive when I have exactly three hundred and twenty-six options to choose from? And that's just my shoes!"

"I'm pretty sure you only wear black, and no offense, it all looks the same to the rest of us," Levi remarked, taking the bottle from Jimmy's clenched fingers, and drinking a bit himself without asking permission. If Jimmy had protested, his words were too slurred to understand.

"A wardrobe fit for a funeral!" he exclaimed as he took back what was his, however dwindling its supply. "For mourning that last shred of humanity left in me, before Charlene goes ahead and throws it in the trash with an evil fucking grin, like she would with a barely touched plate of food in front of some homeless lady, just for shits and giggles!

"Maybe I'm just doing the same thing! Maybe that frost queen's blood really *does* run through my veins, and I'm not adopted like I've been telling myself all these years—and these absolutely jaw-dropping, stunning blue eyes aren't just a fortunate coincidence! Here I am, dangling a bottle of expensive, Swiss alpine spring water in front of a shriveled, dying, dehydrated wretch, just like *she* would!"

He tore at his handmade Italian shirt and tried to rip it in two, but it was too finely stitched to be so easily rent. With the furious bellow of a toddler he slipped off one of his dark designer shoes, barely scuffed by the ancient dust of the railroad tracks, and threw it hatefully at Levi's undecorated feet. It wasn't clear if it was Levi's plainness that he hated, or his own empty life. But Jimmy, destructively loquacious to the end, wasted no time in making it perfectly clear.

"God, what the fuck *is* this? I think I'm gonna be sick. It's this shit vodka, Thompson! I *knew* I should've spent that extra hundred on *Bespodobny*! This garbage is wrecking my stomach—I'll sue, I swear! Even my goddamned *chest* is killing me! The whole point was to black out from this pointless existence, not give me a fucking *coronary*!"

Levi smiled, almost cruelly, with the unspeakable satisfaction that a sadist enjoyed at his submissive's first cathartic scream. "I think that's guilt you're feelin'."

"Guilt? *Guilt?* I don't even know what that word *means*! I hate it, I hate it, *I hate it*! Guilt for *what*? Von Brauns don't feel *guilt*! It's the fraudulent stigmata of the weak and the Democrats!"

"Guilt toward treatin' the rest of us like footstools all these years—maybe even me in particular."

"You? *You?* Levi Thompson, the source of this useless, obsolete emotion? I don't think so!" Jimmy guffawed with tears running down his cheeks, either the mark of his own overwhelming sense of the comically absurd, or the first trickle of water from an emotional cistern that Charlene had tightly sealed since he'd slid screaming out into the light. "If I'm going to feel any guilt in my inevitably short lifetime, it's gonna be when I cheat on a six-foot-four, muscular Latin supermodel with one who has even bigger biceps!"

"Well, until that day, all you got is me."

"The hell I do!" Jimmy barked as his aristocratic tantrum reached its climax. It was the tantrum of a singer who'd been given the wrong brand of bottled water before a show, and who tore out random audio cables as retribution; it was the outburst of an actor whose dressing room was four square feet smaller than promised, and who ruined every subsequent scene until the grievous insult was rectified. It was the meltdown of a model who beat her agents with cellphones and high heels, rich sixteen-year-old girls with hooked noses who cursed their parents when they were gifted with a Maserati instead of a Lamborghini, and sniveling boys who gunned down their families for no reason other than to end their insufferable boredom. It was both terrifying and morbidly gratifying.

The symphonic release came in the form of shattered glass; shards flew through the air like a percussionist's broken drumsticks. Jimmy threw the vodka bottle to the ground and smashed it upon the rusted railroad tracks with a primal roar.

"That's it! I've got to get out of this shithole!" he declared in a voice that had become as raspy as an eighty-year-old chain smoker's, not from his cigarettes (they were far too expensive to be so harsh), but from the screaming he seemed to have no intention of quelling, even for the sake of avoiding laryngitis. "I've been shipped all over this country, and for what? To help that bastard father of mine avoid the Feds? So my succubus mother can round up another cult of basic bitches to worship her? And now I can't even find a train out of here, let alone one to jump in front of!" He started to lunge at Levi, reaching out to grab his shoulders and shake some elusive answer out of him for all his problems, crying, "Maybe your mama could run me down, being such a train wreck—"

Without warning he caught his foot on the rusted rail and hit the ground hard; his tirade came to a halt as he lay in the dirt, unconscious. As his body settled all Levi heard was the crunch of broken glass beneath him. Then he saw the blood running from a gash in Jimmy's thigh, and the shard that jutted out from his flesh, gleaming in the moonlight. When he came to, it wouldn't be the wound that horrified him. It'd be the unsightly tear in his designer pants, and the knowledge that, for the first time ever, he didn't look much better than the poor, Southern bastard who stood over him, looking down with unexpected pity.

••

It was Hannah Young's lucky day. The vice principal's call had come in the early afternoon, sounding out from the house phone on the kitchen wall, just above the small, shaky table that sat only four. Jonah shuddered when he saw the caller ID; that instinctive anxiety rapidly shifted to seething resentment. He was no stranger to those damning messages on their answering machine, having been the unwitting subject of them all in years past. His grades had been dwindling, he'd been absent from trig or Earth science, or, most commonly of all, his focus had been waning, as he had more interest in hands-on, extracurricular anatomy than plunging scalpels into the soft bellies of cold, dead frogs.

His parents had chastised him accordingly, though their tired lectures and feeble attempts at grounding him did little to keep Vice Principal Chapman at bay. If anything, the man whose otherwise tanned hands were speckled with unsightly vitiligo had grown fond of making those calls. Each voice message he left on their tape was an interaction with other human beings that he rarely had the chance to engage in, save the sitting-down of delinquent students. Perhaps it was his standoffish wife's fault in the end. He really just needed someone to talk to, even if it was a beep after a young mother's generic family greeting.

*"Good afternoon, Mr. and Mrs. Young. This is Vice Principal Chapman calling from Israel Pickens. I'm sorry to say that this is concerning your daughter, Hannah. She was absent from all but her first morning Social Studies class today; unfortunately, this is her third such absence this week. Needless to say, this strikes the administration as rather odd. She's always been one of our model students."*

Jonah scoffed at Chapman's notorious desire to cover up his native accent. All the vain attempts at feigning sophistication would do little to get his wife to pay attention to him. After all, she was hardly upper-class herself. Any woman who repeatedly cheated on her husband by getting railed by aging, Cialis-fueled janitors in the utility closets at lunchtime was far from refined. It was even more repugnant that she was in her late sixties.

*"If Hannah has one more mark of absence on her record, we will have no choice but to enforce an out-of-school suspension, for at least three days, and Hannah will have a permanent mark on her academic record."* How ironic it was that voluntary absences were punished by involuntary absences. If anything, Hannah would enjoy it. *"Unless, of course, there has been a justifiable reason for her absences, in which case the blame falls on the parents for failing to provide the school with a formal notice. Thank you for your time."* Beep.

Before he could stop himself Jonah had pressed the lifesaver button and erased the message forever. He didn't know why he did it; he even cursed himself for it. The spirit of his younger self had possessed him, having waited in limbo for the opportunity to right the wrongs committed against him. He'd never had the opportunity to save himself from Chapman's prerecorded death sentences, and like a dog turning circles before lying down, he acted on pure, biological instinct, the innate drive for self-preservation. But it wasn't himself he was saving: it was his brainless little sister, who'd wrapped him up in her lies once again, though she didn't even know it. Maybe he couldn't even blame her—but he could sure as hell track her down and give her the good, old-fashioned sibling beating with which even

Vice Principal Chapman couldn't punish her. Backing away from the answering machine with clenched fists and a scowl he'd sported far too often over the past weeks, Jonah decided that Hannah's day of reckoning was at hand.

His sister's delinquency had gone from naturally adolescent to outright pernicious, but it was maddeningly difficult to catch her in the act. With access to Gabe's rusty pickup, she had far too many options for Jonah to ever track her down, and unfortunately, a tracking chip planted under her skin wasn't in his budget. He knew his chances of finding her that day were slim at best, even if he were to follow every rule in a hunter's handbook, checking plants for stray hairs and the ground for traces of an underweight teenage girl's faint footprints. Even so, he pulled on a shirt, grabbed his phone and stepped out into the sunlight, intent on trekking down Main Street in a brotherly soldier's determined march toward Midian Lane.

The house was only a few steps behind him when he slowed his pace, his attention caught by a strange melody that, at first, he thought was playing in his head. Red-eyed and a little unfocused, he was stoned, after all; even if it wasn't an auditory hallucination, it wasn't uncommon to faintly hear Lenore Thompson's old records through the fence of trees between their houses. This tune, however, was anything but classy jazz enjoyed by a less-than-classy alcoholic. It was that haunting song sung by ghostly children in horror movies, delicate and disturbing. It gave Jonah the chills, even in the scorching heat of a Southern summer.

There were no words, only sweet, soprano tones that rose and fell in the wind. Though invisible and intangible Jonah saw the frail echo like an outstretched hand reaching out of the trees, its finger curled to beckon him into a dream or a nightmare. Having seen enough ghost films that warned against placing trust in child spirits, for devils were wont to present themselves as innocent angels of light, Jonah was reluctant to accept the invitation. But he knew this was no demon, and no angel. It was his little sister.

The curtains of lush foliage parted to reveal a tranquil yet tragic stage, upon which lay Hannah, waist-deep in the stream, playing the role of a dreamer lost in her chemical dreams. Ripples spread across the water as she traced her finger over the surface, as if she were painting with literal watercolors. She was the artist, and Jonah, just an observer, could never know the thoughts that guided her hand, for like so many artists before her, she was slipping into unknowable madness. Her song was a disquieting symptom, as were the scratches on her arms left by bitten fingernails, and the lifeless eyes that once gleamed with a youthful spirit. Those windows of the soul had been clouded by the hot breath of her abuser. Jonah told himself he'd be the Windex to clear them, and the toxic bleach to be poured down Gabe's throat.

"Do you like that song?" Hannah asked, propping herself up on a broken branch. It jutted out of the water, having fallen from the trees that masked the sun with glowing, green leaves. Her hand slipped on the wood's mossy surface and she slid back into the water with a girlish giggle. She was lucky she didn't break a brittle bone, as she looked thinner than ever. Even the gnarled branch seemed to have more substance than her body.

"It's creepy as hell," Jonah criticized, approaching the edge of the creek.

"Well *I* think it's pretty. Made it up myself. Mother Nature likes it so much she's singin' along," she declared, her words murmured with a singsong lilt that made it seem as if she were reciting lines in a musical with no spoken prose. "The sun's a harp up there and all those rays are gold strings and the birds are tweetin' a chorus and the water's a cymbal and the moon even though you can't see her is dancin' since no one can see her and she can't get embarrassed if no one can see her." She gazed up at the sky in wonder, with pupils so dilated that her hazel eyes, the proud family trait, were as black as Gabe's lungs. "Just imagine her, Jonah! Why can't you get yourself to dance with Mother Nature? She's our *real* mama, anyway."

"Well, Snow White, you got yourself a Ma 'n Pa, and they're gonna beat your ass bloody once you pull yourself outta that there creek and get yourself inside. I ain't in the mood to drag some fucked-up Disney princess out myself."

There was a time when she would have looked rather fay, being such a petite girl lying in the water. Her skin in the sunlight would have been luminous, and her large green eyes, sparkling like crystal. But now her complexion was too dull to be magical. No self-respecting Disney cartoonist would have ever drafted a fairy princess in her likeness. Tim Burton, on the other hand, might have sculpted her from clay and meticulously moved her fingers frame by frame as she picked apart a bouquet of wildflowers that she clutched in her trembling hands.

"Don't you ever get tired o' playin' Big Brother?" she asked as she sprinkled a handful of white petals over the water. They drifted in the current in Jonah's direction and settled in a bunch at the edge of the stream. "I'm tired o' playin' Lil' Sister to such a damn downer."

"You'll know what a real downer is once you start comin' down off that high."

"Don't you worry 'bout me," Hannah insisted coolly, tossing aside the naked stem. She sorted through her bundle of blossoms and held one up with an excited squeal. "Look!" she exclaimed, as if Jonah should find some significance in it. "This one's yours! Here, take it!" He dismissed the gift with a wave of his hand, but didn't dissuade his sister from trying once more to grant him her peace offering. "It's your color. You're red, you know. Not like blood or even anger even though you sure get mad sometimes, and not like red for a slut or anything even if people have been callin' you that behind your back all your life."

"Guess you learned it from somewhere," Jonah grumbled. She didn't hear him.

"Yeah, definitely red. I dunno why exactly, but you've got red all around you right now, like a cloud or somethin', maybe an aura, I don't know, I ain't thought much about bein' a psychic but maybe I am, y'know? Red, red, red, Jonah's painted red, not by the sun 'cause the sun's yellow and everyone knows it ain't red, but your spirit's in this flower and I think you should take it and keep it close 'cause it'll remind you of who you are and God knows I think you're startin' to forget it. Don't forget it, Jonah." She thrust out the blood-red flower one last time with tears in her eyes, and for once, he saw a glimmer of life in them; he had no choice but to reach out and accept it. He slipped it into his back pocket but didn't smile appreciatively. Instead, he plunged his leg into the creek and waded toward his little sister.

"C'mon," he urged, more softly than he'd spoken to her in some time. "Let's get you home." He slipped his arm behind her back and lifted her out of the water with unsettling ease. She was a small girl, but not small enough to be so lightweight. He felt like he was carrying a dying child as she fell asleep in his arms, her breathing so shallow as to be completely silent. Her flowers fell to the ground and she sighed in her sleep, and though it was a hot summer's day, he clutched her close to his body to keep her warm, as her pale skin felt clammy and cold.

He paid no mind to his sopping wet clothes, or the way his jeans became abrasive and uncomfortable when soaked three shades darker. All he wanted was to set Hannah down on her own bed, toss a blanket or two over her spindly body and let her sleep it all off. He didn't even plan out what he'd yell at her when she woke up. In fact, he didn't plan to scream at all. That tactic had failed time and time again. And as he sat in an old wooden chair watching her toss and turn and whimper in unconscious pain, he cursed himself for his brazenness, and for not offering her the compassion she so desperately needed, but which a sadistic Gabriel Skinner withheld for his own pleasure, if he even had any at all.

*Kill 'em with kindness,* thought Jonah as he quietly shut her door behind him. *Guess Sundays ain't been lost on me, after all.*

••

Main Street was silent and still at that hour, without even a single parked car to be found resting beside the sidewalk. The cicadas had stopped their droning, and the ever-present chirping of crickets had given way to nothingness, reminding insomniacs that they often took such nocturnal songs for granted. The pointed steeple of the Southern Mercy Bible Church was a darkened tower, one just begging to be struck down by lightning in a scriptural apocalypse, cloaked in the same shadow that veiled the Reverend Shaw's heart from the light of modernity. A yellow streetlight exposed the only source of the startling disturbance that echoed down the sleepy road, past the black windows of struggling businesses: Levi, pounding his fist against a locked door, with a wounded Jimmy von Braun clinging to his other arm, his dark pants stained even darker with blood.

The front door of Family Medical caved slightly with each forceful knock, and the metal American flag that hung upon it, dangling from an old nail, clattered against the soft, faded wood. Even with all that noise, Levi elicited no answer. He'd known it was a longshot, expecting to find a doctor past midnight at a tiny private practice, but Jimmy didn't have the luxury of an emergency room. There was no such hospital to be found for miles in any direction.

"Come on, you old, chain-smokin' bastard," Levi muttered as he hit the door harder. "I've got your first real case in years standin' right here."

*"We're closed!"* shouted a crotchety old man from the other side of the door. *"Put a Band-Aid on it or take a goddamned Tylenol! You'll be fine!"*

"Ain't gonna be enough! He's bleedin' out right on your doorstep!"

*"Get yourself a sewin' kit, then! I'm sleepin'!"*

Jimmy groaned and worked up the strength to bark, "Open the fucking door, you useless, old fossil, before I sue you for medical negligence and have my parents' lawyers beat the shit outta your wrinkled, liver-spotted ass in court!"

Silence ensued; few dared to cross an irate von Braun, whose threats were rarely idle.

The door slowly opened to reveal a disgruntled Dr. Noah Lee, who stood at the threshold with a shotgun gripped tightly in his hands. Levi had half expected him to be wearing a floppy, pointed nightcap and carrying a dripping candlestick, hunched over with eyes squinted in elderly suspicion. Instead, Levi was met by a stocky, tan-skinned man in his early seventies, who'd fallen asleep in his black slacks and a plain T-shirt, his white lab coat draped over a desk behind him. He had an unusually full head of hair for a man his age, which had barely begun to gray; neither did he wear the oversized spectacles expected of a senior with ailing vision, but sleek, modern glasses that didn't comically enlarge his brown eyes like thick magnifying lenses. The doctor smelled of liquor and cigarettes, and there was a smudge of gray ash on his pant leg. He lowered the shotgun and pulled his dented pack of Byron Clays out of his back pocket, and ushered the two young men inside with a grumble and a scowl.

"Put 'im on the table," Dr. Lee instructed, shaking his head at the trail of blood across his carpeted waiting room. "His parents had best pay for a new carpet," he complained, and snatched up the round bottle of cognac sitting on the desk that should have belonged to a secretary, but had been unmanned for years.

"Fuck off," Jimmy cursed as Levi helped him up onto the exam table, before Dr. Lee could drape a sheet of thin paper over the cold metal. "Don't act like you're so poor. Being a doctor, you're second only to my family in this shanty town's social hierarchy."

"Ain't no one in this town pays their copay," the doctor explained, pulling up a rolling stool next to the table. He rummaged through a drawer, pushing aside an array of stainless steel surgical tools—knives, hooks and all sorts of instruments of torture—until he found what he needed: a cheap convenience store lighter.

"Thompson, give him my insurance," Jimmy said, struggling to pull his wallet out of his soggy back pocket. "This isn't socialized health care. Take my money and treat me, already."

"Put that shit away," demanded Dr. Lee, who waved away the shiny insurance card that Levi planned to offer him. "Billing those bloodsucking companies is too much of a hassle."

"There it is," Jimmy scoffed. "Like I always say, Thompson, poverty is the poor man's fault."

Dr. Lee put a cigarette to his mouth and lit it, blowing the smoke right in Jimmy's face; to his surprise, Jimmy wasn't bothered, and neither were his lungs. He plopped down on the stool and spun to grab long forceps out of the drawer, as well as a pair of scissors. As he guided the open mouth of the shears toward Jimmy's pant leg, his bleeding patient cried out in horror.

*"Not the pants!"* Jimmy screeched. *"They're worth more than your practice!"*

"Quit bein' a bitch," Dr. Lee grumbled with the cigarette still in his mouth. "It ain't like I'm amputatin' your leg or nothin'. And besides, your precious pants are ruined, anyway. They ain't even torn along the seam."

"Face it, man," Levi added, "they're a goner."

"Well, get it over with, then," Jimmy whined, "but gimme that cognac first. This is the most painful procedure I've ever had in my life."

"I ain't even started yet—"

*"The bottle! Now!"*

Dr. Lee shrugged and handed over the liquor, but before Jimmy could take his first gulp he asked the obligatory medical question: "Any medications or drug use, little girl?"

"I'd have an easier time remembering what I *haven't* dabbled in, grandpa."

"Pot?"

"When I can't sleep. Which is often."

"Pills?"

"Oxys, Vicodin, Percocet, Prince Valium—"

"Ecstasy?"

"Not since last Friday."

"Crack?"

"*Cocaine*, asshole," Jimmy corrected. "Crack's for blacks."

"Heroin? Meth?"

"God, no. Even *I* have a shred of dignity."

Dr. Lee's cigarette had burned out; he tossed the butt behind him into the sink and lit another, then continued with smoke rising from his nostrils, "I ain't prescribed painkillers in a damn long time, kid. Where in God's name are you findin' all this shit?" He cut Jimmy's slacks just above the wound and slid the severed fabric off his leg like shed snakeskin. His noncompliant patient winced in excruciating pain, and chugged what little was left of the cognac.

Jimmy snatched the cigarette out of Dr. Lee's mouth and took a deep drag. Seeing the doctor's disdainful glare, he tried to return it, but Dr. Lee asserted that he'd never had a cold sore in his life and wasn't about to get one in his old age. Though mildly offended, Jimmy answered the question: "That Skinner trash has got a whole pharmacy's worth in their living room."

Levi cut off the doctor's response and remarked, "I know you well enough to know y'ain't the type to knock on their front door."

"Of course I'm not. Do you *really* think I'd ever be caught dead with the likes of them? I've worked hard for my reputation as the baddest rich bitch in town, and I'd sooner let the paparazzi find me on the welfare line than handing the Skinners even a single, crisp dollar bill. These soft, manicured hands won't be getting scabies on *my* watch." Jimmy noticed Dr. Lee lighting up his third cigarette of the impromptu appointment, just before reaching for the forceps; he held out his hand, expecting the doctor to gift him with what most doctors would have harshly condemned. Sighing, Dr. Lee surrendered a fresh Byron Clay, and placed his lighter on the exam table.

"So no," Jimmy continued, swooning with the rush of nicotine to his brain, "I don't go there myself. When you're as popular and disgustingly wealthy as me, you send your emissaries to do that kind of dirty work for you. I don't need anyone thinking that I'm shooting up whatever it is those bottom feeders use, and I *especially* don't need my sexual prospects thinking I've got AIDS from sharing needles with the lower classes."

Then without warning Dr. Lee pinched the menacing shard of glass and yanked it from Jimmy's flesh, producing a dramatic howl that woke up all of Clemency. And worst of all for Jimmy, he dropped his half-finished cigarette right onto the floor. It was immediately snuffed out by the drop of blood it so fatefully fell upon.

*"Jesus fucking Christ!"* Jimmy blasphemed at the top of his lungs. "This is malpractice! I'll have your license revoked, you incompetent bastard!"

The funny thing was that most in Clemency suspected Dr. Lee had gotten his medical license revoked years earlier, for his consistent refusal to provide any sort of medication to even those patients who truly needed it. In his own words, it was "about time the human immune system got put to work again." If anything, he was simply tired of prescribing azithromycin to teenagers who woke up with a burning sensation when they took their first piss of the day. But even if he had been stripped of his legal right to call himself a doctor, he continued to practice anyway, as there was no one in the sleepy little town who had the nerve to call the Alabama Board of Physicians, if any of them even knew such an organization existed in the first place. After all, prayer was the best medicine.

"The worst is over, you petulant, little brat," Dr. Lee snapped. He turned away from a pouting Jimmy toward Levi, who'd been holding back laughter through the entire ordeal. He pointed toward a drawer on the far end of the room and instructed him to open it and find the sutures.

"I dunno what I'm lookin' for," Levi admitted.

"What, ain't you ever seen a needle and thread before? You'd better learn fast, kid, 'cause you're gonna be my nurse for this session, and I'd prefer not to give a blood transfusion today. Christ knows it's been years since I've stuck a patient." He waited impatiently as Levi produced a random assortment of medical supplies, rolling his eyes with each incorrectly identified tool. "And this is why helpin' a doctor out is a woman's job. Jesus H. Christ hangin' off the cross, if only you boys coulda been around for the good ol' days when ladies were nurses, not doctors."

Eventually, Levi found all the instruments they needed to stitch Jimmy up like a rag doll. Pulling the overhead light closer to the wounded leg, Dr. Lee asked, "You sure you don't need a bullet to bite on?" Instead of giving his patient a chance to express his concerns, he plunged the needle through Jimmy's split flesh, drawing out a startled grunt and a grimace, but little else. "I'm a little surprised you ain't refusin' treatment just so you can go get yourself a fancy Hollywood plastic surgeon," Dr. Lee chuckled. "I'll do my best not to leave much of a mark, not for your sake—I don't give two damns about your vanity, kid—but so your parents don't freeze my bank accounts."

"Smart man," Jimmy remarked, "even if you're on the verge of senility, which might even work as a defense in court. But don't get your colostomy bag in a twist about those stitches. This isn't my first scar, and at least I can cover it up." He held up his left hand to draw attention to a rough swatch of skin that was noticeably darker than the sun-starved fairness around it, which vaguely resembled the drooping, phallic shape of Florida. "If I can handle having this monstrosity in public view every day, I can take a scratch on the leg."

"That's a mean-lookin' scar," Dr. Lee said while he made another pass with the suture needle. "Burn yourself on a crack pipe? I'm sorry—*cocaine* pipe, as if there's a difference."

"There *is* a difference, and you'd know it if you hadn't taken chemistry class in the Dark Ages when they taught you how to turn lead into gold, and I bet you dropped outta that, too. For your information, *I* didn't burn it, my bitch *mother* burned it, when she slammed my hand on a hot stove after I called her 'old.'

"And this one!" he declared while pointing to a small dent on his brow, barely visible except to himself, as he was one to stare critically into a mirror for hours on end. "*This* is from when she tossed me in an empty bathtub and beat me bloody with a broom after I caught her secretly eating white bread." There was another souvenir from her alleged abuse: a tiny black spot on the fleshy part of his palm, just beneath the skin. "And *this* is what happens when your thundercunt mother stabs you with a pencil after you catch her cooking your father's books!"

Lucky for Jimmy, Dr. Lee did a fine job of stitching up his laceration, despite the long time it'd been since he'd had to treat such an injury, and over the weeks he would come to find that he couldn't add it to his collection of battle scars. He'd insisted on forking over whatever cash he had on hand as payment, since the doctor couldn't be bothered to file the paperwork required for reimbursement by his exclusive private insurance. Dr. Lee refused, however, although he eyed the two-hundred dollars with a tempted look; he found the strength to turn down a handout he called patronizing, but couldn't resist caving in to Jimmy's uncouth demand for another cigarette for the road. After all, his pack was lying in a pile of broken glass on the railroad tracks, and he was too concerned for his own safety to go back and retrieve it.

"Tell your skanky, disease-ridden friends I'm closed today," Dr. Lee requested as they walked out the door into the light of early morning. "I'm sleepin' in, and this ain't a free clinic to begin with."

"Thank God no one works in this town, and they're all still asleep," Jimmy sighed, pointing down at his embarrassing state of dress. "I'm walking around with one pant leg."

"Ain't no one's judgin', anyhow," Levi assured him. "They might even call you a trendsetter."

Jimmy smirked in agreement, but for such a talkative loudmouth, he suddenly fell uncharacteristically quiet. An awkwardness ensued as he struggled to find a way to express a sentiment he rarely made public, if ever: gratitude. "I guess I owe you a thank you, Thompson," he confessed, leaning forward as if to hug his friend-cum-enemy, until he regained composure and jutted out his open palm for a cordial, man-to-man handshake. "I'm not one for apologies, so don't expect one, not now, not ever. But I promise not to run you down next time I drive by during your pathetically pedestrian commute. Hell, maybe I'll even buy some seat liners so I can give you a ride home."

"I'll hold you to it," Levi promised, trying to hold back a satisfied smile, but with some difficulty.

"Trust me, I keep my word," Jimmy assured him, reaching into his pocket to find his car keys. He cursed when he realized he hadn't driven down to the railroad tracks in the first place. "I just hope you can keep a secret. I don't need the public knowing I have a generous side. So you'll keep your mouth shut, won't you?"

"Will do. Ain't no one to tell, anyhow. The poorest in town ain't got no peers, neither."

# 11

Sunday morning started like any other, marked by the rise of a pale sun on a yellow horizon, which soon glared above the swampy tree line, ready to oppress sleepy townsfolk for another long day. People rose from their beds with a stretch and a yawn, some cursing the blare of their alarm clocks, others praising that alarm as a call to prayer. Men donned suits and ties and slipped handkerchiefs into their breast pockets; women meticulously applied appropriate makeup with their hair still in plastic curlers, their tasteful, pastel dresses draped neatly over their beds, ready for wear; children found themselves forced into bathtubs, and stood on stepstools before bathroom sinks with toothbrushes jammed into their mouths. Main Street heard the ring of the church bells and the hushed scolding of uncooperative children, and all was familiar and routine. But it would prove to be a fateful day, which no one ever could have predicted. It marked a historic event in Clemency, Alabama, one that would go down in history, and infamy, forever: the von Brauns made their first, and probably only, appearance at the Southern Mercy Bible Church.

Their arrival was not nearly as elegant as they had hoped. The royal family sat idling in their polished Bentley on Main Street, waiting for the throngs of churchgoers to get out of the road. Jimmy fiddled in the back seat, his $1,500 sunglasses shielding his eyes like an insectoid Halloween mask; hangovers made such opulence a dire necessity, as the sunlight was just as bad as the flash of a paparazzo's camera. Sprawled out on the leather seat, he had his wounded leg thrust out the open window, and he tapped his foot in the air to the painfully loud electronica he blasted through his headphones. Devout mothers shook their heads in disgust and envy as they passed by wearing unflattering scowls, sickened by Jimmy's uncensored flamboyance, and painfully jealous of Charlene and her perfect blond hair.

For the first time in their lives they parked their car in the front of a parking lot. With so few cars in the lot next to Israel Pickens High School, it was a low-risk area for careless nicks and scratches on George von Braun's European-made pride and joy. The clicking of towering designer heels ushered the family in like the sound of approaching war drums. Having taken their time to adhere to the unspoken rule of fashionable lateness, they arrived at the front steps after the congregation had already taken their seats, sitting in specific spots they defended like animals protecting territory they'd pissed on. George and Jimmy swung the church door wide open, invisible to the pious inside; it was as if God Himself had held the door for Charlene von Braun. She crossed the threshold in a jet-black skirt and a black jacket, a black leather clutch in one hand and a white glove slipped over the other, with pursed lips and massive, dark glasses to block out the divine light of the God who was simply grateful for her presence that day.

Gracey DeRosa gasped in fear and snatched her rosary out of her handbag, frantically passing each red bead through her trembling fingers. SSG Eddie Sharpe threw his rucksack over his shoulder and headed cautiously for the door, willing to risk offending the Lord in order to avoid what he thought to be the signs of impending martial law. Abigail Foster held her hand to her forehead and fainted, falling back upon the pew with no one to catch her. Kneeling women who'd been gossiping with God opened their eyes and cut short their conversations just to lay eyes on the Whore of Babylon and her Beast of a son.

Jesus Christ himself couldn't have made a more spectacular appearance, even if shining white with the light of the Transfiguration. The von Brauns were royalty who never walked among the peasants, drawing stares and whispers from most, with rumors following them from New York to Birmingham. Had they finally come to church to repent for their life of meaningless excess in the North? Had Charlene decided it was time to step out of the way of righteously thrown stones? Or were they offering their son up to God, hoping that prayers and fiery sermons might straighten him out?

Over the course of the Reverend Shaw's illustrious career as Clemency's local Vicar of Christ, he'd never allowed himself to become distracted during a sermon. Even when ill-mannered little babies squealed for an hour, he maintained his composure; the one time a mother with a respect for propriety stood up and slapped her teenage daughter for slipping a curious hand into the lap of the grinning boy beside her, the Reverend didn't skip a single word. A message delivered in the glorious name of God could have been heard over rolling thunder, as it was as impossible to ignore as a blinding lightning bolt. A listener could have heard it on the battlefield booming over the agonizing cries of soldiers for their mothers, and the percussion of bullets from the jungle. His sermons had the terrible force of hurricanes that could level a household, the power of an earthquake that shook one to the core, and the same twistedness of a tornado barreling through Middle American towns. With dramatically ejaculated words, he could smite a reputation just as easily, unstoppable. Apparently, however, Charlene von Braun could quell a tsunami with a glance. For a second, the Reverend was at a loss for words. It was the most unnerving reaction of all.

Maybe the church really did fall silent, or maybe it was all in Jonah's head, but the world froze as the slender patricians made their way down the center aisle. He felt like Joshua staring up at the sun, held at high noon for a full day, with all sense of time erased by the hand of God. Charlene von Braun said nothing as she stood at the end of the pew of her choice: Jonah's, right in the center of the flock, with only the DeRosas at the end seat to separate him from whatever horrors might pour from Pandora's box, though Charlene would never be caught dead wearing a cheap Pandora bracelet.

*Shit*, he thought, looking to Levi. For whatever reason, he didn't seem bothered. If anything, he seemed ready to crack a smile, and that was just as disconcerting.

Charlene merely stared down at Gracey DeRosa with any hint of emotion obscured by her sunglasses. Gracey flinched, as though the baroness's eyes were two pistols held to her head, but avoided looking up at her prim assailant whose license to kill was issued by David Yurman himself. The von Braun matriarch soon grew tired of Gracey's fearful charade and coolly pulled off her shades, and slipped them into her clutch; her icy blues chilled the old woman to the bone, the color of the frozen lake in Hell's innermost circle. Gracey slowly turned her head and had no choice but to acknowledge her. Before Charlene could even utter a single, succinct command, Gracey obliged her and motioned for her husband to shift farther down in the pew, starting a domino effect that left Jonah with his little sister practically on his lap.

"The end seat's mine," Jimmy declared in a harsh whisper. "I plan on being the first one outta here after story time's over."

"The hell you will," Charlene snapped. "You'll repent to their imaginary friend for all the bullshit you've put this family through, and this nice, elderly couple will make sure of it." Without a simple "excuse me," she ordered the DeRosas to stand, so her family might slip in farther, with Gracey and Joe serving as an arthritis-ridden barricade to prevent any evasion of punishment on Jimmy's part. Charlene paid no mind to Gracey's shaking knees or Joe's tired grimace. Instead, she laid her eyes on Jonah and lingered at the edge of smiling, but never bared the teeth that Jonah half expected to be fangs.

"Hold my coat," she demanded, slipping her slender arms out of the jacket that cost more than the Young family's car. "You look clean enough."

Charlene draped it over Jonah's arm and sat down beside him with no intention of offering even a word of gratitude. He was her inferior, after all, and born only to serve her lofty kind, as a natural butler, or doorman, or footstool to be used at her leisure. As such, he kept his mouth shut, more out of concern for ecclesiastical propriety than respect for a woman whose physical beauty was obscured by the sickening cloud of smugness that followed in her wake.

Though she only bared skin on her long, slender legs (which seemed to make up roughly seventy percent of her full height), Charlene von Braun still managed to find sex appeal in her conservative, though fashionable, attire. Her high-necked blouse hardly contained her surgically engineered tits, and her pencil skirt accentuated a waist that was so unnaturally small as to be nearly invisible. She glanced over at Jonah, her manservant; for a second, in a rare show of unpreparedness before a woman, he froze. Charlene might as well have stabbed him in the heart with two menacing icicles. The frigid, rare blues were paralyzing as they scrutinized his body. She was the most intimidating feminine force he'd come to encounter, with a dark abyss for a soul that beckoned men to wander closer, so she might lock them in an icy cage. He felt guilty knowing that even in his fear, he was carnally curious. He forced a grin before looking away. With the Reverend's modest daughter as his new focus at the front of the church, he immediately began to feel warmth in his extremities again.

*"A schemin' slut like that will cut a man down like it's nothin', since people are just her pawns,"* Susan had warned Jonah at the library. He did his best to keep it in mind.

A pervasive and awkward silence ensued. The Reverend abruptly cut short his sacrosanct spiel on the intrinsic evils of gender integration in schools, because as much as he hated bearded Muslims and their multiple veiled wives, he still held in common their strictest and most medieval values, maybe more than he knew. He stared down with an unnamable fire in his amber eyes, leaving them with the alluring sheen of molten gold. Was he furious that he'd been so rudely interrupted by the 21st-century Jezebel (who was late for Sunday service, as well), or was he, too, enticed by an upper-class, nipped-and-tucked beauty who considered the word "modesty" trite and outdated? Certainly, his wife Victoria suspected the latter, as she stood to seize the podium and continue the sermon that had already slipped the minds of most.

Charlene von Braun laughed with a lilt that made even the most patronizing chuckle seem sophisticated. "Don't stop on my account," she advised the dumbfounded Reverend and his scowling wife. "Carry on."

On cue, the Reverend did as he was told. And as he carried on about the lost virtues of a golden age, when little boys had little to do with little girls in the classroom and at home, Charlene turned to Jonah and flashed an unfamiliar and somewhat unsettling smile. She gingerly patted his knee with a white-gloved hand and offered him a tidbit of privileged advice.

"Tone is everything," she suggested in a controlled, unwavering whisper. "With just the right intonation, you can get anything you want." If Jonah didn't know better, he'd have thought she subtly winked. A woman of her status, however, would never have done such a thing, at least while sitting next to the help.

Susan had said something else to keep him cautious: *"A girl like that don't give a shit about what others want or need, and she sure as hell won't stop harassin' a man till she gets what she wants."* It seemed Susan might not have been a crazy, old bat after all.

Together (or, less intimately, side by side) Jonah and Charlene suffered through what remained of the Sunday sermon. This was, unfortunately, quite a bit, as the Reverend had regained his faithful fervor, shaking his fist with newfound conviction. Charlene subtly leaned over to whisper in Jonah's ear, asking if the Reverend Shaw was always so verbose; when he nodded his head, too uncomfortable to speak aloud, she commended him for knowing the definition of verbose, because he was at such a linguistic disadvantage, after all— "Poverty can be a terrible speech impediment," she noted unapologetically.

For once, he wished he had less distractions to take his focus away from the sermon. Charlene proved to be an unmatched annoyance with her unwelcome commentary. The awkward stares she shot at him reflected silent criticism of his Sunday wear, and perhaps a bit of piqued interest in his youth, which her husband George no longer shared.

Jonah flinched when she grazed her slender leg against his, and he winced at George von Braun's suspicious glare when he noticed his statuesque wife offering a playful chuckle of an apology. Her sly grin was the worst of all, as it preceded her feigned adjustment of her stockings, which required the peeling back of her pencil skirt just an inch or two. That inch or two might as well have been a mile for a young man of Jonah's age, and he felt such guilt for looking.

Coffee hour came as it always did, with bespectacled, liver-spotted grandparents funneling into the social hall with boisterous grandchildren. Jonah felt like one of those first-graders, practically running toward Sophia as would an anxious little boy to his guardians. More self-reflective than usual, he found it curious that, consciously or unconsciously, he'd begun to turn to the preacher's daughter for refuge, both from the judgment of others and his own sordid past. She took him in, but not with open arms, of course. To extend her hand to take his in public would be an egregious breach of etiquette, bringing deep, traditional shame upon the pretty, amber-eyed girl whom the parishioners held in such high regard, and, even more detestably, the pious parents who reared said pedestal-worthy angel. A smile was the best she could give to Jonah, at least at that time.

"I ain't never been sexually harassed before," he confessed, glancing over his shoulder for fear of his assailant. "But I think I came damn near close today."

"How the tables have turned, Mr. Young," Sophia jested. Jonah frowned; she apologized.

"Pray your mama's got her eyes on the von Brauns today, and not me, her precious baby girl's white-trash suitor. I don't want no trouble from neither."

"Suitor?" Sophia snickered.

"Love interest. Not-so-secret admirer. Aspiring boyfriend. Whatever."

"I'm glad to see your sexual assault didn't damage your confidence," she joked in mildly bad taste; she apologized again. "Who's the perp, anyway? Please tell me it wasn't Jimmy. I'd be highly disappointed if an athletic young man like yourself could be so easily subdued by an uppity twig like Jimmy von Braun—a ridiculously tall twig, but a skinny little stick regardless."

"No, not that there freak o' nature. His bitch mother."

"Watch your mouth. We're still on hallowed ground."

"If that was true, she'd be a heap of ashes right about now—her son, too, and I ain't seen no flames lightin' up the place."

"I'm sure she's boiling up on the inside."

"I reckon you're right, but she ain't boilin' 'cause o' the power o' Christ."

"The power of Jonah Young, then?"

"You better believe it."

"Well, I don't," Sophia countered, cocking her head and squinting an eye with suspicion. "You're not as fiery as you think you are. Or maybe that fire just burned out."

"It's 'cause you done dumped holy water all over me, Miss Shaw. So what am I now, then?"

"A gentle light. But I won't lie: you're still bright enough to leave me blind."

It'd been a damned long time since Jonah smiled as wide as he did right then.

"And no wonder," he laughed, reluctant to let his heart bleed so publicly, "for Satan himself masquerades as an angel of light."

"I'm a better judge of character than that, and you know it. Besides, even he couldn't hide that hellfire in his eyes, and yours are anything but smoldering. I've never seen a flame with that pretty shade of green in my whole eighteen years." She looked across the room and scowled with distrust at the slender blonde who sipped her black coffee through a straw. "Maybe a nasty shade of blue, though. I hear it's even hotter than the Devil's red."

"Better grab the lidocaine, then, 'cause that one ain't dyin' down anytime soon, 'specially since she's fueled by steel-meltin', ultra-premium Deutschland gas at thirty bucks a gallon."

"I think you mean 'liter.'"

Then, like a bloodhound bred to sniff out the gamey scent of iniquity, Victoria Shaw, that raven-haired Lady Macbeth, tore through the crowd with the deranged eyes of a hungry carnivore. Jonah, however, wasn't just potential prey. He was forever destined to be eaten alive by the Reverend's ravenous pet, so long as he insisted on getting to know her daughter just a little bit better.

"If I stand real still, y'think she won't see me?" Jonah whispered through the corner of his mouth like a ventriloquist, his eyes locked on the snarling tyrannosaur whose stomping sent nervous ripples through his stomach.

"Just fix your face and you'll be fine," Sophia suggested quietly before greeting her mother with questionable enthusiasm. And as Victoria pulled away from daintily embracing her daughter and raised a finger to accuse Jonah of trespassing against her, she was interrupted by an evil from which no God could have delivered her.

"Victoria!" Charlene von Braun boldly declared from behind, not only catching the preacher's wife by complete, startling surprise, but simultaneously belittling her by using the first name of a woman she'd never met before.

Victoria, a two-faced master of courteous deception, turned to face a nemesis she never knew she had until that very moment. "Mrs. von Braun," she almost sighed. "I don't believe I've ever had the pleasure."

"Please, Victoria, call me Charlene. You don't have to act like I'm your superior."

"Well, Charlene, we have only one superior, and His name is God."

"I have to admit, I always thought his name was supposed to be Jehovah. 'God' is just a title, isn't it?" Charlene mused. "Much like 'Reverend's wife,' it can apply to more than just one person. It isn't necessarily unique."

"It is unique, with a capital G."

"I suppose it's really only useful on paper, then. Speaking of paper, how's the family business doing? Times are hard, I hear."

"I'm sure I don't know what you're talking about."

"Oh, please, don't be so modest. Success is nothing to be ashamed of. And if there's anything the two of us have in common, it's that we're both prosperous businesswomen driven by our desire for the finer things in life."

"'It is easier for a camel to pass through the eye of a needle than for a rich man to enter the kingdom of Heaven,'" Victoria quoted with a log in her eye.

"Well, with the right plastic surgeon, I'm sure you'd have no trouble fitting through," Charlene quipped, turning next to Victoria's daughter, who sported a look of abject terror quite unlike her mother's seething glare. "Your daughter's a very beautiful young woman, Victoria. You should be thanking Christ that she'll never need the bank-breaking amount of lipo it took to get my son down to a reasonable size." She held out a hand to Sophia, who accepted it timidly. "Very nice to meet you, by the way."

"Likewise."

Then it was Jonah's turn. Charlene smirked as she addressed him, as if the two of them shared some dirty secret that Victoria would no doubt assume to be fornication. "I haven't caught your name yet. Even with the handicap of that shirt you picked up at Good Will—no offense—you're still the only young man in this room handsome enough to court the Reverend's pretty little daughter."

"Jonah, ma'am. Jonah Young. And I ain't courtin' nobody, just to be clear." He insisted this with his eyes set on the Reverend's wife, not the platinum blonde he was both flattered and embarrassed to have been complimented by.

Victoria sternly agreed. "That's absolutely right, Mr. Young. You're not courting anybody, now. As you've so convincingly declared on many an occasion, those days are over for you, aren't they? And even if they weren't, a respectable woman like my daughter Sophia would never be so senseless as to let you even try."

Charlene scoffed at the thought. "I certainly hope that's not true, Mr. Young. If a boy your age isn't engaging in some healthy extramarital activity, then this country really has gone to hell. Just one more tragedy wrought at the hands of the Democrats."

"I swear, I ain't," Jonah reiterated, fearful for Sophia's reputation and his own personal safety.

"He's not," Sophia agreed, keeping the Fifth Commandment in mind (to not honor her mother was suicide), as well as the Seventh (adultery was a death sentence, at least in her family), while praying that she wasn't breaking the Ninth (was it false witness?).

"He'd best not be," Victoria concluded with venom on her tongue, ready to smash those sacred tablets right over Jonah's head.

"If you say so," Charlene replied with an incredulous shrug, but, for real this time, winking unnoticed at Jonah, who flinched. "You're certainly a conversationalist, Victoria. I must say, I've rather enjoyed this. But the Reverend Shaw's wife naturally must mingle with the rest of the flock now, I'm sure. Don't let me keep you from your followers."

"Congregation."

"Well, whoever they are, you won't get a dime out of them if you don't sweet-talk them. Don't let those tithes slip through your fingers on my account. It was a delight to have met you. Perhaps we'll meet again under less pious circumstances."

"Till then." And as Victoria Shaw walked away with clenched fists and teeth gritted, she experienced the humiliation of public defeat for the first time in her life.

"You're welcome, Mr. Young," Charlene said smugly, adjusting her jacket as if she'd just thrown a punch and disheveled her ensemble. "I think it goes without saying that you owe me one."

"And yet you said it anyway," Sophia interjected, exuding that primal, feminine jealousy that caused all women to defend a living territory even if they'd never really claimed it in the first place.

"And why wouldn't I, Miss Shaw, when a verbal contract is binding in the State of Alabama? I do hope we cross paths again, you two, and not in court, should Mr. Young choose to shirk his legal obligations to the generous woman who rescued him from public damnation. It was a pleasure. You can go back to taking those purity rings back off, now. There isn't a suit or a dress on earth that would match such pointless antiques."

She made the faded wood floor into an haute couture runway as she glided off without a second glance, her back turned, rendering Sophia a soon-to-be-forgotten acquaintance and Jonah merely a memory to be recalled while in bed with her impotent husband. There was no denying that Jonah was grateful for Charlene having sabotaged yet another attempt by Victoria to keep him on his side of the line in the sand. But despite that welcome relief, he couldn't help but worry that he'd been saved from the sinister clutches of one woman just to wind up in the wandering hands of another, when all he wanted was to be in Sophia's arms.

He knew this to be true, harboring not a single doubt; it was his faithfulness that made the slight stirring in his slacks all the more painful. He was a man, after all, subject to the whims of biology just like anyone else, but he would fight his instincts with every Bible verse he could dig up in his head. They were evolutionary (or creationistic) impulses that he could not act upon: not with a high-class cougar, which would break what little of Sophia's heart he'd managed to win thus far, and not with Sophia, whom he would never defile so brazenly.

"I think you might be right about her. Where can we get a list of sex offenders in this town?" Sophia joked, though her tone led Jonah to believe that if she had the chance to brand Charlene with the title of sex offender, she would, simply to keep him chaste and available.

"Ain't enough water in the Jordan to make me feel clean right about now," Jonah muttered, in need of a good shower to wash away the psychic filthiness of Charlene's advances, the lingering dread that was iconic of any run-in with Victoria Shaw, and the nervous sweat on his brow that his long hair did little to hide.

"Is it a baptism you need, or an exorcism?"

"Don't matter. Either way, we're gonna need a shitload o' holy water."

••

"You've gotta get rid of those shoes, Thompson. Those atrocities are so beat up that even going barefoot would be a better look for you. After all, you've got that whole blond farm-boy thing going for you, even if you don't have a tractor to ride to work. Or a sheep to fuck and call your girlfriend."

Jimmy von Braun had turned on the cruise control to match Levi's walking pace as the two of them slowly made their way southbound on Main Street, with AlaCo's flickering sign behind them and the pointed steeple of the Southern Mercy Bible Church ahead. He pulled down his car's sun visor instinctively, not to block out the glare of the sun, but to hide that looming edifice, to which he reacted like someone to a dog who'd been bitten as a child.

"But seriously, though, those shoes have got to go."

"Seein' as I ain't got no spares, I reckon you gotta have plenty to lend out to the poor and needy," Levi replied, looking down at the shoes he hadn't replaced for far too long.

"Give a man a fish, he eats for a day; give a man free shit and a welfare check and he'll vote Democrat the rest of his life. No handouts from Jimmy, no sir! But you should count your blessings on one hand, Thompson, because today's the day I make an exception."

"I don't care if one pair outta thousands—"

"Hundreds. Because of my cheap mother."

"—Okay, *hundreds*, is gonna go unnoticed from your closet. I don't want 'em."

"Good God, Thompson, even I'm not so cruel as to give season-old shoes to charity. It doesn't matter if no one in this Southern slum would know the difference. It's a matter of principle! No—we're going shopping."

"Ain't got the time."

"You're off the clock, now! After an honest two hours' work! I deserve to feel good about doing something spontaneous and nice for the voluntarily less fortunate!"

"You ever consider I might have a social life?"

"Oh, you're meeting that hot, white trash boy you're always running around with? Well, he can't come. There are limits to my generosity, naturally, unless he's promising some sort of physical repayment, in which case I'd buy him a completely new wardrobe and force him to sign a prenup."

"I doubt he'd accept a deal that fair."

"His loss. Come on, Thompson, if you want me to admit the shameful truth once again, then here it is: I owe you one. And a von Braun never owes anyone shit. Other than the Feds. Don't you dare repeat either of those unsavory facts—especially the one about my interpersonal debt."

"I release you from your debt. There—happy?"

*"Just let me buy you some goddamned shoes, Thompson."*

Taken aback by Jimmy's uncharacteristic, hardheaded intention to drop a few hundred dollars on someone who would have been satisfied with the cheapest pair of Nikes he could find, Levi conceded, "Alright, alright. I'll humor you just this once. But I'm returnin' them the second I get the chance."

"You do that. By all means, spend the money on whatever it is people of your class spend it on—toilet paper, maybe. But that'd be a hell of a lot of toilet paper for what we're gonna be spending today."

They traveled southbound, flying down Main Street; Jimmy rolled down the window and thrust a middle finger in the direction of the Southern Mercy Bible Church. Clemency soon gave way to untamed woods and open road, which soon gave way to open windows, violent blasts of humid summer air and vicious disco beats, which soon gave way to the contraction of twenty-two miles into about eight, maybe seven (had Levi not been gripping the door handle for dear life, he might have paid more attention to the time). Stepping through the hole in space-time that Jimmy had torn open with his lead foot, Levi found himself striding across the parking lot of the only mall within fifty miles of Clemency, toward which all desperate teenage girls across the region turned to face during prayer.

"Of course, we've got limited options here, but I'll make the best of what we're working with," Jimmy promised as he grimaced in abject disgust at the passing throngs of chunky girls in offensively short shorts. He glanced at the mall directory, a glowing map freestanding between two overfilled trash cans, and groaned, "Jesus Christ, we're in an even worse situation than I thought."

"What, no Express?"

"I'm insulted, Thompson. No—this is gonna be the shortest shopping spree I've ever gone on, which might be a good thing for your sake, because you didn't pack the tent, water bottles and sleeping bags required to survive how long I'd normally keep us here."

"Well, what's first?"

"Follow me, and don't ask questions. I've never been in such a barbaric shopping center before, so I don't think I'd have any answers for you. We're in this together, Thompson. Grab your machete and get a move on it."

The shoe store they (or rather, Jimmy) chose had a sign crafted of tinted red plastic letters that were meant to have a backlight, which someone had forgotten to turn on. It was called SOLE PURPOSE, and it was packed with young local athletes in shorts and black high socks who ogled sneakers that promised to make them run faster on their college tracks, though their price made such a claim fairly dubious. Jimmy went straight for the rack along the wall that presented the most expensive merchandise, which Jimmy lamented as being pathetically economical. He even went so far as to apologize for bestowing such a worthless gift upon Levi, who couldn't have cared less about how cheap the selection might be, because he never wanted a pair in the first place.

"How about these?" Jimmy asked, pulling off the shelf a pair of dark blue tennis shoes with white highlight stripes. Before Levi could even answer that it didn't matter to him, his imposed stylist threw the pair of shoes on the ground, muttering, "They'll be out of fashion in a matter of weeks, I'm sure—if they're even in now. *These* are much better." He presented a second pair, which he immediately rejected on Levi's behalf. The third rejected pair made its way into the hands of an employee who was quickly growing tired of Jimmy's willingness to disdainfully litter the floor with unused merchandise. The entire display had been emptied by the time Jimmy stumbled upon a pair he felt he could stomach, saying that it was far from ideal that he'd have to bite the bullet and charge such mediocrity to his platinum Visa. He spoke as if he himself would be wearing them. It was the least he could do, of course, to let Levi take a walk in his shoes for once, even if those shoes were disposable in his eyes.

They were black, simple but refined, at least as far as Levi was concerned. They did seem the most practical, as he was guaranteed to suffer the daily spill of any number of automobile-related substances on his feet, and their dark shade made such embarrassment a little less public. Jimmy insisted that they were waterproof enough to deflect any stain that threatened to ruin his day, though Jimmy sought waterproof shoes for protection against spilt alcohol, and perhaps vomit, should his Percocets prove too hard to keep down.

He slapped the shoebox upon the counter and swiped his card without even checking for a price. "Give us a pair of scissors, while you're at it," he instructed the cashier, "because my friend here plans to wear these out the store." After snipping off the tags he demanded that Levi surrender his old, desecrated pair for destruction. With Jimmy holding the shoes delicately by their untied laces, a look of complete revulsion upon his face, and Levi sitting on a bench pulling on his new ones, the moment of truth had arrived.

"Excuse me, would you happen to have an incinerator out back?" Jimmy asked.

"…No," grunted the pimple-faced Hispanic boy at the register, whose nametag identified him as John ("You're not fooling anyone, *Juan*," Jimmy grumbled)—John the employee with no furnace with which to placate his bossy customer and rid the world of Levi's old sneakers once and for all.

"A box crusher? A trash compactor? *Something* to erase these shameful abominations from history forever?"

"*No.* "

"Fine, I'll settle for a trash can."

John held out a small plastic bin that he kept hidden beneath the register, filled with crumpled receipts and scraps of tissue paper;

Jimmy turned to Levi, asking, "Any last words?" to which Levi had no response and no eulogy, and in a split second, Levi became a little less poor, as a sign of his poverty disappeared into the depths of a plastic bag.

"What a burden to have lifted off your shoulders!" Jimmy exclaimed, more outwardly pleased than Levi. He had, after all, just performed an act of disingenuous charity, but it was charity nonetheless, and he could easily write it off on his taxes that year. Levi, on the other hand, merely looked down at his feet and couldn't help but crack a subtle but noticeable smile.

There were many things of which Levi had yet to be convinced, like a future free of his mother's vices, or the prospect of a job that paid him more than just enough to starve a little more each day. The one certainty he recognized and embraced, however, was that he looked damned good that day, walking on rubber air, not once comparing himself to the heir to the von Braun fortune who strode beside him not as the hero, but as the sidekick. And as girls smiled coyly at the pair, he thought, for once, their blue eyes were set solely on him, the young man who so willingly made himself an object with no higher thought or feeling than an honest satisfaction with himself, and with the God who created beauty, loved beauty, and blamed not His children for loving the same—the beauty of others, of the world, and of themselves. After all, what good was modesty in a town where belief was measured in gold on a beaten breast, by the size of a Sunday hat, and not by the length of time a poor boy spent in the dark, in unconscious prayer, away from the glares of those who judged with blind eyes wide open?

••

Sophia the Reverend's daughter likened it to willingly entering the lion's den, stepping unattended into Jonah's bedroom. She had no male chaperone, save him—no father to protect her from hormonal predators, no brother to defend the honor that she could easily defend herself, if it even needed to be defended at all. Jonah had only just begun to tidy up his room before her arrival. He held the already open door for her and offered her a seat on the edge of his bed, the one feature he'd actually prepared, however sloppily. He pulled up a chair that looked suspiciously identical to those out at the kitchen table. It had occupied an empty corner of his room that he hadn't managed to fill, flanked by a neatly stacked tower of worn paperback novels, and a used guitar he'd never learned to play.

"Play me something," Sophia requested, drawing attention to that neglected instrument whose only use was to collect a thin patina of dust. Had it been some antique classical guitar, such a sight might have been appropriate. Sadly, it wasn't.

"Never learned how," Jonah admitted, plucking two untuned strings before sitting down.

"How about those?" she said, pointing to his growing literary Tower of Babel. "I hope you've at least learned how to read."

"Just 'cause I ain't much of a Bible reader don't mean I'm illiterate, although your mama'd beg to differ."

Sophia leaned over to grab hold of the guitar and strummed a chord; the dissonance made her cringe, like she'd just been subjected to the screech of nails on a chalkboard, but much more offensive, because at least one expected nails to sound unpleasant. The off-key strings, however, were an insult to her ears and to the God who made them.

She quickly went to work and tested each string, tightening them as needed until she came as close to harmony as such a beat-up instrument could allow. Finally, the notes fell into place, each assuming the necessary vibration to turn Jonah's room from a house of aural horrors to a recital hall, which Sophia filled with perfectly plucked melodies, to which she hummed softly, without words. She did not need them.

"Y'ain't never told me you can play," Jonah said, pulling his chair closer.

"'Sing to him, sing praises to him; tell of all his wondrous works!'" she quoted, though she sang no prayers. The delicate, precise movements of her fingers were writing scripture in sound, transforming the Word of God from a divine whisper in her mind into a form the whole world might experience and embrace. Her dark hair fell over the guitar and swept across its resonant strings. Jonah didn't recognize the song she played, and without words, he couldn't hope to guess its name. But at that moment, he was in sync with the rhythm of life itself, carried by the current of its music across universes and ledger lines.

Then she sang, timidly at first, sweetly, like a trickle of water not from the stone of Jonah's heart, but over and upon it, eroding it into a smooth, shining gem. Anyone else would have deemed it the voice of an angel, but Jonah couldn't bring himself to utter such a cliché. It was the voice of a devil, echoing in those dark places deep within him, leaving him quaking with fear and despair: fear that he no longer knew who he was, having been redefined by one, pure note, and despair that he could not bring himself to reach out and touch her, that girl who'd torn down his walls with a word and left him naked, not immodestly, but like a newborn, vulnerable and blind to his bright new world.

She sang of a God whose eyes fell upon the smallest and most common of birds, who smiled upon such a creature with joy; her song was a sparrow's song, to be sung as she took to the skies, carried on humble wings, not those of an eagle. Around her, within the walls that could not cage her, not a single sound rang out; the shaky, rattling fan in the parlor quelled its tinny clatter, and the grumbling of the old ice maker in the freezer fell silent for the first time in Jonah's life, all out of respect for that girl's crystalline voice, and in awesome reverence before the Almighty she praised with simple sincerity. Jonah, too, felt his mind grow still, and all he could do was watch, as though there were nothing else in the world, save her. She sang of God, but God seemed almost an afterthought. That day, Jonah became an idolater, and Sophia was his graven image of the most numinous perfection, before which he would prostrate until she commanded him to rise.

"Don't be quiet on my account," sneered that smiling chanteuse, bringing her spellbound listener back to the here and now. "I know you're used to talking like it's going out of style."

"Only when there ain't nothin' else to fill the silence, Miss. But with a song like that, ain't no reason to be loquacious."

"Loquacious? Compulsive garrulity isn't going to get you the girls."

"Ain't it the truth. Ladies like big boys, not big words, don't they?"

"The type you're used to, at least."

"And a hell of a lotta good that got me," he groaned, rolling his eyes at an old high school jersey hanging on the wall. Its once bright ultramarine had long since faded to a gray that hinted at a bolder past, the color of the sky that unstoppable jock once thought to be the limit. The surname Young, however, was the same white it'd always been. It was the one thing left unchanged, stitched permanently upon a uniform that could have been a gown worn proudly at a college graduation, but instead was a reminder of a young man's misplaced priorities, and the trophies that now proved to be little more than shiny plastic.

"Athletic ability isn't anything to be ashamed of," Sophia insisted. "It's good to be well rounded. You'll live longer because of it, too, if the Good Lord doesn't strike you down before you're thirty for your self-admitted transgressions."

"Academic ability ain't nothin' to be ashamed of, neither, but at the time, I thought an A on a paper was like a goddamned scarlet letter."

"If it weren't for your casual blasphemies, I'd admire your basic awareness of 19th-century American literature."

"Ain't like I read it by choice."

"But you did read it, didn't you? That's more literate than most."

"Yeah, I read it," he admitted, as though reading an old staple of American education was as shameful as submitting it to a book burning. "And when the teacher read my paper on it, she decided I didn't know a lick of English, and probably learned to write my name like I was copyin' a sloppy drawing, not writin' real letters."

"Bad handwriting doesn't mean you don't know your own language. And besides, you're a boy. It isn't really your fault. That'd be like blaming a crippled person for not running an eight-minute mile."

"In that old bitch's defense, two-hundred misspelled words out of a total o' seven-fifty'd make me think I was gradin' a mongoloid's essay, too. And the word goal was a thousand. I ain't tried at all."

"I'm sure you had your reasons," she remarked with a crinkle in her brow that didn't imply judgment, or even pity. It almost looked like she was peering through a window into a past best left behind, with every intention of shutting it, but no means to do so. Her glance was so removed that Jonah felt she was reflecting on her own memories, not the ones he recollected for her in a tone that revealed nothing but regret. She refocused her eyes and returned her attention to him, and only him, asking, "I'm not casting stones here, but I have to ask: why'd you do it?"

"Fail on purpose?"

"Let everyone think all you had going for you was on the outside. That you were nothing but a dumb jock who couldn't even read an issue of Playboy without a tutor, not that you'd ask for one."

"Everyone wants to make a name for themselves. I just picked a shitty name I can't shake to this day. Ain't no one's gonna forget it when I made such a fuss about them rememberin' it."

"Fair enough, but you haven't answered my question."

Jonah paused, at a loss to explain the motivations he'd never had to identify before, to himself or anyone else. He was generally the type to act on impulse, and saw little use in analyzing why he did something, or why anyone else did something, chocking it up to a basic desire to be happy and not be second-guessed about it. Now he imagined Sophia sitting with a yellow notepad, scribbling observations as he rambled on, considering what chemical compound might be appropriate for a condition of his sort. Surely the good Reverend and his wife would prescribe him a mega-dose of religion, written on a page out of the Bible. But if Jonah were to self-medicate as he was inclined to do, he'd say the only course of treatment was sitting right before him at that moment, on his bed, with no carnal intentions.

"Y'ain't never really knew my sister back then, did you?"

"I barely even knew you. And that's who I'm asking about, not your sister."

"Everyone always knew she was the smart one, even when she was in diapers. She could draw, she could do math real early, and she played a mean recorder in elementary school."

"You're deprecating yourself again."

"Ain't never said she was actually smarter than me. But she was the baby o' the family and everyone watched what she was doin' way closer than what I was. When she got good grades they came to expect it from her. Poor girl got put on a pedestal with no way to climb down."

"Setting standards for your children isn't what I'd call bad parenting."

"Funny, since it ain't like I set the bar that high before her. Maybe her teachers just wanted her to prove they ain't failed in teachin' the

Youngs after they got nowhere with me, 'specially as I got closer to graduation. And maybe Ma 'n Pa saw it comin' that my halcyon days were about to end, so they pushed her into havin' a future, since mine had nothin' in it 'cept for dirt pay and a crazy ol' spinster for an employer."

"You know you've got more than that, and even more in store for you."

"Yeah, but I can count them blessings on one hand. One finger, even."

"And what's that, then?"

"You."

She smiled, but did not blush. He'd told her something she knew, had always known, not because it was predictable, but because it was as certain as a sunrise. But she was not one to take such things for granted, though she'd been lauded her whole life for being the Reverend's daughter. They viewed her as an unsullied example for all lost youth, whom churchgoing parents both praised and envied, as she was the child they could not raise, nor even conceive. She was a reminder of their failures and own daughters' flaws. Had she not heard that she was Clemency's truest blessing, who would deliver the townsfolk from a nation that taught its sons to be heartless, and its daughters to be whores? How foolish might a lost boy like Jonah be, should he have the arrogance to assert that she was a blessing unto him, and not all of mankind?

But even with such knowledge of her own importance in the hearts and souls of men, she expressed not even the slightest hint of conceit, no sardonic giggle at the compliment she'd no doubt been paid before. She did not reject such a compliment, but neither did she agree. There was something in her eyes, however, that made Jonah think that this time, this instance of genuine flattery, meant something more: like that sunrise, guaranteed and often dismissed by those who saw it every day, had finally been seen not as clockwork, but as the giver of life it had been all along.

"If there's one thing I'd ever ask of you, Jonah Young, it's that you don't go and end up deriving your worth from someone else, especially not me," she said softly, her amber eyes locked with his hazels, not tensely or with intensity, but shining with the compassion and wisdom her saintly parents could never offer to anyone, him least of all. He listened more closely than ever, smiling in understanding when she went on, "There's a poem I think you'd like—one line comes to mind, if I remember it right: 'Give your hearts, but not into each other's keeping… And stand together yet not too near together: For the pillars of the temple stand apart, and the oak tree and the cypress grow not in each other's shadow.'" He grinned; she mistook it for slyness, and added, "No, it's not biblical. And if you tell anyone, I'll just deny it."

"Might as well be—an improvement, even: *The Prophet*, right?"

"You're always so close to impressing me, and then you blaspheme."

"Surprised the good Reverend's wife ain't snatched it off your shelf and burned it. With a name like Kahlil Gibran, I reckon she'd think you're readin' some Muslim shit."

"A Maronite might as well be, since they haven't paid their dues at the Southern Mercy Bible Church." She looked to the pile of books on the ground, scanning up their spines from floor to near eye-level: *Misery*, *Animal Farm*, *Brave New World*—*The Prophet* was not among them. They were a hodgepodge of themes and genres that revealed his multifaceted soul, which too few had sought to see, or were permitted to. She inquired as to its absence; surely he'd read it, and not just read it, but had taken a part of it with him.

"I lent it out to Levi," he explained, gripping the bottom of his faded blue shirt. "Thought it might do him some good and give him a push, but he ain't never read it. His choice, and loss." To Sophia's surprise, he began to pull his shirt up and over his head. A girl of her unrivaled modesty should have averted her eyes as though he'd shamelessly shown his nakedness, but she only half looked away, peeking out of the corner of her eye. "Don't worry, I ain't about to show you much. Left my fig leaf in the drawer, anyhow. But look."

She immediately recognized the words that decorated the smooth skin of his torso, running line after line in colonial cursive down his ribs. The black letters against fair skin, ornate, but not ostentatious, spelled out the beautiful thoughts of a poet long since passed. His words were lost to many, who could have learned so much from them, had they chosen to fill their emptiness with eloquence, not reality TV. She read them aloud, but in a whisper, as if reading from scripture, inscribed as permanently as stone upon the living, sculpted marble of Jonah's warm body:

*"Forget not that modesty is for a shield against the eye of the unclean.*
*And when the unclean shall be no more, what were modesty but a fetter and a fouling of the mind?*
*And forget not that the earth delights to feel your bare feet and the winds long to play with your hair."*

Unconsciously, she ran her fingers along the path of the words, like a blind girl reading braille, finding new sight in the verse he read backward in the mirror each morning. He gave it little thought those days. But her fingertips, tracing the loop and flourish of the letters, etched his skin like the first pierce of the tattoo needle years earlier, searing with that same intent, but without the pain. He felt she was writing those words upon his body for the first time, and the only agony he felt was in not being free to pull her close and kiss her.

"Ironic it's hidden, ain't it?" he jested.

"Maybe just a little too metaphorical," she proposed as an alternative, without taking her eyes off his body. They reflected no lust or teenage hunger, but simply adoration, as one would adore something beautiful, though Jonah couldn't discern if that beauty was that of a dead poet's words, or his own uncovered form. "Keeping your passions hidden from everyone else like that. If only they knew what you were carrying with you all along."

"Well, consider yourself part of a select few," he concluded, pulling his shirt back on.

"I'm honored, Mr. Young," she professed with her head bowed in humility. In reality, she was looking down upon her own body, with an air of scrutiny and wistfulness. "You know, high school would have been a lot easier if I could just cover up some unwanted 'gifts.'" She did her best to allude to her undeniable bustiness, without crossing the thin line of tastefulness she hadn't fully drawn with Jonah yet. She'd never worn anything to accentuate them. In fact, she'd tried for years to draw attention to her eyes alone. She was lucky she needed no makeup to make their amber hue warm and bright. Sadly, both boys and girls in Clemency rarely looked up.

"Ain't no girl in Heaven or on Earth who'd reject such a blessing," Jonah insisted, fighting the innate, male impulse to admire the subjects of her grievances. He was proud of his newfound ability to do so without the blushing and a tortured wince.

"If they got called the things I was, then they'd be knocking on a surgeon's door at three in the morning to get them removed."

"Don't tell me you tried that."

"No, I didn't. My mother would never suffer her daughter to mutilate God's perfect creation. Not that she didn't tell me to cover myself like a Saudi to deter the prying eyes of men—and jealous women with a penchant for gossip, for that matter. Did me little good with that."

"There couldn't have been that much to talk about. Pardon my manners, but you're a virgin, ain't you?"

"Of course I am," she snapped defensively. "Do I need a signed affidavit from an OB/GYN to get anyone my age to believe me in this town?" After seeing the surprise and immediate regret in Jonah's eyes, she promptly apologized. After all, he meant no offense. He didn't even lower his gaze in shame, for fear of looking like a pervert—that is, a normal young man in Clemency, especially of the churchgoing kind.

"Look at me, years later and I'm still on high alert," she sighed in frustration at her own defensiveness. "I guess being called a slut every day for the majority of your adolescence is enough to keep any girl on edge." She rolled her eyes and scoffed, "And Heavens, imagine the rumors that'd fly if I'd been seen with the likes of Jonah Young back then."

"Hate to break it to you, sweetheart, but them rumors are probably spreadin' all through town as we speak."

"Idle hands, idle talk."

"The Devil's playground."

"Then Clemency's the Devil's Disneyland, I figure."

Never had a truer statement been spoken; God knew Jonah had made that wretched town his amusement park for too long. But those tickets came at a steep price, one he'd paid in self-respect. He'd never get it back by demanding repayment, a refund in dignity. He'd have to earn that wealth himself. Sophia, however, as the Reverend's heir to the keys of Heaven and Clemency's most beloved daughter, didn't have such an expendable reputation, and Jonah was terrified that if she were to associate with his name, she'd find herself out in the streets without a dime in her pocket. His heart in that pocket had little value and couldn't pay for what she'd need to survive in the harsh world he'd come to know over eighteen years, covered in graffiti with words and names they both hoped to wash away with blood, sweat or tears, whichever was necessary.

"At the risk o' soundin' like a broken record, I'm gonna say this again: bein' with me won't bring you nothin' but trouble." He'd changed, and they both knew he'd never mean to hurt her. But regardless of his personal transformation, he couldn't ever change the town. Clemency was stuck in its ways, and they were ugly and cruel. Leviticus looked like a slap on the wrist next to the merciless flogging of a church lady's gossip.

Sophia grinned and declared, "It's about time a good girl got herself into some trouble in this town by her own volition."

"Wouldn't be the first time."

"Maybe not, but you might prove to be the best thing for me. Let the past be the past, and let's face the future together. After all, if Jonah Young can change, why can't I?"

••

The sun was low on the horizon when Jimmy von Braun pulled his luxury car up to the very end of Shiloh Path, and it gleamed off the pearly paintjob he refused to tarnish by traveling down that bumpy dirt road. "One smudge and I'll be forced to take my beloved to a car wash, where I'll risk having her leather-lined pockets picked by thieving Hispanics," he explained as Levi opened the passenger door to disembark, clad in sharp, new shoes. "I'd walk you to your door like a true Southern gentleman, but then I'd risk an equally horrific smudge on these shoes, and no amount of manners is worth desecrating a pair of Pradas worth more than a lifetime's wages in this glorified homeless shelter."

Needing no escort, Levi didn't protest. He bid Jimmy farewell, offering an obligatory "see you soon" that, despite everything his gut told him, he actually meant to some degree. And as he made his way home down that quickly darkening path, with its dried mud and tire-track moguls, he realized he was stepping with unconscious caution, because he was just as concerned for his new shoes' safety as Jimmy would have been. He debated cursing himself for it. He chose not to.

No, he wasn't rich, and he'd likely never be. Wealth wasn't in the cards for a young man of that place, that time. In any other nameless dot on a roadmap mistakable for a pencil mark or fleck of dirt, someone his age would have looked upon the world around him and declared it teeming with possibilities. Every road was a pathway to a big city and big dreams, and every run-down public bus that passed by was just a mobile stepping stone to his own shiny, imported sports car, earned through bloody, worn fingers, and long nights spent fighting the nightmarish urge to give in and surrender to life's innumerable obstacles. Levi was no such man.

He had little doubt that somewhere across the country, in a crowded city bustling with suits and showbiz, or a quiet suburb with uniform houses and immaculate lawns, the American dream hadn't given way to simple, inane daydreams, dreamt pointlessly at gas station pumps in the scorching midday heat. Those who'd attained the success promised to the displaced children of many nations couldn't possibly accept the validity of his experience, his reality. If he'd found himself slaving away just to afford a life of sheer stagnation, it must have been due to some fault of his own—that is, if he wasn't outright lying about his failures, simply to undermine the ambition required of all patriots, which was as obligatory as a salute to Old Glory.

He refused to believe he had any part in it. He did not necessarily blame his nation, but Clemency, an ugly tear in the Bible belt, was just as guilty as the sinners it condemned for sport and self-assurance. It held him back like St. Peter's fetters or coarse ropes that bound one to a whipping post, while his mother, as drunk as a Roman soldier, gave him thirty lashes a day with the whole bloodthirsty town watching idly from their bedroom windows. The guilt fell on those sadists and psychos around him. Without them, he'd surely have escaped by now.

In a sick way such powerlessness was comforting, like when an ill man, wasting away from some unknown affliction, finally finds a name for the condition he can do nothing to cure. If Levi were to die in Clemency with the cancer of zealotry choking every organ, at least he'd know there was nothing he could have done differently to save himself, for the laying on of hands was just holy snake oil, and his mother kept his chemo pills locked away in the liquor cabinet.

*No matter,* he told himself as the moldy floral cushions of the porch bench came into view, lit by the fading twilight. *If I'm gonna face my death here, I'mma be dressed to the nines.* Or at least his feet would be. After all, who could dress him better for his own funeral than Jimmy von Braun, whose entire somber wardrobe was made for delivering eulogies, if not just for last season's couture?

With death on his mind he passed his foot over a fat, brown beetle, leaving it hovering above the graceless creature. Had it been inside the house he would have labeled it a cockroach, worthy only of swift extermination by whatever means necessary. But outside, it was just a beetle that mistook the looming podiatric death threat above it for the shadow of a cloud. Levi was prepared to drop the anvil on the unsuspecting insect, but refrained, unable to do so. Of course, the virginity of his shoes was his primary restraint, but his hesitation ran deeper than mere vanity. The bug was beneath him, and not just beneath his foot. He pitied it. It was short-sighted and barely conscious, subject only to its most basic biological drives: eat, reproduce, defecate. It was all too reminiscent of the mindless townsfolk who would lay waste to its kind without a second thought, but their instincts, programmed by biblical writ, were only superficially more complex. They ate of Christ's body and drank of His blood, and devoured the mangled carcasses of their social prey; they reproduced in large numbers, being fruitful and multiplying, to breed an army for God; they defecated in the form of bastardized verses and judgments antithetical of their Messiah's most fundamental teachings. Levi had always resented them. But now, for the first time, he called them cockroaches.

The creaky steps he ascended were unworthy of the feet upon them, as were the pale green lichens that grew among their bald spots of peeling, white paint. The aging mosquito nets were unforgivably inadequate, as the holes in their mesh allowed biting insects to draw his blood like homeless thieves, of which they were undeserving, as a common drunk was of a fine wine. And the squeaking front door was too plain, its past white now sullied with dust and gray streaks of mildew, with no ornate glass portal to distort the image of its resident with frosted panels and muted colors. And to think, he was just wearing one pair of expensive sneakers, the only ones he'd ever owned, and didn't even buy with his own money. He had no money.

But on that day, he was a young, sandy-blond patrician among mousy-haired plebeians. Jimmy had made him that way. Levi wasn't really grateful for it. It was a reward he knew he'd always deserved, but thought would be denied to him by all those who were jealous of the potential they saw in him, but that he did not recognize until then.

If two shoes, not even designer ones, made him feel so superior, then how powerful did the von Brauns feel, with closets filled with thousands, and a mansion in which to hide them, like lofty misers hoarding chests of glimmering gold?

All his life he'd been told his riches awaited him in Heaven, to which no amount of money on earth could ever compare.

The meek were never as meek as one was told. At noontime in the boisterous school cafeteria, under the watchful eyes of mummified lunch ladies who were as snippy as they were shaky, Levi, Jonah, and two other dirt-poor kids would congregate and engage in the most bizarre form of competitive dick-measuring: fighting for the title of the most destitute. It made little sense, neither then nor in hindsight. The red-headed Paul Leister claimed victory one month after having completed a two-and-a-half-week streak of wearing the same pair of ratty jeans. Gad Robertson, a chubby sixth grader who eventually quit drinking soda, shed the weight and grew up unexpectedly handsome, was the poorest for a few days when he repeatedly used only a single, folded slice of white bread for his grape jelly sandwiches, because there wasn't enough left at home to last till Friday, should he eat traditional, two-slice sandwiches. Jonah triumphed when he didn't eat lunch for two days straight, although Levi had always suspected he'd done it on purpose. But in the end, Levi held the record, and no one even came close to challenging his legendary status. This was after his father was out of the picture. Before then, he'd have won far less often, though still enough to stay in the game.

He supposed they'd kept up the competition to cope with the sobering fact that they'd never have the nice Gap button-downs guys wore to the school dances, where boys and girls stood an enforced minimum of three feet apart at all times. Earning the title of victor was better than being called a loser, even when both referred to their parents' embarrassing income. Had Jimmy known him then, he would have been appalled by their pride, as if they were white trash boasting about whose house had the most cockroaches, counting down to the very last unhatched egg in a darkened drawer. And certainly Mama would have chastised him for his behavior if she'd known, because he was not praising his own material lack as a virtuous state of spiritual grace, but for his own selfish insecurity, and this was a slap in the face not only to his overworked single mother, but to God.

However, that evening, Mama was enjoying a break from her fruitless labor, though how much of it she would recall in the morning, no one could say.

The parlor couch was her throne, but she was no queen; she was the evil sorceress who'd poisoned the rightful monarch or left her in a dungeon somewhere beneath the Southern Mercy Bible Church. And just maybe the holy seat of her own mind had been usurped, and she'd been stripped of her divine mandate as queen mother of their home by the stinging demon in a bottle that sat before her, prideful and mocking upon the coffee table. Whiskey's victim, a slave who didn't know she was enslaved and thought her chains were lifelines, was not dressed in garments fit for a woman of her potential. She reclined in a housedress, a pale pastel reminiscent of her waitressing apron. She propped up her feet on the cushions, her nails still painted the same bright red that complimented her bold, classic lipstick on Sundays, but the polish was beginning to chip, and she was in no state to touch them up without staining the sofa red, like blood. And when her son stepped through the rickety front door with footsteps lightened by quality footwear, she was ready and eager to draw such blood.

"It's late," she began calmly enough, taking a cursory glance at the small clock hanging on the wall, above her collection of worn records. It'd been her mother's, his grandmother's, and they'd only recently fixed the old thing. After Pap had gone, the clock began to tick a little slower each day, until it came to an eventual dead stop.

"The sun ain't all the way down yet," he noted, as if it made any difference.

"Real perceptive, ain't you?"

"I try to keep at least one eye open, if only to dodge whatever train wreck's headed my way." He was feeling a little feisty that evening, like he could outrun her with ease should she bolt at him with a knife or an open palm. After all, his shoes were made for sprinting, and his fight-or-flight drive was always primed for takeoff.

The brittle springs of the old couch whined as she began to sit upright, though she had some noticeable trouble. "Count yourself lucky, boy, that I'm tired as all Hades," she advised, her words crawling sluggishly through the unconditioned air, as fatigued as she was. "I been workin' since last night and ain't got no rest on account of it."

Her jaded son knew it was a lie, but it was one she believed. A woman of God never lied to others. She only lied to herself—about the cruelty of those who cursed her, and her own fictitious innocence.

"Wish I could say the same o' my own son," she lamented, not as a failure of a mother, but as a good mother who was at the end of her rope with a lazy, undisciplined child, "since he ain't man enough to put in the work to take care o' his own mother, when she ain't gettin' any younger." It seemed she only aged when it was convenient to do so. Under all other circumstances, the good Lord stopped the passing of time just for her, like the sun over Gibeon.

"Y'ain't stinkin' up the house like an Arab oil field tonight and I don't see no stains all over them clothes I bought you"—she hadn't bought them—"so don't bother tryin' to tell me you been half-workin' for two whole hours today. You're about as good a liar as y'are a child to be proud of."

"Ain't no one in this family got a damn thing to be proud of. Y'can't go boastin' about your son's college degree or how much money he's makin' and God knows I can't brag that I had a happy childhood and lovin' parents. Instead I got me a martyr. So we're in the same sinkin' boat, ma'am."

"Y'had a good childhood, till your Pap gone and left us. Now I got me no choice but to pick up the pieces, so count your blessings," she commanded with a half-empty glass in her hand, the ice clinking as she subtly wagged it at him. "I ain't the softhearted type and I ain't sorry for it, even if y'didn't grow up to be the disciplined man anyone else woulda been. I followed the Bible and done raised you right, but there just ain't no hope for you, and now I don't know what to do with you, takin' up space and air without doin' nothin' in return."

"Y'could let me leave and never look back."

"I'd sooner sell my soul to Satan," she snapped without a second's hesitation. "I got me a right mind to board up these windows, put a padlock on the door and toss the key in the Gulf."

"Just toss it in the collection box. You'd never see it again."

"And that's the kind o' worldly thinkin' I shoulda been shieldin' you from all along. This ain't a godly world and it's gone and corrupted you, boy. Children don't show their parents a lick o' respect, they goin' round drinkin' and cussin' and adulteratin' when they think ain't no one's watchin', and I swear, boy, I curse the day you gon' tell me you been lyin' with that good-for-nothin' best friend o' yours. And look!" she barked with a hint of condescending laughter, pointing at her son's new pair of shoes. He didn't look down to acknowledge them and embrace them as anything out of the ordinary, because for anyone else, sporting fresh kicks would have been as routine as a snake shedding its skin. "Where'd you get them shoes from? I trust and pray, boy, that you ain't gone and spent what little money you got on those, when we got bills to pay, which you done run up in the first place."

"I didn't."

"So you stole 'em, then? I took you for simple, but not a criminal!"

"I didn't steal 'em, neither. Didn't even ask for 'em. But I got me some friends who ain't so poor. And even if they were, they wouldn't be droppin' their paychecks on liquor."

"I taught you better than to take handouts from no one but God," she hissed through gritted teeth, like air pressure from a just-cracked can of cheap beer. "You let 'em give you an inch, and they gon' take a mile, one way or another. Only a matter o' time before they come lookin' for somethin' in return, and it ain't never nothin' good. You ain't never gon' see me in debt to no one person"—banks weren't people—"and I ain't never gon' let us get chained to this wicked world. Thank God I ain't let your Pap take us outta this here town or you woulda come out even worse."

"That's just like you, ain't it? Well, y'can hold on to the past as long as you want like it's a goddamned rock in a storm, but y'ain't gonna keep me there with you to rot. What kinda person lets herself get so comfortable bein' poor, anyways?"

Mama scoffed at the sound of her son patronizing her, as if he himself weren't in the same sinking canoe. "Y'think your life woulda been so different up north? Lazy is lazy, no matter if it's in the country or the city, and God's a-watchin' ever-where y'go, shakin' His head at that lost sheep who sold 'imself off to wolves with a stinkin' smile on his face."

"Call 'em what you want, but I'd rather die with 'em than live in misery with you—ma'am," he sneered with a cutting boldness. His mother's eyes grew wide and her fists clenched with what was as close to hatred as a mother could feel toward her own ungrateful child. Had she not been held hostage by that small amount of poison at the bottom of the glass before her, she would have hurled it at his feet like a grenade. He walked away unscathed, untouched by a blast of shattered glass shrapnel, and took refuge in his darkened bedroom, so confident (or brazen) that he felt no urgency in even closing the door.

When he woke up the next morning blessing the rising sun for the first time in a decade, he found his new shoes in the kitchen trash can, doused in sour milk and the putrid slime of black bananas. He had no choice but to wear church shoes to work, and a look on his face as sour as Mama's garbage.

# 12

THE CLOCK STRUCK SEVEN and the Reverend took off his priestly ephod, for the Lord's Southern tabernacle was to become the town hall, where he would preside over its hearings as its divinely mandated Judge of Israel. He served as their leader in all spheres of life, and this was just and fair: there was none other among them worthy to carry such a burden, and what a heavy and frustratingly dull burden it was.

They were weak, spineless and pathetic, incapable of making any choice beyond choosing what to wear for when they'd stand before their beloved Reverend. Their eyes reflected their inadequacies more than their jumbled, simple utterances ever could. One bloated woman in the front stared at him with the look of a rejected child, who believed that no one but God would ever love her—she was probably right, as no man could stomach the thought of lying with her. An astigmatic man in the second row nodded his head in mindless agreement at every declaration the Reverend made, no matter how insipid—every line he ever read from the screenplay of his life had been written by others. They were just two of many, who were helpless without Jeffrey Shaw. He found it unsurprising. To lead was his lot in life. It disgusted him.

"When are we convertin' the cellar into a Sunday nursery, for the lil' ones durin' services?" asked an old man whose wrinkles were like the Mariana Trench, and who wore a pale red T-shirt bearing the name of an old football team that didn't exist anymore. "We put our money in for that collection two months ago, if memory serves me right."

"Victoria and I realized that services are for e'eryone, no matter how young. If y'can't get your lil' ones to behave on Sundays, then perhaps y'ain't bein' the right 'n proper parents the good Lord done charged you to be," the Reverend scolded, striking insecurity in the hearts of Clemency's young mothers and fathers. Distracted by their parental failures, the thought of wasted donations passed out of their minds. Their money wasn't wasted, however. Victoria was looking stunning as ever with a new diamond necklace strung about her slender neck.

"How 'bout that new back door?" a lifelong smoker croaked, her dry, puckered lips radiating a circle of fine cracks. "We been pushin' through that there front door for years, now, and it ain't no simple task with so many of us."

"Think of it as time for socializin' and greetin' your brothers 'n sisters in Christ Jesus while you're waitin' patiently in line," the Reverend countered, inspiring guilt among the pious but antisocial, and those who simply didn't care to stand on the two cankles God had blessed them with. The two handsome, gold cufflinks he sported that evening were a worthier purchase than a new doorway, anyhow.

Were they really so naïve, or were they just outright stupid? It was as though he were cursed to be an eagle-eyed prophet leading the blind, or a frustrated, once well-intentioned teacher trying to make a class of bumbling retards just a little more normal. He'd known such anthropomorphic fleas all his life, since the first time he was presented to his father's congregation as a newborn, ready for baptism in the name of the Father, the Son, and the Almighty Dollar. It seemed he was destined to plunge others in the same waters of baptism just as his father did; there were times, though, that he felt Satan holding his hand on their heads just a little too long, and on his weakest days when his flock's simplicity really irked him, he thought of keeping them underwater.

Death always played a prominent role in his religion (what was resurrection without it?), but his father's, especially: he put his own life at risk every Sunday evening, holding a hissing, striated snake in his two hands before a small parlor filled with gullible, devoted sheep. He was the Divine Wrangler, God's appointed head of the cultish Sect of the Conquered Serpent, who was immune to snake venom and impervious to total poverty, as the only thing deeper than the basket he kept his sideshow pets in was his collection basket. He toured the mountain regions of southern Appalachia with a band of straggly bearded disciples; all he was missing was a covered wagon plastered with fantastical ads for some bottled cure-all. His beloved serpent Lucy always stayed with him in the passenger seat in a wicker basket. She was his money maker, and a far greater asset than the plain-faced wife whom he made sit in the back seat, whose only use was in giving him a son with his father's striking eyes, and in cooking some mean roadkill.

Lucy had an understudy, a snake of a similar species, though not a single soul could tell the difference, save the Reverend Simon Shaw and his young son Jeffrey. This second hissing stage prop had the same distinctive stripes of red, black and yellow, but in a different sequence than good, old Lucy's. The simple people of the Smoky Mountains never noticed, not once in all their years of profitable proselytizing through farms and foothills. Now, any zoologist could have told them that Sadie, the red-yellow-black body double, was frighteningly poisonous. The members of the Sect of the Conquered Serpent clearly knew this as well, as their invincible preacher demonstrated with sacrificial rats and rabbits, before swapping the snakes to prove his own supernatural immunity. But that same zoologist would have promptly dismissed Lucy as a harmless milk snake. This the faithful did not know, and that was the Divine Wrangler's greatest trick.

He taught his son Jeffrey everything he knew, which his own father, Saul, had passed down: how to fake tears at key points in a sermon to drive in some profound revelation, and when to make his voice shaky and likely to crack, to show the overwhelming emotion that came with divine communion. Perhaps his most ingenious act was the use of potassium thiocyanate, loaned to him by a friend in the film industry, which he painted on his palms before service to make himself a bleeding stigmatic on cue. With that clear chemical on one hand and a bit of ferric chloride on the other, he'd clap his hands together in celebration at just the right moment, and then— Praise the Lord!—he'd instantly suffer the holy wounds of Christ Jesus himself. After all, the marks of the crucifixion were as vital as a man's signature on a personal check. Lying was a violation of the Ninth Commandment, of course—not even his father would deny that. But lies for the sake of promoting the faith and kindling spiritual devotion were permissible, even admirable, and the money that came with such pious fraud was just an earthly reward for those good and godly deeds.

"The pagans lie to their chil'ren 'bout that damn Santy Claus," he used to grumble when his innocent, young son questioned their sanguine subterfuge. "Ain't nothin' wrong with a white lie, 'specially when it's for the flock's own good."

One thing Simon Shaw wouldn't lie about, however, was his distaste for his son's girlfriend and bride-to-be: a raven-haired girl named Victoria McCrimmon. That was one light of truth he wouldn't hide under a bushel basket, even for the sake of his horny teenage son who'd rather get married than fornicate outside the bonds of holy matrimony.

Her family had heard of the Divine Wrangler and his power over the most lethal of serpents, and his miraculous faith healings of planted paralytics and people with colds, not cancer. When they came to one of his services, they were not the perfect, impoverished parishioners Simon would have hoped for and preyed on. Mr. McCrimmon showed up in a pinstriped suit of unspeakable cost, and the Mrs., a surprisingly matronly woman who was likely a rich Georgian dowager, sported so many iridescent pearls that it seemed she'd singlehandedly driven all species of oyster to extinction. They sat quietly in the back row, never shouting a socially obligatory *"Amen!"* or even mumbling a personal supplication under their breath. They only stared, their dark eyes smoldering with some hadean judgment, as though they were agents of the Devil himself, sent from the lowest depths of the Pit to discern whether the Reverend Simon Shaw was a good enough liar to serve the Prince of Lies. Their presence at his small revival left him unnerved and insecure. His sermon that evening was the most lackluster of his career.

The McCrimmons approached him when the last religious hyperbole had been declared to thunderous weeping and applause, waiting patiently in line behind a crooked young woman with cerebral palsy who would have given up her meager life's savings to receive the Reverend's gift of the Holy Spirit. Seeing the stoic couple behind her, Simon refused the meager wad of bills the girl tried to slip into his hand; for the first time, his outstretched hand was stopped by a crippling guilt. The McCrimmons shook their heads in silent disenchantment. Simon was taken aback. Even the poor girl on wooden crutches who left unredeemed harbored less disappointment than that cold-hearted couple.

"There's a story from Scripture I'm sure you're familiar with," Mr. McCrimmon began with no introduction but a tug of his silk tie, as if to remind Simon of his fortunes. "A poor widow put two small, copper coins in the offering box, and Christ Jesus himself called her the most faithful, because she gave everything she had in good faith. It isn't right to reject such an admirable offering. If anything, you may have just denied her her just reward in Heaven."

"I pray her faith isn't shaken," Mrs. McCrimmon sighed. "Nothing can dismay a believer like finding out that her preacher's a faithless hypocrite, or that his little pet snake couldn't even kill a squirrel, let alone a man."

"She doesn't have to learn all of those unsavory facts, though. Neither do her family, her friends and the whole congregation. In fact, you can keep Appalachia in ignorance without a worry in the world," Mr. McCrimmon promised without making eye contact with the nervous Reverend, polishing the face of his pocket watch with his thumb. "We have a proposition for you. And we think you'll find it quite compelling."

While the three prophets of the Most High went off to a back room, where the McCrimmons strong-armed the Reverend Shaw into surrendering a third of his followers' tithes in exchange for their keeping his shameful fraudulence a secret, a curious Jeffrey meekly approached their statuesque daughter Victoria. She held a black Bible in her left hand and a tall glass of iced tea in the other, from which she sipped casually while Jeffrey spoke his graceless salutation, peering at him cynically only through the corner of her eye. She largely ignored the useless banter that tumbled off his teenage tongue, until, in his desperation without even realizing it, he began to speak in a tongue that she readily understood.

"…And my father's doin' so well in his ministry, he's set aside $20,000 for me. 'Course, I'll only see it on my weddin' day, and that ain't anywhere close to bein' set yet."

From that moment on, they were deeply and inseparably in love.

Every month his father wrote a check to the McCrimmons that might as well have been signed in his own boiling blood, while Jeffrey and Victoria held private Bible studies so frequently that they should have had the whole book memorized. And every month, the Reverend grew more disgusted by his son's infatuation with the toxic fruit of his masters' loins, and on the day that they declared their engagement with a fetching diamond ring (formed of metamorphosed coal, the same coal mined by the faithful who paid for it), the Reverend finally disowned his son and declared him worse than an apostate, for he had disobeyed his father, and had wounded him more fatally than a rattlesnake bite to the heart.

"Envy can tear a family apart," Victoria said to her silent fiancé, stroking his hair while he lay pale with stress in his bed.

"Is that what it is? Envy?"

"You'll be a better preacher than he'll ever be, and with the right woman at your side, you'll be unstoppable."

Jeffrey awoke in the middle of the night to her absence; he found her in the back parlor, the color of fiery candlelight dancing upon her face, which sported a smile that would have looked natural on both angels and devils alike. Lucy slithered up her arm as though it were a slender branch on the Tree of Knowledge of Good and Evil, her basket open and empty upon the ground. Deadly Sadie was still trapped in her wicker prison, but Jeffrey could hear her hissing. Before long, he couldn't tell the difference between that serpentine hissing, and Victoria's entrancing words.

"I've always been told I'd be a preacher's wife. And this beautifully wretched creature knows it. God has kept me safe, so I might make my vows before him with your hand in mine."

"Lucy's harmless," Jeffrey reminded her. "Sadie's the one to watch out for."

"And so are we, my darling."

The next day, the Reverend Simon Shaw lost his favor with the Almighty God, and like a flash of lightning, the serpent in his hands lashed out and sank her fangs deep into his arm. He didn't worry for his health. It was his pride that sustained the worst injury, as he froze before his congregation, who looked as though they might reach into the collection basket and take back their donations, as he was no longer worthy of their faith. The Divine Wrangler had been stripped of his divinity, and showed his true identity as little more than a cheap magician. No one noticed the subtle change in Lucy's characteristic colors that afternoon. Simon broke into a cold sweat and collapsed to the ground, dead as a doornail.

Women screamed and jumped atop their folding chairs; one brave man stomped his boot upon the serpent's head, crushing Satan beneath his feet. The Reverend's homely wife fell to her knees in despair, crossing herself in Christ's name, and choked out a prayer of repentance for her dishonoring her husband, who was no doubt smitten by God as a punishment for his wife's disobedience (she was in favor of her son's engagement). No one in that chaotic room knew that Lucy had been an innocent creature all along, hidden away in a back room in a basket—no one but Jeffrey and his young bride-to-be, who consoled her fiancé with a hand on his knee, but displayed little reaction other than a subtle grin, as easily overlooked as Sadie's ominous rings of red, yellow and black.

The faces of those broken believers, frozen and contorted with the fear of God, never left Jeffrey's memory, burned into the back of his eyelids with the same hellfire his father promised to all those who disbelieved. But if there was one face he'd never proven able to erase, no matter how hard he tried, it was that of his pitiful, cowering mother, who submitted blindly to her husband as the Bible commanded her, up until the very end, and then blamed his death on her own disobedience: that is, quietly approving of his son's choice in a woman, more readily in her head than out loud. For the rest of her tragically subservient life she harbored unshakable guilt for the part she played in his defeat at the hands of the Enemy. Every wrinkle each year brought to her hardened face was another line in the sand, on the wrong side of which she'd always stood, but never endured the final stoning she felt she so undeniably deserved.

The ever-frightened and trembling people of Clemency were no better than the desperate fools his father had duped into faithfulness and serfdom to his godly title of Reverend, which he handed down to his son like thin blood in a dynastic family line. Their lives were as irrelevant and meaningless as those of the poor farmers and tired coal miners that made up the sickly body of the Sect of the Conquered Serpent; it was his job, his duty, and his curse to give them meaning. He knew better than they ever could hope to, the meaning of life beyond the impenetrable cloud of all its painful mysteries. They were Hebrews wandering in the spiritual desert of the American South, and he and his kin were the family of Moses and Aaron, the sole mortals deemed worthy enough to look upon the face of the Lord and not perish.

Yes, his pillar of cloud might as well have been produced from a fog machine, and his pillar of fire just cheap fireworks. Their money bought Victoria gifts of gold and jewels that even the Queen of Sheba would have coveted, and he and his wife shifted their accents as effortlessly as a prophet allowing his tongue to be guided by the Holy Spirit of God. But it was all for the greater good. They all had riches waiting for them in the next world, both those who followed his word as law, and he who judged them in that sleepy Southern town. It was unfitting for a leader to reject a leader's pay, even if it was thirty pieces of silver for the betrayal of honesty. They needed him, and all the white lies he shed along the way like Sadie's pale snakeskins. And they should have counted themselves lucky that they'd never had to see that venomous serpent bear its fangs, save when he and his wife spoke that one hour each Sunday morning.

••

The crack of the shaky front door against a dusty wall broke the solemn silence of the old farmhouse. It was as blasphemous as the clatter of a crowbar smashed into the stone portal of an ancient tomb. But unlike a duo of brazen tomb robbers, Levi and Jonah would enter through that cobwebbed doorway safe from a dead pharaoh's curse, as the farmhouse harbored no royal bodies, nor priceless treasure to be guarded by arcane magic. The only curse upon Levi's head was the guilty reluctance he felt while standing at the threshold, over which Jonah stepped without a care. It was, after all, Jonah's foot that kicked open the door that he'd expected to give far more resistance, hanging on rusty hinges.

It was his idea, not Levi's. He was scoping out somewhere new to bring the Reverend's daughter, for nothing more than quiet conversation and hand-holding far away from the Pharisees she called her mother and father. If she were anything like Levi, she'd advise Jonah against violating the memory of those who once lived there. Levi, however, couldn't ever hope to get him to listen. He didn't have the anatomy for it.

Any good tracker would have read his footprints in the dust and judged that he'd entered slowly, with one of three mindsets reflected in his steps: great caution, paralyzing reluctance, or pitiful cowardice. Caution was a necessity when walking on rotted floorboards, their weak spots hidden beneath green mold and dirt; reluctance was natural for anyone who believed that trespassing on a once beloved home was as sacrilegious as desecrating a corpse. And was he a coward? He didn't think so. Cops rarely made an appearance in Clemency. The Law of Moses was readily enforced without blue shirts and handcuffs. Crotchety, old Judges with a penchant for gossip did their jobs just fine. And besides, a nice tie or bonnet on Sunday was a more intimidating sign of authority than a gold badge, anyway.

The cloudy windows, through which Levi had peered countless times, offered a limited view of what really rested in morbid silence inside that forsaken farmhouse. They were the milky white eyes of a dead man, which once reflected every emotion, thought and memory he held dear and personal in life, even at the hour of his death. Now that the light of life had left them, they obscured any sign of who he was, whom he loved and held close, save those vague and superficial details that one could infer from picking his pockets and rummaging through his wallet.

"It's a damn shame," Levi muttered. He could have been talking about many things.

More than one timeline ended at that house: a personal history, and an untold story stretching as far back as the Civil War, both of which converged sometime in the mid-20th century then hit a dead stop at the edge of the page. It was easy to imagine that the pictures lying amid broken glass had been shaken from the walls by the thunderous rumble of cannons out in the field. The floral sofa, with pink flowers faded to a mildewy brown, still had a familiar depression in its left cushion, where the master of the house sat to watch his sons and daughters play with rag dolls and wooden guns on the parlor floor.

These were modern additions, of course. But even in those modern times, there was no television, and nor had there ever been one. In place of a TV stand there was only a single bookshelf, tall and slender. Levi ran his fingers across the brittle books and found a good number of cookbooks, teaching the culinary arts of diverse cultures across the world; one book on traditional American tarts and pies had the most damaged spine, broken from years of loving use. That baker's husband collected an entire shelf's worth of World War II history and reflections on Christian thought. They had their hobbies, as well, like origami and kite building, and distilling whiskey from corn grown in their own backyard.

"Ain't as much of a damn shame as Levi Thompson taggin' along with the most spoiled douche in town," Jonah quipped, testing the sofa with his hand before sitting down. The second he touched his behind to the soggy, stinky fabric, he stood straight up. The wall he opted to lean against was in danger of collapsing from the force of his shoulder.

"Ain't like I got much to show for it. The one perk I got out of it is sittin' in the garbage out back."

"Waste of a perfectly good brick o' Colombian coke, wouldn't y'say?"

"Coke or clothes, I still ain't a dime richer."

The shards of broken glass jingled delicately as he dragged his foot through the pile on the floor; the thought of a piece getting wedged in the treads of his worn-down shoes made no difference. He'd have almost preferred to go barefoot. Bloody, cut-up feet would heal. Scuffed, beat-up shoes would only get more scuffed and beat up, and no amount of bandages, not even a mile-long strip of gauze, could cover up that ugliness. There really was no one to impress, though, other than himself, and he normally wouldn't have cared. There was a very fine line drawn between self-respect and vanity, and he was just a child learning how to hold a crayon.

"You just watch yourself," Jonah warned as Levi trod through the broken glass that looked like cut diamonds. "When the upper classes come down from their tower to start mixin' with the likes of us, it's 'cause o' one o' two things: fake charity, or exploitation. And either way, they're takin' advantage, for praise or slave labor."

"Ain't no one in this here town's praisin' him unless he takes up the cross and repents, and I'm sure as hell not workin' for him—already a slave at the gas station, and I can't serve two masters."

"Neither can he. Money ain't a solid base for friendship when there's only so much to go around. Sooner or later, someone's gonna get shorted."

The unmistakable scent of Jonah's cannabis drifted across the parlor, the air of which was already hazy with dust; sunbeams pierced the cloud of curling smoke, invisible until just slightly obscured. It was like incense lit in the name of the departed, to be burnt in the silent tomb of the farmhouse, though those blessed dead—if they'd even really died—were anonymous, completely forgotten. He held out the once virgin joint whose cherry glowed red in the haze, but Levi was unreceptive, too busy sifting through debris. A faded photo had caught his eye, one of several lying at the base of the wall, still in broken frames. He'd found faces to put to the nameless.

He held the wrinkled Polaroid reverently in his hands. Rainwater, like warm tears, had blotted some of the ink, turning the summer shore in the background into soft watercolors. The woman in the foreground stood in a dreamy Monet painting, her mocha skin lit by pastel sunlight. The white polka dots on her navy-blue dress were clear as day, untouched by the elements that made the edges of the photo fade like tunnel vision. Most striking of all were the gray eyes that looked straight into the camera, or perhaps at the man who held it, seeking to preserve their rare hue forever. He'd artfully succeeded.

"Pretty lady," Jonah remarked after a quick glance, and just as quickly, he returned to inspecting an aging, dark wood liquor cabinet, topped by a fragile bouquet of dried daisies. Not a single bottle had been taken off its shelves. They hadn't been opened in quite some time.

*Summer, 1970* read the delicate cursive note on the back corner of the photo, written in pencil. It committed to memory what might have been the young family's first seaside holiday: a baby, sporting the defiant grin of a two-year old, sat in the alabaster sand at his mother's sandaled feet, encircled by a coral reef of plastic shovels and polished seashells. A wide-brimmed cloth hat covered his dark curls, striped with white and the pale shade of the sea foam right behind him. All he needed was a catamaran to carry him off to some island Neverland, where the sun might darken his skin and the glass soda bottles his mother held would never go dry. No such island existed for Levi, who took in every detail of that immortal photo as though he'd been there and couldn't quite remember it without help. Of course he hadn't. There were no whiskey bottles buried in that warm sand.

He tucked the photo away in his pocket. It was his one act of grave robbery that afternoon. Had he been asked, he would have said he was rescuing it from being forgotten by history. Otherwise, it would slowly be wiped clean from Clemency's memory by worms and rain.

••

There was something missing on one middle shelf in the Christianity section of the Swayne Public Library. For the sake of graceful symmetry, it had to be found. It was imperative. The maddening, empty space mocked the librarian from between two other books: the one on the left, penned by the medieval proto-Nazi Heinrich Kramer, was a translation of the *Malleus Maleficarum*, a witch-hunting field guide; across the mysterious divide, the book on the right was a transcription of the perpetually pissed-off theologian Jonathan Edwards's "Sinners in the Hands of an Angry God." In all likelihood, that vacant spot between them was reserved for some antique commentary on the righteousness of repaying an eye for an eye. But there was always that slight chance that maybe—just maybe—it was meant for a book on Christian mercy, or brotherly forgiveness. That was what was missing from the heart of Clemency's faith, at least.

There was plenty that was deserving of being purged from the soul of that small town, which one was inclined to call sleepy, though it was quite vigilant in the face of heresy. The first book Jonah pulled from the cart of strays might have helped in that urgent cleansing: *The Complete Idiot's Guide to Demonology*, shamelessly titled as an appeal to bored kids, overweight paranormal researchers, and Protestants who were too proud to seek out a Catholic's expertise in rescuing their teenage sons from the unclean spirits of chronic masturbation. It was possible, however unlikely, that the superstitious garbage it contained had the power to rid Clemency of its demons once and for all. Out of the curiosity that arises in the stupefying fog of boredom, Jonah opened it to a random page to see if he might glean some insight into the mind of a self-proclaimed demon hunter, who peddled his knowledge for the price of an oversized paperback.

It seemed that a brass crucifix, two pints of holy water and a dose of blind faith were all that was needed to banish most evil spirits back to the outer darkness. However, for those rare few regents of Hell who had the strength to endure an amateur's remedial incantations (Gabe Skinner came to mind), such an exorcism required nothing less than a comprehensive demonology kit, available on the author's website for a modest $79.99. It was a small price to pay for the ability to free oneself from the Devil's snares and from greasy white trash who frequented methadone clinics in lieu of Black Masses and had a wicked lust for underage souls.

Jonah had a cheaper option than an overpriced box of worthless trinkets: in fact, it was free. It was a baseball bat hidden beneath his bed that he hoped he'd never have to use. But as time went on, he started to think more and more about just how hard he'd swing the bat at the back of Gabe's head, and hit a home run straight back to Hell.

Jimmy von Braun was next. Levi had opened the doorway, and as any good demonologist could tell you, it is far easier to open a door than to close it.

The much more mundane library door swung open to the sound of shaking bells, and through the rows of bookshelves passed a head of perfectly coiffed blond hair, like the fin of a silent shark on the prowl in a book-lined chasm.

*…Speak of the Devil's mother.*

There was nowhere to hide: she could smell male pheromones like blood in the water, and God knew he reeked of them. There was nowhere to run: he'd leave an airborne trail of chemical breadcrumbs in his wake no matter where he slinked off to, and with each step in primal pursuit Charlene would be driven further into a predatory frenzy, thrashing and gnashing in the deep. He had no choice but to stand his ground and hope that the Bible-lined bookshelves might serve as a steel cage of guilt, and deter her long enough for Susan to get the hell out of the bathroom she was busy desecrating, since she always wielded harpoons of the most lethal sarcasm.

Pretending not to notice the approach announced by the clicking of designer heels, he picked up the next drop-off in the pile (aptly named *Magdalena: A Harlot Redeemed*) and reached up to slip it onto its appropriate shelf, right beside *Jezebel Preyed* and *Rahab: A Hole in the Wall of Jericho*, by the same author, Norman O'Shaughnessy, who clearly had a fascination with loose women. O'Shaughnessy could have written a ten-part series on Charlene von Braun.

"Impressive balance," she noted with icy eyes set on the tightened muscles of his outstretched arm and calves, as he teetered on a shaky stepstool. "I must say, I admire your flexibility, Mr. Young. I daresay I'm starting to lose mine from lack of practice in this black hole of physical fitness. Are you offering weekly yoga classes? Quite modern of you."

"The only stretchin' you'll find in this here town is stretchin' the truth, and that's just on Sundays, Ms. von Braun," Jonah replied, stepping down to meet her eye to eye. She was a tall, slender sylph, even without heels, though she wore such heels to hold herself above the level of the worms and rats that kept company with young men like him. "What brings you down here?"

"This is a library, isn't it? Most people, I'd assume, come here to find a book or two. Unless you and Mrs. Lewis are offering some other services, of which I am completely unaware."

"Can't say we are, ma'am."

"Well, that's too bad. I should have figured as such, given your lack of Orientals, and what would a massage parlor be without them? Besides, your hands look far too rough and rugged for such business." She winked, then took a cursory glance at the perfect nails that could only have been painted by a Dragon Lady with no grasp of English. "And please, I'd prefer you call me Charlene. If my mother ever builds up the willpower to leave her tasteless gated community in Boca and visit this even more tasteless town, you're welcome to call her 'ma'am.'"

"What would your son say if he knew he was the only one abidin' by good Southern formalities?"

"Oh, that bratty little queen? He's been calling me Charlene since he was old enough to taste the difference between Grey Goose and Belvedere, just before his eleventh birthday. That is, if he isn't opting to simply call me 'bitch' instead. Very uncouth of him, but what can a mother do?" she sighed. "He certainly didn't get that word from his prim-and-proper father. Like I've always said, such derogatory language is best left for the bedroom. Though my husband is far more likely to bore me with endearments, if anything."

"Well if *we're* on a first-name basis, *Charlene*, then it'd be fittin' for you to use mine."

"Rightfully so. Mr. Young must be your father, and when it comes to cars and men, I always prefer the newer model." Another wink—another uncomfortable pause.

The subject of business was always like an ice water bath, at least for him, so he turned right to it. "So, what is it you're lookin' for today? Romances? Recipes? Maybe a better gossip magazine than a Sunday church bulletin?"

"Romances are for bleeding-heart liberals, and I've got three master chefs on call to cater every meal at home—Gucci knows I haven't touched a saucepan since I used it to beat some sense into my disobedient brat of a son. But I do declare, Jonah, that it's now perfectly obvious what you think women should do and read. Should I simply go back home to my kitchen and lament my weight and failing marriage?"

Jonah knew he wasn't a sexist but didn't have any evidence to present to the contrary other than a beet-reddening of the face, which could have been used either in his defense or by his stylish prosecution. For a moment he actually questioned if he might, in fact, harbor some unconscious resentment of women, a silent misogyny imbued in him by his father, and his father's father before him. He shook the feeling, knowing that he didn't treat women as objects, and respected them for their personalities. Granted, even sofas and lamps were said to have character.

"I'm only joking, Jonah. The Bible outlaws a lot of fun things, but humor isn't one of them," Charlene reassured him as she gingerly caressed his arm. Her nails felt like sharpened fish hooks; Jonah wondered if she'd misinterpreted the Bible's promise of making one a fisher of men. "In reality, I'd just like to browse around, if that's alright with you. Or do I need a man's approval to walk unattended through your little library, vulnerable and ripe for the ravishing?"

"I doubt you'd let him tag along, anyhow."

"Now there's that smartness you've been hiding," she sneered through her porcelain white veneers. Pushing back a rare stray strand of platinum hair, she drew attention to a diamond earring of considerable size, which glittered in the library's otherwise unflattering fluorescent lights. It was so heavy that it threatened to stretch out the fleshy lobes it'd pierced many years ago, perhaps enough to pry open her ear canals, which she'd kept shut to the voices of peasants for most, if not all, of her life, save that one strange day when she decided Jonah's plebeian words were worth listening to. "Now, go back to sorting through this town's intellectual trash. I've kept you from your menial duties long enough, and I wouldn't want you to get in trouble with a crotchety, old spinster like Mrs. Lewis, of course. Who knows what kind of punishment you might deserve?"

She winked a crystal blue and batted flytrap lashes one last time, then disappeared, like a fleeting memory of a dream he'd had in the middle of the night, in which he was a rich gentleman being tempted by a shiny trophy, which turned out to be a woman with gold hair and a penchant for humiliating the loser.

No matter: he didn't need that prize, anyhow. The daunting race for Sophia's heart was the most exhilarating championship in which he'd ever competed, and he was winning it with flying colors, leaving his opponents in the dust. He was just yards away from seizing the gold. Jesus, her Lord and Savior, might end up being left with a silver medal, as unsatisfying as the thirty pieces exchanged for his betrayal. Jonah didn't want to one-up him, though. Respectfully, he hoped for an honest tie, with no tiebreaker other than the breaking of her parents' steely fetters.

He was retrieving the next book from the cart when Susan's smoky voice broke the perpetual silence he was destined to endure until they found his dusty skeleton by the back shelves, clinging to even dustier tomes. "Ain't no sense in takin' out Jenna Jameson's sex guide when she's already got it committed to memory," she groaned, taking a look at what was left to be sorted. "What's that bitch doin' here?"

"The hell if I know. I reckon her maids do her reading for her."

"You know as well as I do that we ain't got no Spanish fiction section. Hussy ain't up to nothin' good, I can tell you that, sure as shootin'. Ain't no fresh meat here 'cept you, kid, 'cause I'm just some old, dried up jerky. Let's pray that uppity bitch is a vegan, for your sake."

"Library ain't that big, y'know. She probably done heard you by now."

"Eh, let 'er," Susan huffed with a dismissive sweep of her hand. "Tramp's so skinny I could break her in two if she tried to start somethin'. Ain't no one's gonna disrespect me in my house. And I know y'can take care o' yourself on your own, kid, but I got a bit of a soft spot for you over these past few years, and I'll be damned if I'm about to see some disease-ridden whore with a good dye-job violate your honor in front o' me. Lord knows you done violated most of it well enough on your own, and take it from me, that shit don't grow back."

# 13

THE GIRL HAD THICK SKIN. Gabe hadn't expected it. He thought the needle would slip in without a fight, but it could have been a little dull. He did use it often.

Her body was draped over the pale green couch: the itchy tweed one his father had found on the street just a few blocks away from their mobile home, waiting to be picked up by trash collectors in neon vests. "Git outta here!" his father had shouted at his children, the eldest of which (that is, Gabe) had just reached his twelfth birthday, "This fine furniture ain't gon' move itself!" He pulled the youngest away from eating the greasy crumbs at the bottom of an empty bag of potato chips; Gabe helped his father drag the couch with an empty stomach, having gone without food since last afternoon. His guts rumbled worse than the heavy sofa over gravel and chipped pavement. And when they finally pulled it gracelessly into the house, dumping it in the middle of the parlor as though it were still awaiting garbage day, Gabe never even got to use it. His mother claimed it as her bed, upon which she'd collapse after a quick shooting-up.

And now Gabe had an equally useless girl on that couch, looking just like his mother did. She slept with shallow breath in chemically induced unconsciousness, oblivious to the hungry boy looking upon her with desperation and disgust. He once needed food. He now needed something more satisfying, but just as scarce, though the hunt was far more rewarding when his next meal came in warm skin and not a puffed-up plastic bag of Cheetos.

He flicked his finger against the side of the syringe, and white sediment swirled about in the liquid like flakes in a snow globe, for a Christmas he'd never had. He was strangely hesitant. There was really nothing special about this girl: she was painfully ordinary. She didn't talk about it much, but Gabe eagerly assumed she'd been in the retard classes when she was young. Actually, she didn't talk much at all, which was fine by him, since he didn't spend his time with her, or anyone, for the conversation. When she did speak, she did so carefully, even more slowly than was to be expected of someone from that part of the country. She didn't want to make any mistakes. Most wouldn't have noticed if she had, since they lost all interest after only a few short sentences. Missy treaded through speech like thick, stinking mud. She was so inept that she could barely pronounce her own stupid name without getting caught on the "s" like a hissing vacuum cleaner, and she was a disposable fleck of dust.

Missy was so forgettable that Gabe struggled to recall how he'd met her. In all likelihood, it'd been at a grocery store. He frequented supermarkets and fought his hunger by pickpocketing at Walmarts and dollar stores, walking the isles with his hand plunged into bags of pork rinds and pretzel sticks. She could have been working at the deli, giving him a container of buffalo chicken bits that he should have paid for at the register but had eaten before ever getting anywhere near the line; maybe she'd been the quiet greeter who meekly waved him goodbye as he marched triumphantly out of the store, his fingers slick with the remnants of spicy sauces. He could have met her any number of times. They were blurred in his mind, indistinguishable, just like all his girls, and most like Missy in a crowd.

Why waste good chalk on this girl? He could keep it for himself, and buy him some time before he'd have to truck his way down to

Hebron to pick up some more in a Dollar General parking lot. He could leave Missy there, disappear. She'd be left alone, emotionally abandoned, just as she'd been her whole life. God knew she was a disappointment to everyone she'd ever known. It was no secret her father had wanted a boy. It was the one thing Gabe remembered her having said, and only because she said it all the goddamned time. But unlike most fathers, he held it against her, as if she had any choice in that last chromosome carried on the back of his sperm.

Her mother had made more of an effort. She was the type of overbearing parent obsessed with early learning, who watched from the sidelines of her child's crib like it was the soccer field she'd one day force her to run on. She'd bought into all sorts of popular, fraudulent trends that promised to teach infants to read Camus before they'd naturally figured out how to clumsily crawl. The dining room table was littered with stacks of classical music CDs: Mozart, Bach, Beethoven, the works, all composers whom her mother had never taken the time to appreciate before deciding they'd hasten the expansion of her unborn daughter's brain. When her husband wasn't home to laugh at her, she stretched a pair of cumbersome, padded headphones over her swollen belly, in hopes that the shapeless blob growing inside her might hear even a few muffled melodies. According to the fanatically amassed collection of books and DVDs on her bookshelf and the front seat of her car, the baby would be born a genius. She'd be reading and speaking well before her peers, at a level unattained by some of that small town's high school dropouts. She'd be a baby to be proud of.

Missy got older. Her mother didn't know what to do with her. She had tried to remain patient through elementary school—Missy was still young, she'd catch up. She never did. Her mother never really forgave her for it.

Shaking his head, Gabe brought the needle close to her skin a second time. Still, he hesitated. He never pitied his girls. He never felt a thing for them. Fuck them, leave them: that was his MO, a plan he skillfully executed time and time again, turning his back to them while they desperately begged him to stay. "You told me I was beautiful!"; "You said I was different!"; "You promised you'd changed, just for me!"; their parting words might as well have been pulled from a set list of pathetic one-liners. There was something wickedly empowering in fixing the price of a sorry little girl's sense of value and self-worth. He loaned them compliments and inflated flattery like gold from the vault of his heart, to which they thought they held the only key. Little did they know it'd been emptied long ago.

For those he got hooked on more than just his love—on ice or angel dust—the supply ran out in an instant. He was their only dealer, and they weren't street smart. The image of a broken girl weeping in pain, both heartache and withdrawal, was the sweetest of all.

*Missy's no different*, he told himself. *Why spare her?*

He hadn't been spared. He'd been through tougher shit than her. She deserved it—she was lucky to have had him, even for a time just as brief as her next high. What she didn't deserve was independence. He knew all too well how much of a curse it was to fend for oneself. If anything, he was saving her from it. Maybe he'd saved all of them all along. He wasn't their punisher: he was their savior, from the loneliness of free will.

He tried to dig up old anger and rummage through foggy memories of what he could call his childhood. *Think of what you've been through,* he thought. *Push the needle with it.*

Gabe couldn't remember ever being given a toy or having eaten a Christmas dinner outside of a McDonald's (that one up in Lillian had since been bulldozed). He played with burnt-out lighters and empty matchboxes, pretending they were spaceships and freight trucks. He drew stick figures on scraps of hamburger wrappers with his bitch of a mother's lipstick and imagined they were action figures. Empty beer bottles were skyscrapers in a city made of slightly flattened packs of cigarettes. He played unsupervised, as his father was either out somewhere unspecified or getting drunk in the yard with his beer-bellied cousins, and his mother was almost always incapacitated on the couch. Her son was second to her fix. Dad had gotten her hooked right after they left the hospital with him in her arms.

At least she had her husband to depend on, in one way or another. Their son had nobody.

His search for friendship proved fruitless, even when he'd moved on from invisible ones among his beer can cityscapes to real-life boys his own age. He was that Salvation Army–dressed kid that no one liked, since their parents had warned them of the Skinners; their quiet, socially inept son was more dangerous than an adult stranger with candy. Over time he chose to prove them right. He didn't need a windowless van and chocolate bars to get the PTA to pick up their torches and pitchforks. All he needed was a lighter, and a flaxen-haired cheerleader named Amber Calhoun.

Even years later he recalled the distinctly sweet smell of that preppy bitch's hair. Like all Ambers throughout the United States, she was a Grade A cunt. If she had anything fossilized inside her like her namesake, it was a repulsive, bloated tick. A mosquito bite was nothing compared to the bleeding lesions she left on a loser's reputation. She chugged the blood of the poor and nameless, draining their social life away with each witless insult. Thinking herself impossibly clever, she'd nicknamed him "Raggedy Gabe" (a moniker which was lackluster and not even a smart play on words). He was, after all, dressed in thrift store junk. When he got older he realized their clothes probably came from the same discount source. Her parents just washed hers more often.

She was his most logical target. She took great pride in her long, blond hair, sweeping it from side to side as she walked from one classroom to another. A band of horny, smitten jocks always clustered about her, carrying her books and personal effects, throwing themselves beneath her feet in hopes that she might one day lie beneath them. Her perfect, straight locks were just long enough to make the peons on the ground think they could possibly climb up into her tower, but she only hung it down mockingly. It smelled of warm vanilla and baked peaches, and all the boys wanted a slice of that pie. If that slut had stripped anything away, it wasn't her undersized tees or ripped jeans. It was Gabe's dignity and pride, and he had a sense of personal justice strong enough to do something about it.

One morning he snatched a butane lighter right out of his mother's hand while she was passed out on the couch. He sat behind Amber in chemistry class with a clear shot at her proud mane. She had an irritating habit of flipping her hair before incorrectly answering a teacher's question, blasting a wave of fruity fragrance right into Gabe's scowling face. While Mr. Templeton rambled on about ionic bonds and Amber smacked her gum like a golden cow without a care in the world, Gabe slipped the lighter out of his pocket and held it just beneath the long hair that hung over the back of her chair. No one noticed. As usual, his classmates ignored him.

He snapped the safety down and watched as a strong, hissing blue flame sprung forth from the lighter and lapped at Amber's then-intact ends. The flaxen strands began to coil back as they smoldered, transforming from silky gold to a crumbling, brownish mess. Her hair was long enough that she hadn't begun to feel the heat yet, but the smell quickly became overwhelming. As she whipped her head around to find the source of the biting stench, the lighter's bright flame dragged straight across her hanging hair, severing it halfway in a crackling swoop, and the fire spread higher toward her scalp. The principal at the other side of the school could have easily heard Amber's screams of abject horror.

Her shame reached its glorious peak when Mr. Templeton snatched the fire extinguisher off the wall, pulled the pin, and unleashed a flurry of white, chalky foam all over her and her precious ensemble. Too shocked and shaken to even start crying, she merely stood there in the middle of the classroom, an abominable snowman beginning to melt in the heat of her own embarrassment. She simply stared at their teacher, eyes wide and mouth gaping open in the kind of surprise that lobotomizes the language center of the brain. No one said a word. Not even a whimper.

Gabe was the one to break the silence. His laughter began softly, rising up from the depths of his being in delicate murmurs, but soon the floodgates of his newfound cruelty burst open, never to be repaired as long as he lived, and a violent fit of hysterical gasping exploded from his lungs when he saw Amber start to sob in unfathomable embarrassment. At that moment, he knew how God must feel when He sees the unrepentant sinner weep at the mouth of Hell. No one ever treated him rudely again. But they were far from accepting him: they feared him now, and he remained a loner. God, too, stood alone. His plan had been a success. It was better to be feared than loved.

If Missy loved him now, then he'd need to make her fear him.

"Fuck!" he cursed, falling back to sit against the sofa. He put down the needle and nestled it in the thick fibers of the moldy shag carpet, slipping a bent Newport between his fingers instead. He lit it quickly. With the amount of time he'd wasted, the solution was probably settling by now. Sure enough, he held the syringe up to the flame of his lighter, only to see chemical sediment gathering at the bottom of the reservoir.

*Could that kill her?*

She'd be no good to him dead. And besides, he'd have to touch her more if she were a corpse than if she were alive, if he wanted to dump her somewhere out in the woods.

*It'll be fine. Just a little dust.*

He flicked the syringe again and shook it a bit. It looked like an intoxicating glimpse of a white Christmas, one he'd never seen firsthand. It was beautiful, elegant, even. What a waste of beauty, giving it to a girl who, for the first time, thought she could actually be beautiful. Gabe had lied. She didn't know. None of the girls did, and that's just how he liked it. Especially that new one he'd picked up from the schoolyard, the skinny one with the hazel eyes who did what she was told, even if it meant being shared with his friends. What was her name again?

It didn't matter, really. She'd be gone in a month or two, with track marks on her arm and his pickup's tire treads trailing from her family's front porch. But first, Missy had to go.

••

The sons of light did not sleep in Clemency, but kept watch, sober, except on caffeine after Sunday service. They were not of the night, or the darkness; they were vigilant, alert, ready to greet the Second Coming with their pants up. But there were those who were content to sleep at night, naked as they came, beside another warm body. And there were those who eagerly drank themselves into a stupor well past midnight, in a bacchanal behind the closed doors of Gene's, who figured that if Christ were to show up in all His glory in the middle of the night, it didn't matter if He caught them with their pants at their ankles. After all, He saw them when they took a piss every morning, and they hadn't exactly come screaming out of their mothers' wombs dressed in a perfectly pressed Sunday suit.

Sweating beer bottles scattered about the room glimmered in the dim light like candles in a church. Drunk on the blood of the Antichrist, men and women raucously gave each other the sign of peace: clumsy high-fives upon hearing the news of a new sexual conquest, handshakes to seal some ridiculous bet, and the occasional punch to the face. They were the hedonists who knew they needed saving, but figured repentance could wait for another day, after an aspirin and a Bloody Mary in the morning. They knew they stood on the far side of the line in the sand. They were those condemned by the moralists down the street, but not by God, at least not yet.

The way they saw it was that there was less danger in the sins of the body than the sins of the soul. Drunks and adulterers could find redemption, since they knew they were in the wrong. There was always time to come crawling back to God. On the other hand, the pious and mighty thought they were entitled to redemption. One didn't need to repent when he'd already bought God's grace through public works of righteousness. But in the end, all were sinners. And only those who acknowledged this would come to walk with God.

That was for another time, though. That night, they didn't walk, but stumbled in their stupor.

"I'm tellin' you, man, the bitch won't leave me be," Jonah complained as he slammed down his fourth beer onto the shaky table. "Four trips to the library in a week and a half, and there's still two days left till Sunday. Ain't no one reads that quick. And ain't it interestin' she's only takin' 'em from the shelves I'm busy sortin'? Latin reference books? Fuck me, she don't know a word o' Latin— 'cept maybe 'coitus.' Bet she's right familiar with that one."

It'd been a long time since he'd seen Levi struggle so hard to stifle his laughter, and he wasn't doing a very good job at it. "It ain't like you to keep a secret so long," he snickered between desperate swigs of beer meant to keep his chuckles down, like trying to fight hiccups with sips of water. "The whole school knew who you was doin' before you done finished doin' her. How's it this is the first time I'm hearin' about all this fuckery?"

"Folks care a whole lot less now when y'ain't in the Friday night lights no more. And besides, I ain't screwin' her. Don't start no rumors. That's the last thing I need."

"Funny you got such a problem with me talkin' to Jimmy when you're practically in bed with his mama," Levi noted, coaxing the last drops of piss-warm beer from the bottle onto his tongue. He held his hand high and snapped his fingers like some nouveau riche asshole summoning the help. "You made it real clear you think all that snobbery's contagious. If it's airborne and I'mma get it just from talkin', think o' how much faster you'll catch it from fuckin' Typhoid Mary herself."

In place of an enticing French maid, a Southern swamp-thing in rags was at his beck and call, crawling out of the stinking bayou to please that delusional aristocrat and his poor best friend. As quickly as he'd summoned her Valerie Skinner slinked over to their high top with two fresh bottles, her blotchy, red lips peeled back over a receding gum line. Her crudely cut tank top hung repulsively low as she leaned over to try to force a familial kiss on Jonah's cheek, exposing an unwelcome glimpse at what gravity had been quite cruel to over the years. He winced. She didn't care.

"Trust you me, in my eyes, she ain't no better than that withered husk of a whore behind the bar," Jonah insisted with a rough, brown napkin scraping away at his cheek. "I know what's good for me, so I'm resistin' the bad. And if you were just as self-aware, you'd be resistin' her son's 'friendly' advances just the same. You know as well as me they've got some ulterior motives here, whatever those might be, and I ain't about to take the plunge just to find out."

"Her motives seem pretty obvious. I reckon she had a whole slew o' young dick back in the big city, and now that she's in short supply, she's tryin' to jump on the first one she finds. Christ knows I'm probably next. There's only so many of us here in Clemency."

"Don't get cocky. Y'know I'm the first and the last."

"Well, I gotta say, I'm real stunned y'ain't goin' along with it. But for the sake o' your own safety—and I don't mean just your bill o' reproductive health—it's a welcome miracle you got yourself some temperance. The only thing worse than screwin' the Reverend's daughter is screwin' her over, 'specially with some ritzy cougar. Guess you're really into her, if y'ain't goin' off on a week-long pussy bender like the Jonah we all known and loved woulda."

"Y'know, it's real troublin' that of all the sorry cynics in this here town, the one I been havin' the most trouble convincin' is you, my own 'best friend.' Can't y'have some goddamned faith in me, for Christ's sake? I'm a changed man, man."

Finally, on a much-needed serious note, Levi declared earnestly, "I do—really. I believe you, and I believe y'can keep it in your pants for once. Sophie's a real nice girl, and I know y'ain't enough of an asshole to do her wrong. *But*,"—of course, there was always a condition to such understanding—"all I'm askin' is that maybe y'put some o' the same faith in Jimmy. He ain't as bad as we thought back in school. Or maybe he really was that bad, who knows? All that matters is he ain't so bad now."

"Y'ain't about to go and take credit for that, are you? Levi Thompson, the best influence a friend could ask for." Jonah figured if that really were the case, then all his problems would have been fixed long ago, and he wouldn't have had to earn his way into Sophia's arms to find out that he'd been in need of fixing all along. Levi hadn't ever told him he was broken. But he supposed it was hard to see the cracks in someone's window when your own window was practically shattered, smashed by whiskey bottles thrown violently in a fight at home.

Ready to call it a night, Jonah stood up to slip his wallet out of his back pocket, and as he tossed some uncounted bills onto the table that teetered precariously on uneven legs, he proclaimed, "Well, if y'really are the village Savior, you're sure as shit runnin' outta sinners to save. Maybe you're just too good at it." He glanced over at the old, drugged-up trollop standing behind the bar, who stroked wet, empty bottles like they were peckers: the same sorry chick who sold shots for six bucks and handjobs for two, but always sold far more liquor than happy endings. He'd sooner take her up on that offer than let Hannah follow in her footsteps. He groaned through gritted teeth, "But get to work on my little sister, Lord Levi, 'cause that's one lost sheep y'ain't tried hard enough to find."

"Can't very well get her back when she's old enough to choose the wolves over her own family. That one's on you 'n your folks, in one way or another. Someone drove her out, and it wasn't me. A taste o' the gritty and dangerous is bound to keep her cravin' when she's been eatin' bagged lunches her whole life."

As they left the bar without saying much more about anything, Jonah worried Levi had eaten the caviar, washed down with a shot of top-shelf vodka. Now the rest was just peasant food.

••

"You know, you're lucky I don't hate you as much as I hate most people," Jimmy stated as he passed through the door of Backwater Spirits. "You dragging me here is as degrading as asking Heidi Klum to pick out the best-tailored T-shirt at a dollar store. Granted, I'm better: that Kraut couldn't spot a broken seam if the Führer asked her to. But what can you expect from someone who didn't even notice the holes in her ex-husband's face?"

He let the door slam shut behind him. After all, he had to make his presence known to that one person in the store, Mr. Green, smirking wisely behind the register, because he lacked the dancers and full orchestra required for an entrance fit for the heir to the von Braun family fortune. "If you're here to buy more whiskey for your mother, you could have left me out of it. I'm proud to say I'm not well acquainted with the toilet water you people drink out here in the sticks. Besides, you've been doing it perfectly well on your own since you were three, right?"

"I think I'mma broaden her horizons today."

"Levi Thompson, the cultured risk-taker!" Jimmy scoffed without even eyeing the scowling subject of his mockery. He kept his focus on an eight-dollar bottle of Pinot Grigio, which he examined with a sickened grimace as if it were an embalmed fetus in a jar. "Trying something imported, like Kentucky instead of local?"

"Before you're too drunk to recall and you black out like some slutty co-ed, what kind o' liquor gives you the least angry sort o' drunk?"

"Well, I can tell you with absolute certainty that anything sold here would leave me as belligerent as a slut who just lost her favorite cock." He looked over to Elijah, who shook his head disapprovingly, but sported a subtle smile that detracted from his disapproval. "No offense," Jimmy added. "For the subterranean-shelf liquor comment—not the promiscuous one. That's not a joke. It's a warning."

"No need to apologize," Elijah replied warmly. "I'm no stranger to them demons in a bottle."

"Don't try to one-up me, Papa Midnight," Jimmy snapped, his cutthroat, competitive spirit riled up at the thought of being outdrank. "I'm the town's proud Courtney Love, here. But a hell of a lot richer, I can tell you that."

"Wasn't always so," the old man chuckled. "But the past is the past and I done moved on. Give it some time and you will, too. But for now, have your fun. Mr. Thompson, you were lookin' for somethin' a lil' easier on the soul?"

Levi was browsing the cognac shelves, inspecting each rounded bottle as though he even knew the difference between them; really, they were all the same shade of brownish orange, and he worried the French names might offend his mother's sensibilities as a red-blooded American. "If y'even got such a thing," he murmured. "Probably wastin' my time here."

"Y'know, kid, if she really gets that fired up each 'n every time, it might not be the whiskey doin' the talkin'. Some damage can't be covered up with a cleaner cocktail."

"Don't listen to this aging A.A. cultist. He's walked his miserable Twelve Steps to a duller life," Jimmy insisted, holding a plastic bottle of gold tequila—"Fool's gold," he muttered under his breath. "In my experience, there's nothing a bottle over a hundred dollars can't fix. Listen up, amateurs," he scoffed, snapping his fingers to command Elijah's attention, which, like everything else he'd ever demanded throughout his eighteen ostentatious years, he promptly received.

"Steer clear of this shit," he advised, thrusting the bottle in question up into the air. "Tequila's nothing but trouble—gold, silver, doesn't matter. I ended up getting engaged to the son of a cartel boss after fifteen shots of Cuervo at some seedy spic bar down in Mexico City. Cheap beaner didn't even get me a ring—just a few months in witness protection, half a million in legal fees and two painful trips to my proctologist.

"Rum's out of the question, too," he added, brandishing a bottle of pirate grog. "Never trust anything out of the Caribbean. That's how I ended up wrapped up in a Puerto Rican flag and tied to the hood of a Chevy Impala down in San Juan and paraded through the streets like a statue of Santa Maria on a Sunday.

"Don't even get me started on absinthe," he groaned, pointing across the aisle at a lone, greenish flask of poison; the fear in his eyes was genuine and raw. "Do you know how terrifying Paris is while you're tripping balls at two in the morning after you've been abandoned by your uncircumcised French interpreter? By the time I came to, there was a trail of knocked-out mimes all the way down the Champs-Élysées, and my right fist was all bloodied up. In my defense, the pale-faced freaks were asking for it. Never trust the quiet ones.

"So, lucky for you, I've ruled out all the spirits that'll just serve as rocket fuel for your burning train wreck of a mother. I guess this is the best we're gonna get," he declared without much enthusiasm, ashamed he was even making the suggestion that Levi buy a bottle that cost less than a Wall Street banker's biweekly paycheck. He presented a blown-glass version of brutalist architecture, tall with hard edges and little adornment, save a plain label marked prominently with Cyrillic typeface; the military memo–style English print beneath it offered a transliteration of the second-world brand name, *Amneziya*, giving the buyer an idea of the mental blackout a few wretched shots promised him.

"She won't remember a thing," Jimmy assured his doubtful friend. "I'm pretty sure Stalin kept his inmates in check with this bad boy while they slaved away in the gulags: no one's gonna stage an uprising when you can't remember your own forced labor. Now, your mother's no Soviet dictator, and she's sure as hell no Charlene von Hitler, but maybe more like a second-in-command—either way, give her a glass or two of this Russki baby formula, and you'll drop an iron curtain right over her head. Problem solved. You're welcome."

"Just be careful, son, 'cause that there's some city liquor, and if there's one thing that can go to a country gal's head faster than a vodka tonic, it's remindin' her of her place in the food chain, and what she is, and what she ain't," Elijah cautioned, "and she sure ain't a martini gal. Years o' ringin' you up done convinced me o' that."

"Consider yourself lucky," Jimmy muttered. "She doesn't have to fall too far off the social ladder each time she embarrasses herself."

"Wish she'd gone and climbed it back before she done wasted her whole life away," Levi grumbled. "Now she's just a drunk, Bible-thumpin' waitress without a penny to her name. But God knows I ain't in a position to judge. Ain't even got a glass house to throw rocks in. Can't afford it."

"Don't waste your time thinkin' about how the other half lives. Trust and believe they got their fair share o' bitter drinkers, too."

"You're looking at one of them," Jimmy snickered.

"So if there's one thing y'should take to heart, it's this, Mr. Thompson: maybe down here in sorry, ol' Clemency you got yourself some empty pockets, but up north you'd have yourself an empty heart. And it's a heck of a lot easier to fill a pocket with loose change than it is to fill a void."

"I never expected to say this, but I've gotta agree with old Papa Midnight here, Thompson. My bitch of a mother has a goddamned black hole for a heart, and all she can do is go around draining our liquor cabinets, my happiness, and my father's bank account. And no amount of upper-class drama, cocaine or young cock is gonna satiate her."

"More money, more problems, right?" Levi sneered, unconvinced.

"Thompson, you have no idea." Jimmy held out the bottle of vodka. "So do you want it or not? A blackout's a blackout, rich or poor. And think about what a relief it'll be for the bitch to forget how apparently useless you are."

"I'll take it," Levi declared without a second of hesitation, grabbing the bottle of vodka out of Jimmy's hands only to set it down frantically at the register, where Elijah looked upon it with doubt. "Don't matter how much it'll cost me."

"Y'ain't never gonna solve the problem by knockin' her out cold all the time," the old man said as Levi passed him a stack of bills fatter than any he'd exchanged before. Despite his wise reluctance, he slipped it into the open register, sliding it closed to the clatter of bells. None of it made any difference to Levi, and this seemed to disappoint him a little. Maybe a lot. He didn't appear the type to judge harshly enough to evoke that haunting emotion.

Jimmy adamantly rejected that advice on Levi's behalf, preaching that Levi's problem in the first place was his refusal to sweep everything under the rug. "Granted, that witch went and stole the broom a long time ago," he conceded, "so what can you expect him to do? He's out of options."

"I've swept up a lotta dust in my day, and what I took from it is there's always another way out. 'Knock, and it shall be opened to you,' no matter how heavy the lock, or brittle the key." He passed the paper bag across the counter and shrugged. "But what do I know? Such are the ramblings of a crazy, old man who's had one too many cups o' moonshine in his day. Ain't no one in this here town's fit for dolin' out advice. You gotta turn to God for the good stuff."

••

Every time Charlene looked out her bedroom window, she saw the white church steeple rising up like the mighty middle finger of God.

That evening, He held it especially high. In her mind, she returned the gesture. It did little to make her feel better, but it was better than letting Him get the last word. She flipped that perfectly painted bird right in the air, and let it soar up to the heavens, where it could take a watery shit right on God's eternal throne. If she'd had enough fingers, she would have sent Him a whole flock of them. But alas, she only had two; she wouldn't let Him kill them with one stone.

"Sit down, Charlene," her husband suggested, his eyes lowered, fixed on the novel he held in his hands. "It's like looking at an ant farm. You won't find any surprises there. Let them go about their simple lives, and put away your magnifying glass. You could burn someone."

She wished she could feel any smoldering at all those days. Instead, George's words had that same cool aloofness, unlit by the scorching sun he once called his ambition—that is, the very beacon that drew her to him in the first place.

"This useless Valium hasn't kicked in yet. You know I can't get a good night's sleep without it," she muttered, still peering out the window. The tension in her shoulders hadn't improved. She'd always known her doctor had been stingy with her dosage, and her husband was an unreliable neck-rubber.

"Get a new doctor, then. Or chase it with a nightcap," George sighed with disinterest, or disdain: it was hard to tell the difference. He licked his finger and turned the page. He adjusted his reading glasses and coughed.

"As is my usual routine," Charlene quipped, pointing a polished finger at the empty glass on her vanity, resting neatly on a coaster. "Am I really that predictable, George?"

"Of course not, dear. Just consistent." He didn't seem to be sarcastic—that would have required a shred of regard. "These townspeople are predictable, and we can both agree that you have no intention of assimilating."

"I'd sooner don a sombrero and chat in Spanish with the maid."

"And if anyone could wear something so avant-garde, it's you, dear." He turned the page.

It was doubtful he noticed what she wore anymore—or even what she didn't wear. After all, she was standing across the room in a sheer, cream negligée, through which the light of the moon passed unobstructed, revealing the admittedly tantalizing silhouette of a near-perfect woman. It went unnoticed, just like the black one the night before, and the scarlet one the night before that, though all three (and the rest of her intimate wardrobe) flaunted what was meant to be George's alone, who she truly was beneath it all.

She was the unattainable desire of men, and the primal envy of women. Surely her picture was held fondly in the adolescent memories of men who'd grown up during her modeling days. It was pinned to cosmeticians' mirrors as an example of what clients could pay to look like, but fall short of. Her beloved husband George, on the other hand, only kept her photo on his office desk, allegedly. She'd never seen it herself, but she knew there wasn't one in his wallet—only tired-looking credit cards with which she paid good money for her figure.

George turned the page. He didn't look up once.

"You know, I'm fairly certain I saw that Bible-thumping bitch Victoria driving around in a Mercedes out of town the other day," Charlene remarked in an attempt to strike up some idle conversation, the gossipy kind that Victoria herself would have gobbled up like communion bread after a Lenten fast.

"Well, you can't expect the woman to ride into Jerusalem on a donkey, now, can you?" George quipped without a hint of a smile. He backtracked a page to check a line he must have missed.

"I'm sure that bitch has been pocketing some of those church tithes—I should have our private investigator do some research. Apparently there's money to be made in the business of saving souls. Maybe you should look into it." She turned away from the window and slipped into bed beside him, sneering, "It seems safer than *some* investments you've made in the past, and you get a weekly payout every Sunday."

At last, George set down his novel on his barrel chest, still open, because he wasn't finished with it. He slipped off his reading glasses and hung them from the neck of his pajamas. "I'm in the business of saving this *town*. By the time I'm done with it, Clemency's going to be born again—a new economy, a new Main Street, a new goddamned heart and soul. And if the Governor values my money at all, this train station will be reopened soon enough and then all our progress will skyrocket with the whole state watching." Picking up his book, he resumed his evening reading; it didn't take long before he realized he'd forgotten his glasses, without which he was blind to the words. "This time, I won't be making a profit off of something I can't see: no clear, clean-cut results. How do you expect me to keep track of how many of my consumers end up in Heaven?"

"None of them, George, because there's no such thing. But who cares about salvation? You're selling them peace of mind. And they'll pay whatever you want to get it."

"I'd be selling them snake oil."

"Wouldn't be the first time, George."

The George von Braun she'd married never would have turned down such a golden opportunity for profit. Who was this man lying beside her, letting his new bleeding heart soak their designer sheets? If she didn't know better, she'd think she'd been betrothed to a Democrat. It was like *Invasion of the Body Snatchers*, and George was just a hollow shell of a former unfettered capitalist, whose ruthlessness had been eaten away by an illegal alien worm in his once beautiful brain.

Eighteen years ago he was a free man, a free thinker, the ruler of a corporate empire built on the backs of anorexic models and caged lab animals. George von Braun, the CEO of Bellatrix Cosmetics, was universally praised in the business world, lauded by prominent magazines like *Forbes* and *Fortune*, while cursed by the lazy and socially parasitic. Leftist college professors called him a despicable bastion of selfishness and greed, and their later unemployed students, struggling to enter any relevant industry with a degree in English or Women's Studies, lambasted him for not hiring them. Labor unions sought to crucify him after continuously scourging him in conference rooms and town hall meetings. George was reviled simply for working harder and earning more than those who aspired to mediocrity. His hefty bonuses, however well deserved, only served as further evidence against him in the court of jealous public opinion. The boom of a private jet's liftoff might as well have been the crack of a judge's gavel.

He was just inches away from the peak of his career when Charlene first met him on the set of a commercial photoshoot. She'd just celebrated her twenty-third birthday two days prior; she still tasted vodka in the back of her mouth. The product she presented to the camera with a brilliant smile was some variety of face cream, skin serum, or collagen booster—eighteen years later, she couldn't remember exactly. Whatever it was, she surely had never used it. But she flaunted it as though it alone had spared her from the shameful stigma of fine lines and dark circles. For all the consumer knew, she was actually seventy-something years old, but after having smothered her face in the stuff for just two weeks, she'd miraculously transformed into a nubile maiden. The outrageously flamboyant photographer practically worshiped her, throwing his hands upon weak wrists into the air with squealing glee with each flash of the camera. If it were a film, she would have easily seized an Oscar.

Charlene noticed him standing there after the temporary blindness began to subside: a distinguished man, taller than the assistants around him, with blondish hair that was subtly graying in a matured tonsure. The arch and dip of his eyebrows created the semblance of a dissatisfied frown, but his eager grin betrayed the illusion. He crossed his arms. In Charlene's next pose, she smiled just for him. She had no idea that he was George von Braun, that wealthy executive who had no one to share his wealth with. Even with three rolodexes of contact cards on his desk, all he could dig up at that point were withered heiresses and gold-digging whores from the Upper East Side.

He saw her across the crowded room at one of many star-studded launch parties, mingling with braindead male models in her short white dress. Those walking, talking, well-groomed vegetables pinched at their suits as though the concept of clothing was abhorrent and cruel, like they were forced to wear sackcloth at a funeral of their own nakedness, or irreverently throw an overcoat on a Grecian statue, sculpted in their perfect likeness. Charlene, however, couldn't have looked more comfortable in her elegant formalwear, carrying herself so naturally in that white dress as though it were her own skin.

She and George caught eyes by chance, and though he knew he was a handsome man, he was nonetheless proud that he'd drawn her attention away from younger, more sculpted men. He approached her with his cognac neat in one hand, and an ever-safe champagne in the other. The fluted glass she had been cherishing that whole time suddenly vanished. It reappeared on a table behind her, abandoned half full to make George feel more accommodating. It was the least she could do for the man of the hour.

Her parents had raised her a right and proper lady, but by the end of the night, she found herself tossing aside her inhibitions in the stairwell, her white dress dirtied just a little on the third step up.

The fire between them raged on for a few years, and in it was forged a crushing 8-carat diamond ring and a pudgy, ungrateful son. That is, until eleven years later, when the company burned to the ground overnight.

Perhaps it was because she was a natural-born cynic, but she never expected George's next big project, *Graal de Jeunesse*, to actually work. Preliminary trials confirmed that it was a genuine, over-the-counter solution to wrinkles, managing to transfigure even the wrinkliest of naked mole rats into tight-skinned (though still unsightly) rodents. Animal testing alone was enough to cause Bellatrix Cosmetics' stocks to skyrocket overnight. George von Braun, his finances already more stable and formidable than ancient bedrock, became an unfathomably rich man.

But then FDA scientists woke up one morning to find their lab rats covered in hideous tumors. As it turned out, that miracle product, Bellatrix Cosmetics' claim to fame and fortune, was a dangerous, topical carcinogen: forty-five percent of test subjects developed sebaceous carcinoma after a month's regimen. Beauty always did come at a price.

It was the middle of the night when George got the call—he almost didn't answer it. Though his first instinct was to evacuate his bowels right then and there in the silk sheets of his bed, he managed to overcome that bodily urge and dump all his stocks instead. Within minutes, he'd phoned his personal assistant and arranged for the sale of all his shares in Bellatrix Cosmetics.

This was before the days of rampant wiretapping and government voyeurism. It took a few weeks before the SEC came knocking at his door. At that point, the company was drowning in lawsuits, and with all its executive leadership having dyed their hair and disappeared into the jungles of South America, it had no hope of survival. George was the only one who stayed, albeit locked away in the basement of his multimillion-dollar fortress, biting the nails off his once manicured left hand and gripping a shaking glass of scotch in the other.

Charlene was the one who cautiously greeted the SEC officials in the foyer. It was probably her tits that disarmed them. To the present day no one but her and those two agents would know what went down in the front hallway that morning to drive off the men in black suits, though anyone who'd seen a softcore film on HBO about pizza boys and moms in bathrobes could have at least gotten an idea. She would never admit this, of course. Her husband, hidden away downstairs, knew nothing, and never asked once about it over the next decade. They had both done things they weren't proud of. At least she'd never make the headlines for it.

The federal penal system never managed to get George in handcuffs, but by the time his fifteen minutes of infamy had run out, he would have preferred a sullied record over his now permanently tarnished reputation. And even with half a dozen prescriptions for anti-depressants, mild sedatives, muscle relaxers and stool softeners, he never really shook his paranoia. Every time the phone rang, he knew it had to have been the SEC. When the mailman came by to deliver Jimmy's illegal diet pills imported directly from Guangzhou, he was convinced it was a federal agent in disguise.

"They're still building a case on me," he insisted every night as he milked his nightcap. "We'll have to leave the city soon enough, mark my words."

Charlene shrugged it off each time, and disappeared under the sheets to silence him in the best way she could. After a while, even her particular set of skills couldn't stop his rambling. And eventually, she started to believe him when he promised their inevitable exodus from the city that never slept, just like him, and even like her, who was kept up all night like a veteran's wife, enduring her husband's violent night terrors.

Then one day she woke to her own worst nightmare: she was speeding down I-95 at 83 miles per hour somewhere in the backwoods of Georgia, following signs for the exile state of Alabama, then Birmingham, then some irrelevant town, then another, and another, until she and her family reached their shameful destination. The armada of moving trucks on their tail did little to comfort her. The cost of shipping their entire lives hundreds of miles across the country amounted to more than the combined value of all of Clemency's homes ("Extra-wide outhouses," Jimmy had so aptly declared). While their bank accounts could have handled the price of forced relocation a thousand times over, it saddened Charlene to know that that was the last thing she would truly be dropping real money on, because Clemency had no designer stores, and bottled water was as rare as a married couple who weren't at least distantly related.

One morning she found herself ordering return address labels for her and the family. When prompted to enter her street address, she almost wrote *"The Middle of Nowhere."* She then poured herself a vodka double and smoked a menthol-100 or two.

Most husbands took up hobbies like painting model airplanes or starting a short-lived microbrewery, but George decided it was befitting for a fallen corporate giant to buy out a local textile factory. Perhaps he was just sick of being surrounded by the unemployed. He didn't seem to consider that he'd just go from seeing trash in the streets to seeing trash in the workplace.

Jimmy bitched and moaned his way through high school, stealing the overvalued virginities of two or three deeply closeted defensive linemen along the way, and after he'd donned a cheap cap and gown made of the same wrinkled plastic of dollar store tablecloths, George miraculously decided that they'd weathered the worst of their legal storm, promptly sold his pet factory project and bought three one-way tickets to New York for his graduation gift. Their endeavor didn't last long.

"What do those human tapeworms want this time?" Jimmy groaned after the Feds paid them a visit a second time. He'd answered the door wearing nothing but his underwear and a pair of oversized Prada sunglasses, a Bloody Mary in his left hand and the stinging smell of last night's cocktails on his breath. He scared the suits off for the time being, probably with his abrasive personality. However, Charlene wouldn't have put it past him to follow in her footsteps when it came to effective blackmail, as the rotten apple didn't fall far from the tree, especially when men were crawling all up in her branches.

"Your father, in an act of either Casey Anthony–style negligence or complete white-collar shrewdness, never legally changed our address back to the Upper East Side," Charlene coolly explained as she prepared her usual breakfast of Metamucil and two shreds of romaine lettuce. "He's been sparing us the Democrats' fetish for taxes up here in the city this whole time. If Clemency had one thing going for them, it's that they pay about five dollars a year to the government, if they can even afford it. I'm sure they'd prefer to spend that money on a pack of stale Byron Clays, or a Big Mac."

"That's what they have EBT cards for, Charlene," Jimmy quipped.

"Well, unfortunately for us, we don't have a government dole to go on to pay all these New York taxes we may or may not owe those pinko commies. So, your dear father's left us with two equally unsavory options: go by the books and surrender to the Democrats' demands, or ship us off to the sticks once again."

"I'll never forgive the bastard."

"For which one?"

"Doesn't matter. Either he kills my social life like an illegitimate black baby at Planned Parenthood, or he lets the Leftists get the best of him."

It was unsurprising that George chose not to bow down to the thieving gods of socialism. They left for the South two days later. And George, struggling to find meaning in a post-capitalist world that bruised his ego time and time again, seemed to have left their marriage, having checked out the moment they checked their bags at seedy LaGuardia Airport.

Now Charlene stood in her bedroom with her attention torn between the simple town outside, which was perfectly and pathetically (maybe admirably?) content with its own simplicity, and her husband, a once complex and ambitious man, who was determined to make something great out of said simplicity. No matter how he spun it in his newfound sympathy for the underprivileged, he still found something wrong with that town. If he didn't, he wouldn't strive to change it and its backward priorities: God before money, and small-town gossip before God.

If only he had even a shred of concern for the undersexed, he would have seen that the beautiful woman who'd just slipped beneath the sheets beside him was in deeper need than even the poorest of trailer-dwellers just a quarter mile down the hill.

Each scandal—and there were many, some less noteworthy than others—pushed them further apart, and over the years they became harder to swallow, like horse pills they were force-fed by some quack liberal doctor. Charlene just got headaches from them, the kind that only Belvedere and Xanax could dull; for George, however, they were some kind of anti-Viagra, so potent that even the sight of his wife's bare breasts and black lace panties wasn't enough to steal his attention. She wanted his hands on her body. Instead, he filled them with that damned book.

It was nothing short of baffling that her competition was a bundle of paper and not some melon-breasted, comically vocal porn star hidden away in an untitled folder on his PC. She would have preferred the latter. At least she'd have known what she was up against, and how high, or low, the bar was set. But how could she possibly outdo his entire library of classic novels, which unfairly became even more appealing with age, while she, on the other hand, became more overlooked with each new wrinkle? The more lines those books had, the more time George poured into them. The more fine lines she had, the less likely she was to catch even a passing glance when she stepped out of the shower.

Deep down, she knew her age wasn't the problem. But it was harder to acknowledge a travesty that couldn't be measured like a sagging arm: her husband's rejection of what it meant to be a red-blooded, masculine American.

"Those hairy-legged feminists can go to hell," she'd always told her son when he lamented the machismo of his exchangeable Latin lovers. "The patriarchy is the best thing that ever happened to women—and your kind, I suppose." After all, what woman wouldn't want a man to pay for her every want and whim, when all she had to do was offer a few minutes of sex in exchange, and not a forty-hour work week?

But apparently such a sweet deal wasn't enough for George anymore. He footed the bill for all of Charlene's increasingly extravagant desires, and wouldn't even accept a simple, two-minute handjob in return. It disgusted her. If there was one thing she hated in this world, it was a moocher. And that's exactly what her dear husband George had forced her to become.

# 14

THE SUN SHONE LOW through the woolly moss hanging from the trees that flanked the Thompsons' driveway. It cast flickering shadows on Levi's skin as he briskly walked toward the house, bottle in hand. He looked down at his father's watch, strapped loosely around his left wrist. Pap had thicker wrists than him. At the hour it pointed to, it was doubtful Mama would be working. Instead, Levi assumed she'd be sitting, or lying, in the parlor, tired enough to ignore his arrival. He hoped that Ella or Billie would cover the sound of the squeaking door like they'd done before. Apparently the only favors he got at home were from the voices of singers long since gone.

That evening, the sultry sirens were quiet. There were no fleeting blues notes slipping through the tired porch screens. Instead, Levi heard the scratching of a finished record, an unmistakable static that Mama never would have allowed if she were around to suffer it.

As he opened the front door, he thought he might be in the clear. He didn't smell fresh smoke, but only the lingering staleness of airborne tar trapped in the couch upholstery. If Mama were up, he would have been immediately assaulted by the stench of her vices upon cracking the door. He found her asleep on the sofa, completely unaware of his presence. It was a rare blessing he'd learned not to take for granted. It didn't happen often.

He set the bottle before her on the table, where it stood with an aristocratic grace never before seen in the parlor; with her tired eyes half open, Mama might have thought it were an angel, sparkling like pure crystal in the room's warm light. She reached out to grasp the glass guardian's hand in semi-conscious desperation. Someone had to pull her out of the perilous chasm between the sofa cushions in which she'd recklessly caught herself.

"Pour it," she groaned sleepily, but still with enough wakefulness to carelessly push a glass in her son's direction. "I ain't in no state to do so."

Levi turned away to fetch some ice, but didn't manage to take a single step. "Don't need none," Mama whined, half her face buried in a worn, frayed pillow, permanently stained with blotches of mascara and the salt of tears. "Just top it off 'n go. Don't need no more grief today, least of all from you, boy."

She'd given him an out. Hastily he wrenched off the cap and touched the mouth of the bottle to the lip of the overused glass, like a Wall Street banker kissing a back-alley hooker. Aptly he meant to pass it on to someone else, dirty and covered with oily fingerprints.

"And turn on that there record player again. Only thing more irritatin' than you just standin' there all useless is a scratched record."

It was his last task before he was free to go and leave her to her useless business. He pinched the stylus with his fingertips and swung it over, setting it delicately between the inner grooves of the well-worn record. It began to spin; after a crackle or two, Bessie Smith, the Empress of the Blues, opened with a song that cued Levi's welcome exit.

*"Trouble, trouble, I've had it all my days,"* she sang. *"It seems like trouble going to follow me to my grave."* Bessie Smith never told lies. No matter the song, Levi heard himself in it. Maybe Mama did too.

"Tell me this ain't some kinda joke, boy!"

She gripped the bottle with white knuckles, waving it in his direction like evidence of a crime he'd committed. In her anger she mustered up the will to sit up and touch her feet to the floor, but she struggled to stand. It was unnerving, seeing her so tired and frail. Her words, however, hadn't lost their sharpness, as slurred as they might have been. Levi did his best to withstand them.

"Somethin' different today, ma'am."

Mama shot out a sputtering laugh. "I ain't blind, boy—but maybe the Lord done struck you down 'n made you deaf 'n lame. I ain't never told you to run and fetch me 'somethin' different.'"

Without warning she threw the bottle. It hit the wood floor hard and shattered. Its clear, lukewarm poison pooled at Levi's feet and flowed along the cracks in the floorboards like eye-stinging streams. Levi jumped back to save his only pair of sneakers from the practically caustic liquid.

"I ain't drinkin' no city liquor, boy!" Mama yelled. She kicked a piece of glass toward Levi, her shoe scraping through the wet, gritty puddle. "You best remember where you done came from, too! Y'ain't nothin'—and this place ain't nothin', 'cause God done forsaken it before you was born! And there ain't a thing y'can do to make it any different, 'specially not drinkin' like a city boy!"

He meant to back away but knew she'd only follow. His feet almost began to walk on their own and carry him off to temporary refuge in his darkened bedroom, but the puddle of vodka surrounded him as if he were marooned on a raft of wooden floorboards, unable to escape. Standing his ground with little choice, Levi snapped, "Maybe it'd do you some good to try somethin' else for a change, since your usual drink ain't done nothin' but leave you piss-drunk and knocked out on that there couch."

A look of shock washed over Mama's face, the kind that exuded such furious hate that it could have been mistaken for genuine, innocent surprise, like extreme heat feeling cold to the touch. "If the Lord ain't already gone and struck you dumb, mark my words, boy, He sure as Hades gon' do it soon. Who do y'think you're talkin' to with that lip o' yours? Lemme tell you somethin', boy: I ain't your friend, and I ain't never gonna be. You wanna talk to somebody like that 'n act like you ain't below 'em, go run off to that 'friend' down yonder and do whatever abominations y'all partake in when ain't no one but God's a-watchin'!"

She let him go, but not without using up what little air was left in her tired lungs. She was his mother, not his friend, but it seemed he wasn't meant to have friends at all, because to have friends was to mean certain fornication—a sin that, even when borne in false witness, could never be shaken from Clemency's collective memory. According to her, even the big city wouldn't accept him, in spite of all its vulgarities. He'd been born in a no-good town, to a no-good father, and grew up to be just as devoid of value as the man who begot him. There wasn't a city in the world where he could make something of himself. To create something out of nothing was God's job. Anything else was just cigarette smoke and broken mirrors.

••

The train station was the quietest part of town, though it wasn't far off Main Street. The tracks never rattled from the approach of a distant passenger train, and pebbles hadn't jumped up in excitement since before Jonah was born. Rumor had it that George von Braun was paying off the governor to get the station reopened, to speed up the development of his little pet project of propelling Clemency into the present. If he was dabbling in a bit of bribery, it hadn't yet paid off, and no one saw a single train proudly brandishing the von Braun family name.

Instead, the tracks stretched on untouched into the distance, where open fields turned to dark forest. The trees obscured exactly where that steel path led. It was the road least traveled, un-traveled, which, for all Jonah knew, could have been cut short at a cliff miles north. At least an escape would have meant a quick death, abrupt and unexpected—a prospect that was almost exciting. Life in Clemency promised only a slow, demoralizing demise, not in the fiery glory of a train plunging into a bottomless chasm, but a quiet fading into the dark.

But for one moment, Jonah appreciated the stillness. The only sound to be heard was the rustling of an old train schedule, tacked to a board over the mildew-slick benches; it fluttered with frayed ends in the breeze, meekly waving the existential words of a teenage vandal written in black marker.

*"What now?"* the defacer had written. It was a question to which Clemency had no answer.

"People's always raisin' questions but ain't nobody got answers," Jonah muttered. His eyes followed the overgrown rails to the horizon, where they faded into nothingness.

Sophia sighed along with him, offering the first rush of air since the last time a train passed through, years ago. "You wouldn't listen to their answers, anyway. And just as well, since their truths are worthless compared to answers you went and found yourself."

"Tell that to your parents' congregation," he groaned. "They think your daddy's got a monopoly on the truth."

"Some people are better off as followers, I guess."

"Well, it's not hard to monopolize on truth when you're standin' at a pulpit with a Bible in your hand. Sheep will believe anything as long as it's from the Book."

"It's the *Bible* that's got a monopoly on truth," Sophia insisted, frowning. "*Not* the person holding it. And how many times have I gotta tell you to watch that mouth? If you get yourself struck by lightning, I'm sitting too close for comfort."

Jonah smirked. "I gave you a way out weeks ago. Ain't nobody's forcin' you to sit here and listen to my habitual blasphemy."

"I choose to," Sophia reminded him. "You can't save sinners without sitting among them."

"Might wanna quit while you're ahead. I'd say I'm a lost cause."

"There's no such thing. And besides, all that sinning hasn't been enough to dampen that light in your eyes. Can't hide that under a basket."

"Even a decade at seminary wouldn't give you the apostolic authority to forgive the kind o' shit I've done."

"I don't need a degree to notice when a rotten little boy's finally becoming a man." She leaned in and gave him a delicate kiss on the cheek; a rush of warmth spread through his body, like an anesthetic, numbing everything but his emotions. It was ironic that Sophia claimed to be witness to some masculine coming-of-age, when one innocent kiss was enough to make him feel like a bashful child.

His voice almost cracked, Peter Brady–style. "Glad to hear that I ain't blossomin' in a vacuum. Guess you can add one more man to the ranks o' Clemency's army for Christ."

"You're not the Crusader type. You're better off with a pen in your hand, not a sword."

"They say it's mightier, I guess."

"No, it's just that your wordplay is better than your swordplay. You didn't slay me with a blade—it's that smart mouth of yours. But you could do a lot more with that talent than just sweep me off my feet. You could get yourself into a good school and get a real education."

"Ain't no school's gonna admit me," he grumbled. "And it's too late for a football scholarship or somethin'. Besides, I ain't been in a single class in a damn long time, and my brain ain't as quick as it used to be." The weed didn't help much, and neither did Clemency's distaste for critical thinking.

"You're just a year out of high school, but you're acting like some kind of old, academic spinster, too past his prime for a suitor or degree."

"Ain't anyone ever told you a gap looks bad on a résumé?"

"You could always tell them you took a year off to contribute at the local parish," she suggested with a sardonic smirk.

"Now I know Sophie Shaw ain't in favor o' bearin' false witness."

"Of course I'm not. But you wouldn't be lying."

"And how's that?"

"You were giving the preacher's daughter the time of her life."

There came that tingling again, back with a vengeance. He closed his eyes for a second and let the chills pass, concerned that he might stammer like a pubescent boy faced with his first kiss. "Why would I wanna go and ruin what we've got goin' by headin' off to college somewhere?" he asked, twirling a lock of her dark hair around his finger.

"I'd wait for you."

"Four years? Trust me, I ain't worth it."

"Yeah, even for four years. And it's not about being worth it. It's a practical issue: you're the closest thing to a handsome boy this whole town's got."

He laughed at her characteristic teasing but posed his next question in all seriousness: "But what about you? Y'could get outta here, too, a hell of a lot easier than I could."

Sophia sighed but didn't look distressed. She had that look on her face that suggested she was at peace with the world around her, even if that world wasn't the good creation God had made at the dawn of time. "My future's already written, as clear as that greeting sign on the edge of town. I'm to inherit the family business. When my parents are too old to stand up and praise the Lord, or their arthritis gets so bad they can't even turn a page in their Bibles, I'll be the one leading the people of Clemency through the narrow gates of Heaven." There was no bitterness in her voice. Wistfulness, maybe—but no grudge, against the Reverend and his wife, or the backwater town that'd claimed one more hostage.

"Well, if I heed your wise advice, then I'll use my impressive new degree to get you outta here." He nodded, affirming his intention to himself. He swore an oath in his mind that day, even if Sophia would never really believe it. "I'll get me a good job and you can find yourself a whole new flock o' sheep to shepherd."

"And buy us a house in the suburbs somewhere, have three kids and a dog, and a big, bold American flag waving in our front yard?"

"If that's what you want, then yeah. I'll do what it takes to make it happen."

"Apply for school, then," she pushed one last time. He knew she was right. That's how he'd get the girl in the end, and that white picket fence he'd never wanted until that very moment.

They spent the remainder of their time at the train station in silence, with Sophia's head set softly on his shoulder, because she knew he needed some time to think about the whole idea, and he knew it, too. He put his arm around her and watched the sky until the tree line scraped the sun and the warm light paved their path home with liquid gold. They followed it together as far as they could. And when the Shaw family house emerged in the distance, they had no choice but to part ways. Sophia melted away into the sunset, and Jonah was left alone in the street, thinking not of the night that was falling all around him, but of the coming morning.

••

Clemency didn't look much different in 1976. That was the year Lenore was born, to a handsome car salesman by the name of Jack Quigley, and a devout housewife, Eileen. Of course, the cars were brand new, though most were still on the road forty years later, sporting rust instead of a shiny paintjob. But back then, the trains ran through the town twice a day, gas was cheaper than milk, and now-vacant storefronts still had names. Nobody was willing to call Clemency prosperous, but there was some hope it might be. Though they didn't envision a bustling commercial center, they certainly didn't expect that it would one day come to make the Great Depression look like a time of great abundance.

Jack Quigley made a decent living by honest means. He wasn't a greasy, sleazy salesman, despite the grease he used to slick back his hair. He was a good-looking man with a natural charm and penchant for small talk that seemed not so small. Jack had a thing for Cadillacs, and always pushed those sales the hardest. They were strong, reliable American cars—a chariot fit for a patriot.

"Proudly made in the USA," he never neglected to mention as he presented young couples with what was clearly meant to be their first car together. If it broke down, surely the owner was to blame, as personal accountability was the American way back then.

He always managed to empty the lot of all its Cadillacs around the Fourth of July. Cars sold at that point in the summer came with an American flag for the buyer's porch, free of charge. Jack felt it was a good-natured touch to an even better-natured deal. He'd playfully slap the trunk of the car as the new owner drove off to live the American dream. It was the kind of smack on the bottom that a man might impose upon an attractive woman. Something about it rubbed his wife the wrong way. Granted, almost everything gave her that mental rug burn.

Eileen was never the kind of woman who could be described as stable. Her only anchor in life was the risen Lord Jesus, who provided the comfort she refused to allow her own husband to provide her. She was, of course, the victim of alleged adultery. If Jack was so touchy with his cars, how much touchier was he with the women he swindled into buying them? It was a question she asked herself over and over again, even on those days when she woke up on the right side of the bed and faced the day with a manic smile. Those were the times when she rushed through the house like a tornado, catching dust and dirty dishes in her whirlwind to be thrown right where they belonged: out of sight, like her husband's sins.

Lenore liked when her mother was happy, as any child would have. There was a certain amount of juvenile selfishness involved, of course. When her mother was having one of her good days, attention wasn't something she'd have to fight for. A new doll might have awaited her, or a few extra minutes of grainy, black-and-white television, and the home-cooked meals tasted better than usual. Best of all, the belt would stay in her mother's wardrobe, and the wooden kitchen spoon in its drawer. They were cruel monsters brooding in their lairs, just waiting to see the light of day when mother's light had gone out.

Each time she felt the humiliating sting of the belt on her body, Lenore looked back at her mother for mercy, but Eileen stared right past her, like she wasn't there. It was as if she were chastising someone else. Perhaps she imagined her husband. Perhaps she imagined herself.

Housewives in those days always gathered for a drink and a cigarette while their husbands were hard at work. Eileen partook in such social activities, but over time, she grew tired of her so-called friends. Clara's famous iced tea was famously unpalatable. It was tiresome to tell constant white lies about Harriet's hideous false eyelashes. Norma was a slut addicted to her dryer's spin cycle, Laura's knitted blankets were itchy and ugly, and all the Best Flower Garden awards in the world couldn't make Bernice a pretty trophy wife. Drinking alone offered a much better repose. After all, she couldn't expect her bridge partners to believe anything she said, when they themselves lived in a delusional Stepford world where hair curlers were tiaras and men kept their word. They were too self-absorbed to even consider her problems.

She let the suspicions fester for a while before she finally confronted Jack. She expected he'd deny the accusations, and he fulfilled her jealous prophecy. Being a kind man and a proper Christian husband, he reacted with tenderness, and did not raise his voice even half a decibel. Most would have called it touching. Eileen, though, found it condescending, and her bitterness grew with each gentle embrace. That smell on his shirt—was it perfume? Or was it just that new car smell, which men found as captivating as the scent of a beautiful woman?

He still had the aura of the handsome twenty-six-year old he was when Lenore was born, which drew in married women like moths to a bug zapper. Eileen, on the other hand, was stuck at home in a housedress, with hands permanently smelling like Pine-Sol and breasts to whom gravity had not been kind. If he were being unfaithful, could he really be blamed? She struggled to accept that she'd suffered the curse of Eve, like every woman before her: to have a screaming child ruin her body, to sustain the physical torment of being torn apart and the emotional pain of facing herself in a mirror, all while her virile husband gallivanted around without a single stretch mark to his name.

No one would ever believe her. Everyone knew he was a good, honest man, who would never do such a despicable thing. Somewhere deep down inside her, Eileen knew it to be true. But each time she popped open a bottle, she put a lid on that inner wellspring of wisdom.

Accusing him did little to ease her fears. She turned to God for help, kneeling at her bedside whenever she had a minute to herself; Lenore would never forget the sight of her mother's hands folded and set upon the floral comforter, like a bed of roses for a Marian devotion. To question her husband was to break her vows as a submissive wife, and this was an egregious sin, of which only a contrite and humble heart could be absolved. But even after appealing to God's merciful nature for her shortcomings as an upright Christian wife, she still tacked on an addendum to her prayer, asking for evidence of his adultery so she might be vindicated before the eyes of the community. Her testimony as a woman, after all, was worth half as much as his.

"There is nothing covered that shall not be revealed," she preached to her daughter as she put her to bed. She scorned secrets. Though she should have left her daughter out of it, she decided that her marital cross would be more easily borne with the help of a third-grader.

A girl that age wasn't fit to play the role of therapist, confidante, and spiritual counselor, but one could have fooled Eileen Quigley. She lay sprawled out on the parlor sofa, a drink in one hand, a cigarette in the other, relaying her entire life's narrative to a little girl who just wanted to go play outside in the sun, and not in the ever-shifting shade of her mother's unpredictable mood swings.

Eventually, one of Eileen's old friends caught wind of her volatility, and showed up at her door with a bottle of red and white pills that she got from her doctor for her own traditional housewife's depression. Eileen swallowed her pride and the pills that night, after much prayer and liquor. From that day on, she popped them like the candy she never bought for her daughter. It did seem to help, at least at first. Young Lenore hadn't seen her mother so uplifted and whimsical in a long time, if ever. But for every psychological high came a devastating low, even worse than those crashes that came naturally to her, and those that came with the last drop of an exhausted bottle of whiskey.

When those contraband pills finally ran out, she cleaned herself up as she would have on a Sunday, and headed to that same doctor to get her own prescription for a medication that the federal government banned a decade later. Studies found that it caused debilitating birth defects, and, despite the manufacturer's claim that it would stabilize the emotionally unstable, it permanently altered the brain's serotonin receptors, and consequently, Eileen Quigley's relationship with her own family.

No dose of medication was high enough to fix her paranoia, and her suspicions of her husband's infidelity proved to be a self-fulfilling prophecy, as she drove him to disappear more often over the years. His alleged overtime at work reached a point of violating labor laws, if he were telling the truth, because nearly every night he left his daughter alone with the insufferable woman who was too drunk to help her when she got her first period, was too heavily medicated to attend her junior high graduation, and simply too numb to read the blurry, unintelligible words on her college acceptance letter. She was, however, coherent enough to realize that she would be left alone with her husband without the buffer of her daughter, if Lenore were to head off to nursing school.

"You'd leave me alone with that lyin' cheater, just for your own selfishness, girl?"

"Divorce him, then, and leave me be," Lenore suggested, finally uttering the word "divorce," which had lingered like a pink elephant in the room for years.

"I'd sooner risk my sanity than my immortal soul. Divorce is un-Christian."

She preferred hell on earth over eternal damnation, even if it meant dragging her daughter into the pit with her—a pit of her own making. Jack had crawled out of it a long time ago.

Later that night, the letter ended up in the trash, crumpled up beside an empty beer bottle and Eileen's wedding ring. Like she did every night, Eileen went back to retrieve the ring, having succumbed to the guilt that got her every time. Lenore never went back for the letter. She honored her mother, despite the dishonor her mother brought on the family name.

She used to be excited for the prospect of graduation, counting down the days till she could see a cap and gown instead of her mother's housedress; now, the date she'd marked on her calendar was routine, without significance, like an annual physical or a dental exam. Every day was indistinguishable, blending into the next, separated only by the six hours a day she spent at school, which were just as mundane. There were no classmates to bring over for sleepovers and teenage gossip. If she were to expose any girl her age to the train wreck that was her mother, she'd destroy any hope of a social life, and the five months of school she had left would be as tortuous as the hangovers her mother awoke to each morning, but impervious to aspirin.

Life was one long cloudy day for a while, until Lenore found a magazine slipped into the weekend newspaper, left at her front door. It was a shiny, new issue of *Cosmopolitan*, to which she was sure her mother had no subscription. Maybe it was God trying to put a smile on her face, as she was too pretty of a creation to frown so often. Granted, it was unlikely that God cared much for fashion or celebrity gossip, though at that time the periodical still had a shred of dignity.

As it turned out, it wasn't God's doing, at least directly. That magazine was delivered at the hands of Sam, the local paper boy, who had brought it to her doorstep personally, instead of tossing the paper from his bike at the end of the driveway, as was his usual routine.

The next month, the newest issue fell into her possession. And the month after that.

In the privacy of her darkened room, Lenore flipped through the pages of the magazines, careful not to rustle them too much, lest her mother catch her reading something other than her Bible or schoolbooks. She ogled photos of beautiful women, dressed to impress young men, and to encourage young girls to aspire to a level of beauty they were unlikely to ever achieve. She swore an oath that night that she would one day look like them. Those women weren't flaunting perfect bodies and flawless makeup to shame her—she felt no shame. All she felt was admiration, aspiration, and a longing to catch Sam Thompson in the act of leaving that gift on her front porch.

In matryoshka doll fashion, handwritten letters began appearing tucked inside the magazines, which were tucked inside the weekly paper, and ultimately tucked away in a shoebox beneath Lenore's bed.

Penned by the unsteady hand of a teenage boy, the letters narrated a love story that, by today's misanthropic standards, would have been considered stalking at best. But in that decade, in that small town, it was endearing to know that she'd caught the eye of a quiet young man who was as handsome as he was kind. He was a far cry from those self-obsessed, middle-American macho types with hormonal imbalances due to their mothers' smoking during pregnancy and their coalmining fathers' mutant sperm. He played trombone, he was a Rain Man for trigonometry, and spent his free time at home with his impossibly Christian nuclear family.

Just the thought of them was enough to crush the child of an average, broken American home under the weight of a deep shame. Then came natural envy, then bitter, sick jealousy. In the end, it was always just disappointment in one's own imperfect life. She ended up meeting them much sooner than she'd have hoped to.

She met Sam's father for the first time at the Thompsons' front door, after she'd decided that his periodic kind gestures were driving her insane. It was early on a Saturday morning, and she should have known that the whole saintly clan would be home to answer her knock on the door—after all, it was the true biblical Sabbath, beginning on a Friday night without a drop of alcohol. As soon as the door began to swing open Lenore caught the scent of a traditional American breakfast, which teased her empty stomach with the undertones of melted butter in a cast iron pan. It'd been quite a while since her own mother had cooked such a meal. She'd almost forgotten the popping percussion of crackling bacon on the stove.

"Can I help you, Miss?" asked Mr. Thompson without a hint of suspicion or reservation. He stood there in the doorway already dressed in a checkered shirt, tan slacks, and well-polished shoes. His son had inherited the freckles that spread faintly over his nose, which was rather small for his face. Behind him, his wife sat down to eat with her teenage son, to whom she'd just served a portion of scrambled eggs twice as big as her own.

Lenore paused, immediately embarrassed to have interrupted them, probably while they were saying grace, given her luck. "I'm sorry—I can come back. I didn't mean to intrude."

"And I didn't mean to make you feel like you're intruding. Come on in, if you'd like. I assume you're here for Samuel?" He smiled and stepped aside to allow her to enter, without even asking her name. Sam grinned from the table. Mrs. Thompson went to retrieve another plate.

There really wasn't enough food to accommodate a guest, and Lenore quickly realized how careful they'd been to fix their plates with just enough to satisfy them. They all surrendered some of their untouched eggs to Lenore's plate, despite her protests. They gave up what little they had just to make her feel welcome, and they did it with smiles on their faces, without bitterness or reluctance. It was a kindness she'd never felt at home. Until then, the greatest act of generosity she'd ever seen was her mother choosing a drunken sleep over an undeserved beating.

Beneath the table, Sam grazed his foot against hers. It was the first time she'd felt the tingling warmth of human contact on her skin that wasn't the lingering numbness after a backhanded smack by her mother. She wished she'd been wearing a pair of heels out of one of her magazines. Instead, Sam touched her worn tennis shoe, but to him, they might as well have been sparkling ruby slippers.

From then on, they were inseparable. But she did her best to keep him and her mother as separate as possible. For a good while, she managed to.

Her mother was in no shape to meet anyone new, given she could barely recognize her own husband sometimes. In her defense, he made few appearances at home toward the end of their marriage. He'd go off to the dealership, she'd pour herself a drink and ruminate on his alleged infidelity; she'd pour another, and obsess over the brigade of shoulder pad–wearing secretaries he could be womanizing at that very moment; by her fifth drink, she was ready to go out to catch him in the act and smash a couple windshields, if she were able to actually get up off the couch. The sofa smelled like her husband, since that's where he'd been sleeping for weeks. It made her want to cut out the upholstery and burn it in a trash can out back.

Her husband practically had to hold the pen for her as she signed their eventual divorce papers, because she was four drinks in on an empty stomach, as Lenore hadn't made her breakfast that morning. When all was signed and initialed, there was only one spot of running ink on the last page. It wasn't from a tear drop. It was a hot day, and her glass had been sweating.

"My soul is blameless," she muttered one afternoon with words slurring one into the next. "It's your damned father's doin', and he's gon' pay the price for it, sooner or later." Her hands were clean, and his were soaked in blood. Whose blood that was, no one really knew, since both professed contradicting stories to the church congregation that shook their heads at the thought of their marital failure.

Eileen, still waiting in fear for the return of Christ Jesus and drinking to pass the time, never put herself back on the market. Her ex-husband, on the other hand, found himself a woman named Bev who had been flirting with him at the dealership for longer than he could remember. She wasn't the greatest catch, but when he'd been denied his masculine needs for so long, he was willing to stick it to anything with tits and legs, as would any man.

Bev was occasionally attractive, but permanently plain in terms of personality. Jack started bringing her around after admitting her existence to his daughter and her new boyfriend Sam one evening, while they were eating a poorly cooked dinner at his new apartment across town. When they first met her, she offered the usual pleasantries: a hug with two feet between them for Lenore, and a weak handshake with press-on coral nails for Sam. And as they sat there pretending to relish the burnt, charcoal taste of her father's proudly home-cooked meal, Bev had only the most tepid questions to ask them, those few times that she actually opened her mouth for anything other than a spoonful of clay mashed potatoes.

"How'd you two meet?"—as if it wasn't perfectly obvious that they went to the same high school in the same small town, where it was impossible to deny even facial recognition, at the very least.

"What'd you two do today?"—they both had their bookbags sitting on the floor by the sofa, a dead giveaway that they were, in fact, at school all day, and not sneaking around like teenage delinquents.

"Got any brothers 'n sisters?"—she knew damned well Sam didn't, since he'd answered that question twice before during that same dinner, but Bev seemed incapable of recalling it.

Neither of them bothered to get to know her, because from the very beginning, Bev was more like an object in the room than an actual human being. She was a plastic trophy that was far from boast-worthy, not even unique enough to be called a pink elephant, who must have had some sort of exceptional value in the bedroom, because there was nothing publicly impressive about her.

Lenore made two life decisions that night, inspired by Bev's blandness: first, she would never allow herself to be so dull, no matter what the cost; and second, if she were to ever have a future marriage end early, she would not remarry. She understood why Jesus professed remarriage to be adulterous. In trying to forge a new relationship completely opposite of the first, one would only end up with a lackluster reflection of her own fears. It was cheating on one's own dignity, an unfaithfulness to self-respect, and a reduction of a serious vow into a white lie.

Her father rashly put a ring on Bev's finger, then tossed his own in the trash half a year later. It was the second time he had to sign divorce papers like a death certificate. His pride shattered, he packed his bags and moved to Pensacola. He offered to take Lenore with him, but she declined without a moment's hesitation. After all, she had a new engagement ring that some parts of Clemency had yet to ogle.

That small, sparkling rock on her finger became the cornerstone of her self-confidence in those days, when she was still living at her mother's house for the sake of old-fashioned propriety. But even at her wedding, she had to treat her mother like one of the infant cousins, constantly keeping an eye on her to make sure she didn't light her napkin on fire or retch behind the bushes beside the Southern Mercy Bible Church. Miraculously, she didn't cause a scene. Surely God had intervened when she shakily stood to offer a slurred toast to her daughter and the handsome groom, because she immediately forgot what she had planned to say (if she'd planned it at all), and fell back into her seat, exhausted. Sam's best friend gave a short speech instead. It was short, sweet, and unoriginal, and they wouldn't have had it any other way.

They both knew they didn't have the money for a proper honeymoon, so neither expected to be lying on white sands in the West Indies. Sam worked hard, though, to save up the kind of money required for such a romantic escape. He slaved away at the post office, working the extra hours that the federal government said he couldn't work, and picked up side jobs doing manual labor in their neighbors' yards. Lenore missed seeing him as often, but she knew he was working for both their sakes, and when that day came that they could hop on a plane for the first time and flee to the tropics, it'd finally be clear that all the wistful longing was worth it.

Four weeks after the wedding they were living in a basement apartment on the west side of Clemency, with Lenore vomiting at 7:26 AM like clockwork. She didn't need a urine-soaked strip to tell her she was pregnant. It'd be like needing a radar map to tell it was raining right outside their tiny cellar windows.

It would have been helpful, however, if someone had given them fair warning five months later that their landlord was about to be arrested for failing to reconcile over a hundred unpaid parking tickets, and that they'd be given twelve hours' notice to vacate the property.

The pickings were slim when it came to housing, but even if they hadn't been, it was impossible to find a new place to live in the middle of the night. They didn't own much at that point in their lives: a cheap mattress on an even cheaper bedframe, an end table or two, and a hefty bag of paper plates and plastic cutlery well suited for frozen meals. As Lenore stepped out into the dark of the driveway, an old blouse fell out of one of the bulky garbage bags in which they'd stuffed their clothing. She picked it up and realized it was a hand-me-down from her mother's youth. At that moment, she knew what, or who, their only option was.

Her mother had coral-colored curlers in her hair when she answered the knock on her door. Upon seeing her daughter and son-in-law standing meekly on her front porch, she instinctively touched her fingers to her mouth, as if to take a drag from a cigarette, only to realize she had no such cigarette in her hand. Grumbling, she held open the door for them. She told Lenore to fetch her a pack of Byron Clays from the coffee table while she went to put on a pot of coffee. It wasn't so much of an act of hospitality as it was a necessity on her part. It was one o'clock in the morning, and she reeked of cheap liquor.

Over a cup of offensively bitter black coffee Lenore and Sam recited their sob story, though there was no sobbing. Lenore was anxious, for sure, and it came through in her voice. Sam took over the narrative when necessary, interrupting his new wife when she began to ramble on about how she'd make sure to get a job, and would do everything her mother wanted around the house, all to make a stronger case as to why their staying with her would be both transient and helpful. Eileen was quick to draw attention to her daughter's conspicuous baby bump, which she insisted could never be hidden, and would be instant grounds for rejection during any job interview. Of course, this was all coming from a woman who drank and slept professionally.

In the end, it was an appeal to the Word of God that swayed Eileen into taking them in, seeing as it was her duty as a Christian mother to support her child in times of need. Though it may have been a spiritual obligation imposed by the Lord God Himself, the idea of mandated compassion left such a bad taste in Eileen's mouth that she looked as though she'd just taken two straight shots of vinegar.

"You owe me," she warned her daughter as Sam moved their belongings into the spare bedroom. Just thankful for a roof over her head, Lenore gave it little thought at the time. But as she lay in her childhood twin-sized bed, crammed in with her husband sound asleep beside her, she couldn't help but reflect on her mother's bitter declaration of debt. Most mothers would have offered up their home unconditionally, but hers had a right mind to leave a bill on her pillow.

If Eileen were to thrust an invoice into her daughter's hand, it would have come out of a formidable stack she'd already accumulated before her new tenants' arrival. Lenore discovered the mountain of envelopes one afternoon while Sam was out working at the post office and her mother was out cold in the parlor. It was hidden in a cabinet near the back door, where Lenore had hoped to find a mop and bucket so that she might clean the kitchen's dingy linoleum floor. She did get her hands on said bucket, but behind it loomed a two-foot tower of unopened letters. They were addressed to her mother, and those at the top were clearly marked as time sensitive, branded with red ink; they certainly weren't love letters from an estranged husband. Morbidly curious, Lenore reached out to take one. She slipped it into the apron she had wrapped around her waist, and meant to read it later, in the relative privacy of her bedroom.

"Y'know, it's a federal offense to open mail that don't belong to you," Sam reminded her while they sat on the bed that evening, the envelope in Lenore's lap.

"Are you gonna report me, Mr. Postman?"

"Ain't no way I'm lettin' you rot in jail. Then I'd be left alone with your mama and her cattywampus life." He grinned and rubbed his young wife's shoulder. Her attention, however, was fixed on the unpaid electric bill in her hand, and the staggering amount that was left overdue. They both knew that it likely wasn't the only utility she hadn't paid in months. All sorts of bills could have been mixed in the pile she'd hidden away in the broom closet, having literally swept them out of sight. They said nothing further on the matter, and clicked off the light to go to bed, and to spare her mother a few future pennies.

Two weeks later, the lights stayed off for good. Eileen claimed it was a power outage, a freak incident out of her control. Three days after the alleged blackout, the water ran cold as Sam was taking his morning shower; it was one of those rare times when Lenore heard him cuss. The sun hadn't even set by the time the water was shut off completely, and the pipes lurched and groaned, dry as bones. In the span of four days, they found themselves set back an entire century, when a dim candle on the kitchen table was their only lamp as they discussed what might be done about it.

"I ain't payin' them thieves a dime," Eileen vowed, like the late fees she'd incurred were predatory, even unlawful. "That hot water was unreliable, anyway. Bad service don't deserve to be paid for."

"I'm sure if we called the utility companies, they'd be willin' to start up service again, if you at least give 'em some kinda minimum payment," Sam suggested.

"Phone's dead," Lenore reminded him.

"I could call from work. We can fix this."

"No—*you* can fix this, seein' as I been lettin' you two squatters stay under my roof this whole time without payin' me a cent o' rent," Eileen hissed. The candlelight left her looking something devilish, casting fiery colors on her face, before which rose ghostly wisps of smoke from her cigarette.

"No disrespect, Mama, but we didn't rack up this debt. Them bills date back an awful long time, and we ain't been here long," Lenore reminded her. She should have been more careful with her words. The glow of her mother's cigarette flared up as she took one more drag, then she unleashed smoke from her nostrils like a dragon, and swiped her claws across the table, knocking her glass of brandy to the floor with a startling clatter.

"I done told you, girl, *you owe me*. Y'ain't givin' me no choice but to hold my hospitality over your sorry heads with *that* kinda ungratefulness. Y'come to my door in the middle o' the night, beggin' me to take mercy on y'all, and all 'cause o' me, y'aint been left out in the cold like a pair o' dirty, good-for-nothin' vagrants. No good deed goes unpunished, don't it?"

*"Consider it done,"* Sam barked over her deranged diatribe. He didn't give his wife a chance to protest, or propose an alternative. He stood up, retrieved a small box from their bedroom, and tossed it on the table without a word. The lid slid off when it landed before Eileen. It was filled with cash—his entire savings. In an instant, he surrendered their honeymoon to a selfish, unfixable woman who didn't even have the decency to recognize the sacrifice he'd just made for her, let alone thank him.

Lenore was in shock, unsure of whom she should direct her anger at—her bloodsucking, useless mother, who'd stolen her dreams in a shoebox like a greedy child, or her husband, who was so rash as to offer it up as tribute without her consent? And as they lay in bed after her mother had retired for the night, probably clutching the box of cash to her chest with a smile, they said nothing to each other. Even Sam's shoulder against her was more contact than she wanted with him.

As soon as they were able to, they moved out of her mother's house. She watched from the parlor window, drunk and confused as to whether they'd return. Lenore didn't say goodbye, thank her, leave a note, or any trace that they'd ever stayed there at all. Her mother had given her an inch, and took a mile in return. So as they drove off from her house, with its hot water and functioning lights (for the time being), she blessed every mile marker along the way. She refused to look back. And she swore to herself, to Sam and to God that she would sooner die than chain herself to someone else's favors. Mercy was deceptive. Unconditional love was God's alone.

••

"I swear to whatever uncaring God might be out there, Thompson, that if you tell *anyone* I'm smoking these glorified bundles of woodchips, I'll let the whole town think I took your virginity freshman year of high school in the chemistry lab," Jimmy threatened as they sat back down at their table at Gene's, having shamefully exchanged a few dollars at the cigarette machine for a pack of Byron Clays. Levi threw his hands up in the air in surrender. The cheap, domestic pack on Jimmy's side of the high top would be their secret—as secret as one could hope for when sitting in a crowded, degenerate local bar.

"You're drawin' too much attention to yourself already," Levi noted, and pointed at Jimmy's choice of attire that late afternoon: a metallic gold T-shirt with a V-neck that plunged far too low, white skinny jeans, and a pair of handmade Italian black leather shoes with a heel a little too high for a man. Not atypically, he kept his insectoid sunglasses on, even in the dim light of the smoky bar. He figured he might as well make at least a small effort at anonymity, no matter how predictably ineffective.

"Eh, screw it," Jimmy muttered, pulling off his shades, having abandoned his efforts to drink incognito. "These backwater crackheads won't remember a thing, anyway." He drew attention to the hometown queen of drug addicts and lechers, Ms. Valerie Skinner, who'd been eyeing them at the bar ever since they walked in. Whether the look in her eye was one of suspicion or of carnal intrigue had yet to be determined, if one could ever really know. Her stare could just as easily have been attributed to the coarse, white powder that still clung to her untrimmed fingernail. If Levi had been a betting man, he would have put his money on the latter.

"I'm surprised you'd even look her in the eye. Ain't that an honor reserved for the upper class?"

"Not always the upper class, but the sons of Colombian cartel bosses and Arab oil barons, for sure. Unfortunately, Thompson, it's too late for me to start ignoring her now."

"And why's that?"

"Since she caught me on her front lawn two days ago, if you can even call that barren plot of dirt a lawn."

Levi could hardly contain his laughter. Struggling to swallow his mouthful of beer without spraying it all over the table and Jimmy's gilded joke of a shirt, he shook his head in total disbelief. "And what the hell were you doin' down there with the slime o' humanity? You swore up 'n down that you'd never be caught dead buyin' smack off the likes o' them."

"Trust me, Thompson, it wasn't my proudest moment. I wore gloves, at least. I wasn't about to catch anything through physical contact with what might as well be a walking corpse. And so far as I know, no one saw me. I made sure of that—I had on quite the disguise. No one could have ever expected that the sultry hooker in a mink coat and red heels was none other than Jimmy von Braun."

"You still ain't said why you were there in the first place."

"Charlene took the last of my stash and left me high and dry. Naturally, that bitch blamed the maid, but we both know that Latinas steal jewelry, not coke—you can't make a quick buck at a pawn shop with a dime bag. And it was just my luck that my usual sources wouldn't take my calls," he lamented, rolling his eyes. "You know, I'll never understand that. If being a drug dealer is your only form of employment, what could you possibly be doing that'd make you too busy to answer the goddamned phone? *Especially* when it's your most important client calling! Without me, those little white brats would be out of a job!"

"And somehow the shit Gabe's sellin' didn't wreck your nose?"

"Thankfully no, but I did spend most of the time worrying that I'd wake up looking like La Toya Jackson. But I survived, Thompson, and lived to tell the tale, as sorry and humiliating as it may be. Now I've got a new appreciation for what that hot white trash friend of yours has been going through all this time with his little tramp of a sister. If ever I hit rock bottom, it must've been then."

"Sounds like a damn shame."

"And *that's* why I won't be playing in the snow anymore, Thompson. I'm declaring it to the world: that part of my life is over." He finished off his double shot of vodka in one swift gulp and exhaled sharply. "This, however, I'll be enjoying till the end. In fact, when I'm gone, if you can replace the embalming fluid with 100-proof vodka, then by all means, do it."

Levi was hesitant to sing Jimmy's praises, but remained cautiously optimistic. A declaration of chemical abstinence was something he'd never expected to hear coming right from Jimmy's mouth. At a loss for words, he replied, "Guess there ain't much sense in gettin' high all the time when you're livin' the high life with them rich folk up on that there hill."

"Clearly you don't know much about the high life, Thompson, even after all these weeks of me giving you a glimpse into how the other half lives! You might think drugs are a lower-class problem, and you wouldn't be totally wrong. Poor, hopeless trash do it to escape their problems and their sad, bleak, and probably self-inflicted lives. But the wealthy do it to escape their *lack* of problems."

"Ain't sure I follow."

"It's an empty life, don't you get it?" Jimmy snapped in frustration. "All the poor trash in this country thinks is that a big bank account means a perfect, goddamned life. Well, I hate to break it to you, it doesn't. My bitch mother hasn't smiled once ever since her savings hit seven figures. Why do you think all these school shooters are pampered white kids? Because they don't feel a damn thing, since they've never had to struggle for anything their whole lives, and have never had a bigger problem than getting the wrong Christmas present. Gunning down a classroom full of first-graders is a *thrill*, Thompson—it makes them feel something for once, even if it's something morally detestable. And since not all of us are sick, twisted fuckers like them, then it's drugs for the rest of us. And what can I say, Thompson? It wasn't until I started letting myself be seen in public with your run-down yet inexplicably cute ass that I realized any of it. I guess you're proving to be more of an influence than I thought."

He paused after they both realized that he'd just uttered something profoundly intimate. Who was this Jimmy von Braun who gave a damn what others thought, and let himself be changed— maybe even *fixed*—by someone else, especially someone who made less in a year than a five-year-old Jimmy made on one week's allowance? And Levi, who had never had the chance to become familiar with the feeling of accomplishment, prided himself for the first time on helping to put someone's life back together. Maybe one day he'd mend his own. That day seemed a long way away, but he smiled with satisfaction regardless, knowing that he was off to a good start.

••

The ear-splitting crash of the rusty back door was even louder in the dead silence of the library, so offensive to the ears that Jonah cringed and gritted his teeth until the echoes had fully faded. Blameless given the circumstances, Susan barked from the front desk, *"Make it quick, kid!"* She was on to him. Years of cigarette smoking had probably left her sense of smell dull as ditchwater, so it wasn't the skunky joint in Jonah's pocket that had betrayed him. Susan had a sharper mind than even she cared to admit. What else could he possibly be doing out back by the dumpsters? No matter how promiscuous she thought him to be, she couldn't possibly have thought that even he could get it up amid piles of musty, wet paper pulp and week-old lunches.

Again, he heard her smoky voice sound out from behind the bookshelves. "I don't give a tinker's damn if you need a toke or two, so long as you don't go mixin' in the smut with the Bibles!" She slipped in one final word as he carefully closed the rusted door, leaving it just slightly ajar: "And maybe even save me some! I hear it does wonders for the glaucoma!"

He shook his head, and cupped his hand behind his lighter to block the slight breeze. The thought of Susan blazing up was enough to make him simper, and he had to fight the muscular instinct to smile as he put the smoldering joint to his lips and took his first hit. He'd rolled it conservatively before he left the house that morning, sprinkling only a fraction of what he normally would into the curled paper pinched between his fingers. It burned quick and hot, and before he knew it, the glowing embers had eaten their way down to his fingertips. Feeling the heat of an imminent burn, he dropped the clip to the ground. The flame was snuffed beneath his shoe.

Maybe smoking was a habit that was well overdue to be stomped out of his life. What had started as some harmless high school lawbreaking had turned into a flimsy lifejacket that was becoming harder to justify or even slip out of. Of all the injuries he'd sustained playing football back when his athletic prowess still mattered, none required a crutch quite like that of a freshly rolled joint in his hand, which supported him as he hobbled off the field and into the bleak, motionless parking lot he called life. It was becoming embarrassing, knowing that he had chosen not to overcome his career handicap and instead became increasingly complacent with it one dime bag at a time. Every dollar he slipped into the pocket of some white country drug dealer was one that could have been invested in a brighter future: a college degree, an apartment of his own, an overall better life.

*How 'bout an engagement ring?* he mused, possibly for the first time in his life. He'd spent more time fearing that he might end up in a Planned Parenthood waiting room than at a jeweler; for the sake of his social life, he was lucky to have avoided both. But now he had a girl in his life who wasn't eager for a mutual dismissal, in which both parties could fuck once or twice and walk away without a shred of resentment or regret. And while he didn't want to trade one addiction for another, he had to admit that he was growing more dependent on her than he had any person, female or otherwise, in his adult life. After all, who else could have shaken him out of the sleep into which he didn't even know he'd slipped? And was there anyone in the world who could have made him question the smudge of ash and weed on the pavement that day, or the euphoric sensation of floating that, for once, felt like a shameful fall from unearned heights?

The steeple of the Southern Mercy Bible Church scraped God's cloudy footstool just a few buildings away, and Jonah looked up at the small, white cross at its pinnacle, and decided right then and there that he would face his problems head-on with a clear mind and clearer conscience. He made no promises, neither to himself nor to the universe. It was uncharted territory for him, and he figured he'd just see where the wind took him, and try his best to breathe fresh air instead of smoke.

"Y'can smell that from a mile away, y'know," Levi noted from a distance. He came walking around the corner of the building, shoes freshly soaked with gasoline.

"No more than those old shoes o' yours," Jonah countered. "Watch your step or y'might catch fire."

"Put that lighter away, then, before you hurt someone."

"Gotta protect myself somehow," Jonah muttered, flicking the lighter a few times just to see the sparks. "For all I know, you coulda been Charlene von Braun sneakin' round the building to violate me back by the dumpsters."

"Ain't no rape for the willing, I reckon."

"And I sure as shit ain't willing. She's come round here more times than I care to count, always lookin' for a book but never checkin' one out."

"She's checkin' you out, bud."

"It's harassment, at the very least. But seriously, how'd you find me?"

"Other than followin' the stank you done left all the way down Main Street, Susan said you'd be back here. Also said if she didn't have a chest cold, she'd be out here joinin' you. Looks like you done blew right through it, though." He looked down at the smudged remains of what was meant to be Jonah's last joint, and kicked it aside. His shoe was slick against the pavement and squished under his weight.

"I'll probably be takin' a break from it, anyways."

"Y'mean, till your next lunch break."

"No, man, for good."

Levi's look wasn't so much one of surprise as it was suspicion. But after a moment of assessing whether Jonah was pulling his leg, he shrugged the bare shoulders that were tan and freckled from slaving away in the afternoon sun, and sighed, "Looks like everyone's cleanin' up their acts these days."

"It's some Twilight Zone shit, I know."

"Sounds like it's about time for me to get the hell outta this town," Levi muttered. He licked his thumb and tried removing a small black smear of oil or tire rubber from his knee, but only managed to spread it even farther across his skin. "If the world ain't comin' to an end, then this place is sure as shit gonna be more boring than I thought it'd ever be."

"Y'ever thought about leavin' for real?"

"You know I've thought about it—we both have, plenty o' times."

"No, no more fantasies this time. I mean the real deal. Packin' a bag and never lookin' back."

It took a second before Levi's face revealed that he no longer thought Jonah might be joking. He helped himself to a seat on an empty plastic crate by the rusty door, assuming the semblance of *The Thinker*, who was pondering a scenario he'd mentioned a hundred times but never lent much credence to. "Lucky for you you'd be travelin' light, since y'ain't got much shit to pack at home. But where'd you plan on goin' with one bag over your shoulder?"

"College came to mind." Then, having decided to give proper credit to the mastermind behind his newly considered options, he admitted, "Or to Sophie's mind, rather."

"You done met yourself a nice girl and now you'd leave her to rot in this shithole town?"

"She don't see it that way. It's more of an investment than a loss."

"No offense, but it's a risky investment on both your parts."

"I dunno if my résumé's good enough or not, but might as well give it my best shot. It'll be more than I've done in a long time."

"Go ahead and do it, then. Ain't nothin's stoppin' you, 'cept your pathological fear o' rejection."

"Gettin' shot down by a school ain't the same as goin' home with blue balls. One's got a way simpler solution than the other. And if I don't get that acceptance letter, I'm back to square one, stuck in Clemency with no future other than maybe a beer gut and a few kids down the line."

"Hard to picture you with either, seein' as you've been avoidin' both like the plague."

"As any guy well should."

"Then do yourself a favor and send out a goddamned application. And if it don't work out, then pushups and rubbers will have to do for now." Levi stood up, snatched the soggy joint clip off the ground and tossed it coolly into the dumpster behind him. "Don't go makin' me hound you 'bout it, neither. Me 'n Sophie can push you and you bet your ass we're gonna, but in the end, you're gonna have to be the one to sign that form and mail it out. Word on the street's that I'm a good influence these days, but even I've got my limits. But you don't, man. You're goin' places."

# 15

It had been decades since Main Street had seen anything as new as the von Brauns' Bentley idling by a defunct parking meter. Back when that town's cars sported new paintjobs, not rust-eaten front wings, even the best of them, inflation considered, paled in comparison to that British luxury chariot. Its engine purred coyly as it rested beside the sidewalk, terribly out of place. It was meant to be illuminated by the light of skyscrapers and neon signs, not streetlamps that hadn't offered more than an electric flicker in over thirty years. Charlene von Braun would have preferred to risk broken windows and a stolen purse in New York than to allow even a single piece of white trash to look unworthily upon its beautiful chassis, which she guarded more fiercely than her own body, for which she'd charged just as much on her husband's American Express card.

Passers-by stopped dead in their tracks to admire (and covet) the shiny black vehicle, inspecting it closely as though they could ever hope to comprehend the superior craftsmanship of a $400,000 work of art. Charlene was in no mood to suffer their pedestrian intrusions, and she greeted each with a cold, territorial scowl that prompted most to scurry off like frightened animals. She didn't even bother to remove her designer sunglasses, which she'd donned in the false hope that she could go incognito for her stakeout. When no one was looking, she took a quick peek in the mirror to check the artistry of her blood-red lipstick. It was impeccable, as always. She pursed her lips and relaxed in the leather seat, tiny, polished opera glasses held up to her eyes, and peered across the street through the windows of the Swayne Public Library, stalking her prey like a perfectly groomed lioness in the tall grasses.

That carpet-wearing clam dam Susan Lewis was hunched over the front desk, stamping what were probably children's picture books, given Clemency's apparent widespread illiteracy. It was nothing short of insulting that Susan would be so abrasive each time Charlene stepped through the front doors, jingling the tiny bells that, for a woman of her wealth and class, should have been a full orchestra. Never mind the fact that Susan's faux fur coat looked like it'd been woven from a homeless Yeti's back hair, or that her crude, blotchy makeup bore a striking resemblance to marks on a shroud in which was wrapped a crucified clown—Charlene was the customer, and therefore always right, and deserved at least a modicum of respect from the manager of the failing establishment. No one read books anymore, in that town especially. A celebrity appearance by Charlene von Braun was the best advertising such a library could have hoped for.

Really, Swayne's only saving grace was its sole employee, Jonah Young, whose potential as an exclusive source of commercial sex appeal Susan had been wasting for years. His being hidden away from the world in the shadow of bookshelves was even more evidence against Susan's business savvy, if running a taxpayer-funded hand-me-down bin could be considered a capitalistic enterprise. If that withered, old Sasquatch really wanted to have her library practically overflowing with the town's fifth grade–level readers, all she had to do was plaster the walls with posters of Jonah in his old football gear, or, better yet, in little more than a jockstrap. Or perhaps she could draw some inspiration from Abercrombie & Fitch's iconic marketing ploys and have him stand on the sidewalk half naked, clad in jeans that hugged him in all the right places, saturated in overpowering cologne and his own male pheromones.

Charlene could practically smell those sex chemicals wafting from across the street, which in her olfactory delusion were even more delectable than the scent of chocolate surrounding the Godiva factory. She was perfectly aware of the absurdity of what she was feeling, smelling, and craving. Was she going completely crazy? A madwoman with a legitimate mental illness was incapable of recognizing her own insanity, and yet Charlene not only acknowledged it, but embraced it. She hadn't felt so awake in years—not just awake, but alive, with the vitality of a teenage girl who'd just discovered the earthshaking glory of the female orgasm.

She was well familiar with the sensation of stimulants plowing through her veins, though it was lab-synthesized, prescription compounds she'd grown accustomed to ever since she entered the orgiastic world of modeling. However, this was something different. It was a raw, primal instinct, evoked by rushing hormones that kindled a primordial lust somewhere in the depths of her reptilian brain. She'd been accused of being cold-blooded before, and her surrender to that ancient, serpentine consciousness did little to contradict it. At the same time, the searing heat radiating from her flushed skin said otherwise.

Her hair fluttered in the cool breeze of the car's air conditioning, which she had no choice but to crank up to full blast, in defense of the flawless makeup that could be utterly ruined by even a single bead of sweat from her brow. Her husband hadn't taken notice of the new, amaranthine eye shadow she'd delicately dusted over her lids, or the superior-quality false eyelashes she'd ordered online from Madrid. This was nothing new; she didn't know why she even wasted energy on harboring a wife's disappointment anymore. Had he recognized her white belt with the gold buckle as new to her wardrobe, or the fresh French manicure she had to drive fifty miles away to have performed by a proper Vietnamese stowaway? Of course he hadn't. He didn't even seem to catch those purchases on his credit card statement. His obliviousness, or purposeful lack of concern, knew no bounds.

Jonah, on the other hand—there was no way he would overlook a new accessory or cosmetic element, no matter how subtle. After all, how could he? Anything Charlene wore would be a sight to behold for a young man who grew up in a place where Walmart was considered high fashion. Should Charlene choose to show up in pajamas, he'd still think she were dressed to impress. It was simultaneously pathetic and endearing, and most of all, refreshing. Compliments poured from Jonah's mouth like water from the Fountain of Youth, and Charlene had a thirst for it that she couldn't quench. It drove her to stop by the library numerous times in the past two weeks, to replenish the leaky cistern of her confidence each time she heard him utter his charming flatteries in that primitive, backwater accent. Not once did she leave with a book in her hand, but she never left empty handed.

What tangible object she did hold, however, was a thin, discreet dossier, printed plainly but with the utmost secrecy. No one knew its contents, or even of its existence. She'd made sure to keep it tucked away in the ultra-secure diversion safe she kept in her cavernous shoe closet, the combination to which not even her husband knew. In a perfect world, she would have stored it in her anonymous safe deposit box in Zürich, but such ironclad security was a luxury of the past. Only once before had she brought the file out into the light of day, and that was when she'd acquired it in the first place, having made the clandestine exchange with a plain-faced man in a black suit off the side of the road out in the uncharted middle of nowhere.

"Here's what you asked for," the private investigator had said without further explanation, as none was needed. She'd been waiting in agony for the results of his sleuthing. The man reached out his car window and passed the file over to Charlene, who snatched it eagerly out of his hand and immediately began to scour the documents and photos he had tucked inside it. She grinned devilishly and thrust a bulging envelope back at him, packed full of hundred-dollar bills.

"I ain't never seen a broad take such an interest in her estranged kid before," the investigator admitted after lighting an unfiltered cigarette. "That's who he is, ain't he? I didn't do much diggin' into his family background. Can't think of any other reason why a bird your age would want to know about an eighteen-year old's social life."

"He's not my son," she snapped, her icy blue eyes flaring like halogen headlights on a darkened road. "Not that it's any of your business."

"It *is* my business, lady. Literally."

"One phone call and I could shut your business down in a New York minute, smartass. Keep prying and I'll make sure you never work another day in your life," she threatened. There was little reason for her to seek his services again: he'd gotten her Victoria Shaw's tax records in the past, simply for her own personal satisfaction, and now he'd brought her the real prize. But unlike those documents that proved the Shaws' priestly white-collar crimes, she'd keep her intel on Jonah top secret, far away from the prying eyes of her son, who'd managed to find the Shaw records while snooping through her drawers for Valium. This time, she wouldn't be so reckless.

She lit her menthol cigarette and blew the smoke straight through his window. He coughed with stinging eyes as she drove off, her car engine growling with the same ferocity of her words.

While the rest of Clemency spent their evening hours reading Bible passages before bedtime, Charlene made it a habit to scour the dossier religiously, committing every word and picture to memory. She'd paid good money for such information. After all, there was only so much she could gather on Jonah Young from their interactions in the frustrating silence of the Swayne Public Library. Her only option was to build up a library of her own, stocked full of privately funded biographies on Clemency's ex-football star, and apparently reformed playboy.

The redneck private investigator had dug up a mountain's worth of dirt, piled higher than the mound of hearts and rubbers Jonah could have built up over the course of his adolescence. He compiled an impossibly thorough list of sexual conquests, with approximate date ranges for many such torrid affairs, preserving the notches on his bedpost as bullet points on paper. There were report cards going all the way back to grade school (which were not nearly as impressive), pages of innocent text messages between him and his best friend, as well as less-than-innocent sexts with nameless phone numbers who used far too many emojis and LOLs to be male.

Of all the intrusive material the hired sleuth had gathered, Charlene most enjoyed shuffling through the dozens of glossy photos he took of Jonah's everyday activities, no matter how mundane. She was given a tantalizing glimpse into his admittedly dull life, which she somehow found fascinating, even titillating: high-res images of him smoking behind the library, bored but relaxed; early morning jogs down Main Street, sweaty and shirtless, his athletic body glistening in the light of dawn; intimate conversations with the Shaws' pretty daughter that Charlene briefly considered hiring a hitman to take care of; she saw all of it. Charlene only wished she could have witnessed such things with her own eyes, and not through the lens of a camera, taken from the safety of a stranger's used car with tinted windows.

It most certainly wasn't desperation, or some form of psychosis, she told herself. It was scholarly diligence. She would be an expert on the subject of his past and present, strengths and weaknesses, if she wanted any hope of success when the time came for her to finally make her move. That day was fast approaching, even more swiftly than her next Botox appointment. If he had an Achilles heel, she would find it, study it, and exploit it.

Failure was not an option: she had suffered it too many times already. She would rather be handcuffed and thrown in jail for criminal stalking than be rejected by another man. In a gamble for whatever fragile sanity she had left, she was all in, Jonah was the dealer, and it was ten minutes past last call.

••

The library was always darker when Jonah stepped back inside from his outdoor breaks, a shadowy graveyard of bookshelf tombstones lit only by the eerie, greenish tint of eyes adjusting to the rapid reduction in ambient light. Susan's fur coat, too, became imbued with that same sickly color, serving as a natural palette upon which his dilated pupils could paint their optical illusion, due to its dingy white color. She manned her post at the front desk with two stacks of books before her, one to her left, one to her right, which she was in no mood to stamp at that moment. Instead, she licked her ink-blotted thumb and turned the page in one of the library's far-outdated magazines; Jonah thought he saw a bluish stain on her tongue. It was probably a trick of the light.

"I'll do it," he declared without introduction. Susan lowered the magazine and leaned over in her chair, peering around the tower of books that obstructed her view.

"With you, kid, that could mean a whole shitload o' things, and I ain't in the mood for riddles. I only just now learned that Brad and Jen are splittin' up, and I daresay it's gone and blown my demented, old mind." They had divorced over a decade ago. "If they couldn't work it out, then there sure as shit ain't much hope for the rest of us."

"College," he said bluntly. "I'll do it. I'll apply. Right here, right now."

The magazine fluttered in the air as it flew across the room and flopped onto the floor. Susan pushed back her chair with such force that it nearly punched a hole in the wall behind her, and she leapt up with an excitement Jonah had never seen her exude. His shoulders were close to being dislocated when she forcefully laid hands on him and exclaimed with a startling joy in her eyes, *"It's about fuckin' time!"*

Her coat dragged along the floor as she rushed over to the dusty computer at the far side of the room; with it she dredged up a litter of dust bunnies in her wake. She swept her hand over the filthy monitor and blew as much air over its surface as her aging lungs would allow, and the thick film of dust exploded into the air and sent her into a coughing fit. Nothing happened when she pounded her finger on the power button. Desiring a dramatic flash of light and the whir of a cooling fan, she was left unsatisfied, and smashed her fist against the computer tower with little regard for the damage she might cause. After three solid swings, she realized the damned thing wasn't plugged in.

"You got yourself a résumé, kid?" she asked with a tone that expected an affirmative response. She paused and realized the foolishness of her question before he had a chance to disappoint her himself. "Course you don't. Get your ass over here. I'm not about to write up your life story all by myself."

He pulled up a chair and took a seat beside her. It was an old computer—so archaic that it could be called a sexed-up abacus—and booting it up was an excruciatingly long process. In the meantime, Susan slinked back over to her command station, unlocked a cabinet normally hidden at her feet, and pulled out a bottle of vintage whiskey with a grin.

"Close the blinds," she ordered while she set down the bottle and two small plastic cups. "We're closin' up shop early today." Jonah gladly turned over the sign that normally read OPEN during daylight hours, and shooed away what few potential readers the day still held with a bold, long-overdue WE'RE CLOSED—that is, LEAVE US THE HELL ALONE, YOU BARELY LITERATE BASTARDS.

"Been savin' this bad boy for a while now," Susan said, pouring a generous serving of dark liquor into each cup. She handed one to Jonah and raised her own in celebration. "Took you long enough, you stupid, wonderful kid!" They drank to the ambition he never knew he had.

They began with his high school career, which was nothing to be impressed by. "We'll focus on your football. Always looks good on paper. Red-blooded Americans only care about field goals, not life goals, and lucky for you, you got plenty o' the former." She played up his athletic achievements as she typed up that portion of the résumé, just short of saying that Tom Brady played football like a blind ten-year old with cerebral palsy when compared to the undiscovered sports prodigy Jonah Young.

"You got any other extracurricular activities to put down?" she asked. She cracked her knuckles and prepared for another flurry of keystrokes.

"Nothin' G-rated."

"No shit, kid. I know you fancied yourself the town's junior gynecologist. Anything else?"

"I used to babysit every so often, off the books."

"Wasn't your kid, right?"

"Don't got none. It was for some family friends."

"Thank God you got enough sense to use protection, even as a dumb, young man-whore. How often did you watch the little shits while their parents were out?"

"Maybe once a month."

Susan sighed. "It'll have to do. Don't you fret, though. I'll make it sound like you were practically their surrogate parent." By the time she'd finished adding "child supervision" to his list of activities, history had been revised to suggest that he'd been watching the Foresters' kids four days a week for a good two years. She lied and added in that their parents were neglectful, toothless meth addicts, just for good measure.

"You know, I can draw, too," Jonah added without much confidence.

Susan eyed him with suspicion. "I ain't never seen you in an art show."

"That's 'cause I ain't been in an art show."

"Witnesses, kid!" Susan barked. "We need some goddamned witnesses! Someone's gotta vouch for *some* o' this, and ain't no one but God's watchin' you sketch naked ladies in your bedroom. Good to know you ain't wastin' your time jerkin' off all day when you ain't here bullshittin' me, though." She paused and considered his options. "Y'know what? Fine. You're a goddamned artistic savant." In succinct terms she added it to his résumé. "Okay, it's official. Da Vinci ain't got shit on you."

A few hours and three quarters of a bottle of whiskey later, Jonah had officially applied to three schools, with no idea as to what he might major in or how he'd pay tuition. He knew he didn't want to live in a dorm—he'd find his own cheap apartment, far from date rapist fraternity douchebags and brainless sorority girls in beer-soaked T-shirts, where he might be left in peace to study and take himself seriously for once. Susan leaned back in her chair with a satisfied grin, her good mood fueled by pride and liquor, and maybe the realization that she'd soon get her smart-mouthed employee out of her hair. She denied that that was the case.

"Ain't gonna lie, kid, I'll miss you when you're gone. This wretched library won't be the same without you. I'll probably shut it down for good."

"I don't like this sentimental side o' you, Susan. It's givin' me the creeps."

"I don't like it any more than you do, smartass, but facts are facts. And the fact is, I knew this day was comin', sooner or later, even if you took your sweet-ass time gettin' there. I'm proud o' you, kid." She tried to excuse her being so maudlin, blaming it on the whiskey. They both knew she wasn't a very good liar.

"All I've gone and done was apply. I ain't leavin' yet," Jonah reminded her.

"The deal's sealed. You'll get in—I'd bet my shriveled old tits on it. And you just made the deadline—you got real lucky—so it won't take long till we get ourselves an answer. And you better get to packin' the second that letter comes in the mail. I ain't about to give you the time to overthink it and change your mind."

"Y'know, if the von Brauns get that train station up and runnin' again, I could drop by whenever I damn well please. This won't be the last you've seen o' me."

"It better be, goddamnit. 'Cause if you come crawlin' back here lookin' for a job, failed outta school and desperate for someone to take pity on you, I'll pull my shotgun out from under that there desk and blow your useless head off."

"Is that a threat?" Jonah scoffed, raising his cup to the thought of righteous murder.

"Count it as a promise, kid. I ain't gettin' any younger, and at my age, you ain't gotta put up with nobody's bullshit. And trust you me, when my time's up, I'm goin' out with a bang. You, on the other hand—" She took one last swig of whiskey, this time straight from the bottle, her eyes locked on something out in the street. "—you better make your exit real nice and quiet, 'cause that von Braun hussy's been out there casin' the joint for hours now, and she sure as hell ain't lookin' to steal my pearls."

••

Jonah made it a habit to show up at Sophia's bedroom window under the light of the moon, uninvited, more often than not. Of course, there was nothing stopping him from texting her those nights, as he did in the daylight. But to see her face to face, that gentle face shining with pale skin under a paler celestial glow, gifted him with an intimacy that radio signals and backlit screens never could. He saved his visits for the auspicious peaks of the lunar cycle, when the full moon watched over them like a pregnant goddess, who blessed each innocent rendezvous as not just secret, but sacred. Jonah knew the Hebrews of the Old Testament observed the cycles of the moon as a calendar for temple sacrifice. He liked to think he was doing the same, but for the honor of his own idol of flesh and blood, and not the God who watched over them with a smile.

Night had fallen over Clemency when he awoke from his nap in the back of the library, of which Susan was perfectly aware. Charlene von Braun was loitering across the street the entire time. It wasn't until Susan called the police that the coast was clear. The squad car, red and blue lights flashing in the dark, pulled up behind the prowling Bentley and scared her off within seconds. The coast finally clear, Jonah strode through the front doors with a sigh of relief, and made his way up the hill, wiping the sleep from his eyes the whole way to the Shaw residence. By the time he slinked over the grass and rapped lightly on Sophia's bedroom window, he was feeling fully conscious, with the mental sharpness required to charm a girl with her stratospheric standards.

"Whatever you're selling, I'm not interested," Sophia jeered through the open window.

"Y'know I ain't peddlin' nothin' but flattery."

"That's even worse," she jested, leaning out into the open air. "I'd sooner accept a Book of Mormon than cheap compliments from a traveling salesman."

"They're free, though," he reminded her. "You're a smart girl. Don't you like a bargain?"

"Of course, but I don't see one here. All I see is a scam."

Smiling, she slid her legs over the windowsill and waited for Jonah to open his arms to catch her. The delicate kiss on his cheek was an instant sedative, and he felt the muscles in his shoulders and back soften into jelly, so much so that he almost dropped her. The urge to touch his lips to hers was tearing him apart, and had only grown worse over the past weeks. At the same time, his resolve had strengthened as well, and he felt himself finally becoming the young gentleman he'd always been told to be, but rejected out of spite and lack of self-discipline. Finally, he had found it, and had something to show for it.

"I did what you said," he said as they sat upon the lush grass. "Sent out the applications today—three schools, 'cause I was feelin' ambitious." What made him most proud wasn't his own initiative, but the light in Sophia's eyes that he'd sparked with just one line.

"That's incredible!" she exclaimed before covering her mouth in regret, realizing that in the neighborhood's nightly silence she'd just made quite a clamor. In the forceful whisper of a true churchgoer, she continued, "This is a big deal, Jonah—you should be really proud. Prouder than I am right now, and that's saying something." He thought he heard her murmur a prayer of thanksgiving under her breath, praising God's Son for His answering her sincerest petitions. For a moment, he found himself thanking that same God whom he'd never really gotten to know.

"Pride's a sin, Miss Shaw. A deadly one."

"No deadlier than your charms, Mr. Young."

They rested there with his arm around her, their whispers carried on the balmy breeze; their excitement ruined any chance at being unheard. He wished more than anything that they could crawl back through the open window above their heads and curl up in her bed, a place he'd never been to, and might never. He would not defile it. She believed him, but the good Reverend finding his daughter beneath the sheets with a boy would be a scandal no man of God could ever survive. They had a reputation to uphold, and she owed it to them, by mandate of the Mosaic Law. And though she insisted that she wouldn't want to be so uncouth, anyway, Jonah could see a look of restrained disappointment in her amber eyes, and knew she held just as much regret.

"By the way, there's a church concert Saturday night," she announced after much conversation. "I know social functions aren't your cup of tea, but I have a solo. I was hoping you'd come see me." Her tone was nonchalant, but her body language expressed deep longing.

"Course I'll go," he whispered, beaming. Her hair fluttered in the soft rush of his breath as he whispered close to her, "Wouldn't miss it." A light kiss on her forehead sealed the deal, and his hand against her cheek was like swearing an oath on a Bible. It was a promise he wouldn't break. Heaven and Earth would pass away, but his words that night would never.

The force of gravity had no hold on his feet as he walked back down the hill, weightlessly gliding to the corner of Main Street with the kind of cerebral high he was accustomed to getting from good weed, not chaste women. One day he'd give her a real goodbye kiss, he swore to himself, the kind that made her foot pop like a classic beauty in a black-and-white film. Maybe it would happen on the day he left Clemency in pursuit of higher ambitions. It was too soon to say if that day would ever come, of course. But at that moment, with the moon goddess's swollen white belly ready to give birth to dreams, anything was possible.

If the summit of that hill was Heaven on Earth, then the run-down crack house at its foot was the deepest pit of Hell. Just the sight of the Skinners' rathole was enough to drag Jonah back down to the heaviness of reality, and there it was, looming ahead at the end of Midian Lane, lit only by a yellowish lamp by the rickety front door, and the sporadic, electric blue flicker of a bug zapper claiming victim after victim. The night seemed darker around it, like the house were a churning black hole devouring light itself. Even at high noon, the

Skinners' property dampened the daylight, and crossing over the threshold of the curb made time accelerate from midday to an eerie, dim twilight. Jonah clenched his fists, knowing that his little sister had been led into the shadow of dusk, and left there abandoned to find her way back, refusing the flashlight he offered her again and again.

The door swung open on shaky hinges and a pack of gangling degenerates made their way down the three uneven steps, howling in amusement. They shoved each other and drunkenly stumbled over the sparse, withered lawn with the kind of camaraderie only sex or sports could encourage; he saw no bats or gloves. The one who led the crew wasn't Gabe Skinner, but someone of a similar build, wiry and desiccated, strolling out with a bare, skeletal torso and a damp shirt tucked into his belt. And even with figures distorted by the strobe of the bug zapper, Jonah immediately recognized the two behind him: the bare scalp and ill-fitting death metal shirt of the one and the unsightly neck tattoo of the other identified them as none other than the two twisted fuckers who'd shown up at his front door once before. Had Jonah not caught sight of them, he would have kept on walking. But the last time he'd seen them they were intent on finding Hannah, and as he stood his ground in the middle of the street, he worried they might have found her.

Gabe stood in the doorway leaning back against the frame, reducing himself to little more than a spindly silhouette, around which wafted a ghostly cloud of cigarette smoke. A generous host, he tossed an unopened can of cheap beer to one of his slimy cohorts, and offered a smoke to polish it off. It was repulsive, but nothing criminal. That is, until Jonah saw something through the open door he wouldn't ever forget.

She lay like a corpse on the moldy sofa behind Gabe's shadowy figure, stirring subtly in her opiate high. Stripped down to her bra, she was shivering; her wrinkled skirt was pushed up above her knees, and her underwear strung between her ankles. The rubber band around her arm left her skin pale and track marks even darker with contrast. There were no tears, and she let out no sobs of pain or despair. She only stared out the open door, staring lifelessly straight at Jonah, who froze in his tracks when he saw nothing behind her eyes: no hope, no will, and no love, for others or even herself. In those eyes, he saw his sister's future. His blood boiled. Storming down the Skinners' driveway, he had Gabe right in his crosshairs.

*"The fuck's goin' on in there?"*

Gabe and his rotten-toothed friends could do nothing but laugh. He looked back over his shoulder and realized the girl was lying in plain sight, so he coolly shut the door and stepped down to meet Jonah eye to eye. "Well, if it ain't everyone's favorite big brother! Y'know, if you wasn't such a closet faggot, I'd invite you in to get some for yourself."

*"If she's in there, Skinner, I fucking swear—"*

Folding his arms, Gabe scowled. "No, she ain't in there, so quit causin' a scene. You're embarrassin' yourself, man."

The freak with the neck ink tossed a beer can behind him onto the lawn and added, "We was havin' some fun with Missy today, wasn't we, guys?"

"That's right, she's our Thursday girl," said the one whose shirt hung limply from his belt like a tail, which wagged as he stepped behind Gabe like an obedient, mindless dog.

"Hannah hangs with us on Fridays," Gabe sneered. "So we'll be seein' 'er tomorrow night, then. Get outta here, Young. And when y'get home, tell that sweet lil' sister o' yours to rest up. Ain't much fun when she's fallin' asleep on us. Ain't that right, boys?"

The world around him became little more than a blur, and all the sounds that were once so clear gave way to a piercing ringing. His skin was on fire, his pulse pounded in his head, and with adrenaline controlling his every move, Jonah barreled straight at Gabe and swung his fist with as much force as his twitching muscles could exert. He didn't care that he was outnumbered, or that Gabe was the kind to fight dirty with a switchblade. That night, he learned what love and hate really were. His mind knew the difference. His body, however, made no distinction. Joy or rage, affection or rancor—both turned a person into nothing more than an animal, a beast driven by instinct, not thought, for whom there was no good and evil, no right and wrong, but only life and death, nature's only two absolutes.

Gabe stumbled back but didn't hit the ground like Jonah had envisioned when he made his move; his hollering cohorts grabbed Jonah by each arm and pulled him back before he could swing all the way through. He did manage to drive his knuckles into Gabe's chest, and they sank into the fleshy gap just below his collarbone, drawing out a startled grunt but not the howl that would have gratified Jonah's rage. The third junkie sidekick stepped out and gave Jonah a solid punch in the stomach. It knocked the wind out of him, and he struggled to breathe. He felt little pain. His body's fight-or-flight response rendered him impervious to it, but it didn't take the edge off his pride being shattered, or his heart breaking over his sister. He coughed and caught his breath. He spat at the bastard's feet.

Gabe grabbed his associate by the wrist as he prepared to drive his fist into Jonah's stomach one more time, and pushed him to the side. "Let's give 'im a free pass this time," he ordered, strangely calm. It wasn't a reassuring kind of calm. It was like the peace a nation experienced when its enemy's nuclear arsenal matched its own, assuring mutual destruction; it was peace in a technical sense, but it was all superficial, and bound to end with time. One wrong move and it could all be blown to hell.

"He's Hannah's big brother, after all. He musta done somethin' right with 'er, 'cause she's the best we got, 'n she don't bitch or talk back like the rest of 'em. Lettin' him off easy's the least I can do." He motioned for the three nameless goons to get out of there and head back to whatever cesspools they slithered out of, and pushed Jonah toward the road. "But you best mind your business from now on, Young. 'Cause this here's the only second chance you're gon' get."

His deranged smile was yellowish in the moonlight, and the color of flames danced on his pale, sickly face as he lit another cigarette. "And I wasn't jokin' when I said tell your sister to sleep good tonight. She's gon' need it." The smoke followed Jonah down the driveway like an unwanted spirit, haunting him until dawn.

"We'll be seein' 'er real soon."

# 16

CHOIR PRACTICE WAS A TRICKY THING for any church. Music was one of Christendom's many ways of glorifying God, and all were encouraged to sing their praises unto Him. Then there were those few who chose to go a step beyond simply singing by ear each Sunday, by joining the local church choir. There were no auditions or callbacks. If you wanted in, you were in, no questions asked. Some, however, were better than others. And sometimes, it was frustrating to forbid partiality.

Victoria Shaw had endured years of such frustration. There were a select few whose voices were nothing less than angelic. Others were far less heavenly. They had the tone of nails on a chalkboard, inexplicably produced from human vocal cords, which even on their worst days should have at least had some semblance of musicality. Instead, they were discordant and offensive to the ear. Victoria herself had told the choir that God found all voices pleasing when they sang of Him. She, on the other hand, was not so easily pleased, and she questioned God's taste in music quite frequently.

That evening was no different. It was the dress rehearsal for the upcoming choir concert, and the kinds of aural failures she heard were simply unacceptable at that final hour. The withered crones with voices as cracked as their skin were taking too long to kick the bucket—the only way she'd ever get them to stop ruining the repertoire. Children, too, were lauded as being adorable when proved that they were talentless in front of their parents and neighbors. *'Let the little children come to me, and do not hinder them,"* the Son of God had said, *"for the kingdom of God belongs to such as these."* Clearly, those in the Kingdom must be deaf.

Her daughter Sophia was another story entirely. She surpassed Victoria in musical talent, in beauty, in all the ways a mother could ever hope for her own child to exceed what she herself had proven to be. The upcoming concert would be a testament to it. Sophia had a solo she'd perfected over the past five months, and Victoria made sure that no one would overshadow her. Unfortunately, it was far too easy for ineptitude to eclipse true talent.

*"Stop!"* Victoria screeched, violently throwing her hands in the air to cut the music. She glared at the guitar player, an aging ex-hippie with straggly gray hair and a goatee like a rabbit's tail. She couldn't remember his name. Like so many others, it was irrelevant, but right then she wished she'd bothered to commit it to memory, just so she could hiss it in front of the entire choir while she lambasted him for so poorly tuning his strings.

"Now in Jesus's name I pray, sir, that you'll tune that darned instrument so we can all hear my baby girl sing her part and not cringe the whole way through," she said with hands held together in prayer for dramatic effect.

"Sorry, ma'am," the patchouli-scented bard replied. "I'll tune 'em right up. Won't happen again."

"Don't apologize to me," she corrected him. She pointed a polished finger at Sophia, who winced. "Apologize to my baby girl, for holdin' up her rehearsal, and to the Lord, for insultin' the beautiful gift o' song He gave this human race."

The man looked to Sophia, but she was too patient to accept an apology. Victoria didn't know where she got it from. If she had one criticism of her daughter, it was her insufferable modesty.

"And you, sweet Sophia," she continued. "Don't hide that voice under a bushel basket. Sing a lil' louder next time, won't you?" She approached her daughter and covered the microphone with her hand, whispering in her ear, "I can barely hear you over the breath of these mouth-breathers."

"I don't want to steal the show. They've been working just as hard as me."

"Don't be ridiculous. It's not stealing if you're taking what's rightfully yours. And just like your father and me, you deserve this town's full attention." In a rare show of affection, she kissed her daughter on her forehead. "Just remember: all eyes are on you, as they well should be."

Like the Son as the sole reflection of the Father, Sophia was the mirror of the Shaw family's identity, and all those who watched her were really watching the good Reverend and his wife. And any time Sophia allowed that mirror to be fogged with whatever worldly things might influence a girl her age, she jeopardized Clemency's chance at seeing just how pure and pious their spiritual leaders really were.

Over the course of the Shaws' reign as high priests of that Southern temple there had been several occasions when their righteousness came under public scrutiny. Tithes were allegedly misappropriated, routine maintenance of the old church was forgone while the Shaws' installed a new bathroom at home, and the list went on. When Victoria and her husband were unable to inspire enough guilt in the congregation to dispel an imminent scandal, they drew attention to their darling Sophia, their pride and joy, and the only proof they needed of their innocence. Christ Jesus said that true disciples will be known by their fruits, and Sophia was the most perfect fruit of their loins, a living testimony to the Shaws' uprightness in the eyes of God.

Her whole life Sophia had been a beacon of hope in a lawless world, a lamp for those young boys and girls lost in the shadows of adolescent indiscretion. But much to her mother's chagrin, that light was being dampened, and the one who was snuffing the flame was a reprehensible little failure named Jonah Young.

Victoria knew what they were up to—she had eyes and ears everywhere. In the pathways of communication, all roads led to her in that town, and she fancied herself more gossip-savvy than the Almighty. The omniscient Creator did not enjoy such talk. She wished she could say the same. But this was different, as the degrees of separation between herself and the subject of chitchat were growing smaller by the day. Soon enough, the fly stuck in her web of small-town gossip would be just a little too close to the center, and one forceful beating of its wings might knock the spider right out of her own treacherous design.

The Youngs' eldest son had a murky past, and that water under the bridge was still turbid no matter how many months passed since his high school graduation. Sophia's, though, was spotless, as dazzlingly white as the Transfiguration. Victoria wasn't terribly concerned about her daughter's purity, as there wasn't a chance in hell that she'd follow in Hester Prynne's footsteps and brand herself with a permanent mark of shame, least of all for a boy as unremarkable as Jonah Young. Her husband the good Reverend, however, did not have as much faith in their daughter's sense of propriety, or her fortitude in the face of teenage hormones. Victoria did her best to keep him in the dark about Sophia's relationship, which had lasted far longer than anyone could have imagined. Either the Lord had reformed Jonah's heart and soul for the better, or Jonah simply viewed Sophia's virginity as the summit of Mt. Everest: a long, arduous endeavor that a man endured simply for the sake of saying he'd tempted death and came out the victor.

Regardless, the currently innocent affair could all too easily prove to be the Shaw ministry's coup de grace. One impulsive act of foolishness on Sophia's part could bring down the kingdom her parents had built up from nothing but the desperation of the economically crippled and lame. Outright fornication was the worst scenario, but it was not the only killing blow. Simply being caught with Jonah in the wrong place at the wrong time could be enough to condemn her, and through Sophia's condemnation would come the Shaws' day of judgment, which they had staved off since the day they first reached their hands into the collection basket. Accusations would fly, and in the court of public opinion, no solid evidence was necessary. The biblical word *diabolos*, that is, *devil*, meant "slanderer," and in that original sense Jonah could most certainly prove to be the Devil himself.

The Devil took many forms—an angel of light, an irresistible temptress—but his most ancient guise was that of the serpent, coiled around the branches of the Tree of Knowledge. He sibilated in the hearts of weak women, promising all sorts of wonderful lies; Victoria could all too easily imagine Jonah Young's susurrations in her daughter's ear, and what ungodly things he might be whispering so she might betray her parents, before he himself betrayed her.

He was the serpent whose head Victoria meant to crush beneath her heel. She'd seen snakebites before, and they were an ugly thing. And even the most God-fearing men were not immune to their venom. It was a morbid fact the Shaw family knew all too well.

••

The Swayne Public Library had a modest collection of books on pre-Columbian Mesoamerican history, spanning the length of half a shelf, and few had touched it over the years. Like many of the more academic subjects, which did not involve juvenile drama or outrageous religious themes, those eight or nine books might as well have been written in Mandarin, or simply invisible. Jonah, however, made it a habit to read what was otherwise doomed to be perpetually unread. He learned a great deal of useless knowledge, and if anyone in Clemency played Trivial Pursuit, victory was inevitable. Not surprisingly, no one did.

What he did learn from one of those history books was that many cultures viewed time as cyclical, and not the Western world's endless line that stretched forward until its eventual end. They crafted their calendars in the likeness of wheels, forever turning in the abstract fourth dimension; ends were always beginnings, in a universe that knew no moment of creation or inevitable day of destruction. The historian who explained this praised it as a beautiful concept, more elegant than the West's bleak temporal road that stretched for billions of years, only to be cut off at the edge of a cosmic cliff. Life was a cycle of seasons, not meaningless and arbitrary blocks of time, and a man's life was a reflection of nature: birthed among the blossoms of springtime, peaking in adulthood at the height of a golden summer, and finally death in the cold darkness of winter, only to be reborn again at the solstice of resurrection.

For a long time, Jonah hadn't shared the author's sentiments. He'd always known life to be cyclical, with each day coming and going like the one before it, repeating the same mundane events over and over again with little to tell them apart. The same alarm went off, he made himself halfway presentable in the same manner as yesterday, he dragged his feet to work while the same cicadas were just beginning their distant droning, he greeted Susan and robotically carried out the same duties with the same disinterest until it was time to walk out that same door and take the same walk home. Sometimes Levi swung by to propose an afternoon drink, but he didn't come around as much as he used to.

Thoughts of Sophia kept him going. She never changed, but he welcomed that. It gave him a sense of stability. Work, on the other hand, had given him only a sense of stagnation, like being stable in a pit of quicksand: nothing was going to knock you off balance, but the price was steep. It wasn't so much of an endless cycle as it was a rigid line plunging straight down into the muck.

The only time the spinning wheel of his existence came to a halt was from the occasional rock in the road, an obstruction that rattled his progress but with no serious consequences. That day, he wished something would just crack the wheel altogether. He wanted spokes to break and wood to splinter.

A college acceptance letter would do the trick. The road ahead looked refreshingly unpaved. And if it were an allegorical rock in his path to shake up the boringly smooth ride of his adult life, then Sophia was nothing less than an earthquake. He waited eagerly for her next aftershock. It would come in the vibration of her voice in just a few hours' time, in a solo he was sure he'd never forget. He was ready for the last season of his life to come to an end, and for a new one to begin, the first signs of which were blossoming ambitions and a twinkle in Sophia's eyes.

The last displaced history book was back in its place and he clapped the dust from his hands. The cart behind him was empty, marking that he was done for the day. He had a bit of time to kill and had decided that an afternoon run was just what he needed. Levi would be out with the ever-obnoxious Jimmy, a quick text had informed him, and Sophia was surely busy preparing for her big moment. An invigorating run about town and a quick shower would be his own preparation, to get his blood pumping in a warmup to the excited palpitations he never failed to feel in his chest each time he laid eyes on the Reverend's daughter.

With a small bag of workout clothes slung over his shoulder he made his way to the claustrophobic bathroom at the back of the library, shut the door with a bit of struggle against the warped doorframe, and clicked on the light. His worn dress shoes hit the tiled floor with the clatter of objects twice their size, and he gracelessly kicked off his slacks into a pile as he rummaged through the bag. He emerged from the bathroom ten times less formal but a hundred times more comfortable, and relished the softness of black nylon shorts swishing against his thighs with each step, and the freedom of a loose tank top over muscles that were otherwise denied a chance to see the light of day.

Then he noticed a small, unopened box of subscription magazines he'd somehow missed, and decided he had the time to spare to sort them on the periodical display before heading out to break a healthy sweat. The tape tore off with a sound more painful than waxing a leg and he opened up the cardboard folds to reveal a coincidental stack of fitness magazines. Like history books and Latin dictionaries, they would find little use there. But Jonah organized them regardless, slipping each glossy issue out of the packaging and onto the magazine rack. The bottommost shelf was reserved for their genre, boasting a row of svelte swimsuit models and heavily muscled men in tiny shorts, where few would see them. He was about halfway through when he heard the crude signal of an incoming customer up at the front.

The tiny string of bells at the front door jingled and Susan groaned a rather unwelcoming salutation; even from behind a barricade of bookcases, her disgust was as unmistakable as a puddle of warm vomit at the customer's feet. The click of heels on the floor was all Jonah needed to identify the walking emetic. He began tearing through the remaining magazines, practically throwing them at the shelves. The box slid across the floor and stopped at perfectly pedicured feet when he kicked it aside. It was not his lucky day.

"Mr. Young, if I wasn't so fond of you, I'd sue you for a new pair of shoes," she quipped while holding out her foot for both of them to inspect the damage. "Your improvised one-man soccer game has gone and scuffed the toe box. I won't be wearing these again."

There was a smudge of dust but nothing more. Jonah sighed and took a closer look just to appease her. "Real sorry, Charlene. I can get 'em cleaned for you, if you want."

"Don't trouble yourself. I never wear a pair of heels more than once, anyway. Best to think of them like houseflies—twenty-four hours of flitting around town, then years in a garbage bag. Enjoy them while they last." She was neither the recycling nor the charitable type.

"Well, they looked real nice on you while they lasted. Sure your husband'll go 'n buy you another pair twice as costly, though, so all ain't lost." Bringing Mr. von Braun into the conversation was sure to be like a bucket of ice water dumped over her head. The plan backfired. He might as well have been waving a red flag in front of a raging bull.

"That bastard has bought me so many shoes that he should just save some time and open up a sweatshop full of Cambodian six-year olds. I'm sick and tired of his gifts, so no, I won't be wearing another pair tomorrow paid for by a man who barely even looks at me these days."

The conversation was headed in an uncomfortable direction, but Jonah had to pay a compliment when it was due. "Sounds hard to believe, Charlene."

"What, that I'd refuse a new pair of Louis Vuittons, or that the mighty George von Braun is as impotent as an inpatient geriatric with a catheter up his useless, shriveled penis?"

"No, that there's any man in this here town that don't look at you."

For a second, it looked as though she actually blushed, but such an involuntary response would have suggested that the woman had even a shred of modesty. Her manner of dress was far from humble, $4,500 designer heels aside. A string of diamonds hung around her slender neck, given to her no doubt by the husband she accused of intimate neglect, and the neckline of her form-fitting cream dress plunged low enough to boast a deadly amount of cleavage. There was an inappropriately small distance between her Italian leather belt and the cutoff of her skirt, which, had she bent down to take a look at the magazine rack Jonah had frantically tried to organize before her ambush, would have unapologetically revealed what little she wore for underwear, if anything at all.

Inching a little closer, she thanked him for his flattery: something she claimed to be in short supply those days. "Are you one of those men, Jonah? You can be honest. I never blame a man for looking at a woman, no matter what his intent. I only blame him when he isn't man enough to tell her what he wants."

"Guess you could say I was one of 'em, for a good while."

"*Was* one of them? A man with a sharp eye and good taste never loses either."

"It ain't polite to look at pretty women when you're happily seein' the Reverend's daughter."

Charlene stopped her gradual approach upon the mention of Sophia, and she scowled. Jonah backed up just a bit farther, with the back wall only a foot or two behind him, plastered with posters of Pulitzer Prize winners. Charlene gingerly pushed a lock of platinum blond hair behind her ear and remarked, "Oh yes, that pretty little thing, Sophia. She seems like a nice enough girl, but don't they always? The religious ones, I mean."

"Not all of 'em. Her mother ain't too nice, I reckon you're aware."

"A two-faced bitch if I've ever seen one. Lucky for you, I suppose, such a quality apparently skips a generation in the Shaw family. But just because your good Christian girlfriend isn't a thieving, backstabbing harpy like her mother doesn't mean there can't be trouble in paradise. Is she giving you everything you need?"

"Course she is. She ain't jealous or petty, she sees me for who I am, and she's always pushin' for me to go farther in life, even in spite o' herself."

"You know what I meant, Jonah. Men have only one real need, one that's always there in the very back of their minds, even if they won't admit it. So I'll ask you again: Is Sophia giving you everything you need, *as a man*?"

"I'd never make her go back on her religion like that, no matter how bad I wanted it."

"But you *do* want it, then," Charlene accused with a wag of her finger. "Maybe you're trying your hand at monogamy for now, but sooner or later, Jonah, that animal inside you is going to show itself in whatever way it wants. There's no stopping it—it's human nature. You don't need to be ashamed of it. Just be a man."

"People change," he insisted, but then his back hit the wall, and he had no choice but to accept that there was nowhere to run.

"Oh, please. You're not a born-again virgin, Jonah. No amount of divine mercy will be enough to expunge your long list of sins."

"God'll be the judge o' that, not you. How would you know, anyway?"

"I've done my research. Meagan Brown, behind the football bleachers back in 2013, during her fifteen-minute break from cheerleading practice. Laura Delaney, that same year in October, in the vault of the foreclosed bank just after 10:00 PM—" She took one step forward, then another, with the wild look of a blue-eyed tiger about to pounce on her prey. "—Veronica Reynolds, spring of junior year, out in the woods where you got caught by a deer hunter and managed just the tip. Even Ms. Jackie Graham, your high school biology teacher fresh out of grad school, for some extra credit anatomy homework. So please, Jonah, spare me your newfound chastity. We both know it's bullshit."

"How the hell—"

Face to face, she put her finger to his lips and cooed, "I know a lot about you, Jonah Young, and I like what I see. But there's more to learn, and I've got all the time in the world. George doesn't care enough to get in my way."

Her painted claws traced down his body and left a trail of numbness as though they were needles filled with poison. His muscles stiffened and he found himself paralyzed by her feminine venom. Clenching his fists but putting up barely a fight, he watched as her fingers slid over the strong crests of his torso and fluttered over his stomach, her sharpened talons lightly catching the fabric of his shirt. Her heavy sighs sent a cascade of hot air over his neck, but he held his breath until his lungs burned as intensely as the blood beneath his skin. Then she grew tired of the tension and broke it with her hand slipping beneath his shorts; she wrapped her soft fingers around him, that part of him that had not felt a woman's touch in such a long while, where blood rushed to make him grow in the grip of her hand.

He didn't know why he didn't stop her immediately—the spirit indeed was willing, but the flesh was weak. Her eyes grew wide and she giggled devilishly, and squeezed tighter, until he was throbbing in her hand.

"Oh, my… such a big boy," she murmured in sick delight.

"Charlene, don't do this—"

The thud of a book striking her skull startled them both, and with a shriek of pain she let go of him and fell to the ground in shock. Standing there victoriously over her writhing body was none other than Susan Lewis, clutching a Bible like a brick in her hand, ready to swing it once more and knock the bitch's lights out. Her fur coat hung like Superwoman's cape. She pressed her foot into Charlene's side and rolled her over onto her back, and commanded her, "Get the hell outta my house, you rancid hussy, or God as my witness I'll kick them implants right outta your tits."

Struggling to catch her breath, Charlene sputtered, "You'll regret this, I promise—"

"Sweetheart, at my age I can't be bothered to regret a goddamned thing," Susan scoffed. "Call up your hotshot New York lawyers and sue me, for all I care. Alabama prisons don't take too well to sex offenders and child molesters."

"He's no child, I can tell you that," Charlene muttered as she tried to get up off the floor. Susan drove her foot into her side and knocked her back down. She wasn't done with her yet.

"Balls dropped or not, he sure as shit ain't given you his consent. Now you've got twenty seconds to get outta here and drive off in your fancy car, or I'll pull my shotgun off the wall and fire a warning shot right in your bony ass." She let Charlene scramble across the floor and shakily get back up on her heels; the door slammed shut behind her when she dashed out into the street and almost got hit by a passing car. Clutching the back of her head in pain, she hadn't looked both ways.

"You alright, kid?" Susan asked. Jonah was sitting on one of the library's stepstools to catch his breath, at a loss for words. She put a hand on his shoulder and set the Bible down on the empty cart beside her. "If you're blamin' yourself, don't. You're too proper a gentleman to clock that whore in the face, so your options were slim pickin's."

"I coulda stopped her. Guess I ain't changed much after all."

"There's a lotta things I can't stand in this world, kid, but victim blaming's near the top o' the list. Y'ain't done nothin' wrong. Go for your run then head off for that church concert and forget all about it. If y'ain't really gone and cleaned up your act, you wouldn't be feelin' so damn guilty about all this. Hold a grudge against that hooker and not yourself. Besides, no one's gonna know about all this anyway, 'cept for me and the Almighty, and I can assure you that the both of us care about you a great deal.

"She'll get what's comin' to her one day, and if God's takin' too long for your likin', I'll take care of it myself. So if the bitch comes back lookin' for you or for a fight, trust and believe I'll be goin' down guns blazin' in your honor. This old library could use a new paintjob, anyway, and I think red might suit it real nice."

••

The fateful text came right when Jimmy was in the middle of one of his characteristic diatribes. He was cursing his parents for their stinginess, his genes for his endless battle against gaining two unsightly pounds, and his shoes, for which he didn't pay, for being so last season. Inexplicably, the uneducated, ignorant Shaws were shrewder than his own parents, and Jimmy claimed that their darling Sophia lived a better life than Charlene and George ever gave him. A folder full of tax records tucked among his mother's personal boudoir pharmacy proved it. The fact that the documents were incriminating evidence against the Shaws was only an afterthought. Their real value was in proving to him that Charlene was a cheap, miserly bitch.

Perhaps he was right to curse his mother, but for the wrong reasons. Just ten minutes earlier, Charlene von Braun had accosted Jonah Young in the back of the Swayne Public Library, shoved her hand down his shorts, and found herself rejected by a teenage boy everyone thought was incapable of keeping it in his pants.

Levi nodded and played the part of attentive listener. If Jimmy had taken even a second to really examine the look on Levi's face, he would have realized that he'd checked out mentally a good ten minutes ago. The tightness of his lips suggested that he was holding back laughter. The redness of his cheeks implied a similar restraint. The ruddy sunset over Main Street, however, cast a colored light that made such flushed skin difficult to notice.

They were both reasonably drunk and had decided to take a breather in the Israel Pickens parking lot on their walk up the hill. Jimmy might have taken a vow of abstinence from all sorts of pills and powders, but classic ethanol was still on the table, and Levi couldn't let him drink alone with a clean conscience. Levi admitted that he himself never imbibed as often as he'd begun to as of late—

Mama turned him off from that. But for once he decided it was about time that he celebrated his own existence, which did not seem to be as miserable as it used to be, thanks to a series of events he never would have anticipated while pumping the von Brauns' gas not too long ago. Besides, he deserved a toast in his own honor, for all the good works of the Lord he'd done recently in the lives of those who didn't believe in the Lord anyway.

"The bitch wouldn't even cough up the money for me to get a new car," he lamented. "They've got enough money to buy the Governor a first-class call girl every day of the week just so they can get a train to run through this shithole, but they can't even upgrade my ride."

"Your car's pretty damn new, ain't it?" Levi asked, not looking up from his phone. The hysterical text from Jonah was still there on the screen, taunting him like someone telling you a secret you didn't want to know in the first place, but were then were forced to keep against your will.

"*New?* I just hit 40,000 miles, Thompson. I can't drive anything that's been so used and abused. I might as well be driving a salvage vehicle! *Shameful* and *shameless*." He saw Levi snicker and had enough sense to realize it wasn't his fickleness in regards to automobiles that had amused his informal therapist. "And what's so funny that you can't have a little sympathy for someone driving around in a six-cylinder death trap?"

Levi held the power to utter the epitome of *Your Mama* jokes. How often did one have the opportunity to tell a friend that his mother had just sexually assaulted someone his own age? And if one did find himself in such a position, would he do it? If he hated the person, then yes, but Levi didn't hate the cougar's son. Should he do it? Probably not, especially in a town that small, where gossip spread faster than the clap in a whorehouse. And could he do it? Absolutely, especially with a few drinks in him, and with the right amount of provocation. It was against his better judgment, of course, but alcohol delayed judgment till the next morning, when one would judge himself according to the strength of his headache.

"*Spit it out, Thompson.* I spill my guts to you about all the myriad problems I have in my life, and you don't even have the decency to read me one badly spelled text message? It's from that hot white trash friend of yours, isn't it? Tell him if he's so goddamned jealous of me, he can take me out to dinner and spend some time with me himself."

Levi sputtered his laughter and said, "He ain't goin' on a date with you anytime soon, seein' as he done turned down the date of a lifetime."

"He rejected an advance from Prince William, before he lost all his hair?"

"Not exactly."

"Prince Harry, then. Dye his hair brown and I'm sure you could find that ginger a soul."

"He ain't gay, y'know."

"Honey, slip a guy a couple Benjamins and he'll try anything once. I can tell you *that*."

"Well, his suitor's got a hell of a lot more than a couple Benjamins in her purse, and even that wasn't enough for him."

"Melania Trump!" Jimmy concluded with absolute confidence. "It *has* to be!" Levi shook his head with a smirk; Jimmy scowled, then gave up with a sigh. "Eh, I'm losing interest now, anyway. Didn't take my Adderall today and my ADD's flaring up like mental herpes. No one in this town's got that kind of money, anyway, except Mrs. Charlene von Bitch, and she's too frigid to pull that kind of stunt— on anyone but a Manhattan CFO with a brownstone and no offspring."

Levi's awkward silence was all that Jimmy needed.

*"What did that crazy bitch do?!"*

"She didn't get too far, if it makes you feel any better. Just some unsolicited advances and a lil' bit o' gropin' and dick-grabbin', but nothin' more than that."

*"Unsolicited advances?! Groping and dick-grabbing?!"*

"You're lucky Jonah's gone and cleaned up his act, 'cause a year ago he woulda left her with bookshelf marks in her back," Levi chuckled with little concern for the aneurism Jimmy was thirty seconds away from suffering.

"And to think, I detoxed and threw away my prescription crutch just to end up dealing with *this* bullshit! We didn't drink *nearly* enough for me to handle this kind of fuckery, Thompson! How would *you* react if you finally got irrefutable proof of your bitch mother's whoredom? It's one thing to speculate all these years—it's another thing to know *for sure*!"

"I don't see what's the big deal. There ain't no harm done, and don't nobody know about it."

"I wouldn't expect you to understand this, Thompson, but in the civilized world there's a touchy little thing called a *prenup*, and my cheap Jew of a father's got himself an ironclad one. He had his lawyer draw up that legal masterpiece the same day he got his receipt for Charlene's engagement ring. Now that reckless bitch is giving him perfect grounds for divorce on charges of adultery and overall wretchedness, and if they sign those divorce papers, we'll get *nothing*."

"*She'll* get nothin'. Your father'll still pay for your shit, I'm sure."

"You don't know these people, Thompson. They're barely human, especially Charlene, because with all the work she's had done she's basically just plastic and crazy glue at this point. She'll get sole custody in a heartbeat, probably from screwing the judge, and that vindictive harpy will make damn well sure that I don't see a dime of George von Braun's fortune. We'll be *poor*, Thompson, *poor!* Impoverished, penniless, destitute, impecunious, indigent—*poor!* All because she'd rather me *starve* than let her ex-husband get involved in her life in *any* way."

"You starve yourself already, don't you?"

"*That's not the point!* I will *not* be stuck here the rest of my life, just because Charlene thinks that getting some young cock is worth living in an illegal basement apartment with worn-down last year's Prada shoes and a head full of bad memories. So I'm gonna get the fuck outta here, Thompson, at least for tonight, till I can figure out how to get back at that old whore for what she's about to put me through."

"And where exactly are you goin'?"

"To find the best blow this shithole can offer."

It seemed that Levi didn't fix him as thoroughly as he'd thought. Jimmy stormed off with his hands thrust stiffly into his pockets and the light of sunset gleaming off his blond hair. He stumbled as he made his way up the hill in a drunken rage, and his elongated shadows, stretching across the road, shifted and wobbled with each clumsy step. They looked like they were cast by something inside him, and not by his body eclipsing the sun that sank lower on the horizon: something twisted and misshapen, dark as night, the shadow of a creature driven by cocaine and resentment. Seeing it was an ice bath of reality for Levi, who was too drunk to fully realize what he'd just done.

It reminded him that he did need a cold shower. The church concert was in two hours, and he had beer on his breath. Clemency was already at risk of being burned to the ground in a wildfire of gossip, and the public library was where that first match was dropped. He didn't need to pour alcohol on those flames. His own mother had done enough of that already.

••

The entire flock was gathered and all the sheep were waiting patiently in their pen: the four walls of the Southern Mercy Bible Church, a spiritual barrier that kept the prowling sinners at bay. The ones that arrived early claimed the pews, the most pious taking the places of honor at the front, as they had missed the memo that those who humbled themselves would be exalted in the world to come. But that night, they received their earthly reward for punctuality.

The Youngs had managed to find seats for themselves somewhere in the center of the crowd, in the middle place between the demoted first and the promoted last. Hannah was looking sickly as ever. Her mother had tried her best to doll her up for the occasion, so the congregation might not assume she carried the bubonic plague or, worse, demons inside her. She even went so far as to paint her face with makeup in spite of her household ban on cosmetics; her lack of familiarity with more youthful looks made Hannah appear rather matronly, and it did little to help her cause. Instead, the eye shadow only drew attention to her sunken eyes, and the red lips and her skeletal figure gave her the semblance of a haunted marionette, animated only by the Devil's invisible strings.

Her older brother, however, thought he looked dashing as ever. Boasting his Sunday best half a day before Sunday, he drew compliments from no fewer than three old ladies while taking his seat. Levi, too, was dressed to the nines, or rather the nine hundreds; he was smugly sitting two pews away in a slimly tailored shirt that he by no means would have picked out himself or been able to afford. No doubt it was a gift of the von Brauns, doled out to the less fortunate to make the rich and bored feel better about themselves. Or maybe Jimmy just fancied himself some sort of upper-crust Prometheus who sculpted his pet peasant out of a clay facial mask.

Jonah seethed upon seeing Jimmy's own terrible creator sitting among the hoi polloi. Charlene was incapable of hiding, as she always stuck out like a sore but perfectly polished thumb, but she kept as low of a profile as her dark attire and darker sunglasses would allow. Jonah didn't need to be able to see her eyes to know she was staring him down. He saw himself in their black mirrors, the afterimage being slowly but gleefully burned into Charlene's retinas. She had the perfect vantage point, while a black wide-brimmed hat rudely blocked the view of those who sat behind her, and fashionably concealed the swollen bump on the back of her head.

Fortunately she was far enough away for Jonah to ignore her with partial success. Victoria Shaw, on the other hand, wouldn't let Charlene out of her sight. She scrutinized her with brows furrowed in deep suspicion, knowing full well that nothing good could come of her presence. Surely she'd not come to honor the Lord by honoring the Southern Mercy Bible Church and, ultimately, honoring the Shaws. What Victoria refused to accept, however, was that both she and Charlene bowed to the same green Beast, without whose presidential marks there was no buying or selling.

"Before we get started, folks, don't forget to put a few bucks in the basket so we can keep this wonderful music program goin'," the Reverend Shaw implored, standing at the front of the church with his finger pointed at the straw basket making its way down the rows. It was already filled to the brim with wrinkled dollar bills. Jonah was doubtful that the rickety old piano or the failing monitors would ever see a penny for repairs.

The Reverend gave his introduction but Jonah didn't hear a word of it. His attention was fixed solely on Sophia, who was sitting humbly in the choir with her ankles crossed and hands folded in her lap. In her pearly white dress she looked nothing less than ethereal, but she held her gaze low in spite of her beauty. Her modesty wasn't a virtue she upheld out of a sense of feminine shame, or a lack of self-confidence in the presence of those who watched her closely. It was her badge of personal strength, of independence from the opinion and approval of others. There was little point in boasting, as she understood that men and women could never be pleased. Her only responsibility was to put a smile on God's radiant face, and not the fickle crowds that were content for a moment then derisive at the next.

Where such wisdom came from, Jonah couldn't say, as Sophia's parents were more dependent on the praise of others than the old gods were on petty supplications, before Christ walked the earth. Her holy father raised his hand to silence a crowd that wasn't making much noise to begin with. Clapping his hands together with genuine excitement, the Reverend declared, "Without further ado, let's hear them voices raised up to the Lord!"

After the singing began it didn't take long for Jonah's mind to wander, not out of disinterest, really, but because the lyrics to contemporary worship songs too often sounded sexually charged. He was mature enough to keep from cracking up, but he had to wonder why anyone thought it was a good idea to pen lyrics such as *"Jesus, come inside me,"* or *"Touch me there, Lord,"* or, better yet, *"Can't nobody do me like Jesus."* Their real meaning was obvious to any churchgoer, but to an outsider, or anyone with his mind in the gutter, those songs were baby-making music for a blasphemous communion. The choir sang a handful of such songs, describing the Christ in ways fit more for a lover than the Son of God: did they love Him, or were they *in* love with Him? Or was there really a difference when one was lost in the throes of religious ecstasy?

No matter how suggestive their words might have been from time to time, the church choir put on an impressive performance. One wouldn't have expected it of such a small town with such a motley group of singers, ranging from preteen sopranos to raspy senior citizens of all vocal types. There was the occasional mistake— one child chiming in during a rest, an off-key note lasting just a beat or two—but few took notice of them, save Victoria, who could have burned the whole church to the ground with the fire in her vicious glare.

Sophia poured water on her mother's hellfire and stepped forward into the spotlight. It was her moment of truth. Jonah imagined what it must have been like for the high priests of Jerusalem to humbly enter the Holy of Holies and stand alone in the presence of the Most High. He wondered if they faced Him with fear, with awe, or with silent dignity before the Creator who bestowed it upon them. That night, Sophia looked like one of them. For the sake of the whole sinful town, for all its iniquity and hypocrisy, she was standing in the light of God to offer what small sacrifice she had. Hers was the only honest and true religion. All the rest was folly.

"We all picked this song together," she explained without taking all the credit for herself. She clutched the standing microphone with both hands and spoke quietly, such that her voice over the monitors had the strength of an angel's whisper in the back of one's mind, and not God's thunderous glory. "It resonates with anyone who's from a small town like ours, who maybe feels overlooked or forgotten. But just remember that God watches over everyone and sees into every heart, even the ones who don't stand at the front of the church, or sing the loudest, or pray the longest prayers."

She looked into the congregation and met eyes with Jonah's. Their amber hue glimmered in the light, and for a split second, there was no one in the room but the two of them.

"This is for all of them, and one of them."

The piano began with simple chords, soft, sustained. A hum crested from one side of the choir to the other, starting with the bedrock of baritones and tenors, and sweeping up to the soaring registers of the sopranos. Every note was perfectly aligned, melting into harmonies that were both individual tones and one new, complex sound, collective and unique all at once. It evoked an understanding of God's grand design, in which each lowly man played his part, sometimes sharp, sometimes flat, but in the end, resonating eternally with all those around him; if only for a moment, Jonah saw it for what it truly was.

If the choir was the communal voice of mankind, then Sophia was the voice that echoed through the ether to shape worlds and destinies. She was hypnotic. If ever there was darkness in Clemency, that night, she brought forth light.

> *"I sing because I'm happy*
> *I sing because I'm free*
> *His eye is on the sparrow*
> *And I know he watches me."*

The town's youth listened in a reverent stillness, silenced by the girl they used to tease and snicker about in the halls of their high school; her body, the subject of so many jokes and snide, sexist remarks, was the source of a beautiful voice they could never hope to rival. Their elders closed their eyes and let her song take them away to happier days, when they didn't need hearing aids to capture delicate melodies, and when they moved as swiftly as those sparrows of which Sophia sang. Some shed a tear or two. Others bowed their heads in silent prayer.

All of them jumped when the bang of the doors against the wall brought the song to an abrupt and unplanned close.

"*Brava, BRAVA!*"

Stumbling into the church was the one and only Jimmy von Braun, with pupils the size of saucers, and bleached teeth gnashed like a pit bull's.

The pianist carried on for a few more bars before he realized they'd been ambushed. Standing, he knocked his microphone, and a piercing surge of feedback covered Jimmy's shrill voice for just a painful second. The choir members looked to one another, unsure of what to do; blood trickled from Victoria's fists as she pierced her palms with fingernails in white-knuckled fury. The congregation was audibly horrified but did nothing to stop him. The only thing better than spreading the word of God was spreading gossip like loudmouthed missionaries for weeks to come.

Jimmy gripped the doorframe to keep himself from falling. Sophia, on the other hand, firmly stood her ground, with an expression not of scorn, but quiet disappointment. She kept her eyes on Jimmy, and didn't glance over at Jonah, who thanked God for it, because his face had turned as red as the Devil he wished would stab Jimmy's chest with his pitchfork. He turned his glare to Levi, who'd sunk low in his seat, mortified. He had the look of a guilty man. Jonah needed no further evidence that Levi was behind all of it. Leave it to the son of a drunk to tap dance on a landmine.

"Again, *bravissima, BRAVISSIMA!*" Jimmy crowed at the top of his lungs. "Not to you, Miss Shaw—you're a kickass chanteuse, for sure, but you're not the lady of the hour here. No, that honor goes to the coldest, nastiest bitch you've all ever seen—*MRS. CHARLENE VON BRAUN.*"

With the spotlight forced upon her, Charlene snatched her handbag off the pew and began to slink her way toward the exit. Her cocaine-fueled son had other plans.

"*Don't let her leave!* She has to answer for her *whore* crimes!" he barked, and his mother stopped dead in her tracks. She tore off her sunglasses and glared with the sick disdain of a woman who regretted not aborting her fetus when she'd had the chance.

"That's right, good people! You've got a shameless, old *cougar* in your midst! Don't let her designer wardrobe and overpriced perfume fool you, humble townsfolk—she's about as fresh as a meth whore at sunrise, and with just as much sense. Really, Charlene, how long did you think you could fuck around with an eighteen-year old and get away with it?"

The chatter broke out instantly. Which of their children was bedding the town's most notorious succubus? (*"Not MY son,"* some whispered; their neighbors murmured, *"It was yours, I'm sure. He's never had an ounce of self-control."*)

"It's like a goddamned TV show, with the lonely, undersexed wife prowling around town for some young, dumb, hopefully hung guy to fuck her and pay her the kind of attention she can't get from her own husband! How does it feel to be a stereotype, mother dearest? I bet even *Aunt Jemima* has more dignity than you. But I'll grant you *one* thing, Charlene von Bitch: he's smokin' hot, so well done. But don't let it go to your head, because from what I hear, most of the girls in this town have already slept with big-time quarterback playboy *Jonah Young*."

Jonah's pounding heart instantly stopped and dropped to the pit of his stomach. The uneasy feeling of being watched escalated into an overwhelming sensation that he could only liken to being drawn and quartered, with a thousand hooks pulling at every inch of his body, tugged by the wide eyes of the crowd around him. *It's not true!* he wanted to shout, but no one would believe him. Why should they? His reputation preceded him, followed him and walked alongside him no matter where he went. And as much as Sophie might have fallen for him and given him her trust, there wasn't a chance in hell that she would question what everyone knew right then to be a clear and undeniable scandal: that Jonah Young had been caught wet-dicked in the middle of church, right in front of the innocent girl he claimed to love, but had betrayed publicly not just before the whole town, or her parents, but God.

It took every ounce of courage he had left to look over at Sophia. He couldn't bear to see her, if the image in his head would prove true. He imagined her devastated, tears streaming down her face, mortally wounded by the knife in her back that he'd never actually wielded. He pictured her wearing a broken heart on her sleeve and burying her face in her hands. When he turned his head and looked upon her, however, she did none of these things. She was stoic; she was still. Her eyes were set not on him—in fact, they might not have been set on anything. Sophie was in another world. It was a world that Jonah knew he didn't deserve to ever see or enter.

Jimmy's tirade was far from over, because he still had half a bag of rock salt to rub in Clemency's wounds. "I hope you're proud of yourself, Charlene, now that you've gone and ruined that pretty little Puritan girl's first shot at love, like you ruined all of *mine*. But what would a frigid, cyborg bitch like you know about love, anyway, except maybe the love of money?

"You're in good company, though! Because as much as these holy rolling, Bible-thumping frauds claim to love God and Jesus and all those fairytales, the only religion they *really* know is bowing to the *Almighty Dollar*. So while *you're* on your knees in front of some teenage stud getting dirt on your $4,000 jeans, *they're* on their knees praying to J.P. Morgan and all the riches he holds in his holy vaults. But you already knew that! Did you plan on blackmailing them, Charlene? Or did you get your sticky hands on their tax records just for shits and giggles?

"Well, good people of this backwater shithole!" he declared to the entirety of the congregation. "Since the town hooker won't tell you, *I* will. Your good, pious Reverend and his thieving wife have been lining their pockets with your hard-earned welfare checks!"

Hushed voices spread through the room like ripples on a pond's surface, and Jimmy was that one unruly kid who threw rocks. The people of Clemency were admittedly quick to believe anything, at least when it came to God and government, but these accusations teetered on just too much for them to so easily swallow. To admit one's blindness was no easy task, even after having been led to the edge of a ditch.

"I almost can't blame them! They're just smart businesspeople, but not smart enough to keep those fake accents consistent—you all really fell for that shitty act? Really, it's like you were all *asking* for it!

Did Victoria's brand-new Mercedes *really* not turn a single head in this town? Or the fact that this church is more broke down than a washed up, bald Britney Spears? For God's sake, people, get your heads out of your bulky asses and get a look at what those religious *hacks* really are—petty, thieving *whores*, only a small step above my *whore* mother!"

Victoria Shaw couldn't possibly stand for such heinous blasphemy. She lunged for the microphone and rebuked the devil among them. "Don't listen to 'im! Y'all know he's got a whole legion o' demons inside 'im! Cursed by the father o' *lies*, he is!"

No one seemed fully convinced and they continued to eye her with suspicion. Of course, they knew for a fact that Jimmy von Braun was a demoniac, harboring an entire host of unclean spirits inside him, the kind that love dance clubs and party drugs and make boys want to kiss other boys.

"You know what? You *all* should be ashamed of yourselves, every last one of you inbred fucks. You think you're such good Christian folk? *Not a chance.* I might have my place reserved for me in Hell, but I can tell you with absolute certainty that your precious Jesus would have nailed *himself* to that cross if he knew what *hypocrites* his small-town followers would be!

"That's right—*hypocrites*. You know you're a bunch of selfish bastards when *I'm* the most generous one in town! *I'm* the one who's dining with the poor and destitute, not you. *I'm* the one who's buying designer clothes for the naked and haute cuisine for the hungry. *I'm* the one who's treating sorry-ass underprivileged Levi Thompson like he's worth more than the handful of fat strippers' dollars you pay him to pump your goddamned gas. Meanwhile, all of *you* people haven't bothered to lift one pudgy finger to stop those welfare queen meth head Skinners from dragging this town's kids into the gutter, even though you all talk about it enough while sipping your screwdrivers and calling it orange juice. I see *right through* your bullshit, all of you. I see the *real* Clemency—what you *really* are: nothing more than gossipy, cruel, alcoholic, scum-sucking social *parasites*."

Then, like that dark time before the creation of the world, there was only silence.

The townspeople didn't take up torches and pitchforks and call for the public hanging of the von Braun family heir. They didn't hurl Bibles or rotting vegetables or anything they could get their hands on. There was no reaction at all. They were stunned, lobotomized by Jimmy's razor-sharp lampoon, rendered unable to shout or protest or defend the indefensible. However, one among them retained control over his body: the Reverend Shaw, who was making his way toward the back door as if he were sneaking out of a crowded movie theater.

SSG Eddie Sharpe was the first to notice the rat slipping away to safety. He jumped to attention like a soldier spotting the enemy and barked, "Where does he think *he's* goin'?!"

"The Reverend owes us some damn answers!" Joe DeRosa declared as loud as his raspy, old voice box would allow.

"We ain't done with the likes o' him yet!"

"Somebody stop 'im!"

*"Get 'im!"*

As the men in the front row barreled toward Jeffrey Shaw, whose eyes reflected the terror of a man facing final judgment, Victoria threw herself in their path and stopped them with an open palm. She always claimed to be the voice of reason, Clemency's bedrock and font of sensibility. Somehow she thought that an angry mob, the victims of weekly larceny, would listen.

"Now get a hold o' yourselves!" she demanded while the door slammed behind her, the good Reverend heading for the hills. "There ain't a shred o' evidence to back up them sissy boy's claims! More than anythin', all y'all got is evidence o' this town's *sinfulness*! Y'all just done witnessed the breakin' of not one, not two, but *five* o' the Lord's commandments!"

Gracey DeRosa pointed her cane like a bayonet straight at Victoria and yelled, "How 'bout *Thou shalt not steal*, you thievin' harlot!"

"Never!" Victoria cried. "And how dare you even think it!"

Victoria was cornered and knew there was no escape. In one last desperate attempt, she protested, "That von Braun boy's the abomination here, and he's draggin' all o' y'all down to Hell with 'im! He's bearin' false witness against me 'n your trusted, honest Reverend; he's takin' the name o' the Lord in vain more times than I care to count; Heaven forbid he should *ever* honor his father 'n mother; *and* his mother done *stole* from me by gettin' her greedy hands on my bank statements, not to mention her shameless, repugnant *adultery*!"

No matter how many times she tried to pass the blame, Victoria failed to draw attention away from herself, and Jimmy remained merely an afterthought to the horde that cared only about their own empty pockets. Through the fray Jonah looked to Victoria's scapegoat, the one that no one cared enough to sacrifice: he was hobbling his way out the front doors, held up by none other than Levi Thompson, Jonah's alleged best friend, who made himself a crutch to someone who wanted nothing more than for the world to fall around him.

Jonah cursed every step he took out the door; he cursed him for that night, and for all the lonely nights to come. Most of all, he cursed him for the empty seat Sophia had left by the pulpit, and for the rage that welled up inside him, but couldn't fill his complete and utter emptiness. She was gone. He knew it would be for good.

# 17

IT TOOK ALL OF HIS WILLPOWER for Jonah not to beat the piss out of Levi right there in front of the church.

He stood in the middle of Main Street with the frenzied shouts of the congregation behind him, sounding out from the open doors of the Southern Mercy Bible Church, which may as well have been going up in flames. The air seemed hotter than it was at midday, either from the pure, untamed wrath that rose up beyond the steeple, or Jonah's all-consuming rage. At that moment he understood the Old Testament religion's decree of an eye for an eye. He would only turn his cheek when walking away from a defeated Levi, lying battered and bruised on the pavement.

"Are you really so fuckin' miserable that you had to go 'n ruin it for everyone else?" he interrogated. "You wouldn't be chasin' after such frivolous shit if you're really satisfied with your sorry life. I know you grew up around total messes 'n train wrecks, but this takes the fuckin' cake."

"I'm sorry, alright? Y'know I'd never try and get between you 'n Sophie—I had no idea Jimmy was gonna pull this stunt, no more than you did, and you know damn well I woulda stopped him if I saw it comin'."

"That's 'cause you're blind as shit these days."

"How many times do I gotta apologize before you accept it?"

Levi was practically cowering in Jonah's shadow, his body as tense as someone expecting an imminent assault. It wasn't so much fear on his face as it was remorse, and if Jonah had been in his right mind, he might have recognized it. But he had little concern for guilt or repentance or reconciliation, as those were God's problems to deal with, not his.

"Don't bother bullshittin' me," he snapped. "I don't need your weak apologies. You done gone and forgot where you came from and now you think you're all high 'n mighty since you got yourself a rich patron these days, so sayin' you're sorry to one of us poor, classless peasants don't mean shit. If anything, you're just sorry that someone's expectin' you to be accountable, and ain't no amount of von Braun money's gonna pay off this debt you done racked up."

In an instant Levi's guilt toward his own mistakes turned to resentment, and his defenses shot up faster than a wall on the Mexican border, topped with barbed wire and a sense of superiority he saw no point in hiding. "I ain't never took you for the jealous type, but I guess that ain't much of a surprise given anything you could be proud of is left in the past, bigshot has-been MVP. Hate to break it to you, but ain't no college in the country's gonna take you with such a miserable track record. You're lucky Sophie took you in the first place."

The whole situation was too comical for Jonah's ego to be bruised: who was this Levi who'd suddenly decided it was befitting for an eighteen-year old to actually defend himself? "Now *there's* the Levi the world's been waitin' for! Finally standin' up for himself instead o' curlin' up like a pussy! Ain't it a shame that you couldn't grow that kind o' backbone while gettin' bullied by your own drunk mama?"

"Say whatever you want, call me an enabler or a pussy, I don't give a shit. It don't mean a fuckin' thing comin' from someone who ain't even man enough to protect his little sister from being lost for good."

Without warning Jonah grabbed Levi by his shirt collar and instinctively drew his arm back with a clenched fist, a split second away from pummeling him into unconsciousness. He ground his teeth with enough force to break them, but restrained himself. Had it been anyone else, self-control would have been unthinkable. He would have given in to the aggression innate to all human men, a vestigial drive inherited from the primates that were unfettered by a sense of mercy. He released his grip and pushed Levi away, landing a firm hand on his chest. Stumbling back, Levi stopped to catch his breath. Jonah did the same with little success. There was too much adrenaline in his boiling blood to allow it.

"I got a right mind to do the same with you, then," he muttered, unclenching his fists to let the blood flow back into his fingers. He thrust them into his pockets to keep himself from lashing out a second time. "Lemme just let you get caught up in some shit that'll never satisfy you. There ain't no happiness to be found in it, and you'll learn that the hard way, one day or another. You'll keep reachin' for more and more but end up with nothin'.

"You won't be alone, though—you done made damn well sure o' that. I reckon I got no one now. There ain't no way in hell Sophie's gonna talk to me again, Hannah ain't never gonna be the same, and then there's you, runnin' off to chase somethin' y'ain't meant for and sure as hell don't deserve. So really, what's left for me in this shithole?"

Ready to walk away, Levi showed a shred of humanity and reassured him, "You'll get outta here soon enough. Don't listen to me."

"You're right about one thing. I sure as shit won't be listenin' to a goddamned thing that comes outta your mouth."

"Don't worry about that. From now on, I won't be talkin'."

Levi kept his promise. It was his last trustworthy act.

Jonah was unfamiliar with the feeling that followed the death of a friendship. Anger gushed like blood from the knife wound in his back, but he wiped it away and feigned masculine apathy. Convinced of his own independence, he had a right mind to say, *Screw you, I don't need you, and not just you, because that'd mean you were somehow special—I need no one.* It was one of those times when one could not only admit but embrace that innately human sense of selfishness, the subconscious bedrock beneath all relationships. A friendship wasn't ever really for the sake of the other: it was the product of evolution, when cavemen huddled around fires in the dark with wolves lurking just outside their camp. It was meant to ease the primordial fear of being alone, and nothing more.

••

The rain poured down in sheets that night twelve years ago, heavier than the curtains that billowed before the open windows. It was too hot to keep them closed. The sofa suffered because of it, as did the wooden floor, though those floorboards were so worn that water damage was of little concern. The sheer volume of water overflowed from the gutters and cascaded off the lip of the roof, pooling on soil that had swallowed up as much rain as it could, and the driveway turned to a sea of sloshing, sticky mud. The old Ford outside seemed to have sunk an inch or two into the soft earth. Samuel Thompson questioned if he'd even be able to move it.

It became hard to distinguish his wife's sobbing from the surge of the storm, as she shed tears just as torrential as the downpour outside. Her breakdowns always did have the awesome power of Alabama's summer tempests. They did not fight often, but on those few unfortunate nights that they did, there might as well have been a hurricane rushing through the parlor, tearing down anything in its path—usually cutting short their young son's otherwise peaceful sleep. The bottle of whiskey that rested menacingly on the coffee table did little to quell the storm. So long as it remained within sight, there would be no serene eye to pass over them.

It was because of that bottle that he could hardly remember what he'd said to make her cry, if he'd said anything specific at all. One thought blended into another until he was unable to tell if he was saying them aloud or merely screaming them in his own head. Objects in the room drifted and shifted around him, and even the walls seemed to breathe; Lenore's mascara, running over her cheeks, took on the appearance of pitch dripping from her eyes. Her body melted into the sofa and the pillow that she clung to. The last of the whiskey, however, was clearer than ever, trapped at the bottom of the bottle like Samuel's words, locked away in his throat.

Courageously taking on the role of liberator, he grabbed the bottle off the table and gulped what remained in one swig. He slammed it back down and nearly broke it. Its contents tasted like water.

"Stop cryin', sweetheart," he murmured. "It ain't gonna change a thing."

"If you reject this town, then you're turnin' your back on everything that done made you who you are—who *we* are. You might as well be rejectin' me."

"That's why we gotta go. I ain't about to let this place shape our son. He can do so much better than me if he ain't held back by this place."

"You're a good man, Sam!" Lenore cried. Her words forced their way through her weeping like crawling through briars. "You're just losin' your way."

"I know exactly which way I'm headed, and it's out that door. And you're comin' with me, with Levi and everything we got. There ain't no compromise here."

"It ain't that easy 'n you know it."

"Pray on it," he advised, but it was as if he spat his suggestion at her feet. He snatched the car keys off the coffee table and headed toward the door, which rattled in the howling wind. "I'm gonna get myself a room somewhere, give you the night to make up your mind. But when I get back in the mornin', we best be on the same page."

He slammed the door so hard that it became nearly impossible to firmly shut, even years later. Its ricketiness was a daily reminder for Lenore each time she left the house in her pink dress and weathered apron. Over time, she lost the will to fiddle with it and simply left it ajar.

As he stepped out into the rain and felt his shoes sink into the mud, Samuel was surprised to find that his wife made no effort to stop him. He was more surprised that this bothered him.

The wheels of the car spun vainly when he put his foot on the gas, and he shouted the profanity he always did his best to avoid, but with the windows closed and the sloshing of the mud flung across the driveway, no one heard a word of it. With one final cuss the old Ford lurched forward and slithered its way toward the street. The wipers clapped with each pounding sweep across the windshield. They couldn't keep up with the downpour and the glass remained nothing more than a sloped puddle, through which Samuel, with vision already skewed, peered out over the dark road ahead.

The headlights of passing cars were just glowing, amorphous blobs sliding out of sight. The keys rattled when the tires bounced over a fallen branch with a thud. There seemed to be nothing but static on the radio, and as the needle slid from one frequency to the next, the best Sam could get was the distant, ghostly voices of stations just slightly out of reach. Frustrated, he smacked the tuner and drove in silence, his eyes just as deprived of clarity as his ears.

Part of him wanted to drive on forever, to just keep his attention on the endless yellow lines that kept him from drifting off the road. They were his only lifeline. But soon enough those disappeared behind the curtain of the rain, and he was driving blind, toward whatever lay ahead in his life and on the highway.

It was a lonely road to follow. Of all nights to travel it, that was the worst for a man like him. Not only was his mind miles away, but the rain made it impossible to find where it'd gone.

He thought of the future and the crossroads he'd come to, but not of the darkened intersection through which his car was about to race, nor of the sleepy mother and son who paused at the stop sign, on their way home from an evening at church.

••

Levi paced down the narrow aisles of Backwater Spirits without saying much of anything. Some neurotics went to costly psychiatrists to talk out their insipid personal problems; those with more meager savings turned to the bottle and drowned their issues on the living room sofa. Levi, on the other hand, being neither rich nor the son of a sober parent, sought help somewhere in the middle, staring unfocused at stocked shelves and muttering his grievances to the ever-patient liquor store owner.

"Guess there ain't no point in denyin' it," he admitted in a moment of self-awareness. "I lost sight o' things."

Mr. Green was finishing up with closing out the register for the day. He wrote meticulously in an old ledger, etching records of his small profits in pencil. The orderly stacks of dollar bills looked particularly short that day, and Levi wasn't helping much by taking up his time and not making a single purchase. Elijah, however, wasn't bothered. He offered his advice as if they were as instinctual as breathing or blinking. With such wisdom accumulated over his years, he could be an accountant and a therapist all at once and still have attention to spare.

"Money can do that to you," he remarked. "When you start seein' life through green-tinted glasses, it loses all its beauty. Can't appreciate nothin' when you paint it all the same color."

"Funny thing's that I ain't even had money. It was all someone else's. Turned me into a spoiled brat, and I ain't been raised to take favors and handouts."

"I'm sure your friend played his part, but you'd do best not to put all the blame on him. Temptation in itself ain't the problem. It's the weakness of the one who's tempted."

"I'm pretty damn weak, then."

"We all are. You ain't got a monopoly on it, 'specially at your age. If a teenage boy like you ain't got a small lack o' self-control, then you sure as hell got a real lack o' humanity. Ain't no one's expectin' you to be perfect. Don't get me wrong—I ain't sayin' you shouldn't strive to be. But you're gonna fall short sooner or later, and when you do, it ain't gonna help you one bit to call yourself nothin' more than weak."

"Tell that to Jonah. I'm sure 'weak' is the mildest thing he's callin' me right about now."

"From what I know, it's that he ain't the type to take after the Shaws. He'll forgive you. Give him some time to cool off and then I'm sure he'll be the good Christian this town don't see too often these days."

"Who knows how long that's gonna take? I went and ruined his first real chance at redeemin' himself. It sure ain't gonna be easy for him to let that go."

"It's God's will that we forgive others, you know." It was a maxim repeated often in Clemency, though rarely heeded. Coming from anyone but Elijah Green, those words were emptier than Levi's pockets.

"Jonah ain't one to care much about God's will."

"Ain't talkin' about him, young man. I'm talkin' about you."

It was no secret that Levi felt he'd been wronged by the world for most of his life: exploited by his job, tied down by Clemency, and beaten down by his mother. If he were to try to forgive those he claimed had ruined his chances at happiness, he'd waste a whole year doing it. "And who am I supposed to be offerin' my forgiveness to, since I'm the one at fault?"

"I'm tellin' you to forgive yourself. It's probably the hardest thing you can ask a man to do. The punishments we inflict on ourselves for all that guilt we carry is worse than anything God could come up with. Us humans are the sadists, not God."

"Maybe I had it comin'."

"Not for this long, though," Elijah proposed. "I've seen you bearin' this burden o' yours for the past few weeks, and if you see someone who's hurtin' and beatin' themselves down, then the best you can do for 'em is to make 'em remember that they're not alone."

"God's always near. I've heard it before."

"Yes, but that ain't what I mean. We're all sufferin' in this world and it don't do a man a lick o' good to convince himself he's sufferin' alone. I've had my fair share o' sorrows, young man, and I know a thing or two about 'em. I'm here for you. And I hope you'd be there for your neighbor, too, if you were standin' right where I'm standin'. Let it go, make your amends and don't pay it no more mind. Y'can't expect anyone else to move on if you keep draggin' the past along with 'em."

••

Hannah could barely feel the couch beneath her as she began her ascent to a better world. She was aware that it was lumpy, unsightly and worn down, with loose springs that dug into one's body like a bed of nails. Just a few minutes prior, she might as well have been sitting on an oversized cactus, half rotten and stinking of baby piss and sour milk, found on the side of the road somewhere. Now, it was like a fluffy cloud in the highest sphere of heaven. Angels shed tears of joy where once unkempt cats shed their sparse fur.

The dim glow of dingy lamps, the spoils of dumpster diving, flared up with the brilliance of the sun at its zenith. A warmth enveloped her, one that was comforting, nurturing, and she imagined that this was what babies felt like in their mothers' wombs, swaddled by living, breathing heat. She lay back and closed her eyes. Any problems she once had, or would come to have, drifted off into the distance. Her past and future became two places that she could never reach. They were dark points at the far ends of a white tunnel, and Hannah rested motionless in the light of the present. This, she told herself, was the closest thing to paradise she would ever experience, and sadly, it was a transient state of being.

Consciously she knew that what she felt was fleeting, merely an illusion of complete needlessness and wanting for nothing; she could articulate this if she chose to, but why would she? Every mountain collapsed to less than an anthill when she raised that glass pipe to her mouth. The pedestal her parents had forced her to teeter on sank down into the earth until she could finally play in the mud with the rest of Clemency. When everyone was covered in dirt, they were all the same: none better, none worse, all just sullied and indistinguishable.

Not long ago she was crippled with guilt. Her behavior was childish and stupid. She was a shortsighted, weak-willed little girl, eager to rebel against parents who just wanted the best for her, and to impress her exceptionally impressionable peers. She was a defiant, ungrateful sister, who slighted her older brother every chance she got, all because he loved her enough to try to keep her from mingling with the wrong crowd. But soon enough she threw away her guilt faster than opiates shot through a vein, and convinced herself that the only thing she was at fault for was in ever thinking that she was above the people around her—Gabe, the Skinners, his friends and all those whom the hypocrites of Clemency loved to hate but hated to stop gossiping about. If they'd taken a minute to turn their noses down, they might have noticed what was happening to her. Maybe then she'd give them something else to talk about.

Rumors were what high school girls thrived on: they were natural electrolytes. If it wasn't for her peers' constant thirst for tea and trash talk, she might not have ever gotten mixed up with the likes of Gabriel Skinner. Passing notes in sixth grade about secret crushes turned to backroom bathroom banter that focused on more mature themes as the years progressed, like late bloomers, bra sizes, French kisses and third bases. The subject of virginity, then, was inevitable. When Hannah hit her freshman year it was all the girls her age talked about. Virginity was one of those things that a girl was mocked for holding on to but slandered for giving away too soon, though the line between early and late was hard to pinpoint and even harder to keep from moving. If she kept her legs closed, she was a prude, but if she put out, she was a slut—unless of course it was to an older boy, in which case she was practically royalty, or at least a whore with a tiara.

Hannah's winning lottery ticket to the jackpot of social capital came in the form of Rory Skinner, a classroom acquaintance of hers, and Gabe's younger sister. Of all the Skinners, she was easily the most approachable, though she presented herself with the same gritty style one would expect, except she made it into a fashion statement. Long, unruly red hair, black tank tops, unhidden bra straps and furiously ripped jeans made her look like the lead singer of a '90s grunge band. She filled the bathrooms with cigarette smoke and covered the stalls with ballpoint pen graffiti, all in the manner of the kind of rebellious teen that Hannah had never come close to being. Girls thought she was a trailer trash skank and boys thought she was an easy, no-strings lay. Hannah thought she was intriguing.

Who wouldn't be fascinated by the uniquely dressed loner who sat on the bleachers with a cigarette while the other girls were forced to jog and get drenched in sweat, all because she had forged a note from some no-name podiatrist? And who wouldn't want to become acquainted with the sarcastic, apathetic girl at the back of the classroom who drew crude pictures of their suspected transvestite history teacher in drag, all in hopes that he'd confiscate it and be too flabbergasted to chastise her? She was amusingly different, breaking the mold with a sledgehammer, and a far cry from those uppity bitches who thought that screwing popular athletes was the pinnacle of adolescent achievement.

"Looks like you're good at this shit," Rory noted one day when their teacher distributed the graded results of their last assignment. She leaned over to grab Hannah's attention, having noticed her typical A+ gleefully inscribed at the top of the page. She herself had nearly failed. She crumbled up the paper and tossed it forward, landing a perfect shot in the back of Darla Strauss's bulbous head, one of her many nemeses.

"I could always help you out if y'need a tutor," Hannah suggested. Trying to play it cool and feign disinterest, she neglected to face Rory while she spoke. After all, she couldn't be bothered.

"I ain't about to pay you, if that's what you're lookin' for in return. And I ain't no lez, either."

"A change o' reputation's all I'm lookin' for."

Rory grinned slyly. From then on, they were friends. Her grades, however, didn't improve much, but that was to be expected. Hannah, on the other hand, found herself gaining more respect from those around her, who went from resenting her position at the top of the pedestal to fearing that she might jump off it and crush their skulls beneath her feet. But concern for her stability wasn't really what she wanted. It wasn't until she was introduced to Rory's older brother that she started to gain the kind of respect she wanted from the other girls, who were engaged in a ruthless arms race to see who could be the first to wipe her virginity off the map.

Gabe was unexpectedly charming, more polite than Hannah had been led to believe, given his family's infamy in that small town. He somehow managed to clean up his crass mouth just long enough to convince Hannah that he was, in fact, a gentleman of sorts, one who readily admitted to having seduced a good number of girls, but asserted that Hannah was different from all the rest. Being a teenager desperate for validation, she fell for it with little resistance.

The TV screen in his living room had been flashing with graphic images of bloodied corpses and screaming enemy soldiers when she first met him; he was sitting on the couch with a controller in his hand, cheering himself on as he mercilessly gunned down howling Nazis or ululating Arabs or any number of digital, subhuman bad guys. After winning another round, he held out the controller to Hannah, encouraging her to show him what she's got, and she quickly proved that she most certainly ain't got it. He mocked her reluctance to slaughter even a fictitious human being, but in a playful sort of way. She started going there more often. Eventually, she let him slaughter her sensibilities. They spent more time in his unmade bed than on the couch.

Over time, she stopped caring that he rarely washed the sheets, if ever. Really, she stopped caring about much at all. The shared needles on the nightstand were a testament to it.

"If y'really wanna get the hell outta this town, here's the easiest way to do it," he susurrated like the serpent that led Eve down a dark, one-way path. "Ain't no one's gonna expect you to be perfect no more. And you sure as shit won't care what they think, anyway."

He was the one to slip the needle into her arm that first time; she was too squeamish. She couldn't even watch him do it. To the present day, she closed her eyes when the time came for it.

Hannah kept her eyes shut for many things: some things she did to herself, and others that Gabe, and his friends, did to her.

Gabe was right when he said she'd stop caring about what others thought of her. He showed even more foresight when he told her she wouldn't feel a thing anymore—no worry, no shame, and best of all, no pain. It was the one promise he truly kept, the one thing that proved not to be a lie. When he was thrusting inside her, dripping sweat upon her brow while his friends and suppliers watched and waited their turn, she felt nothing. She was miles away, in a field of paper flowers and purple skies, only vaguely aware of the men who had their way with her limp body and then slipped some cash or dime bags into Gabe's greedy hands.

Despite knowing full well that she was being subjected to something morally reprehensible, or worse, pure evil in a town known for its righteousness, Hannah couldn't help but think that she was somehow to blame in all of it. After all, hadn't she asked for it— not explicitly, but with her silent compliance, and for having allowed her sense of superiority to go unpunished for so long? Maybe it was about time she got what was coming to her. She went from being glorified for her grades to being heralded for her having caught the attention of an older boy. Either way, she'd let the world deify her in some way or another. Hubris sent her crashing down to earth.

In the end, she wasn't so cool anymore. At school, she just got overlooked. She was old news—nobody cared that she was Gabe's girl, because really, it wasn't as impressive of an achievement as they'd once thought. There was nothing glamorous about hiding track marks under long sleeves in the summer, or being terribly pale and underweight. She was fading away into nothingness, both in the eyes of those who once admired her, and in her own integrity.

Her rebellion left her empty handed: she never seized the prize she coveted. And now she was longing to rebel against what she'd become, but knew she had no one to support her cause. Maybe her brother would have taken up her flag once, if only she hadn't pushed him so far away.

With great effort she rolled over on the couch and tried to drift off to sleep. Whatever might happen to her while she was out dreaming was of little concern. With no hope in the waking world, all she had left to do was dream, and escape into subconscious fantasies.

That night, she had only nightmares.

••

Time passed by with the same sense of stagnation that, not long ago, Levi thought he'd left behind for good. It felt like he was wading in some stinking, motionless pond, covered in a slippery film of mold and motor oil. He pumped gas, made vain conversation, and brought home slave wages, as he always had. These days, though, he had nothing else to wear but the dingy beaters he sported in the sweltering heat at the gas station, which used to be white at some point in the distant past, and the few button-ups he saved for Sundays.

With hands slick with axle grease, he'd slid back down the societal ladder and wound up right where he started: on the ground, the wind knocked out of him by life's never-ending blows, too dizzy to stand when looking up at just how high that towering ladder stretched.

Mama was just as crippled, trapped at the bottom of her bottle like a tiny ship that would sail nowhere but into a dusty box in an attic. It was the anniversary of her husband's sudden departure, unannounced and unwanted. She made sure not to let Levi forget it: that day, September 20, twelve arduous years ago, he walked out their front door in the middle of the night and never came back.

"He never even *looked* back," she insisted, taking a drag from her fourth cigarette of the hour. "Kept you outta sight and outta mind, boy—maybe for the best, seein' how you done turned out. But you just remember that when you go on cursin' me for his bein' gone. Ain't no one's doin' but his own."

He took it with a dollop of salt, the same that she rubbed in both their wounds each passing year. She was too drunk to realize that it was best thrown over their shoulders and left behind.

"Make yourself useful and head down to the store," she demanded when the flow of whiskey ran dry. "You pay for it, too. Of all days, here's the one where someone should do somethin' for *me* for a change."

He'd become rather familiar with throwing money at one's problems over the past few months, but this time it seemed he was just buying himself more trouble.

As it turned out, booze and burdens were out of stock that day. Mr. Green was closing up shop when Levi approached with his shadow before him, long and narrow in the afternoon sun. His keys jingled as he slipped them into his back pocket, and he rattled the doorknob to make sure his livelihood was safe and locked up for the day. Having developed an uncanny sense for Levi's presence over the years, he didn't need to look up to know that his most loyal customer was approaching, on the hunt for the very goods that kept his business alive and brought Lenore Thompson an inch closer to an early death.

"Good afternoon, young man," he greeted while pulling his keys back out of his pocket for Levi's sake. "Don't worry, I'll make an exception. Today ain't a day for selfishness."

"If that's the case, then don't sweat it. I ain't about to be selfish, neither. She don't need to know I caught you on your way out."

"You're in for a rough night, then. Might be best to stay outta the house for a while."

"Ain't got nowhere to go, sorry to say. Still ain't got a friend in the world."

Elijah shook his head with sympathy and looked across Main Street, toward the thick and untamed woods. "Well, if y'ain't doin' anything, I was just about to pay my family a visit. You're welcome to join me if you need to busy yourself for an hour or two." Levi took him up on his offer.

One of the sleepy back roads ran through the forest and passed a dirt path, overgrown with rough, hardy foliage. Levi might not have noticed it, except for the post that jutted out of the ground at the roadside, sporting a neon reflector that had become dull with dust and dirt. The rocky soil crunched beneath their feet while they strolled down what turned out to be a lengthy, unpaved driveway. Sparse patches of grass brushed against Levi's ankles, as did the gangly dandelions that had since lost their feathery seeds to the warm breeze. No one had been there to make a wish on them. Perhaps they were simply unseen dreamers, wishing only for someone to remember them while casting their hopes to the fleeting wind.

Ahead was the cornfield, and the old farmhouse, waiting as if only for them. Elijah, however, paid little mind to the house—if anything, he seemed to avoid looking at it entirely. As soon as he was able, he turned off the path to keep his back to it. Something about it made Levi sad. He imagined the cloudy windows as the gray eyes of an elderly relative, looking wistfully at a loved one who'd chosen to walk away from her, as though she were merely a reminder of a lost and painful past.

At the far edge of the woods, Elijah found whom he was looking for.

The two headstones were simple but beautiful. They were honest, not ornate. Emerald ivy curled around them as a living frame. They stood in the shadow of an old rose bush, which shed white petals like tears.

MARY ANN GREEN, read the headstone on the left. BELOVED WIFE, CARING MOTHER.

JACOB ANTHONY GREEN, read the one beside her. ONLY SON, PRIDE AND JOY.

Levi would have been six years old when they died.

If there was anything that could be said, Levi was at a loss for it. The two of them held their heads low, and let the wind in the trees speak for them. The moment of silence lingered for what seemed to be far longer than just a moment. But to pay his respects to everything and everyone Elijah had lost, Levi would have stayed quiet for a year. It was the least he could do for the one wise man he'd ever met, who still trusted God despite the lies His believers told, and who let nothing, not even his own loss, keep him from helping a selfish young man who had lost far less, but thought he had nothing.

"We do everything we can to tell ourselves that if we act responsible and stay safe, that ain't no harm'll ever come to us," Elijah mused. He pulled out a pocket knife to trim a rose from the bush, and placed the flower gently atop Mary Ann's grave. "Maybe we're just foolin' ourselves. Who are we to say our lives are in our own hands?"

"You sayin' that's God's place?"

"At the heart o' things, yes. But the people around us have got a stronger hold on our futures than we care to believe. We might think we're layin' out our own path ahead of us, but it only takes one person with an ax to knock a tree right in your way."

"Find a way around it, then, right?"

"God willin', but sometimes it's just the end o' the road, young man."

"That ain't very reassuring."

"No, it ain't, sorry to say. The best I can tell you is to cherish what you got and to thank God every day for it. Whatever He gives you, He can also take away."

"He probably will, too. Pretty cruel o' Him."

"All the better to appreciate it while it lasts. Ain't nothin' in this world is forever. Whether good or bad, all things pass in time. Remember that, and you'll spare yourself a whole lotta sufferin', wonderin' where you went wrong, or what you coulda done different."

"So twelve years later," Levi asked, "you got any regrets left?"

"Only that it took me so long to forgive. But my anger's gone now, buried in the past, along with all my 'what ifs' and 'if onlys.'"

"And who was it that needed forgivin'?"

It was the one question in all of their time knowing each other that Elijah would not answer.

In the tense silence that ensued, Levi came to understand that though he'd encountered many coincidences in his life, this was not one of them. There was meaning in Elijah's hesitation. It was as significant as the dates on those two graves, and the one day on the kitchen calendar that Mama refused to check off until she was too drunk to care.

"If you know somethin', you can't just leave me here wonderin'."

"There ain't much more I can say with a clean conscience, Mr. Thompson. I've had a lot o' years to find my place in this world, and this ain't it. Your mama's the only one who can answer that and be guiltless before God."

He looked into the sunset and sighed. Dark clouds were crawling over the horizon, their edges painted a fiery orange and soft rose in the fading light. "There's a storm rollin' in," he noted, and put his hand on Levi's shoulder to guide him back to town. "It's about time you head on home." He, however, didn't budge.

"What about you?" Levi asked.

"I'm already there. But you—you're almost there, but not yet. Just a little farther, and you'll be home. Just don't look back. Not for me, and not for no one."

••

The dirt driveway stretched on farther than it ever had in Levi's eighteen years. It was all in his head, and he knew it. But he looked down that dim path and perceived it as never-ending, and each step brought him closer to the flickering lights at the end, but at the same time, nowhere at all. Maybe he didn't want to reach his destination. He would have rather been stuck out in the coming downpour than confront the storm that awaited him just behind his front door. But he knew it was something he had to face. To ignore it would be to let it rage on forever.

This was the moment he'd always hoped for, when his mother might finally scream out the truth instead of the lies she told herself and the world. The answers to all his questions would be uncovered like the engraved heart at the bottom of Mama's overflowing ashtray. He knew it would hurt, more than her whiskey to the wounds that refused to heal, and that it could very well seal shut the coffin of a relationship between mother and son. It was a consequence he neither dreaded nor desired to avoid. If the rumors held any value, then the train station would be opening any day now, and he'd be buying himself a one-way ticket to anywhere with the money he kept hidden away from a world of thieves and liars.

On the creaky porch he kicked the dirt from his feet as a testament against his mother, that backward town, and his own weakness. His fears were best left at the door, where they should have been all along. Living in ignorance had been his lifelong torment, a thorn in his side that could not be removed gradually, but only with one quick, violent pull. He wanted the truth, even if he had to bleed to get it.

The worst was that he'd been speculating for years about what Mama had said or done to drive Pap out forever, never really expecting that his theories might be confirmed one fateful day. But now, he was almost sure. What was to come would both vindicate and rectify: his new suspicion was undoubtedly the right one, but he'd been wrong all this time.

Why didn't anyone ever tell him the truth, or put him in his place?

Was he so childish that he had to be shielded from it, by everyone involved?

Pap had left by his own free will. And he took two innocent souls with him, and left two guilty ones behind.

In the parlor, the record player brought a classic instrumental back to life, a dark, longing kind of blues. Deep, woody clarinets droned beneath the slow notes of a tenor saxophone, which sounded out deliberately, making the musician's melancholy clear and unmistakable. There were no smoky voices to accompany it. Those mellow notes said everything that needed to be said. The saxophonist confessed his loss with his shaky breath and fluttering fingers, telling the tale of a woman long gone, as absent as the sultry singer that graced every song but his.

Mama, though, was present and vigilantly waiting in the jaundiced glow of the lamp behind her. She was expecting her whiskey to be clutched resentfully in her son's hand. He was empty handed, but had a grenade up his sleeve. It was time to say a prayer and pull the pin. He did only the latter.

"Save your breath," he growled as Mama began to raise her hand in protest. "I ain't got it."

"And why's that, boy? You too lazy to do one thing, or just too stupid to remember it?" She lit herself a cigarette without looking up to acknowledge him with anything more than a string of slurred words. Waving the match in the air to snuff the flame, she held back the lashing Levi had anticipated, but with conspicuous struggle. Her face reddened, like the Nile turned to blood as but the first step in a display of God's wrath.

"I got questions, though, and it's about time you told me the truth. I can't live like this, listenin' to your lies when I deserve answers."

"The Devil's a liar, boy, not me. And don't talk to me 'bout what *you* deserve. *I* deserve better than this—workin' like a dog so you got a roof over your head y'don't have the decency to be grateful for, all 'cause my sorry husband done left me alone here to take care o' his even sorrier son. I'm *tired* of all of it," she lamented while reaching for her empty glass. "And y'can't even give me the *one thing* I ask for to help me forget it."

"You mean my sorry father who done got himself *killed.*"

Whatever blood had rushed to her face immediately drained back into her empty heart. She froze, pale-faced and mortified, then rose to her feet like a corpse climbing out of her coffin. Levi had never seen such a look on her face. It was shock, of course—he expected nothing less. But there was another element to it: a hint of the wince Eve made when she realized she was naked. It was a sign of vulnerability and shame. It was the haunting expression of a woman whose glass house had been shattered in an instant, all while having thought her walls were made of stone.

"Who told you?"

"Ain't nobody told me. I saw the graves he left behind."

"He left us behind, too."

"Why'd you lie all this time?" he asked, trying his best to keep his voice down. "I shouldn't have had to figure it out on my own. It was *your* place to tell me, and I sure as hell ain't a kid no more."

"You knew he went 'n abandoned us. Didn't matter how many times I told you, boy. You didn't wanna believe it."

"This is different, and you know it."

"Maybe. But we weren't the only ones to get hurt by 'im. If there's one thing I didn't want for you, it was to go round knowin' Heaven's got itself two more angels, all on account o' your good-for-nothin' father."

"But why'd you let me blame you for it?"

"Cause I ain't innocent, neither," she confessed, and the tears began to fall. "I drove 'im out. I shoulda listened to 'im more. I shoulda trusted 'im when he said we'd be better off elsewhere. I held 'im back, boy, and it killed 'im. So go ahead 'n blame me. I deserve it. I might as well have been behind the wheel myself."

"Y'don't need to suffer like this. It ain't right."

"No, I do. It's God's will for me to suffer—'For my strength is made perfect in weakness.'"

"That ain't what He wants. Mr. Green done taught me that well enough," Levi corrected with the spirit of an evangelist. "He wants forgiveness, and nothin' more."

"There's no one left to forgive, boy. They're gone."

"You're still here. And so am I."

There was so rarely a moment of silence between them: between the lines was only ever senseless shouting and artful weeping. This time, there were no outbursts of rage, no accusations of disrespect or abuse. The tears did not boil. They came quietly, almost indiscernible. Had they been outside in the pouring rain, they would have been invisible.

"I forgive you, Mama."

The stillness that followed said all that was needed. Levi knew better than to expect anything more than wordlessness. Mama couldn't utter a thing, not even a sigh. Her guilt locked away everything held deep within, no matter how badly she might have wanted to let it go. Only she held the keys. The best Levi could hope to do was point her to them.

"You need to forgive him, now—and yourself. Turn to God, do whatever y'need to do. But all this drinkin' ain't helpin' no one. I don't need you dyin' because of it. I can't let you."

*"But you look so much like 'im,"* Mama cried. Her words came without warning, like they flowed straight from her heart, unbridled by thought. "I can't ever forget 'im and forget what he did, with you standin' there with his eyes, his hair, *all of it.* I could burn every photo we got, but *you'd* still be here."

He did his best not to listen. None of it was his fault, and deep down, she must have known it. What she was saying was nothing more than a weak excuse. "Tell me y'ain't never gonna have another drink again," he replied sternly. He wasn't about to let her slip away.

"I done taught you better than to make promises y'can't keep," she murmured in tears.

*"Promise me."*

He never got the answer he thought they both deserved.

He knew he couldn't just stand there with fists clenched, glaring at the hopeless woman who had buried her face in her hands. She needed neither his anger nor his pity. And at that moment, something changed within him. All his life he'd known only broken promises: from his teachers, predicting a prosperous future; from the church, prophesying of heavenly rewards for his complete obedience; from within his own heart, swearing that he would not lose sight of himself. Mama wasn't the only one to have disappointed him. It was cruel to act as though she was.

The front door clattered behind him when he stormed out into the rain, following in his father's footsteps. The wind slammed it shut with more force than his own anger could muster. From that day on, it closed properly. It never creaked again.

••

There really was nowhere for Levi to go. He had left the house instinctively, the way a bird might turn his head south when the leaves had fallen, without ever knowing why. And just like such an animal, guided by something deep inside him that had no name, he asked no questions. His feet carried him forward and he followed them in perfect faith that they would lead him right where he was meant to go. Whether it was his subconscious mind or God that drove him out into the wilderness, it was still just a whisper that he obeyed. His doubts were gone. He trusted in whatever lay ahead beyond the veil of rain.

The railroad tracks were a straight and narrow path, and the slight parting of the bushes was his gate. Soft leaves brushed over him like wet palms sprinkled with holy water. He stepped out into the clearing and stood at the edge of the creek, whose waters flowed high and freely, swollen from the pouring rain.

If ever there was a time for him to plunge beneath living waters and emerge a new man, it was then.

He needed no priest, for something invisible guided him. A church would serve no purpose, as the trees were the pillars of a reverent cathedral. The Reverend Shaw and his conniving wife were nowhere to be found, driven out like unclean spirits. Without them, that place was sacred ground.

Levi removed the shoes from his feet and felt the warm, soft earth slip between his toes. The rain trickled down his face and soaked through his shirt; he could hardly tell when the water rose up to surround him in a gentle embrace. His descent was slow and careful, but he was not afraid. The creek swallowed him up to his chest. He closed his eyes and let his breath flow like rivulets from the font of his lungs. He was mindful only of the current caressing his body, and the sense that, for the first time, every burden he ever bore was being lifted, and swept away to wherever that river ran.

Mama didn't deserve his resentment. For years he'd blamed her for his father's absence. Really, it was something for which she blamed herself. It was a knife in her heart she could not withdraw, so long as his fingers were wrapped tightly around its hilt.

Her punishment was cruel and went unseen by their righteous neighbors. She inflicted it upon herself with every glass, but he allowed it, without ever snatching it from her hands. It was her death sentence, a hemlock brew, a poison that he did not concoct but patronized with his own dollar.

The life he sought in the world of the flesh was fated to decay, as all flesh was. He was foolish to have allowed Clemency to throw him into an open grave. He had let the godly turn him away from God. But in the end, they too would rot in the ground.

The God he wrongly forsook had meant for Levi's true relationships to thrive, for him to cherish his friends and keep them close. Instead, he threw his pearls before swine.

He saw Sophie crying in her room and Jonah screaming into his pillow. He heard Jimmy cursing in the dark with no one to listen. He watched a dozen bridges burn.

He saw the wreckage, the lights of the ambulance that had arrived far too late, and the paramedics who conceded that there was nothing to be done. He heard his mother weep. He listened to Elijah's prayers.

He saw himself. He saw what he had become. And he saw what he could be, if he just let go.

*Repent. Start over. Let go.*

At last, he did.

# 18

IF YOU PULLED OUT A DICTIONARY, ran your finger down through the Vs to the succinct entry on the von Brauns, you would see that they were synonymous with "pride," a much more common noun. In Clemency, however, where a regional dialect skewed various elements of the English language, which the aristocratic von Brauns had difficulty understanding, it was more likely that you would hear Jimmy's name uttered alongside a much wider variety of words. "Abomination," "sodomite," and "shameless" come to mind. But on that one day at four in the morning, he would have labeled himself nothing less than "desperate."

There were a million things wrong with the situation in which he found himself: the dingy dirt path back to the road would desecrate his otherwise spotless Prada tennis shoes; the sharp, chemical stench of bubbling crack pipes would surely cling to the fine fibers of his cashmere pullover. Worst of all, any passer-by would catch him taking the walk of shame down the Skinners' driveway, dime bag of cheap coke and painkillers in his hand, and a scowl on his face that expressed disgust toward his last-ditch dealers, the cesspool town that spawned them, and himself most of all, who'd been reduced to sucking pond scum in place of his usual Cristal.

His car was parked a little ways up the road, sheltered by the low-hanging boughs of a shadowy conifer. It was the best he could do to conceal it, since he didn't have an oversized black tarp on hand to shroud his pride and joy. Even if he were overlooked on foot, his precious, shiny vehicle would have instantly exposed his humiliating affairs, carried out only because he'd run out of options, and found his old sources dry and unreliable. Pills and powdered stimulants had become his best friends once again. The comfort he got from opiates and their kin was more reliable than that of a human being, who could go from building him up to tearing him down in the blink of an eye; besides, friends couldn't make him skinny.

He was willing to admit to a lot of things—that going under the knife was his favorite pastime, or that he personally was the cause of several antibiotic-resistant VD strains in New York, Miami and San Francisco—but the one thing he tried his best to deny, both to himself and his stingy parents, was that he missed Levi Thompson, and all his poor, pathetic, low-class antics. Somehow, Levi had managed to keep him level headed. Maybe because when he was forced to walk on the ground with the insects, it was easy to keep his balance on flat terrain.

Remorse was an alien feeling, as strange to him as embarrassment might be to a goldfish, or svelteness to Michael Moore. He suspected that the heaviness in his chest was a sign that he did, in fact, feel guilty, but he could only speculate. It was a terrible sensation. He hated everything about it, and tried all kinds of ways to stop that sickening tug on his heartstrings, but he couldn't shake it. No amount of booze or boys could rid him of it. Granted, it didn't stop him from trying: if it had, he wouldn't have found himself walking away from the Skinners' hovel in the cover of night, with the light of dawn just barely discernible on the horizon.

It would have been a smooth operation, too, if he hadn't heard a young girl's cries for help coming from the hellhole he was just yards away from escaping.

Of all nights not to bring his headphones, it had to be that one.

*Mind your business*, he told himself. If a girl was stupid enough to get herself tangled up with those degenerates, then she had no one to blame but herself. It was best to leave it alone and call it a night.

She screamed again, begging to be let go. Groaning, Jimmy looked over his shoulder. If some whiny bitch was going to ruin his exit, he might as well see what all the fuss was about.

*"Shut the fuck up, Hannah!"* barked Gabe Skinner, storming back inside to lay down the law. He slammed the front door behind him. It dampened her wailing but not the uneasiness it left behind.

Wasn't Hannah the name of Jonah's little sister?

Jimmy's memory wasn't what it used to be, with drugs having left his brain with more holes than Lindsay Lohan's datebook, but he was sure that was her name. Hadn't Levi said she was getting herself into trouble with the Skinners?

If so, he'd just been witness to it. And she was in more trouble than anyone had thought.

"Goddamnit!" he cursed in the dark. This new penchant for guilt was crippling. The old Jimmy would have coldly gotten into his car and driven off, without giving Hannah's plight so much as a second thought. For better or worse, that was no longer an option. Her screams in his head, replayed over and over again, wouldn't allow it. He had to swallow his pride and do what he'd sworn not to do. It was time to pay Levi a visit. Apologies could wait. A young girl's future was at stake, and Jimmy had to play the hero, a role for which he was entirely unprepared.

No longer concerned about secrecy, he swung closed his car door with a thud and pressed a glowing button on the dashboard to rev up the engine. Fortunately, it was a short drive down Main Street to the Thompsons' house, two or three minutes at most, so long as no zombie churchgoers were wandering around in the middle of the road that close to dawn. Hitting the gas too hard as usual, he was pressed back into his leather seat by inertia, fighting back against physics only when he reached a stop sign, which he meant to pass with only a rolling stop. He would have kept going, if a pair of headlights hadn't menacingly flashed on in the dark ahead. There was someone idling at the intersection, watching his every move.

He would have recognized those bitchy blue halogen lights anywhere. It was Charlene, prowling and waiting to strike.

*"Shit!"* he yelled, and threw the car in reverse, turning the wheel with all his might to swing around and speed off in the opposite direction. Tires squealed, smoke swirled, and the odor of burnt rubber wafted through his air conditioning; he floored it and accelerated from zero to eighty in less time than it took for Charlene to take a shot of vodka before bedtime. If he was going to reach Levi in time, he'd have to take a different route. He punched the address into his GPS and bellowed in fury when the system decided Clemency was too irrelevant to be marked on a map.

By a stroke of luck, he had a sliver of a bar of cell service. The phone rang through his car's surround-sound speakers. He prayed for Levi to answer. Naturally, he didn't. It went to voicemail.

*"Goddamn you, Thompson! We've got a crisis over here!"*

The purr of the Bentley's engine turned to a lioness's feral roar as Charlene closed in, coming in hot. Jimmy glared in the rear-view mirror and slammed his lead foot even harder on the gas pedal, but his car was straining to go any faster. Panicking but trying to remain calm, he glanced at Charlene, who sat behind the wheel with her sunglasses on in the pitch blackness of early morning, lips pursed and face unfazed. It could have been the Botox or the Xanax, of course, but she seemed fully unaffected by being just seconds away from rear-ending her son—so unconcerned, in fact, that she did just that.

The front of her Bentley crashed into Jimmy's bumper and knocked him forward in his seat, slamming his head into the steering wheel. The crunch of crumpled metal was like nails on a chalkboard, more painful than the gash he sustained on his forehead. And just when he thought he might be in the clear, the crazy bitch used her luxury sedan as a battering ram a second time, and Jimmy nearly lost control of the wheel, swerving left and right with the finesse of a drunk while his deranged mother pummeled his car.

Regaining command, Jimmy dialed Levi's number once again, and begged God or Jesus or Lady Gaga to intervene and make him pick up the phone. Charlene's headlights had disappeared behind him. He rolled down his window to get some air, and the warm breeze tussled his sweater and disheveled his hair, but for the first time in his life, he didn't shriek in horror. Besides the tortuous ringing and the clatter of his dangling, twisted exhaust pipe bouncing along the pavement, there was a welcome silence.

Still no answer. His second voicemail was even more frenzied than the first. Hell-bent on being acknowledged and saving the day, he tried a third time.

And a third time, an impact rocked his vehicle, and the seatbelt was all that kept him from falling into the passenger seat. This time, the blow came from the side. Charlene was there, windows down, screeching like a banshee as she aligned their cars and matched his speed with the utmost precision.

*"You ruined everything, you ungrateful, little queen!"*

The shrillness of her voice cut through the loud rush of air past Jimmy's ears with the clarity of someone speaking in a room as empty as her soul. He tried his best to ignore her disparaging tirade. He thrust his middle finger out the window, keeping his eyes on the dim road ahead.

*"You just can't stand to see me happy! You want me to be MISERABLE, like YOU, a SINGLE, UNLOVED FAIRY!"*

"Bitch, you could *never* be this fabulous!" he retorted at the top of his lungs.

*"Well, it doesn't matter NOW, does it?! You decimated my reputation in front of this whole inbred town, and now I'll NEVER have Jonah!"* To drive in her point, she jerked the wheel and sideswiped him.

"I'm sorry you couldn't hold on to that young dick, but you would've lost it sooner or later, *granny!*" He recoiled when she knocked him aside again; he winced to the piercing din of metal scraping metal. The voicemail greeting he reached yet again was even more insufferable. For the fourth and final time, he dialed Levi, and uttered every curse word he could think of, from modern to Shakespearian, as if it would make any difference.

*"Don't you DARE!"* she screamed with her painted talon pointed straight at her son. In one last offensive maneuver, she accelerated and pushed her Bentley's engine to its limit. The whirling pistons rumbled with the fury of a thousand warhorses. She sped ahead of him until he could see her license plate, shining in the hellish glow of her taillights, and swerved into his lane without warning. The red lights flared out as she slammed the brakes.

Shrieking in the likeness of a prepubescent girl, he had only a fraction of the second to decide if he'd instinctively avoid a crash as he would with a clueless, bumbling deer, or barrel into her head-on, risking his own death, but potentially taking her out in the process. When he realized that they'd be stuck in Hell together for eternity, he opted to cut the wheel with the lightning reflexes of a cocaine user and dodged into the left lane. Unfortunately, his maneuver wasn't as clean as he'd hoped.

*BANG!*

His right headlight shattered when he clipped the edge of her bumper, and its glow fizzled out. He whipped his head back and watched as Charlene's battered Bentley spun off the road and crashed into a ditch. Much to his disappointment, it didn't burst into flame. His many fantasies went unfulfilled, as Charlene didn't perish at the witching hour in a fiery wreckage.

"Psycho bitch!" he called out the window, waving his fist in the air in both victory and contempt. He left Charlene on the roadside, smoke billowing from the hood of her car, while she vainly stumbled down the road in her stilettos, screaming obscenities into the dark.

Catching his breath, he soon resumed his own swearing. Levi still refused to take his call. Recklessly he cut the wheel and turned back toward Clemency. It seemed as though he'd driven on for miles, and the ride back was just as long. He just hoped he wasn't too late. His list of grievances against his homicidal mother was a record of many travesties, some insipid, some serious, but if she held him back from rescuing a desperate, young girl in time, it would be something neither he, nor anyone, could ever forgive.

••

All of Levi's sins were in the past where they belonged, put out of the mind of God in perfect mercy. He knew, though, that man wasn't always so quick to let go of trespasses against himself. Jonah was one such man. Levi's soul was almost free, but Jonah's grudge kept him from being raised higher. He needed reconciliation. They both did, for the sake of the future, Jonah's especially. No one should have to go to college with more baggage than a suitcase full of clothes and condoms.

The night's rain had broken the humidity and the morning air was refreshingly cool, as the sun had not yet risen, and there was only the dim aura of dawn spreading behind the trees. For all its faults and shortcomings, Clemency did boast the kind of fresh air that no urban jungle could ever hope to breathe. Levi too often forgot it. Clouds of smog had no silver lining, even if the city folk had pockets lined with gold.

Levi slipped into a pair of fresh jeans and pulled on a plain white tee. He peeked in his father's worn leather wallet before putting it in his back pocket: it held no more than a few wrinkled dollar bills and that old, unclaimed florist punch card, not that he expected anything else. For once, it didn't bother him. He didn't give it a second thought.

The front door made no sound. Mama was asleep on the parlor sofa, the glow of twilight transforming her fair skin to radiant alabaster. He wasn't sure if he'd ever seen her sleep so soundly. She didn't wake when he shut the door behind him and took a deep breath on the porch. He blessed the nascent day and claimed it as his own.

His arrival at the Youngs' front door was unannounced. Granted, this in itself was far from unusual. What was unprecedented, however, was the nature of his visit, which had begun with the swallowing of an unpalatable bolus of pride. Apologies were in order, or rather, disorder, as Levi had little idea of what he would say when Jonah answered the door—that is, if he didn't immediately slam that door in his face, having been ambushed before his morning run, and leave him on the porch with his mouth gaping and words stuck on the tip of his tongue.

Life threw its hundredth monkey wrench in Levi's good works when, after a crescendo of knocks, no one came to the door, even to shoo him away like a Mormon peddling nonsense and unwelcome calls for repentance.

Tapping his foot impatiently, Levi turned around and realized that the driveway was empty. He'd been too preoccupied to notice something so obvious. Mr. and Mrs. Young were out for the weekend, evidently, and their erratic and rebellious daughter could have been anywhere without them as a late-night sentinel. Jonah, on the other hand, was a creature of habit, and with Swayne a good six hours from opening and Sophie having blacklisted him for good, he would no doubt be found inside brooding. If Levi were a betting man (and he wasn't much of one), he'd have wagered that Jonah was in there, shoving his feet into a pair of beat-up sneakers, or groggily filling a water bottle at the kitchen sink with sleep in his eyes and a brutal cowlick on the back of his head. He'd never see Levi coming.

The doorknob didn't resist his grip as he'd expected it to: it'd been left unlocked, as home invasions were a phenomenon wholly unheard of in Clemency. After a moment of hesitation, Levi turned the knob all the way until he heard the lock click, and the door slowly began to swing open without a sound. He felt like a vampire standing there in the twilight, unable to enter without an explicit invitation to do so. The threshold was more than just a clear and everyday divide between inside and out. It was the taboo of his friendship, solidified over many years. But these were strange times, and he was treading uncharted waters. He asked the universe to forgive him for upsetting the natural balance and stepped boldly where he'd never gone before.

Houses were houses no matter the architect, and they all had the same elements—parlors, kitchens, hallways—but in the darkness of an unfamiliar home, Levi was disoriented. As he held his hands out in front of him like a blind man stripped of his cane, moving slowly through the shadows for fear of shattering lamps and picture frames, his eyes gradually adjusted to the environment. Given that this was likely to be his only experience within those four forbidden walls, the wallpaper would forever be a dim blue in his memory, and the furniture, vague, tenebrous forms. His fingers caught the corner that marked the mouth of a corridor, and he followed it instinctively, assuming that somewhere down that obscure path there would be a messy bedroom and an unsuspecting friend to be regained.

In fact, unsuspecting was too mild a term. Really, he was entirely oblivious to the rattle of the doorknob and the tap of the door against the wall. It was Levi's voice that caught his attention, or rather, snatched it and knocked him to the ground.

"Hey," the intruder began, offering one simple word behind Jonah's back—nothing more, nothing less. There was little else to say. Jonah, however, shouted a much more dramatic salutation.

*"What the hell!"*

He tripped over his own shorts and stumbled forward with them caught around his ankles, and he fell to the floor in his boxers with a nasty thud and an involuntary groan. Teeth gritted and scowling, he strenuously turned himself over and growled at Levi with his bare back still pressed to the weathered wood floorboards, "So you gone from wreckin' lives to breakin' into houses now? I ain't got shit for you to steal. Get that rich asshole to buy you somethin' if you're so desperate."

"The door was open, and we both know y'ain't about to take my calls."

"You're damn right I ain't. But the least y'coulda done was announce yourself before invadin' my goddamned space."

"That'd defeat the purpose o' breakin' and enterin', wouldn't it?"

Levi held out his hand to help Jonah off the floor. Begrudgingly, he reached up after a moment of resentful hesitation and accepted, having decided that it was easier to put aside his pride than let Levi literally look down on him as he sat there like an inferior, half naked at his feet.

Jonah always was taller than Levi but at that moment he seemed to tower over him, standing aggressively close with his chest puffed out and fists clenched so tight that they trembled. The air above him seemed to ripple from the heat rising from his head. Despite Jonah's threatening stance and the very real possibility that he might break one of Levi's ribs, Levi didn't recoil. It was a reaction that caught Jonah off guard, as he always took Levi for the type to run instead of turning the other cheek for a punch. He backed away and let the blood flow back into his fingers.

"Put some clothes on," Levi suggested, and pointed to the mess of shirts and shorts strewn about the room. "Y'look a damn mess."

He was in no position to disagree. "So, we ain't talked in weeks and now you just show up in my bedroom," he noted, pulling on the gym shorts that had accosted him. "I've had one-night stands that had more sense than you. Don't tell me: you're lookin' to say sorry for all your bullshit."

"Well, y'just spared me the trouble o' sayin' it myself."

"Go ahead and try me."

Levi waited until Jonah had thrown on a faded shirt and composed himself before taking a deep breath and conceding, "Alright, I'm sorry, man. I lost sight o' things. Ain't much else I can say."

"You're damn right y'did. Got yourself so blind that you went and knocked the rest of us into the pit with you."

Levi's phone buzzed in his pocket. For the sake of saving a friendship, he ignored it.

"Trust me, I'm seein' things real clear now," he insisted. "I cut Jimmy out, and I'm patchin' things up at home. I'm pickin' up the pieces and startin' over, and no lie, you're the one I really gotta make amends with—maybe the hardest one, too. I done made things right with God, with Mama and even the dead, but till you and me are back to where we were before I went and fucked it all up, ain't none of it matters."

The moment might have been more heartwarming if his phone hadn't started ringing a second time. Disdainfully shoving his hand in his pocket, he silenced it. The vibration against his thigh was cut short.

"I'll be honest," Jonah sighed, in preparation for showing too much friendly affection for his own comfort. "This town ain't easy if there ain't no one to bite the bullet with you."

"Worst month o' my life. And that's sayin' somethin'." Levi extended a hand, which may as well have been brandishing a white flag. He held it out in the air long enough for Jonah to accept or reject his truce. "We good?"

Shaking his head, Jonah declined the handshake. He grinned and grabbed Levi in a bear hug, slapped him on the back, pulling a friend not just into his embrace but back into his life. "We're good," he declared. "Just remember your place in the world, and we'll keep it that way."

Levi's phone began to ring yet again, except this time, Jonah felt it. They both tried to dismiss it, with Levi silently cursing the 21st century, but Jonah grew tired of the distraction and said, "Just answer the damn phone, man. It's killin' the moment."

Levi withdrew it from his pocket and groaned when he saw Jimmy's name. He held it out for Jonah to see, who waved it away and changed his mind. "On second thought, better not. Y'shoulda blocked him weeks ago. God knows Sophie done gone and deleted my number."

It sounded like the best course of action until yet another pulse announced the delivery of not one, or two, or three, but four voicemails, all from Jimmy in rapid succession as if they'd been shot from a machine gun, with a bejeweled grip, tassels and feathers. Levi found himself caught in two possible scenarios: first, that Jimmy was in the middle of a brutal bender, or second, that something real serious was afoot. Suspicion trumped Jonah's advice and he checked the last message.

Jonah sensed a change in the air and muttered, "What'd that asshole do this time?"

"Where's your sister right now?" Levi asked. "She ain't answered the door. Tell me she's sleepin'."

"No, with the parents gone, she's pullin' her usual stunts and stayin' out till the ass crack o' dawn. Ain't no point in stressin' over it anymore. Just a fact o' life."

"Not this time. She's in some deep trouble," Levi reported as he hurried out the door. With his back turned, he didn't see the grave look on Jonah's face that had washed away his first smile in weeks. "Grab your bat. This shit's gonna be ugly."

••

It was the first time that Jonah was ever thankful for living in such a small town. His morning run, once undertaken simply for the sake of his own body, was now a race against time. His shoes pounded the pavement as he sprinted down Main Street with his baseball bat in hand, following the road that led to God and the Devil, to the Southern Mercy Bible Church and the Skinners' unholy hovel. The congregation had always considered themselves to be holy warriors. He finally understood what that really meant. By the time the sun rose, he would have a pockmarked serpent trampled beneath his feet.

He knew this day would come. In fact, he had prayed for it regularly, to a God he was only just beginning to know. It was Gabriel Skinner's inevitable day of reckoning, when he would finally answer for all the degeneracy he had brought upon Clemency and, worst of all, into an innocent girl's life. Every daydream of beating him bloody and every sleepless night of worry had led Jonah to this very moment. And tragically, the culmination of all his thoughts and nightmares proved to be a confirmation of his worst fears. When he arrived at the Skinners' front door, he knew his little sister was in there, being violated in ways he, as her brother and protector, never wanted to imagine.

*"Get your ass out here, Skinner!"* he barked as he repeatedly slammed his fist into the rattling door. *"Open the fucking door!"*

No one answered. Bugs flitted about in the air in the warm, yellowish light of the lamp that hung beside the door—ugly gray moths, flies and fat beetles—and their presence drove Jonah crazy.

He swatted them away from his face. For every obnoxious insect he squashed against the wall, he vowed to bash in Gabe's skull twice with his slugger.

"I'll break that damn thing down if I have to," he swore to Levi, and drew back the bat to ready it for one clean swing into the grimy window. Just as he was about to drive it in and smash the glass, a voice sounded out on the other side, whining, "Alright, alright!"

The door opened but it wasn't Gabe standing there to greet Jonah with a reddened face. It was one of his cohorts, sickly and sweaty, who'd neglected to put on a shirt, sporting only a pair of sagging jeans and a lascivious grin. "Too late, buddy," he crooned, leaning up against the doorframe with an unlit cigarette in his mouth. "Party's almost over. These girls can take a beatin' but they got their limits, y'know."

He was the first man to take a beating.

Jonah shoved him inside and knocked him onto the sticky carpet before he even knew what hit him. The scumbag curled up like a dead spider on the ground, withdrawing himself into a quivering tangle of limbs as Jonah gave him a single kick to the ribs. The room was just as foul as he'd imagined, cluttered with fast food wrappers, unfinished beer cans and dirty plates, but the most repulsive filth in that decrepit shack was the wide-eyed human garbage that had lined up before the bedroom door. There were four such men waiting their turn, and not one came to their friend's aid. The sound of the door being opened was louder in their ears than the wounded yelps of their fallen comrade. It meant it was the next one's turn.

Emerging from the room with a satisfied smirk on his face, the hulking lecher zipped up his open fly and held out his hand to give one of his rat-faced buddies a high five. Before they could smack their sweaty palms together, Jonah rushed at him, ready to barrel right into his soft stomach with one shoulder forward like a battering ram. He wanted to grab the guy by his straggly beard and swing him onto the floor, to crack his skull with every swing of his bat, even if it meant getting attacked from all sides by the others waiting impatiently in line. Gabe never gave him the chance.

The ringleader stormed out of the bedroom and knocked Jonah aside when he was just a foot away from landing his first punch in his target's gut. Jonah caught his balance with a hand on the cheap

TV stand behind him. He could see into the darkened room to Gabe's back, just barely. The lights were dim but enough to illuminate the tangled clothes at the foot of the bed. They were fit only for a girl still in high school. They were unmistakable.

"All y'all, get the fuck out," Gabe commanded. In his hand he gripped a switchblade, and held it low, almost as an afterthought. He made his way over to the front door and pushed it open with such force as to make it clatter violently against the side of the house. "We got some shit to take care of."

Levi slipped in unnoticed while the lot of them funneled out into the yard, with Jonah at the front of the line, guided forward by Gabe's knife between his shoulder blades. And as Jonah stood his ground before a crescent of Clemency's worst, he looked to the open door behind them, and saw his little sister come into the light like some ghostly apparition, a white blanket wrapped around her fragile body. Bruises and black, runny makeup covered the pale skin of her sullen face. Levi kept his arm around her, and as quietly as possible, he led her away, gently shepherding her toward the edge of the Skinners' blighted property.

"I told you I ain't one for second chances," Gabe snarled. "You gotta be a real fuckin' idiot to show up here again, 'specially after I went easy on you as a goddamned favor."

"It's over, Skinner. I ain't gonna let you touch her again."

"It's one thing to stop *me* from touchin' her," Gabe replied, toying with his knife. He ran his finger up and down the blade. "But gettin' my boys to stop, all of 'em? I'd like to see you try. They ain't about to give up their favorite girl that easy. Ain't that right?" He looked to his left and his right; every one of them nodded, grinning despicably, with teeth that might as well have been fangs. One grabbed himself suggestively. Given the chance, Jonah would have slit his throat first.

"She ain't much more than a little girl. Ain't nothin' macho 'bout a goddamned pedophile."

"Trust me, she don't act her age. Besides, they're better when they're small, ain't they? Even *you* can't disagree, there. No better feelin' in the world. And your little sister? She's the most—"

The brutal screech of tires on pavement drowned out Gabe's obscenities. A broken bumper dangled from the back of the car and scraped along the asphalt. One of the headlights was out and the other, flickering behind cracked plastic, threatened to die at any moment. It seemed they had company.

*"Can't you answer your goddamned phone, Thompson?!"*

Jimmy von Braun leapt out of his car and broke the battered door; it fell onto the street as a piece of luxury scrap metal. He shook his cell in the air as evidence of Levi's neglect.

Gabe's only reaction was a fit of laughter. Jonah couldn't even blame him for it. "Look!" he exclaimed in the face of hilarity. "The town faggot, comin' to the rescue!"

Jonah was furious. He didn't need the cavalry to come to his rescue, especially not Jimmy, riding on a totaled horse in hopeless disrepair.

"Get the hell outta here," he barked, but Jimmy didn't stop in his tracks. "Y'ain't never helped before and you sure as shit can't start now."

"Listen, bitch: *I'm* the one who found your sister in the first place!" Jimmy snapped. He pointed to his car, wrecked but miraculously still functional, and directed Levi to slip Hannah into the back seat. His phone lit up in his hand when he flicked his finger over the screen and pressed three fateful numbers; in his calmest and most sophisticated tone, he requested that local law enforcement pay the Skinners a long-overdue visit. "You're fucked and you know it, Jonah. It's us three against an army of mongoloids."

"'Us three,' my ass," Jonah sneered.

"Retard strength's a real thing, Jonah—trust me, I've dated my fair share. You're in no position to reject help, even mine," Jimmy retorted.

As much as Jonah hated to admit it, he was right. No amount of pride could have balanced the numbers. He may have wielded his faithful baseball bat, Levi may have been more agile than their troglodytic enemies, and Jimmy may have had a legion of lawyers behind him, but they were no match for the gang of seething, blue-balled goons. If they saw no problem with raping a girl, then they certainly would have had no moral issue with murdering three young men in the Skinners' front yard. With the nearest police precinct twenty miles away, they had plenty of time to clean up the mess. And besides, the lawn was parched. Blood was just as good as water.

Their lowlife kingpin, on the other hand, seemed perturbed by the threat of cops arriving at his front door just before sunrise. He slipped his knife into his belt and dismissed his cohorts with a begrudging wave of his hand. "Go home," he instructed, and one by one they obeyed, however disappointedly. "Let's make it a fair fight—or as even as we can, guys. Me against three queers still ain't fair to 'em, but what can y'do?"

Nonchalantly, he pulled out a gun.

Jonah's instinct was to drop the bat. He tossed it aside and it rolled away into the dark. The three of them stared into the barrel of Gabe's gun, holding their hands up in surrender. There really wasn't any other choice.

"Now, tell your faggot friends to head on home, before they get caught in the crossfire. I got no problem with 'em, least any more than any real man would have with a couple o' fairies, anyhow. They can even take your dear lil' Hannah with 'em, too. She don't need to see her big brother get what's comin' to 'im."

Neither Levi nor Jimmy were willing to budge. Jimmy started to open his mouth to inevitably say something snide, but Jonah stopped him before he could utter a single catty remark. More than anyone could have known, he appreciated Levi's being there; even Jimmy, a thorn in Clemency's side that had snagged Jonah in the worst way, was on the right side of his personal history. But Levi's loyalty and Jimmy's newfound conscience couldn't help him. The best they could do was tend to Hannah's needs, and take her far away, as she sat there in the back seat too weak to cry out and too drugged to understand the dire straits in which her older brother found himself.

"Go," Jonah murmured, despite their opposition. "Take her home. Come back when the sun's up. Let's hope I'm still standin'."

They disappeared into the shadow of twilight, lingering, but unseen. Jonah was alone. He knew he was facing death with no one beside him. This would have scared him once, when he was all talk and hot air. But now he had loved and lost. He was stronger for it, with thicker skin and a steel heart. There was no man braver than one who had nothing left to lose, except the respect he held for himself. And if he were to cower before Gabriel Skinner, the monster who had broken his sister and stolen her innocence, he would never be able to look at himself in a mirror again. He would be just as repugnant.

"So, what am I gonna do with you, Young?" Gabe mused, breaking the tense silence. Besides his grating voice, the only sound was that of the wind in the trees, whose black leaves fluttered before the pale yellow glow on the horizon. "Y'know I can't let this kinda disrespect go unpunished. I got a reputation to uphold."

"I reckon you'd rather be a killer than just the town rapist. I hear they don't take kindly to pedos in the county jail."

"Now, y'know I don't give two shits about a lil' jail time. Wouldn't be my first and it sure as hell won't be my last. What I *do* care about is my girls, and the good thing I got goin' for me 'n my buddies here, and I'll be damned before I let some pretty-boy pussy go 'n ruin my enterprise. Trust me, puttin' a bullet in your head'll be the best business decision I done made in a long time."

"It'll be life for you, this time. Y'ain't gonna get off so easy."

"And that's where you're wrong, Young," Gabe insisted. He cocked the gun and held it with stronger intent. "All those fancy lawyers are gon' see is the poor, misguided son of a broken family, with a junkie mom and a drunk, useless dad, without a penny to their name, left alone to take care o' his many brothers 'n sisters, and got round up with the wrong crowd. Sure I got myself a record, but ain't nothin' like what you're accusin' me of. A couple o' shopliftin' charges, some drug possession, so what? It don't mean shit. And for all they know, this time I was givin' a couple o' drug-usin' girls a place to stay, gettin' 'em off the streets and whatnot. Public defense'll spin it however they need to. It ain't my fault. It's the fucked-up world around me. Ain't gave me no other choice."

"Ain't no one's gonna buy that horse shit. There's always a choice. Any idiot could tell you that."

"What about your good lil' Hannah, then?"

Jonah glared, gritting his teeth. His jaw was so tight he could hardly speak. "She ain't chose this. *You* did it to her. Y'saw a vulnerable girl and took advantage."

"You're right, Jonah: she didn't have no choice here. Someone forced 'er into this but it sure as shit wasn't me. *You* 'n your good-for-nothin' parents done drove 'er to it. You, bein' the jealous brother who was so damn busy watchin' out for 'er that y'couldn't even see what was happenin' right under your nose, and your Ma 'n Pa, who told 'er she was so damn perfect that she'd beat the shit outta herself for missin' the mark just once. Like it or not, I know a hell of a lot about 'er that you ain't took the time to learn yourself. Blame me all y'like, see if I care, you're just wastin' your time. I mighta handed 'er the needle, but you done stuck it in."

Jonah did his best to ignore the one boiling tear drop at the edge of his eye. He didn't know what to say. The pounding in his head drowned out Gabe's words: his mouth moved, but Jonah heard nothing. He certainly didn't hear the crunch of footsteps on the dry grass that came from behind Gabe's back.

"I gotta say, Young, I'm kinda disappointed," Gabe sighed. "I really expected some smart last words outta your mouth, given y'ain't never gon' have another chance to cuss out the guy who's been fuckin' your slut sister for the past year. So, I'll give you one more chance. Got anything to say?"

Jimmy's shadow stretched over the lawn, cast by the flickering lamp at the door. Gabe didn't see it. He had his gaze set between Jonah's eyes, the bullseye he swore not to miss. And before Gabe was able to land that one lucky shot, Jonah muttered, "Fuck off, Skinner."

The bat struck Gabe in the back of the head and the gun flew from his hand. He fell to his knees, groaning in a daze, stars flying past his face as he knelt at Jimmy's feet. Jonah kicked the gun away and it slid out into the road. Teeth cracked when he kicked Gabe's mouth just as hard. One got stuck in the toe of his shoe, a yellow shard from a gaping, bleeding mouth.

"Keys are in the ignition. It's not pretty, but it'll drive," Jimmy said, his face spray painted red with the splatter of blood from Gabe's skull. "Take your sister home, Jonah. The cops will be here soon, and God knows you don't need assault and battery on your record if you're gonna get into any civilized school. Myself, I'll buy my way out of any legal trouble, but no offense, you're poor as shit."

"I've been waitin' to do this for months. I ain't about to walk away from it."

"Fine, one shot, then," Jimmy conceded. He handed the bloodied bat to Jonah and let him take one good swing.

The sound of bones shattering never sounded so sweet.

The sun was rising as Jonah sat in the back seat with his sister, holding her tight. It had taken him a short while to keep from looking back. Everything he had ever wanted to do to Jimmy, all the pain he wanted to inflict for having taken Sophie away from him, was now being wrought on Gabe. His hatred for Jimmy was gone. He had stolen the girl Jonah loved, but had given him back his little sister. For this he was thankful, more than he could ever have hoped to explain. He hadn't just regained Hannah, or his best friend. He'd reclaimed his future, unfettered by the rancor of his past.

It wasn't until weeks later that they learned what became of Gabriel Skinner. Minutes before the police had arrived, Jimmy took one last swing at him, right at the base of his neck. Unfortunately, he survived. But the Skinners' eldest son never walked again. And in his rickety wheelchair, he was nothing more than a disfigured oddity to young girls who passed him by, powerless to prey on them, or even to point their way.

# 19

"YOU GOT MAIL, KID."

Susan held out the sealed envelope, pinching the edge between her thumb and forefinger. It was crafted with cream-colored paper, sturdier than the usual plain, white envelopes that typically enclosed junk mail and bills. Her finger covered the return address, as well as the fateful, metallic seal stamped at the top left corner that identified the academic sender. All Jonah could see was his own name, printed in classic serif font, and the address of the Swayne Public Library beneath it. Susan had insisted he list it as his mailing address on all applications. She was far too nosy to allow any correspondences to pass into his hands without her screening them first.

"Came in yesterday. Kept it on my desk till this mornin', debatin' if I should break federal law 'n open it up myself." She smirked, then handed it over with some reluctance, like she were holding a golden ticket she couldn't let go of. "The goddamn suspense is killin' me."

Its face was branded with the shining emerald seal of Easthampton University.

Of all the schools he'd applied to, it was the one he was convinced would instantly reject him. He imagined wizened, bespectacled administrators sitting at a long table, sorting through thousands of applications, some outstanding, others mediocre at best. He had little doubt that the second they took a cursory glance at his, they'd crumple it up and toss it into the garbage, then laud themselves for landing a perfect shot, as such men were rarely athletically inclined.

"Open her up, already. I'm an old broad, and the clock's tickin'."

Taking a deep breath, he slipped his finger under the lip of the envelope and slid it across its length. He slipped out the single, folded page it concealed from Susan's prying eyes. It opened up like an accordion and revealed the irrevocable words of Easthampton University's admissions office, as profound as a judge's sentence of life or death.

He skimmed over the formalities: the pleasantries just delayed the revelation. And what a victorious revelation it was.

Looking up at a grinning Susan, he stammered, "How'd you know it wasn't a rejection?"

"Faith, kid. Never doubted it for a hot second."

Jonah smiled but resisted the urge to give her a hug. He didn't need his clothes smelling like her musty fur coat. He conceded, "Y'know, I couldn't have done it without you. Or wouldn't have, at least."

"Well, what good is a crotchety, old bitch like me if she ain't there to give you a kick in the pants?"

"Now I just gotta figure out how to pay for it."

"Federal loans, kid, like the rest of America. Y'ain't a real patriot unless you graduate $100,000 dollars in the hole. Ain't no shame in it though—I'd rather my taxes pay for your degree than for some welfare queen's lobster dinner."

"I'll make it count, then. I've been bitchin' all this time about wantin' to get outta this shithole town, and now that I got the chance to, I gotta say, it's perfect timin'."

"Word in the choir loft is that you and your best friend's fairy godmother went and jumped that Skinner sack-o'-shit. Now, y'don't gotta tell me if that's true—I don't need you incriminatin' yourself— but I sure as hell hope it is. Almost makes me as proud as that there acceptance letter. Anyhow, I figure y'ain't gotta run from your problems no more. Your lil' Hannah's safe, and you done served that bastard a heapin', cold dish o' revenge. Goin' away to college is more like chasin' an opportunity, now.

"Speakin' of opportunities," she continued, opening up her desk drawer to take out a single cigarette. "I got myself one, and one more for you. I still call myself an ex-smoker, but this here's an occasion I can't pass up. I'll be outside, enjoyin' this bad boy, lightin' up in celebration o' my late-bloomin' protégé. I'll take my damn time, too—you're gonna need a few minutes to yourselves."

"Ourselves?"

"I took some initiative and called up that sweet lil' Shaw girl for you. Told her Clemency done seen a real goddamned miracle, and besides, there ain't no way she woulda took your call. I ain't about to let you leave this place behind with unfinished business. If you're gonna bring anything with you to that fancy university, it'd better be some good memories and the biggest box o' rubbers you can find."

Before he could bark a single disparaging word about Susan's inability to mind her own business, the tiny bells jingled at the front door. Susan snatched up her matches and cigarette, gave a cordial nod, and headed off for the back of the library, her fur coat sweeping along the floor with an airy swish. And standing in the door, with the light of day gleaming on her raven hair, was Sophie Shaw, hands crossed modestly, and beautifully overdressed for the occasion.

"Hi, Jonah."

Her voice was soft and insecure. Jonah had expected anger, resentment, frustration, any variation of revulsion. Instead, she seemed scared to be there, to face him, like she may have made the wrong decision to walk through the library doors and look into his awestruck hazel eyes for the first time in weeks. Maybe she was scared of what he might say. Or was it that she was unsure of her own resolve, and her ability to resist falling back into his arms, despite all that had transpired between them?

He could only hope so. In the meantime, he just had to come up with something to say. His college career wasn't off to a great start if he couldn't even string together the words to acknowledge Sophie's presence. She caught him like a deer in headlights, and the headlights had the brightness of two midday suns.

"Mrs. Lewis told me about the letter," she began on his behalf, smiling meekly. "I'm proud of you."

"Wish I coulda told you myself," he admitted. He stepped a little closer, but stayed just far enough for propriety. "But I guess that's my own fault. Yours was the last bridge I ever wanted to burn."

"You're not the only one to blame. I never let you build it back up again."

"We both know I don't deserve your second chances. I ain't never deserved you to begin with."

"Maybe what we both deserve is forgiveness," Sophie suggested, and with those words, she approached him and pressed her cheek against his chest, and his heart melted.

He knew it wasn't the same, and that it could never be. This was the reconciliation they both had longed for, the purest act to fulfill God's will. It wasn't the first stirs of a romance reborn. They were picking up the pieces, but they weren't about to build a house together. They were placing them neatly back on the shelves, clearing the paths that led two separate ways.

"I know Jimmy was just telling lies," she said, still in his arms. "Mrs. Lewis explained that, too. It was wrong of me to believe them in the first place."

"She's a meddlesome old bat, ain't she?"

"She means well—and she's really got a soft spot for you. I imagine it'll be hard for her to see you go, no matter how much she denies it."

"Not as hard as it was for me to see you go, I can tell you that. But now I'm gonna have to relive that day all over again," he sighed. Letting her go, he backed away and sat down on a nearby stepstool. Sophie followed and pulled up a chair from the computer desk, the one he'd sat at to gamble his way out of Clemency and into a cap and gown.

"I reckon you'll restore your perfect image once I'm outta here," he predicted. "Probably couldn't get that back so long as I'm still loiterin' on Main Street, stackin' books and wastin' time."

"Actually, I'll have to build up a whole new one—just like you, I'm getting a fresh start. We're leaving Clemency, my parents and I."

Never in his life would Jonah have imagined the Reverend and his wife standing anywhere other than behind the pulpit of the

Southern Mercy Bible Church, their 24-carat rock and hallowed Fort Knox. He raised an eyebrow and replied, "Must be a cold day in Hell, then. Where are they fixin' to go?"

"Somewhere out west. They're looking for a new flock to shepherd. Thanks to Jimmy von Braun, no one's willing to donate to the church anymore. But it sounds like they're going to sell all they have and follow Jesus, like they were called to all along. Something's changed in them, or in my father, at least. I guess I have Jimmy to thank for that."

"Hate to say it, but turns out he ain't half bad," Jonah admitted. "If it wasn't for him, I'd be leavin' my sister alone with a monster. He mighta gone 'n ruined my life, but at least he kept her from ruinin' hers. Even I couldn't do that."

"You, forgiving none other than Jimmy von Braun?" Sophie laughed in disbelief. "So I *did* manage to teach you something."

"Well, God's a-watchin', ain't He?"

"All day, every day, Mr. Young. And I think you just made Him proud."

"How about you?"

She put her hand on his knee and simpered, saying, "More than you know, Jonah."

Sophie stood up and looked to the door. "I should go," she said, and came close to him once more. She placed a gentle kiss on his cheek. "We both have some packing to do. I'm really glad I came today. You know, I almost didn't, but I thought it'd be best to practice what I preach. Wouldn't want you thinking hypocrisy runs in the family, now." His bashful grin was the only response she needed. "Goodbye, Jonah."

And for the second time, she walked away.

"Y'know, I really did love you," Jonah confessed, stopping her for just one more moment. "Ain't never said it. But I still do."

Sophie looked back at him and smiled, her fair skin glowing in the morning sun. It had been too long since he'd seen such light in her eyes, the kind he always hoped to kindle there, and which he knew he'd carry in his own from that day forth. "I know you did," she replied, reaching for the door. She opened it and let the fresh air in. "And to think, I once took you for a shallow little boy. I've never been so thankful to be proven wrong."

••

Levi had made the lonely walk to Backwater Spirits more times than he could recall over the course of his adult life, and racked up enough miles to travel across the country at least twice. It was strange to think that this time could be his last.

It was well past noon and the sun was lingering at the point between daylight and the first hints of a tangerine sunset; the newly erected sign at the level crossing ahead cast a long shadow across Main Street. Things were as they always were, but somehow, subtly different. The air was sweeter knowing one wouldn't be breathing that same air forever.

"If I'mma head off to Virginia, I ain't goin' without a roommate," Jonah had declared earlier that day. "Shit ain't cheap up there, and I sure as hell ain't findin' someone to live with online. That's like playin' Russian roulette, but instead o' bullets, you got yourself crazies, kleptos and crackheads."

Life outside Clemency was expensive, and Levi knew he'd have to find himself a job within a week or two of migrating northeast. He had his savings, but those reserves would only last so long before he reached down into the bottom of his coffee tin and came up empty handed. With such a limited skill set and barely any references, he worried he might be the least marketable job seeker in a new city. At least he'd have a lifetime friend in a place where he didn't know a single soul, but unfortunately, friendship didn't pay the bills.

It was a leap of faith, leaving Clemency behind with no real goal in mind—but he'd stood at the edge of that cliff many times in his dreams, and it was about time he took a deep breath and made the jump in the real world. He'd rather be crushed on the rocks below than die on a mountaintop, alone and starved of hope.

The train station was set to reopen in a few days' time, and Jonah had already bought a one-way ticket to Virginia. It was no secret that it was George von Braun who'd cut through the red tape with political scissors bought with his immeasurable bribes; no one questioned or criticized that fact. The state contractors came unexpectedly, and left just as quickly: they cleaned up the tracks, nailed down some new railroad ties, painted over the graffiti and put up a clean, new sign. CLEMENCY, it read in bright, inviting letters. WELCOME HOME.

Levi, unlike those whose train tickets led to Clemency, was saying goodbye. He would find a new home. And wherever it was, Mama would not be there. Staying with her and buying her whiskey and smokes had never helped her, not once. And even with their having mutually confessed their sins, seeking absolution and finding it in each other's tears, this would not change. The best he could do for her was to leave with his peace upon her and her home, and pray that she find herself, and not drowned at the bottom of a whiskey bottle.

He entered the liquor store and did not immediately acknowledge Mr. Green. His silence was an instinctive response to the awkwardness he was convinced was inevitable, and his averting his eyes was the natural reaction to the guilt he felt, for being the son of the man who'd robbed him of his family, and for knowing this was his last goodbye. With the location of his usual product forever burned into his memory, Levi promptly headed to the trusty spot on the wall, grabbed the whiskey off the shelf without even turning his head, and set the bottle on the counter. Elijah looked up and smiled, awaiting Levi's difficult hello.

"I know everything now. And I'm so sorry."

Elijah looked puzzled, albeit appreciative. To him, Levi was not to be punished for the sins of his father. "Ain't no need, I promise. A man's sin is his own and no one else's, and don't forget, all sins can be forgiven. I just hope you found the answers you needed to hear, sooner or later."

"I was wrong about her, this whole time. She never even stopped me."

"You weren't wrong about the drinkin', son. Not by a long shot."

"Fair enough," Levi conceded. "She still ain't never said she'd stop that, even after we got all them family secrets out in the open, and reconciled as best we could. Even my forgiveness wasn't enough to break that habit—hell, I forgave the whole damn world that night. But I guess I've done what I can, and what I can't do is keep on feedin' into her illness. I owe everyone that, her most of all."

"I'm one hundred percent on your side here, Mr. Thompson," Elijah replied with a smile, but then pointed down at the whiskey bottle Levi had placed right before him. "However, I feel I gotta point out the irony here."

"Might as well give 'er her last hurrah, right? Maybe call it a partin' gift."

"And where are you headed to, that you gotta leave her somethin' behind?"

"My friend's goin' off northeast, and I'm goin' with him."

Elijah nodded, intrigued. "Congratulations, then, Mr. Thompson. I do hope I can keep this place in business, having lost my most loyal patron."

Levi laughed. "Y'deserve a nice retirement, anyway. Me, I'll be strugglin' to find work in a far-off city, eatin' dollar menu food, without a penny to my name, most likely. But it'll be my own life, for once. Don't matter how tough it'll get. My problems'll be my own, not somebody else's for me to deal with."

"And you're doin' this for yourself, I hope? To play a better game with the cards the Good Lord done dealt you, and not to just throw in the towel?"

"All for me, as selfish as it sounds. I guess I ain't never turned into the perfect Christian she wanted me to be, since I won't take care of her anymore. I can't."

"You forgave her for all her meanness, her resentment, and her mistakes; you forgave your father for mistakes you ain't never knew he made, no matter how grave they might've been. And now, you're finally pushin' your mama in the right direction. I'd say that's pretty darn Christian o' you. The future's gonna be brighter for both o' y'all, even if y'all are partin' ways. It don't always have to be good on only one side o' the fence."

"I just don't want her thinkin' she went and pushed another man outta the house, or that she done made the same mistake twice. She'd never move on. It'd kill her."

"Even if you don't go, it won't change the fact that she's been pushin' you away all these years, but in ways she can't see right now. You done your part," Elijah professed, pushing Levi's money back across the countertop. He never took one look at it. "You can make yourself a better life knowin' you got yourself a clean conscience and not a regret in the world. They say to feel guilt is to be touched by God, but sometimes, it ain't nothin' more than the Devil's chains."

Elijah slipped the bottle into a paper bag, but instead of passing it over to Levi, he cordially extended his hand. "It's been a pleasure, Mr. Thompson. I've had a lot o' changes in my day, and now that I've gone gray, I can't say they all been good ones. But seein' your face every week's been my one constant this past year, and it's gone 'n gave me a great deal o' comfort. To be honest, you done gave me the closure I ain't even knew I needed.

"I'm sure you heard it already, but you really do look so much like your father—and though I never really knew him, I'd say any man who could raise a son like you, even to just six years old, has got to be a good soul. And if even just one young man like you could come outta this two-faced town without losin' his soul, then, praise God, there might just be some hope for this place yet."

# 20

It was 10:45 AM on a Tuesday, and if everything was running on schedule, the next train would be arriving in no less than fifteen minutes. Levi was the first to reach the station; leave it to Jonah to be late for the one-way trip he'd hoped for all his life. With an old suitcase in his left hand and his ticket to freedom in the other, he ascended the stairs to the platform, and helped himself to a seat on the one small bench that overlooked the railroad tracks. It offered a scenic view of the white steeple of the Southern Mercy Bible Church, which Levi couldn't wait to see disappearing into the distance.

He wasn't alone on the platform: it was foolish of him to think that he might be the only one who wanted to run away. On the other end of the bench sat SSG Eddie Sharpe, waiting patiently, possibly unconsciously, with his bulging eyes closed. There was an overstuffed rucksack resting on the ground beside him. From its side dangled a survival pan and a metal canteen, and Levi could only imagine what kinds of doomsday gear were hidden inside. He found it funny that Eddie thought he might have a better chance surviving the apocalypse outside of Clemency. Everyone else believed Clemency might be the one town that the Lord Almighty wouldn't smite for its iniquities.

Between the two of them was sitting a quiet woman Levi had never seen in Clemency before. She appeared to be the churchgoing type, wearing a navy-blue dress with white polka dots, and a small, classic hat tipped just slightly to the side. Though she was dressed for a Sunday morning, she wasn't a member of the local congregation, so far as Levi knew. It was odd to see a stranger in that town who wasn't just passing through and maybe stopping for a few gallons of cheap gas at AlaCo. Levi wondered as to what her business was in Clemency, but he decided to mind his own business. She certainly did, waiting patiently with her small purse in her lap, ankles crossed and back straight and poised—that is, until five minutes went by in silence, and she decided that some light conversation would be a fine way to pass the next ten.

"Excuse me, young man—do you have the time?" she asked. Levi looked over at her, and saw her smile politely. She had a kind face, with smooth, mocha skin that made her age difficult to discern. The twinkle in her gray eyes also lent to an aura of youth.

He peeked at his phone and reported the time, and received a nod and a thank you. "These next ten minutes are gonna be the longest ten minutes o' my life," he sighed, though he wasn't sure why he said it.

"Eager to get going?"

"Y'can't even imagine."

"Where are you headed?"

"Far from here, I can tell you that."

The woman opened her purse, took out a tiny breath mint and popped it into her mouth. She offered one to Levi, but he declined. "That can only mean two things," she replied. "Either you're running towards something, or running away from it."

"I woulda said I was runnin' at one point, but now it's different. I'm lettin' go of the past and chasin' the future."

"Very wise for a young man your age."

"Took a while to get to this point, though. Forgivin' ain't as easy as it should be."

"God never said it'd be easy," she corrected him gently. "But it's all that life's about."

"Well, now that I've got that behind me, I can finally start livin' for me. 'Seize the day,' and all that. It's finally gonna be my life, and no one else's."

"You know, my husband did the same. I've been watching him for a long time now, and I don't think he knows I see the changes in him, but I do. My son also. It took some time, but he learned that forgiveness is all that really matters. And it never comes too late. Finally, he's free—just like you, if this train is on time."

Levi looked back toward the staircase to check if Jonah might be on his way up, but saw no one. He rolled his eyes. "Y'know, this wasn't even my idea at first, and I'm the one who's on time. My friend shoulda been here a good while ago."

"So, he's leading the way, then?"

"Y'could say that. He's goin' off to school, and he needs himself a roommate. Life up north ain't cheap, I hear."

"No, it isn't," she chuckled. "Pardon my prying, but what will you do when you get there?"

"Not sure yet. I'mma let things play out the way they will, and trust it'll turn out fine."

"I've always been fond of that verse: 'Take therefore no thought for the morrow, for the morrow shall take thought for the things of itself.' A peaceful way to live, I think. That being said, I've gained a bit of wisdom at my age, and I have to tell you that I'm not quite sure it's God who's leading your way."

"Who then, the Devil?"

"No, your friend. And that's not always a bad thing. But if you're looking to start your own life, on your own terms, then it won't do you much good to be the sidekick. I mean no offense, of course, but it's hard to chase your dreams when you're following in the footsteps of someone who's chasing his own."

And at the eleventh hour, Levi realized she was right.

"What should I do, then?"

"That's for you to decide, not me, naturally," she reminded him with a lighthearted chuckle. "But take your time in choosing. You're young, and there's no hurry. Maybe you'll end up deciding you really should follow your friend—maybe you won't. If he's a true friend, don't think for a second that you're leaving him, or, Heaven forbid, losing him. Paths diverge, and ways part. Friendships, on the other hand, aren't here or there, but everywhere, no matter the distance."

The gates at the level crossing began to lower, and clinking bells sounded. It was 10:58, and the train was right on schedule.

"Sorry I'm late!" Jonah gasped as he dashed up the stairs, a bulky piece of luggage in each hand, arms flexed and brow glistening with sweat. "Dumbass sister was takin' her sweet time in the shower. Detox's a bitch." He noticed the rhythmic ringing of bells and the flashing yellow lights at the level crossing. "Shit, got here just in time."

"I can't go with you," Levi said frankly.

"What do you mean, you can't go?"

"This ticket ain't meant for me. It's your escape, your dream. And I don't wanna hold you back in any way, even if it's at your side."

"You know that's horse shit. I'm the one who wanted you to go."

"And that's just it," Levi continued. "I can't get where I'm meant to go if I'm just a passenger on someone else's journey."

Jonah didn't seem satisfied. He set down his luggage and crossed his arms. His hair was tussled in the rush of air as the train pulled in and came to a stop with a forceful hiss. "Seems real impulsive o' you to turn back at the last minute. Tell me Jimmy ain't said somethin' to change your mind—or your Mama, usin' guilt against you one last time."

"Wasn't either o' them, for once," Levi explained. "A total stranger, in fact. Ain't even caught her name." He turned around to point out the woman who'd opened his eyes right before he made his leap of faith, but was surprised to find that she wasn't there. All he saw was SSG Eddie Sharpe, groggily returning to consciousness with a grumble. The train doors hadn't opened yet.

"What are you gonna do, then? God knows I couldn't survive this place on my own, and you ain't much different."

"I got no idea," Levi admitted. "And I'm okay with that. If I'm gonna wander my way through life, at least I'll be leadin' the way."

"If you change your mind, you know where I'll be. I'll be stuck there for four years, if I don't fail out first, which you know there's a damn good chance I will."

"You won't," Levi laughed. With nothing left to say, he embraced his friend and didn't hold back. "I'll miss you, y'know."

"Course you will," Jonah scoffed, giving Levi a slap on the back. "This whole damn town will, with nothin' else to talk about at coffee hour. But now that I'm gone, at least you'll find yourself a girl without me there to steal your thunder. Silver linin', man. Don't forget it."

As the train pulled away and passed into the far-off cover of the trees, Levi saw another chapter of his life end. The warm air that swept along the railroad tracks was a last breath. He knew and believed, however, without a shadow of a doubt, that every end was a beginning, and every death a rebirth. His faith professed it, his town preached it, and his loved ones lived it. Now, it was his turn to step into the unknown. That would have scared him once, no matter how badly he wanted the escape. That day, he saw no shroud of fog before him. He saw only the soaring clouds above.

••

When Levi tucked his unused ticket back in his father's old wallet, he slipped out the unclaimed loyalty card, and decided, for no real reason, to see if it was still good for one bouquet of flowers.

"Haven't seen one o' these in ages," Mrs. Young marveled at the florist stand in the back corner of the Hometown Market. After expressing her initial shock at Levi's decision to stay in Clemency, she closely examined the loyalty card, counted the ten holes clipped in succession, and concluded that she saw no reason as to why it would no longer be valid.

"No roses, though," she reminded him. "Even after twenty years, they're still overpriced."

He picked out a bundle of bright yellow sunflowers. He felt they would look nice on the kitchen counter, and God knew he needed a bit of sunlight in his home, even if it only radiated off a ring of vibrant flower petals. They were also the kind of gift for Mama he should have been buying her all along.

The old Cadillac was in the driveway when he got back to the house. The front door opened without making a sound, and closed just as perfectly, with no creaks or clatters. Mama wasn't waiting on the parlor couch, cigarette and glass in hand, ready to criticize his choice in flowers. Her old blues were playing, but she hadn't fallen asleep to the voices of sultry singers long since passed. She was in the kitchen, standing at the sink, pouring the last of her whiskey down the drain.

# ABOUT THE AUTHOR

Joseph (Joey) D'Urso is a born-and-raised Long Islander living far from home, and despite his relocation, he has yet to lose his New York accent. He was born to a loud Italian-American family and takes great pride in his surname's apostrophe.

Creative even from elementary school, he has been writing fiction longer than he cares to remember. His published novels include *Devils in Sunday Hats*, a story of dead dreams, dogma and redemption, and *The Aetherverse*, an incendiary space opera for troubled times.

Aside from writing fiction, Joey is an avid saxophone player, having played alto sax for over 15 years. He also has an intense interest in languages (both real and fictional) and graduated from Binghamton University with a BA in Arabic.

**Read more of Joey's work at:**
www.joey-durso.com

**Follow on social media:**

   | @joey_durso